The Collected Short Works 1907–1919

University of Nebraska Press
Lincoln and London

Bess Streeter Aldrich

The Collected
Short Works
1907–1919

Edited and Introduced by Carol Miles Petersen

Acknowledgments for the use of previously published material
appear on pages 243–244.

⊛ The paper in this book meets the minimum requirements
of American National Standard for Information Sciences—
Permanence of Paper for Printed Library Materials,
ANSI Z39.48-1984.

Library of Congress Cataloging in Publication Data

Aldrich, Bess Streeter, 1881–1954.
[Short stories. Selections]
The collected short works, 1907–1919 : Bess Streeter Aldrich /
edited and introduced by Carol Miles Petersen.
p.   cm.
Includes bibliographical references (p.   ) and index.
ISBN 0-8032-1038-8 (acid-free paper : cl.)
I. Petersen, Carol Miles, 1930–   . II. Title.
PS3501.L378A6 1995
813'.52—dc20   94-19005 CIP

Publication of this volume was assisted by The Virginia
Faulkner Fund, established in memory of Virginia Faulkner,
editor-in-chief of the University of Nebraska Press.

Contents

Introduction

In describing how to write a short story, Bess Streeter Aldrich noted the author must "live the lives of his characters, crawling into their very skins. . . . He must be an actor. More than that, he must play all the parts."[1] In playing "all the parts," Bess Streeter Aldrich brought to her readers the pleasure of well-written stories that reflect her own personality: her positive outlook on life, her humor, her understanding of people. The stories further offer the pleasure of recognizing characters and incidents that reappear in Aldrich novels: the revised Mason and Cutter family stories became the books *Mother Mason* (New York: D. Appleton and Company, 1924), and *The Cutters* (New York: D. Appleton & Company, 1926); and Zimri Streeter appears as "Grandpa Stàtler" in the 1915 story of that name, in the 1925 novel *The Rim of the Prairie* (New York: D. Appleton & Company), in the 1939 *The Song of Years* (New York: D. Appleton-Century), and as the hero of the 1944 short story "Soldier Vote of '64" (*Think Magazine,* August). The character of the school teacher in "The Madonna of the Purple Dots" (1907) and in "The Cat Is on the Mat" (1916) appears as that of the protagonist in *The Rim of the Prairie.*

Many of these stories are reprinted for the first time since their original publication. I have included two that were sold but not published—one, "The Madonna of the Purple Dots," because the magazine went out of business and the other, "Concerning the Best Man," because of an editorial policy change. Aldrich wrote more than one hundred short stories and was able to claim the enviable record of never writing a story she did not sell. Many of her stories were syndicated after first publication and many were sold to British magazines; her readership was enormous. All of her novels are in print.

This book contains stories that Aldrich wrote from the start of her career through 1919. That year she turned thirty-eight, and had accomplished a great deal both in her personal life and in her writing. After graduating from college in 1901 she taught for three years, received a second teaching degree, married, moved three times, bore three children and was pregnant with her fourth child, was active in church work, organized the first Women's Club and helped start the first Public Library in Elmwood, Nebraska, and wrote and sold twenty-six stories plus miscellaneous articles. All of this demonstrates the truth of a comment in 1920 by one of her editors that hers was "a case of stored up energy."[2]

Bessie Genevra Streeter was born in Cedar Falls, Iowa, on 17 February 1881, the youngest of eight children. With ten years separating Bess from her nearest brother and fourteen from her nearest sister, Bess learned to rely on her reading and her own imagination for entertainment; she said that the characters she met in books became as familiar to her as the neighbors. Reading meant curling up in the large friendly armchair in the living room or tucking a book under her apron as she went upstairs in the morning to make the beds, knowing that if she got her chores done quickly she could then read until someone began to wonder where she was. Favorite authors included James M. Barrie, whose humor she enjoyed, and Charles Dickens, whose characterizations she appreciated. Along with her personal favorites, there was the Bible, a staple of her Scots-Presbyterian family. From it, she learned the moral principles by which she would live and which her writing would reflect. She also learned Bible verses, which occasionally surface in her novels, rephrased, but with cadences intact.

Relishing stories as she did, Bess began creating her own—sometimes in the playhouse that her father had built for her in the backyard. Probably from about the age of nine or ten and using a lead pencil as she always would for first drafts, Bess wrote fanciful stories; she knew even as a child that "when words are put together right they're just like singing."[3] Also in the playhouse, pedaling with furious speed on a broken treadle sewing machine, she transported herself on adventurous trips; playing with neighborhood friends, she wove tales of exciting balls, beautiful gowns, and handsome knights with their ladies. One of these friends, Grace Simpson, recalls how Bess would begin telling a story peopled by herself and all of her listeners; she would describe the setting, the dazzling people, and her own exquisite dress; then turning to Grace, Bess would say it was Grace's turn. Grace, lacking a flowing imagination, would respond, "Oh, I don't know, Bess, you tell me."[4] And Bess would describe Grace's and any of the other children's costumes in detail. In all likelihood Grace Simpson was reincarnated as Josephine Cutter's friend, Effie Peterson, in "Josephine Encounters a Siren" (*The American Magazine*, December 1922).

Bess won her first writing prize, a camera, at the age of fourteen, later admitting, "It was then I first tasted blood; for the intoxication of seeing my name in print was overwhelming." At seventeen she entered a contest with a story she later described as "heavy as a moving van. It oozed pathos. It dripped melancholy."[5] It won five dollars for her, which she used to purchase a showy umbrella she thought made her look sophisticated and which would later appear as a humorous object in her writing. She wrote articles throughout her college career at Iowa State Normal School, now known as the University of Northern Iowa, from which she graduated in 1901. She then went on to teach in Boone and Marshalltown, Iowa, and then Salt Lake City, Utah. She returned to Cedar Falls, Iowa, in 1906, working as Assistant Supervisor of the Primary Department on the equivalent of her master's degree, which she received the following year. While she taught and worked on her second degree, she wrote articles and published children's stories and had a story accepted for publication just weeks before her wedding.

However, after her 1907 marriage to attorney Charles Sweetzer Aldrich and their subsequent move from Cedar Falls to Tipton, Iowa, she found little time for writing. In 1909 the Aldriches, their two-month-old daughter Mary Eleanor, Bess's mother, and her sister Clara and brother-in-law John Cobb moved to Elmwood, Nebraska, where the Aldriches and the Cobbs had purchased the American Exchange Bank. For the next two years, Aldrich spent her time as wife and mother and became an active member of her new community. Then, in 1911, she saw an advertisement in the *Ladies Home Journal* asking readers to send in stories for a contest the *Journal* was sponsoring. Aldrich's desire to write resurfaced, and the next few afternoons while the baby napped, Aldrich wrote her story. She took it to the bank to type, and when one of the clerks needed to use the typewriter, Bess took out her story, waited until he was done, and then sat down to pick out the letters again until the next interruption. The contest attracted more than two thousand entrants, apparently exceeding what was anticipated, for the magazine dropped the contest idea and instead purchased six of the submitted stories. Aldrich's "The Little House Next Door" was one of those. When the $175 check came, her mother, who was living at the Aldrich home at the time, said, "Look again, Bess, it must be a dollar seventy-five!"[6] It was, indeed, one hundred seventy-five.

Bess Streeter Aldrich then began the transition from occasional to full-time author. With the excitement and impetus of this important sale, she began immediately on another story, sandwiching writing time between the tasks of caring for her husband, her children, and her home. She explained that "the blood that had come from the people who crossed the Mississippi on the ice with oxen began to assert itself, and I determined that if keeping constantly at writing would eventually land one somewhere, I would begin writing in earnest. From that time on I had a manuscript on the road" almost constantly. The next story "wandered around from magazine to magazine making twenty-three trips before it found an editor who would buy it, and it brought only twenty dollars." Because some of her stories went out so often, they became dog-eared, and Aldrich would retype the first and last pages to create the impression that the story was on its first trip. She said that she was "selling one just often enough to encourage me."[7]

In order to sell, Aldrich knew she had to work on the details and techniques of writing; thus she did whatever gave her the opportunity to practice. She entered and won a few newspaper contests, submitted a recipe to *Armour Cookbook* that was accepted, sent a couple of comments to *The Delineator* and received one dollar for each, and wrote some other miscellaneous materials, only two of which are included in this collection. The first is "My Life Test" and the second is "How I Knew When the Right Man Came Along." These both have the Aldrich cadence and character types, and, to the best of my knowledge, are Aldrich's writings; however, they were published anonymously, and no conclusive evidence proving they are hers has come to my attention. Both are recorded in her financial journal.

Every acceptance, whether it garnered one dollar or many times that amount, was recorded in Aldrich's financial journal. In four years, she had earned a total of $638 for her writings; only three sales had exceeded $100. She continued to work at her craft by taking correspondence lessons from a writing school whose director told her that inasmuch as she had already had some success in publishing, he would take her on as his private pupil and read her work himself. It was not long before he told her that she was a born writer and that her work was so good there was little he could teach her, although he would be glad to continue to read and critique any material she might choose to send him. Acceptances for her work increased.

The year 1918 was an important one for Aldrich. Until this time, describing it as a form of writer's print fright much like an actor's stage fright, Aldrich had written as Margaret Dean Stevens, a combination of her two grandmothers' names. She was now confident enough to use Bess

Streeter Aldrich. Proof of her increasing success came in 1918 when *McCall's* accepted "The Box behind the Door," and *The People's Home Journal,* another solid magazine of the time, bought "Their House of Dreams." The letter from *The American Magazine* for "Mother's Dash for Liberty" must have been the most exciting acceptance since the *Journal* had published "The Little House Next Door" in 1911. Aldrich felt this sale was her turning point, for she had long been trying to break into the highly regarded *American,* which had rejected some of her stories that other magazines, such as *McCall's,* had subsequently accepted. *The American* reflected the optimistic ideals of its editor, John M. Siddall, who chose only well-written and upbeat stories. Evidently Siddall understood his subscribers, for by November of 1919 *The American's* paid circulation was more than 125 million.[8] "Mother's Dash" appeared in the December issue. Shortly thereafter, a soldier stationed in Germany wrote that his buddies had worn out his copy of *The American* because "Mother's Dash" reminded them so much of home and their own mothers; he asked for more of these stories. Aldrich already had the next one at the editor's office.

In 1920 her fourth and last child was born, giving Bess and Charles one daughter and three sons. Fortunately, Charles gave Bess "help and encouragement . . . pressed [her] to take more time for writing, encouraged [her] in every way." Continuing to find the time to write was not easy, however, and she struggled with obstacles: "I wrote when the meals cooked, when babies tumbled over my feet, and while I was ironing, in the old days. The hand that rocked the cradle was often the left one, while the right was jotting down a sentence or two. I have had the first draft of many a story sprinkled liberally with good old sudsy dishwater."[9] Nor did the writing itself necessarily come easily, and Aldrich speaks of "walking the floor" in distress over an idea as she would of walking the floor with a baby in distress, and in so doing she reveals how for her the private and the professional, the domestic and the literary, were one.[10]

Not surprisingly, Aldrich's principles for her fiction were those by which she lived. Her writing must be acceptable to everyone, she determined. Her stories are about decent people saying and doing decent things. There is no swearing in Aldrich stories, no sex, no divorce, none of the seamy side of life; indeed, "decent" and "seamy" are Aldrich's terms. She wrote,

> Why quarrel with a writer over realism and idealism? After all, an author is a glass through which a picture of life

is projected. The picture falls upon the pages of the writer's manuscript according to the mental and emotional contours of that writer. It is useless to try to change these patterns. If one writer does not see life in terms of dirt and grime and debaucheries, it is no sign that those sordid things do not exist. If another does not see life in terms of faith and love, courage and good deeds, it does not follow that those characteristics do not exist. . . . I claim that one may portray some of the decent things about him and reserve the privilege to call that real life too.[11]

By similar principles, Aldrich chose to write of domestic rather than of political conflicts. As a granddaughter, a wife, and a writer she knew of war: during the Civil War her grandfather, in his sixties, had gone to Atlanta to bring the Iowa soldiers' votes back to their state to be counted in the 1864 presidential election, and, because all contact with the North had been cut, he had had to endure with Sherman's troops the terrible march to the sea. Her husband had served in the Spanish-American War and had almost died; and Aldrich wrote and published stories during World War I. War was the single topic for which Aldrich expressed unequivocal hatred, and in her own way she devoted herself to eradicating it. As if willing a future free of war, she joined others in believing that World War I would end all wars; and as if erasing it from the present, she expunged it from her fiction. The "Rosemary of Remembrance," published in the *Black Cat Magazine* in 1917, contains no direct mention of the conflict—nor do any of her stories. Only in the subtext of metaphors does armed violence erupt: words are "like a hand grenade" and "shrapnel."[12] The "hand grenade" metaphor also appears in a 1918 story and rain is compared to "shrapnel" in another 1918 story. Perhaps the metaphors took her unaware, for Aldrich consciously dedicated herself to the belief that people read to escape, and that as a writer she should offer an enjoyable respite from war's horrors. It was a principle of literary nonviolence, one might say—a principle Aldrich retained throughout her career. Years later she explained to an editor that she could not believe that during a war people wanted to read about conflict in their leisure time.[13]

An observer of life and people, Aldrich recognized that much of life is lived through feelings. She said that "my type of story is a story of emotion rather than of the intellect. I try to make the reader feel."[14] She also wanted to promote understanding of rural lives by her urban readers. Aldrich lived and wrote in a village, and her stories ring with the life of small towns: the kensingtons (church women's groups), the school activities, the functions and celebrations that were combined efforts of all the townspeople, and the sense of personal history they had about each other. In her stories, Aldrich is protective of and supports those who remain on the farms; her message is that farmers are becoming well educated and often may be college graduates and that the wives are becoming chic and up to date, much as their urban sisters. One reason her work was so in demand was that she offered to her readers the feel of the country, the best of their memories of rural homes known or imagined. As one editor wrote to Aldrich, he and his wife were "small town folks—the big cities are full of us. . . . You don't merely create characters, you create people with whom we are familiar."[15] Aldrich was a fighter for what she believed in, although something of a velvet-gloved fighter, and there was little that could raise her ire as quickly as someone insulting her beloved Midwest, which she inevitably defended. Aldrich believed in the farmers and villagers and in their lives, knew that they experienced the same emotions as their urban relatives, and, while recognizing that they were not perfect, wrote of them with respect and affection.

Always conscious of the distinctions that a choice of language makes, she rejected academic classifications and described herself as a realist, explaining that "sentiment" (that is, emotion) was part of reality:

> Sentiment doesn't lie in soil, or in climate, or latitude, or longitude. It lies in the hearts of people. Wherever there are folks who live and work and love and die, whether they raise hogs in Iowa or oranges in California or the sails of a pleasure boat at Palm Beach, there is the stuff of which stories are made.[16]

My own label for Aldrich's writing is "romantic realist," for she was a writer who affirmed the goodness that exists in everyday living.

Even in these early years as a writer, Aldrich was firm in her principles, but she never felt it her duty to force her ideas on others. She offered her thoughts and words as possibilities or examples, but let each choose her or his own path. She was consistent in her ideals.

Notes

1. Bess Streeter Aldrich, cards on how to write a short story, Box 10, archives of Nebraska State Historical Society, Lincoln, Nebraska, hereinafter NSHS.

2. John M. Siddall to Bess Streeter Aldrich, 22 June 1920, Box 4, NSHS.

3. Bess Streeter Aldrich, *The Cutters* (New York: D. Appleton & Company, 1926), p. 110.

4. Julie Bailey, "Bess Streeter Aldrich, Her Life and Work," May 1965, p. 7, Cedar Falls Historical Society, Cedar Falls, Iowa.

5. Bess Streeter Aldrich, "How I Mixed Stories with Do-Nuts," *The American Magazine,* February 1921, p. 33.

6. Item 20, n.p., n.d., NSHS.

7. Bess Streeter Aldrich, Box 10, NSHS. Box 10, File Misc. and Mss., p. 5, NSHS.

8. John M. Siddall to Bess Streeter Aldrich, 19 November 1919, Box 4, NSHS.

9. "Nebraska Woman Gains Fame as Author," *Fillmore County (Neb.) News,* 12 May 1926.

10. Box 10, File Misc. and Mss., p. 4, NSHS.

11. "There Are Two Viewpoints . . . ," Box 10, File Misc. and Mss., p. 2, NSHS.

12. Bess Streeter Aldrich, "The Rosemary of Remembrance," *The Black Cat Magazine,* 1917.

13. John L. B. Williams to Bess Streeter Aldrich, 18 September 1941, Box 7, Bus. Corres. File 1941, NSHS.

14. Draft of talk "And There Are Times When . . . ," Box 10, File Misc. and Mss., p. 1, NSHS.

15. John M. Siddall to Bess Streeter Aldrich, 22 January 1920, Box 4, NSHS.

16. Lillian Lambert, "Bess Streeter Aldrich," *Midland Schools* (Des Moines, Ia.) 42:8 (April 1928), University of Northern Iowa Archives, p. 299.

The Collected Short Works 1907–1919

The Madonna of the Purple Dots

(Margaret Dean Stevens)

The letter of acceptance from the *National Home Journal of St. Louis* (1907) stated that the purchase price for "The Madonna of the Purple Dots" was five dollars. When the check came, however, it was for ten dollars and was accompanied by a letter saying that the editor decided the story was worth the extra amount.

The story, which does not seem to have been published, is probably the one to which Aldrich referred when she said that shortly before her wedding (September 1907) she had received a larger than anticipated check for a story and the magazine promptly died. The *National Home Journal* was discontinued after May 1907.

This is Aldrich's first piece with a Christmas theme, a theme to which she returned through the years in such works as "The Silent Stars Go By" (*Cosmopolitan*, 1933), "Bid the Tapers Twinkle" (*Ladies Home Journal*, 1935), "Journey into Christmas" (*Christian Herald*, 1947), and "Star across the Tracks" (*Saturday Evening Post*, 1948).

Until 1918 Bess Streeter Aldrich wrote under the name of Margaret Dean Stevens, a combination of her grandmothers' names.

He was the one element of non-Anglo-Saxon material in Room No. 1. Among the thirty-nine who looked aristocratic from the tips of their enormous bows to the toes of their patent-leather slippers, the little beady eyes and hooked nose of the fortieth made emphatic proclamation that he was the son of Jacob Israel, who was the son of Moses Israel, who was the son—but if one wishes to know the line, he should ask old Aunt Sarah Wolfe who lives above the pawnshop and whose eyesight is gone, but who remembers.

Why from the thirty-nine who daily wiggled in the diminutive seats, whose fathers were even the fathers of the city, whose mothers managed the Charity Ball, whose homes stood on Capitol Heights, who, themselves, were everything that was sweet and clean and well-bred—why from these Miss Felicia Brown's fancy did not select some one who particularly charmed and interested her, will never be known.

But as Miss Felicia Brown's fancy was apt to be something indefinite, like a certain unknown quantity in the mathematics of her Wellesley days, this one phase of it, although unexplainable, was no more so than some others along lines less pedagogical. For notwithstanding the big blue eyes of Arthur Stanley, Jr., the bobbing curls of Miss Dorothea Wakefield, or the wiles of any of the other sons and daughters of the elect, their charm for Miss Felicia Brown was as nothing to the charm of Jacob Moses Israel, who was the son of Jacob Israel, who was the son of Moses Israel.

The thirty-nine did not know of this chosen lamb of their flock, and the apples and the flowers and the candy continued to be placed on her desk, offerings to the goddess who was Minerva and Venus in one. But the sticky ginger cookie from which one little bite had been taken, and the colored Biblical card, much the worse for having been carried in a small perspiring hand, were dearer to the goddess when smuggled in to her by the elated and adoring Jacob, than were the roses from the Wakefield hothouse or the box of French bonbons that Arthur Stanley, Jr., was wont to bestow upon her.

Miss Felicia, herself, was a dweller in the social atmosphere of Capitol Heights, and not being a common Brown, but the second daughter of the Spencer-Browns—which makes all the difference in the world—she was, outside of Room No. 1 as well as within its confines, a much-loved, much-adored young person.

When Miss Felicia graduated from Wellesley, she announced her intention of teaching in some sort of settlement, no one knew just where. The Browns and the Spencers wailed and protested. Judge Brown called his daughter to the library and very pleasantly but as firmly, placed a very large foot on the proposed scheme. Then the much-spoiled Felicia teased a little and pouted a great deal, but succeeded only in effecting a compromise that she might teach in their own city schools, which, considering the family's aversion to even that plan, was quite a triumph.

This teaching idea of Felicia's was not only a wholly unnecessary one in the eyes of the devoted relatives, but an exceedingly foolish one as well. Who, they asked themselves, would want to teach forty children several hours a day in a big prison-like building, when one might be Mrs. Graham Stanley of Capitol Heights? Like his nephew, Graham Stanley had long since placed his offering on the shrine of the goddess, but Miss Felicia did not love Mr. Graham Stanley, and therefore did not propose to marry him.

Miss Felicia was walking through Fairview Park on her way to a college friend's. Curled up on the corner of a park seat, the elastic band of a tam-o'-shanter under his quivering chin, a skin-tight red sweater covering his little sobbing body, was Jacob Israel. Miss Felicia had her arms around the little fellow immediately and was making out of his babyish sentences that he was "losted" and "why don't Sadie come?" All thoughts of her call straightway left the tenderhearted Felicia, and her one mission in life resolved itself into an endeavor to find out where the little fellow lived. Thereupon she began to fall in love with Jacob Moses Israel, son of Jacob Israel, who was the son of Moses Israel. The little fat face, the baby mouth, the little nervous fingers that wound themselves around her neck, all won Miss Felicia as Mr. Graham Stanley had never been able to do. More than anything about Jacob did she love his brave little way of pretending not to be frightened when she could plainly feel the baby heart fluttering against the dirty red sweater. He lived by the city hall, he said, and maybe if she'd go with him he "could find it easy." He trudged along for awhile, his hands in his ridiculous pockets, but his stumblings soon conveyed the fact that he was tired, so tired he could scarcely walk.

"Can you walk any farther, Jacob?" asked Miss Felicia, in tones she had never used to Mr. Graham Stanley.

"Easy," he said straightening his shoulders quickly.

"Do you think you will be able to find your house soon, Jacob?"

"Easy," blinking a little but still quite brave.

"Can you find it now, Jacob? There's the city hall."

"Easy," he said between two sobs, and fell over the feet of an extremely broad-shouldered young man, who stopped in surprise, picked him off his feet and said: "Hello, there, young man. Don't blame you for falling over them. One naturally would if they came in one's way." Then seeing Felicia, he held his hat and gave her a very impersonal smile. As the sun was going down, as Miss Felicia was anxious to find the residence of her protege, and as the man stood there with his hat in one hand and Jacob Israel, Jr., in the other, she ventured:

"Do you know where he lives?—or I mean—his name you know is Jacob

Israel and he's lost, and he lives near the city hall, and he can't see it—his house I mean—and he's dead tired."

Whereupon the young man placed his hat back upon a very good-looking head, swung the son of the house of Israel to one of his shoulders and cheerily proffered his services.

"I am Robert Middleton. The youngster can't walk he's so sleepy, and you certainly couldn't carry him," looking down on the dainty Felicia.

"Thank you," that young lady said, "if you would."

It seemed to Felicia that they walked around that city hall a dozen times. It occurred to Dr. Robert Middleton that they didn't walk far enough. It mattered not at all to Jacob Moses Israel, fast asleep with the tam-o'-shanter over one ear.

"It seems too bad, young man, but your advice and wisdom as to which side of said city hall you reside is quite essential in this pilgrimage, so if you'll kindly come back to this mundane sphere and give us a little information, we'll be greatly obliged," and the man gave the nodding boy a shake.

"How perfectly idiotic," Felicia said once, "to build all four sides alike. Of course a lost child could never find his way."

But to every question put concerning the probability of finding his place of abode, Jacob gave his tired, brave little, "Easy."

Suddenly a much-distracted girl of twelve or fourteen came bouncing across the street, crying and yelling at once: "There's Jakie! There's Jakie!" And a mother and father and grandmother followed, all very voluble and grateful.

Felicia kissed the tired, dirty little face good-bye.

"Jacob, I am Miss Felicia Brown. Can you remember me?"

"Easy," came the faint sleepy answer, and with much bobbing of jeweled ear-rings and many effusive thanks the reunited family of the house of Israel disappeared into the costuming house from whence they had come.

"Miss Brown, I believe we have a few friends in common," her companion remarked as they turned on their homeward way, "beside our young friend 'Easy.' The Miltons of Pittsburgh gave me letters to your family when I located here a few weeks ago."

Then a very friendly Felicia and an interested young physician had a short walk to the big stone house of the Spencer-Brown's on Capitol Heights.

"I have the Miltons to thank for their kindness," he said, as she turned a moment on the steps, "but I feel particularly indebted to a small specimen in a dirty red sweater and with an optimistic tendency of looking at life."

"Poor baby," Felicia said, "I want to see him again soon."

"Lucky little beggar!" her companion murmured smilingly. "If your desires for reuniting us were only strong enough to—?" he questioned.

Felicia laughed.

"You may come—and bring the Milton's letter," she finished.

"The name of 'Miltons' is the password?"

"No," as she ran up the steps and looked back at him over a huge stone lion. "No, the password is 'Easy.'"

That night when Miss Felicia's lights were out, she stood by her window a few moments and looked over the buildings to where the city hall loomed big and gray against the sky.

"Wasn't he dear?" she murmured to the clock in the tower. "Jacob, I mean."

The summer passed and the autumn came and Jacob Moses Israel, resplendent in a new red sweater, went to school to Miss Felicia in the big brick building on Thirty-Fourth Street. His nervous little fingers made smudgy paintings and funny drawings. He grew wildly interested in the social problems of the Little Red Hen, and none of the thirty-nine felt as vividly as he such delicious, creepy chills of excitement over the adventures of the Three Bears. To everything Miss Felicia asked him to do, he gave his funny little smile and said 'Easy.'"

"Why he says that all the time, I can't understand," Felicia remarked to Dr. Robert Middleton one evening. "The children were making little gifts this afternoon to lay away until Christmas. You should have seen Jacob's. I gave him a little picture of the Sistine Madonna and he pasted it on a pieced of pink cardboard, painted a big red-and-orange circle around it and dabbed large smudgy dots in the circle. I told him it was very pretty and he should give it to the person he loved best. 'Do you know who that is?' I asked. He gave one more purple daub to it and said, 'Easy.'"

"Good thing his name isn't Mark," murmured the occupant of the big leather chair by the fireplace. He had called long ago armed with the required password, and Felicia had been kind. There had been walks and drives and talks, but of late Robert Middleton had looked things squarely in the face and knew that for his own peace of mind he was with Felicia too much. When rumors began to float here and there that she had relented and that her engagement to the young capitalist would no doubt be announced very soon, Middleton set his square jaw, looked long and steadily into the burning logs in his fireplace, said good-bye to the pictures he saw there and went up to Capitol Heights to tell Felicia that he was going to New York for some special work.

His work took longer than he had expected and only the day before Christmas saw him again in his office. He did not enquire for Felicia—he felt that any news of her would be but the confirmation of her engagement and he felt hardly equal to inviting the fatal announcement.

The young lawyer across the hall, not being snowed under with legal business, strolled in for a few moments talk.

"Oh, by the way, suppose you heard about Stanley?"

"No," answered the doctor shortly.

"Well, old Stanley's crossed the pond. Bundled up his little trunk and gone to Timbuctoo or some other heathen place, and they say it do be Miss Brown that sent him across the briny. You knew her a little, didn't you?" The informant shot a hasty quizzical glance at his tall host.

"Who told you this, Mac?"

"Told me! Town talk for one thing. Besides my little sister who is at the chummy high school stage with Miss Brown's sister Helen says she," he paused mockingly as though for breath, "the Browns and the Spencers an all their ancestors are making particular mincemeat of Miss Brown's feeling by rubbing it in that she's been extremely unwise to ship Graham. And, by George! she certainly has. Why, man, some day he'll be worth. . . ." But Dr. Middleton didn't stop to hear at what the Stanley estates were valued. He suddenly remembered an important errand, and was down to the elevator even while he explained.

Miss Felicia Brown came slowly down the curving stairway, buttoning her long gloves. Could the forty members of Room No. 1 have seen their goddess then, they would have opened their eyes at the dazzling sight and felt in some indefinable childish way that verily the Kingdom of Pedagogy was not of these. The trim figure in the shirtwaist and pretty ties one could love with all one's heart, and even touch if one were very brave. But that was Minerva; tonight it was Venus of the starry eyes who came slowly down the stairway. A lace coat had slipped back from her shoulders, the soft white gown clung lovingly in graceful outline and about her was the vague sweet scent of some woodland flower.

She sat down in the library to wait for her escort. From across the way in one of the big churches came the voices of the choir in "Little Town of Bethlehem."

"Christmas Eve," Felicia mused to the fire. "Christmas Eve and tomorrow I'll get my gifts, everything that heart could wish." She lifted a proud little chin and glanced toward the big chair on the other side of the fire.

A loud peal of the bell startled her from her dreaming, and almost without waiting for admission the door was thrown open and a man carrying a little limp form, white with snow, stepped into the reception room. It was Robert Middleton and he paused a moment with the child in his arms, a tam-o'-shanter dropped to the floor, and the little coat thrown back revealed the stripes of a diminutive red sweater. Through the hall door, which had been left open, crowded a hesitating mob from the porch and steps, among them the gilt buttons of a policeman shining under the porch light.

With a low cry Felicia ran to the boy.

"Jacob, dear," she called softly. But the baby mouth and the little nervous fingers were still. She glanced fearfully at Robert Middleton, who was already asking for a place in which to lay him.

"Tell me, first," she said quickly.

"Knocked down by the streetcar. Can't tell just how serious. Don't worry, Felicia." The name which had slipped out so unconsciously was unnoticed by either.

"Come," she said quietly.

They put him on Felicia's own bed and cut away the little clothes. Then the little bones were skillfully set and word sent to the distracted parents. Sometime during the evening the escort called and was sent away. After the confusion had subsided and they were resting in the library, Dr. Middleton told Felicia how he had been on the car when the boy was hurt. "He must have been coming up here," he said, "for he probably knows no one else up here on the hill,—he started to cross the track when the car struck him."

A maid came to the door and gave Felicia a little box. "I found this on the front steps when I went out to tell the neighbors how the little boy was."

Felicia cut the knotted string and lifted out a picture of the Sistine Madonna on a pink cardboard, a red and orange circle around it, and big purple polka dots in the circle. A new feature had been added, however, since Felicia had last seen it.

Scattered among the gorgeous purple dots were the words "Fr tHe Wun i LuV." She turned with a sudden mist of tears to the grave sympathetic face watching her. "Oh, Doctor, save his little life, his baby mouth, and his brave little smile."

Presently came the moment that the boy was conscious and she quickly bent over the bed. "Jacob, dear, this is Miss Brown. Do you know me?" The head gave a faint nod.

"They said you were so brave and good, dear. How could you be so brave?" Just a faint shadow of the old smile touched the baby mouth as it whispered, "Easy."

It was midnight. Felicia was standing by the fire in the library. Jacob's mother and aunt were in the room with him, and she was not needed. Someone came in and after a moment's hesitation crossed to her side.

"You were going out this evening," he said looking down at the slender girl in the white gown.

"Yes," she said, "the opera. I had forgotten it."

"This has been a hard evening for you. You are nervous and tired, Felicia."

And Felicia couldn't help it. The strain of the evening, the long weeks that had passed, all leagued together to bring the tears, and she put her head over on her friendly old leather chair and let them come, for even a Minerva and a Venus must sometimes be a Niobe. And Dr. Robert Middleton gathered the girl and the lace gown and the woodland blossoms into his arms without so much as "by your leave."

"Felicia," he breathed, "little girl of my heart. The boy and I were both coming up tonight with our Christmas gifts. His was the best he had and you loved it. Mine is the best I can give you, too. It is my heart. Look at me, dear. Do you think you could love my gift, too?"

And Felicia raised a face that was both tearful and smiling, and whispered, "Easy."

The Little House Next Door

(Margaret Dean Stevens)

After the family's move to Elmwood, Nebraska, Aldrich wrote nothing for about two years and then wrote this story, also under her pen name, in answer to a notice about a contest in the *Ladies Home Journal*. Out of more than two thousand submitted, this was one of the six that the editors selected for publication in the 28 July 1911 issue.

It was such a quaint, old-fashioned grape-arbor that the sunbeams lingered there a little longer than necessary. Sunbeams are independent little things; in a dismal spot where dark deeds are hidden they frighten and scamper away; on a bank of nodding white clover where the bees stumble about drowsily they stay long after scheduled time.

The old arbor was a tangle of gnarled vines twisted about the trellis-work with the growth of many summers, while the big green leaves might almost have kept out a heavy rain so dense were they. Indeed the sunbeams, piqued at the refusal of the leaves to let them in, tumbled over each other in their rush to get through the opened archway. Even then they could not quite reach the girl in the hammock, but fell on the white stone flags, where they danced and struggled in a vain endeavor to touch her pink gown.

The girl laughed at their mad efforts, and, throwing her arms above her head, curled herself up more comfortably in an ecstasy of abandon.

Just outside the arbor a bed of Johnny-jump-ups lifted their comical little faces, and long rows of scarlet geraniums smiled brightly on each side of the moss-grown walk. The green lawn stretched peacefully up to the back door of the house and away on each hand to the neighboring hedges. People in Baywood were not packed in city lots, but gave themselves room for lawns, tennis courts and vegetable gardens, while many an old family horse had his half lot in which to shake his clumsy hoofs.

The old Colonial house seemed none the less peaceful than its surroundings. The small-paned windows blinked sleepily in the afternoon sunshine, and the shady porch, with its easychairs and swinging fern-baskets, seemed a haven of rest.

"How peaceful it all seems," said the girl drowsily and half aloud.

Elizabeth Stanford was visiting her uncle for the twenty-third summer. Ever since she had been brought, red and bestowing wails on a colicky world, she had not missed spending a period each summer at Baywood. Born and brought up in a city she had in her childhood looked forward to these visits as the happiest time in the whole year. And now that the harum-scarum days of romping were over—and since even schooldays were over—no less happily did she count on the rest and quiet to be found each summer at Uncle Thad's.

As she sat swaying to and fro, the quiet broken only by an inquisitive robin, the city seemed very far away. Fading with the city went the thoughts of Mr. Ward Van Meter, his money and his social position.

Betty, very much a favorite and very much a beauty, was sought by the fastidious Mr. Van Meter as an altogether tasteful accompaniment to his big, empty house and his big, full purse.

"When I come back from Uncle Thad's I'll be ready to tell you. Please don't say anything more about it now," she had said.

"But, Miss Elizabeth, can't you give a fellow something to think about while you are gone—some little word that he can sort of depend on?"

Betty had been just a wee bit irritated for a moment. "I don't know—truly I don't. But I am sure I can think it all out in the summer down there."

But now that she was here in the hammock ready to "think it all out," she could not seem to concentrate her mind on anything but a fat, old beetle that was laboring up a stalk of hollyhock.

"But of course I will; I know I will," thought Betty; "for life would be so easy—the family expects it—and I could do so much good with the money," she added almost apologetically.

She would have given the subject more detailed thought, she was sure, if Robert Carhart had not come striding over the lawn, his big frame almost filling the arch of the arbor.

"Hello, Midge!" He came toward her with his hands outstretched.

"Hello, Bugs!" she laughed up at him, giving him her hands.

"How's the old, wooden doll?"

"All right. Have you got your turtle-tank made yet?"

It was the way they began every summer—some nonsense in reference to the old days when Bob had followed her about like a big, faithful dog, pulling her out of tight places and championing her cause before a scandalized aunt.

They seated themselves on the garden-seat in the arbor. Betty gave her dainty skirts a little pat, saying comfortably: "Now we will have an old-fashioned visit, won't we?"

"Sure! Fire ahead."

"Well, then, Bob Carhart, have you been good?"

"Mostly."

"Have you been smoking?"

"Just an occasional pipe when the 'blue devils' got me."

"Especially blue, Bob?"

"Now and then."

"What about?"

"Quite a small thing, I assure you," and his eyes twinkled at her.

"How's the practice?" she asked, ignoring the twinkle.

"Pretty fair."

"Any new clients?"

"A few."

"Tell me more about them."

"Well, the Lieutenant-Governor sent for me to do some odd jobs for him."

"Oh, Bob, I'm so glad. I knew you would make good."

"Nothing very exciting financially, though."

"It will be getting better all the time now, especially since you have gone in with Attorney Foster."

"Optimist!" he smiled at her.

"But what makes you blue, Bobbie?" she asked sympathetically.

"You wouldn't understand, little girl," and he threw twigs at the patient beetle.

"I always did understand, didn't I?"

"You were always—just right," and his big hand closed over her little one.

The color surged over her face and faded, leaving it a little pale.

"Class dismissed," she said gayly. "Eighty per cent is all I can give you in this year's quiz, for I feel it in the air that you have concealed dire things from me."

Neither spoke for a time and then it was Betty who broke the silence.

"Well, Bob," she said lightly, "what about *my* yearly catechism?"

He straightened his shoulders and turned toward her.

"Well, then, is it true?"

"What true?" Betty parried, and added paradoxically, "What have you heard?"

"Oh, some of us fossils down here in Baywood read the Washington society items," he answered—somewhat ferociously.

Betty's face suddenly lost its smile and she spoke slowly:

"Bob—honestly I don't know whether it is true or not. I haven't decided. I was thinking it all over when you came."

"And you don't think that fact a little significant?"

"Your coming?" Betty laughed and meant to give her usual mischievous answer, but something in the sincere blue eyes bent upon her caused her suddenly to drop her own and become confused.

Bob arose and strode back and forth in the little arbor. "Betty," he came toward her and took both her hands now. "Oh, Betty, I've cared so long—ever since you were five and I was ten. I couldn't say anything before—I'd have been a cad—Father's debts to cancel—Mother to care for— she's gone now." His voice was breaking a little. "I'm not rich—probably never will be. I've nothing but myself and a heart full of love for you. Nothing could take that away from me—that would be mine whatever happens. I could see you marry him if you care for him. Your happiness means more to me than anything. But you must tell me you do care for him. Tell me that and I'll go away, and not bother you any more. Do you, Betty?"

She was biting her lips, fighting to keep the tears back.

"Do you, Betty?" he urged gently.

She shook her head.

"I don't know, Bob, truly. He has been very good to me, and the liking is so mixed with the liking for the good times—and gay life—and other things—that I can't know for sure."

"Do you care for *me*, just a little, Midge?"

The tears started now, but she nodded bravely.

"I mustn't take advantage of your sympathy, must I? You must decide for yourself. It's your happiness that counts, dearie, not mine. But if you could know just what you have been to me all these years. I'm not a whiner, but the years were hard and no one to care after Mother left me. It was your friendship and sympathy that got me over the rough places. And now, after all these years, I want you, dear—so much. I thought I would be contented with your friendship and what it had meant. But it isn't enough. I want *you* with every fiber of feeling in me."

She put her head on the high arm of the garden-seat.

He walked back of her and patted the black hair.

"But you mustn't feel badly for me, dear, if you care for him. Your happiness is more than mine, little girl—more than mine."

His big hand was stroking her hair as gently and tenderly as a woman's. Nothing was heard but the homely sounds of the old town—a bird or two, a pony trotting along the shady street, the rustle of the vines.

"It's such a quiet old place—you might not be happy here. I know I'm crazy asking you to come, when that other means ease and all the gay life you love. For myself I like the place. I'd love it above every other place on earth if you were here to stay," he continued in his deep, quiet voice.

"Every day in going to the office I pass by the little house next door. For years I've liked that little place. Each time I go past there I think what it would mean to me to turn in at the gate and have you there. Winter nights I've gone by when the lights were low and the shades half drawn and a fire burning in the grate. It looked so peaceful and homelike. I've pretended you were sitting by the fire waiting for me. Summertimes I've pretended you were on the porch or sitting in the window-seat. You would have on a white dress and your hair would be coiled low, like you used to wear it."

The girl was sobbing frankly now. The big man stood looking down at her with all his love in his eyes.

"Now I've made you feel badly—maybe spoiled your visit. That would be punishment enough for me. I'm going to leave you now, little girl, and let you be alone. You must do just what your heart says; for, rich or poor, city or town, Betty girl, the heart must be satisfied. I'm coming back this evening and you are to tell me then."

He stroked the dark, fluffy hair for a moment longer and went quietly out of the arbor.

Half an hour later a big limousine, too aristocratic for Baywood, came up the shady street, and gracefully and silently drew up to the curbing.

Betty, curled up in the window-seat of her room, saw the chauffeur alight and start toward the house, and heard a refined voice saying: "Wait a moment, Trotter; I will go myself."

She descended to answer the old knocker, to invite the caller in, and to tell of her aunt's hurried departure to the bedside of a sick friend that afternoon.

The caller was a woman of middle age with a face of haunting sweetness. She was most perfectly gowned and had that unmistakable air that betokens culture and gentle breeding.

"I am very sorry, indeed, to miss your good aunt," she said, "but I have a favor to ask of you. Could you tell me where I might find the agent of the little house next door? I want so much to go over the place."

"Why," said Betty in her pleasant, girlish voice, "the key is here. The agent, who is a very old friend of Uncle Thad's, is away, and he asked to leave the key with Uncle for a few days. Let me get it for you."

She had seen Uncle Thad put it on the mantel, so getting it quickly she gave it to the stranger.

"I am not a prospective renter"—and the gracious lady smiled—"but just a sentimental old woman who wants to turn back many pages and live for a time in the past. Will you come with me, my dear? I would be very glad to have you."

Betty, glad to accommodate her and just a wee bit curious, too, readily assented, and they passed down the moss-grown steps, across the green lawn, sweet from its recent mowing, and through the opening in the hedge that separated the big house from the little one.

Betty was studying hard on the problem of who this beautiful woman could be, for at no time had she volunteered that information. Like a flash there suddenly came to her mind a name of National reputation, a name of such immense wealth and of such social position that it was, indeed, a name to conjure with. There was no mistaking that beautifully pathetic face. Betty had seen it in papers and magazines many times.

So it was with a feeling of surprise and astonishment that she heard the great lady say: "You see, my dear, I lived in this little house when I was first married. We built it too. My husband was a lumber clerk, so we got the material cheaper."

The story of that lumber clerk's rise, like a fairy story, was known to every schoolchild in the land: clerk, lumber-yard owner, long-sighted purchaser of timberlands, investor in hardwood forests, Wall Street multi-millionaire. And his lovely wife, whose beauty and social triumphs were known to two continents, was saying simply: "So we got the material cheaper."

Betty gave her a sympathetic smile from which she eliminated all curiosity.

The modish skirts of the gracious lady fluttered delicately against the low, green currant-bushes as they passed up the path.

"I made currant jelly that first year," she said smilingly. "There were twelve little glasses of it. I remember it as though it were yesterday. I could have got it all in eleven, but I had twelve cunning little glasses, and I wanted to fill the whole dozen to surprise John, so I put short measure in each."

Betty couldn't resist a smile, too, but her smile was at the thought of "John" exulting over the jelly—"John," whose pleasures now were Mediterranean cruises on an elegant yacht, and a twenty-room hunting lodge in the mountains.

They passed up the steps and the lady paused with the key in the door: "I wonder why I'm doing this. It will break my heart and not do anybody the least good in the world. But for some reason or other I have felt this summer that after all these years I must come back. It is more luck than I dared expect, to find the house vacant. People would not have wanted a foolish old woman poking about their rooms."

She opened the door slowly, as though she were either afraid to meet the past or desired to prolong an anticipated pleasure.

They stepped directly into the living-room, apparently a pleasant one running across the entire front of the house. Although empty it had been left neat and clean. The warm afternoon sun flooding it cheerfully gave it a hospitable appearance, void of that feeling of loneliness usual in empty houses.

"It seems like yesterday," the lady said again. "For years it seemed so very far away—the life here—like it was another girl who had lived it. Sometimes I think it was another girl, for, as I remember her, she was sweet and happy and contented—and I'm not—I'm a cross, discontented woman."

Betty shook her head and smiled, deeming it more tactful to let the lady think she was unknown to her.

"I suppose it looks like a forlorn little house to you, my dear," she said, as she walked over to the empty fireplace. "But to me there is a pretty Axminster rug on the floor and a library-table in the center. The rug cost twenty-eight dollars and a half, and John and a carpenter made the table. The bookshelves are here, each side of the mantel. A vase, the only piece of cut glass we had, is on top of this one, and a little plaster cast of Psyche is on this one.

"Over here is the piano—my father's and mother's wedding gift to us. The little music-cabinet stood here. The music in it is 'The Maiden's Prayer' and 'Angels' Serenade,' and some old songs that John used to like: 'Daisy Dean,' 'The Little Brown Church in the Vale' and 'Ben Bolt.'" She hummed the line, "Sweet Alice, whose hair was so brown," in a singularly sweet and clear voice.

"Ah me! Ah me!" she smiled; "and now we have Sembrich and Melba and Scotti at the house to sing for us." She paused and looked out of the small-paned windows for a few moments, unmindful of Betty, and then suddenly resumed more cheerfully:

"And here on the table are the books. Some say 'From John to Molly,' and some 'From Molly to John.' There were Emerson's 'Essays' and 'Jane Eyre' and Tennyson. I wonder how it ever became changed to Bernard Shaw and Ibsen and Maeterlinck.

"And the chairs: there were just three in this room, John's and mine and the caller's, and when more than one caller came we had to bring a dining-room chair in. The caller's chair was slender and had little fine spindles. I know John sat in it one time and broke the arm off—he was too big for it." And she laughed reminiscently. "My chair was on this side of the fireplace and John's was on this. And we sat there, long winter evenings, and read and talked. Oh, my dear," she broke off passionately, "whatever you do always keep two chairs by the fireplace."

Betty knew the meaning of that little heartcry as well as though it had been explained at length—a cry that carried a world of sorrow with it because they were such a long way now from the two chairs by the fireplace.

"Well, let us go to the dining-room," she said brightly. "Such a wee little house, isn't it, but so bright and cheery!"

Even to Betty's eyes the possibilities of the cozy little dining-room were apparent although it was empty, save for the built-in china-closet and window-seat.

"The table was here," the visitor began. "John sat here, and I sat there and poured the coffee. I had three square tablecloths and two long ones. We had pretty little dishes with pink sprays on them. We only had six drinking-glasses, and in my clumsiness I had broken all but two. I neglected to replenish the supply, and one noon just as we sat down to dinner—we dined at noon in those days—John's cousin walked in. Luckily John had not tasted his glass of water and he quickly passed it to the cousin's plate. Then during the meal he nearly convulsed me at intervals by looking at me and swallowing painfully as though he were choking to death." And she laughed a merry, youthful laugh.

Betty laughed, too, and followed her to the window-seat.

"Here is the place I used to sit and watch for John in the evening," she was saying.

Betty's heart began playing her a riotous tune. "I'd pretend you were sitting in the window-seat waiting for me," Bob had said.

"It is a dear little house," Betty said impulsively.

"Yes," said the lady. "Any one who lives here should be very happy. I think I'll tell you a secret. I never breathed it to a soul before: *I believe if we had stayed here among the vines with the window-seat and the two chairs by the fireside we, too, would have been happy always.*"

They passed into the kitchen and the sorrowful mood of the lady changed to her girlish one.

"Oh! Oh! Oh!" she laughed, "wasn't it funny! I had blue gingham dresses and white aprons with little pockets in them, and I loved to cook. Once I entered doughnuts at the county fair. I didn't get the prize, and John said he didn't know what the judge was thinking of."

Betty laughed and opened the cupboard door.

"What a dear little place," she said.

"Yes," said the lady, "I kept my spices on that shelf, sugar and coffee on that one, and the milk tickets here. How it all comes back. The stove was here and the table there. We ate here on cold mornings. I baked little griddle cakes or waffles. John always liked them so well."

Betty thought of John's reputation for ordering dinners, his titles of "Prince of Diners" and "Connoisseur of Wines."

"I had a little servant girl who came Wednesday and Saturday mornings to help me," the lady continued. "She was a Swede and so neat and clean. We laughed and had such good times together with the work. Her name was Selma Knudsen. She was going to marry a carpenter. I wish I knew where Selma is. I would like to see her."

They had passed back to the dining-room and the lady said: "I must hurry, for the sun is getting low."

"This room," opening a door, "was a little guest-chamber. There were pink poppies in the wall paper, and the chairs had pink cretonne coverings. There were white, ruffled curtains, and in the spring the cherry blossoms looked in at the windows. The first person who ever slept here was my grandfather. He said it was a fine room and a fine house, but none too good for his Molly. When he left he said, 'Always be a good girl, Molly, and keep sweet and true.'"

Tears glistened for the first time in the fine eyes.

"Now," she said, as she put her hand on the knob of a closed door, "I've purposely saved this until the last, for I want to say good-by to my little house from here."

She swung open the door and stepped softly in as though some one lay sleeping.

"This had pale blue paper," she said in a hushed voice, "and a little silver moulding. There was matting on the floor and there were two little blue rugs. The bed had a dotted Swiss coverlet over blue and the curtains were the same. There was just one picture. It hung at the foot of the bed. John gave it to me one Christmas. It was a little copy of a Madonna and Child in a silver frame. I went to Europe last year to get the original."

She put up a jeweled hand and touched the spot where the copy had hung.

"That was the Christmas before the baby came," she said. "She only lived a few hours."

She walked across the room and stood looking down, as though upon a sleeping child.

"If you had lived," she said softly, "I would have been a good mother."

Betty turned away quickly and walked from the room. The other came, too, and together they stepped out on the porch.

The lady placed the key in the lock, but made no move to close the door. Instead she stood looking into the house as though loath to leave. She was repeating something, but Betty only caught the last:

" 'And what if it crumbled away at our feet,
We had our dream—and the dream was sweet.' "

"Love began here. I wonder," she said curiously, "was it here that it ended?" She was speaking slowly. "Maybe we just left it here. Wouldn't it be queer if we simply forgot to pack it—and it is still here?"

"Perhaps it is," said Betty. "Aunt calls this the 'Bride's House.' Ever so many people have lived here and they have all been happy."

The lady's face cleared. "I'm glad you told me that. It is a happy thought. I shall always think of it in that way. We left our love here for others." She locked the door and turned to Betty. "Here is the key. I hope you will give it only to some one who is worthy."

They passed down the little walk, bordered with sweet alyssum and candytuft. At the gateway they paused while the car glided up softly. Already the lady's manner had changed. Although seemingly as gracious as ever, there was a faint suggestion of hauteur about her, as though, coming out of the past, she had again assumed an habitual mask.

"Good-by, dear," she said, taking Betty's hand; "forget the ravings of a passing stranger—and thank you for a charming half hour."

At supper-time Betty was irresistible. She had coiled her hair low, and wore a little white slip of a dress in which she looked eighteen. She laughed and talked and sang and teased the old uncle and aunt like a perfect hoyden. She helped Jane in the kitchen with the dishes and delighted the old soul with her nonsense.

"What's got into you, Midge?" Uncle Thad asked. "Yesterday you were an aristocratic, finished young lady, and tonight you're nothing but a tomboy. And a mighty pretty one," he added irrelevantly.

Betty answered him with an impetuous fling of her arms about his neck. "Oh, it's the air down here in Baywood; it's so sort of sweet and pure and—lovely."

"Auntie," she said a few minutes later, "Bob is coming tonight for—an old-fashioned chat, and if I'm not here you tell him that I'm over at the little house next door looking for—a lace handkerchief I may have lost this afternoon."

She sped through the little hedge even as she heard the click of the gate at Uncle Thad's. Unlocking the house she crossed to the window-seat and dropped into it with her heart pounding from running—and other things.

The moon was up now, flooding the windowseat and casting little silvery ripples on the empty built-in china-closet.

When she saw him step easily over the low hedge she grew frightened and sprang up to run out of the house, but the back door was locked, and as for the front door—to go that way would be sheer folly.

So she dropped back on the seat and——

My Life Test

(Anonymous)

Aldrich wrote this story in response to a *Ladies Home Journal* contest announcement, winning fifth place in a field of almost five thousand entries. The story was published anonymously (in February 1913) because of what the editors called the "confidential aspect" of the material. It was also edited somewhat to fit the length requirements of the magazine.

Aldrich was fiercely loyal to and protective of farmers. She often portrayed them as intelligent and thoughtful college graduates who were as knowledgeable about Shakespeare as they were about silos. "Their House of Dreams" (1918) and "Romance in G Minor" (*Delineator,* 1929) bear messages similar to this story's, as does the concluding portion of her novel *Spring Came on Forever* (New York: D. Appleton, 1925).

Here also is Aldrich's first consideration of the benefits of rural life over urban life, a theme she would examine at greater length in "Mother's Excitement over Father's Old Sweetheart" (1919), "The Old Crowd" (1915), and "The Rosemary of Remembrance" (1917).

Being a college graduate and a farmer's wife it is of the crucial moment in my life wherein the two became reconciled that I write. Some there are who will blame me, calling me narrow that I held such nonsensical views; others will sympathize with the viewpoint from which I saw my life at the time. It is to the latter, and especially to any who might perchance be standing at the crossroads where a like decision awaits them, that I tell my little story.

My girlhood was spent in a carefree way in one of the happiest homes in a college town. Could youth find a more alluring picture? There is ever a healthy freedom under like conditions not to be found in other places.

Of a naturally romantic nature my idea of friendships with young men was based on the same principles of our happy college days, and while I had known many bright young classmates for whom I entertain a wholesome regard I kept myself free from anything of a serious nature, feeling that somewhere, some time, "my own would come to me." When he came, as he did a year later while I was teaching, he seemed everything to me that the college "boys" had not seemed: he was more mature, a rising lawyer, an ex-Consul, a man among men.

We became engaged, and then followed a year of separation in which I was at home preparing for our coming marriage.

In the spring word came from him that his father was lying at the point of death, and that he was leaving immediately for the old farm home, there to meet with his brothers and sisters who were also hastening homeward. A letter that the father had passed away came next, and then this one:

> *Dearest Marian:* We laid Father away yesterday in peaceful Mount Auburn. He was a good man, loved and honored by all who knew him. He is at rest. We shall miss the kindly old face, but I think he is happier to be where Mother is.
>
> There is no one left now to call the old place home. It is like an empty nest, or like a loved body from which the soul has gone.
>
> We sat about the grate last night, the brothers and sisters, saddened both from Father's death and from the impending loss of the old home. We talked a little of the feasibility of keeping it, but there seemed to be no one to see that it was kept up. The girls, of course, have their own homes, Ed has his railroad business, John his Denver church, and Frank his dental practice.
>
> After the others had gone to bed I sat far into the night with a half-formed plan in my mind. I arose this morning

early, walked to a high point in the timber back of the house, where, in my boyhood days, I had threshed out my youthful problems; and there, watching the sun rise, I came to a definite conclusion: I am going to buy the old place from the other heirs. I shall have to borrow a little capital, for I haven't quite enough to cover the amount, and I want every foot of the land. I am going to give up the law, and I am coming here to live as God must have intended men to live. I am going to plow and sow and reap and live in the open. I have felt the call to the land for several years, but it was easier to keep on in my practice than to make the break. I thought it all out this morning, with the song of the birds about me and the spring smell of the rich loam in my nostrils. The office, with its grind and the petty grief of our clients, seemed very far away; the artificial life of S——, with its constant social strivings, seemed suddenly an unworthy thing; and with bared head I thanked God for the wisdom to see my life as it should be.

Then followed a sweet, intimate portion of the letter, concerning our coming marriage, of the happy life we would have together; there would "again be little children in the old home——." But I was in no mood for any of this. I was stunned. That he should make this move without first consulting me seemed incredible. Who was I—Marian Barclay, Professor Barclay's daughter, educated, talented, a social favorite in my home town—who was I, to marry a farmer? Oh, I proved to myself that I was an egotistical little prig, there is no denying that! I was mystified. That a man of his education and standing in the community should deliberately turn his back on an honorable profession, with its social advantages, and choose to be a farmer seemed unbelievable. I was disgusted. "To plow and sow and reap." Yes, and wear overalls, and be dirty and sweaty! Ugh! How could he? And to think that my home-town friends didn't know him; and now, instead of appearing as the distinguished young lawyer from S——, he would come to our wedding in the autumn a sun-tanned farmer. And I to be a farm drudge all my life!

Well, at least it wasn't too late. I didn't have to be a farmer's wife. But I loved him. That was the hardest point to meet. I couldn't give him up. Plainly the thing to do was to dissuade him from this foolish venture, this fad that seemed to be his for the moment and which he would in time thank me for persuading him to relinquish.

I wrote him to that effect. Letters at any time are more or less unsatisfactory, and this one must have seemed a combination of all that was petulant, angry and sarcastic. His reply contained much that was kind and considerate: a steadfast opinion that he was doing the best thing, and an underlying note of disappointment in me that I couldn't fail to detect. One sentence stands out clearly in my mind: "I want to ask you one question, little girl. Do you love *me*, or did you love the idea of being a lawyer's wife and moving in the S—— social set?"

It was a miserable way for things to go on.

I went one afternoon with two of my club-girl friends to a concert in the college auditorium, a famed orchestra having been secured. It was such an occasion as I most enjoyed—the music, the pretty gowns, the soft chatter between numbers. Before it was over I had determined to stay in the environment I loved. There would be my parents and my pretty home, the college life, the concerts and lectures, the little nephews I adored.

Upon returning home I went to my room and wrote the letter, a letter so bitter that it would forever sever the bond between us. I have happily forgotten much that I said, but I know I quoted:

> Let it pass in silence,
>> We'll forget.
> There are, doubtless, things to live for
>> Even yet:
> And Life holds far nobler uses
>> Than regret.

With my heart full of sadness, rebellion and anger I walked along the shady old streets to the post-office. I dropped in the letter—and a sudden panic seized me.

"George," I said to the neighbor boy at the post-office window, "could you hand me back that letter? I've forgotten something—important." I had. I had forgotten that love is the greatest thing in the world.

"Sure," he said with a friendly smile.

I walked to the hill beyond the cemetery. I don't know how long I stayed, and I cannot follow the intricacies of the debate that went on in my mind and heart. But I fought it out—the foolish pride that bound me to the conventions of what I chose to call "my station in life"—and renewed the love for a good strong man whom I trusted implicitly. I came down from my hill a wiser, maturer woman, and I did not go home by way of the post-office.

That night I told Father and Mother of the change in our plans. Father, strange to say, seemed wonderfully well pleased. There seems ever a call to Nature in the hearts of men. Mother was more dubious. She had a "sister who had worn herself out on a farm"; it wasn't just what she had "planned" for me—and, such is the perversity of human nature, I found myself defending before her what I had previously despised.

W̲e were married in the autumn—my farmer and I. Oh, yes! He was tanned from the summer's work, but so was "Charlie" Morgan, who had been "lazying" away the summer down East on his uncle's yacht.

Next to my family I have learned to love the old place, and two children play in the big, grassy yard. We have prospered. We have refitted and refurnished the fine old brick house. We have books and pictures and music. A touring car stands in the garage. We have our friends with us often. My husband's influence is felt far and wide, in country and in town alike. Better than these we have our health, we are happy, contented, tranquil.

I wouldn't make the picture more ideal than truthful. There has been plenty of hard work. I have ironed and baked and sewed, and I think I have canned *tons* of fruit. But I have been happy; and when work and health and happiness go hand in hand what more in life is there to be desired?

If I have worked hard so has Esther Cole, one of the girls with whom I attended the concert that long-ago afternoon. Witness her last letter:

> Tuesday we were entertained at luncheon at the Savoy by Mrs. Emory-Dodge; then from there we went to Mrs. Hambright's for bridge, to the Middletons' for dinner and a theater party afterward. I was nearly *dead*. I'm coming out to "The Oaks" one of these days, Marian, if it's convenient, and try to catch up.

Ah, me! The things that used to seem worth while!

And an extract from Clara Burnham's last:

> I just gave my little annual entertainment, a rose luncheon—and, Marian, it cost us $65, half of Fred's salary. It just makes me *sick,* the *awful* high cost of living. But what is one to do?

Ah, well! "A crucial moment in any life, viewed through a ten-year perspective, becomes softened and mellowed."

What We Think of the Man Who Is Ashamed of His Wife: Is *My* Husband Ashamed of Me?

(Mrs. C. A., Nebraska)

The November 1912 *Ladies World* carried an article titled "Why I Am Ashamed of My Wife"; the following February (1913) the editors acknowledged that in response to it they had received a "most remarkable series of human documents" some of which were "too intimate and too tragic" for the magazine to print. The editors did, however, publish several replies that expressed varying viewpoints and were of general interest. Among the printed respondents was Bess Streeter Aldrich.

In reading my *Ladies World* last night I came across the startling headlines, "Why I Am Ashamed of My Wife." I looked across the library table at Edward, my big, solid, well-to-do, well-known husband.

"Edward," I said, "did you write that?" and held up the paper for him to read.

He laughed his easy, deep laugh.

"Yes, mother," he said; "how did you guess it?" and settled comfortably back in his big leather chair.

It was just our little joke of course, but some way I have thought of those flaming headlines ever since. The article is good and there is contained therein many a good lesson for a young wife. The case is not my own, for Edward never had reason to be ashamed of a neglected house or a tin-canned supper. But one paragraph struck me with a sharp blow. It was the one about how we see in a railway train or a steamboat an alert, well-dressed man with his wife, who doesn't seem to be of his own style. It is in behalf of those wives, and because I am one of them, that I write.

Some of you would know who Edward is if I should give you his name, for he has made a success of his business and has been honored more than once in a political way. I have often thought that he had cause to be ashamed of me, for I am—well, I am just Mother.

Years ago Edward came out to this new country, got some land and started a little store. When he had been here a year he went back to Indiana for me—the girl he loved. I was nineteen. I had never been away from my mother. I never saw her again.

The journey was long and tiresome: the last twenty-two miles was made in an old lumber-wagon.

We went to housekeeping in the room behind the store. I can remember just how cozy it looked with the geraniums in the window and my rag rugs on the floor.

Ellen and Ned were both born there. The day Ellen was born a blizzard was raging, so that the doctor could hardly make the nine mile trip. I was nearly gone before he got there. Ah, well, God takes away the memory of the agony when they place the warm little thing in one's arms. She was eight years old when she left us. Such a little woman! She used to say, "I'll always stay with you, mamma, and help you." She has—she has always stayed with me and helped me. I have often thought if we'd had the means then that we now have we might have had a specialist to attend her and perhaps saved her life.

Well, time went on; we continued to prosper (five other children came), and finally Edward went into the banking business, and was elected to the legislature. We moved to the capital and soon after we built Woodlawn. So here we are, just such a couple as the writer says one often sees: Edward, alert, well-dressed, confident of himself; Mother, faded and old.

Oh, yes, I've tried to keep up. I have been manicured and shampooed and massaged. But the hands that have kneaded bread and made soap and even worked in the garden, the manicurist cannot coax into shape. The shoulders that have cuddled seven babies cannot keep from drooping.

I catch a glimpse of myself in the beveled mirror of some fine hotel, and I know people think of me just what the writer of the article says. I have attended dinners with Edward (from which I should like to have been excused) and have worn expensive gowns (which I have been glad to get off).

I have also entertained at Woodlawn many of the people I have met at those dinners, and my manner is that of another woman. In my house dress and ruffled white apron there is nothing I love so much as to have company and oversee a big dinner. We have parties galore for the young people and I am happiest when planning for their pleasure.

My sole point is this: The author and others must not always take the faded appearance of the wife to mean her defeat *in her own line of business—* homekeeping. She may have grown mentally. No one knows the number of times these prominent men take advice from their faded little wives. If she has raised children to be a credit to their father, she has certainly grown in character. As for dropping her accomplishments, almost any man prefers a good steak to a piece on the piano.

Is Edward ashamed of me? In public he has reason to be, perhaps. But not at home, where the whole machinery of the house runs smoothly under my supervision. And do you know there are some of us who are just old-fashioned enough to believe that is where we really belong anyway.

Mrs. C. A., Nebraska

Is *My* Husband Ashamed of Me?

How I Knew When the Right Man Came Along

(Anonymous)

Ladies Home Journal published this story, like "My Life Test" of February 1913, anonymously, due to the "sensitive" nature of the material. It appeared in December 1913.

When I look back upon my girlhood I shudder to think of the ignorance, the false ideals, the lack of any true conception of the meaning of life that was characteristic of it. I wonder that my mother, high minded and gentle natured as she was, could send me off to acquire that higher education which she had so craved for herself without first making some attempt to instruct me in the fundamental facts of life. But that is what she, the best-intentioned mother in the world, did, and I entered our State university as ignorant as a child from the cradle. That the life there, utterly devoid of any restraints or supervision, did not result in some disaster must have been due to an all-wise Providence, for in the house where I lived with half a dozen other "co-eds" each of us did as she pleased, went where she listed, and remained as long as she desired.

In my Sophomore year I met the man whom I fondly believed to be the one and only love of my life. He was handsome, courteous, deferential, charming, in every way the ideal man—and devoted to me. I was ready enough to return his devotion, but some instinct of maidenly reserve made me slow in admitting my love, so it was not until near the close of my Junior year that I blushingly admitted that I loved him as he did me.

There followed one deliriously happy month—the sweet month of May— and then we were plunged into the vortex of examinations, out of which

I came with flying colors, but not so my Prince Charming. His neglect throughout that glorious May of the exact scientific work that his course demanded resulted in a formidable list of conditions and failures that bade fair to bring his university career to an abrupt and ignominious end.

And then I was suddenly made to realize the difference between the ardent devotion of a happy lover and the cool judgment of a bitterly disappointed and humiliated youth. For my lover was suddenly transformed into a brooding, moody failure who took no pains to conceal the fact that he held me largely responsible for that failure.

I did my best to console and encourage him, but we parted for the long vacation in a most unloverlike way.

During that vacation I thought deeply, and the truth slowly came to me that there was no real bond of union between my lover and myself. That he had proved selfish and even cowardly in his failure to bear manfully the trouble that he had brought upon himself was bad enough, but that he should have been willing to kill the romance of that perfect May was worse. It was a sadder and wiser young woman who returned to the university for the last year and plunged with all the energy of her ardent nature into the multifarious duties of a Senior.

Before graduation I was called home by the death of my father, and the next three years were spent in straightening out his business affairs. His death made me reflect on how little he and I had been to each other, and then it suddenly dawned upon me that he and my mother had never been happy together, and I gradually realized that the reason for this was a lack of congenial tastes and interests. Mother had always been fond of the best in literature, music and art, while Father, utterly indifferent to art in all its phases, had devoted himself to the business of making money, his one relaxation being his club.

In trying to settle my father's estate I met a young attorney who soon became something more than a friend to me. Not yet thirty he had already attained marked success in his profession, and with his gifts, his compelling personality, and his determination to succeed, he bade fair to attain remarkable success. Had it not been for my experience in college I might have succumbed to his somewhat violent wooing. I could not quite forget the bitter disillusionment that I had suffered, so I parried to gain time, and then the man not of the hour but of all time asked me to be his wife.

I had known him ever since I could remember, but had never thought of him except as a friend of the family. He had given me valuable advice in regard to my father's estate, and had formed the habit of dropping in once or twice a week, but I was quite unconscious of his feeling for me until he told me one afternoon over the teacups. Upon the impulse of the moment I told him I never could care for him in the way he desired, and asked him not to speak of it again. He consented in an enigmatic way and left me, apparently little cast down by my refusal of his proposal.

And then I began to think deeply of the subject of marriage. What was the true basis? How was a young woman to know when the right man came? Was there any really-and-truly "right man," or was this merely an idea, sure to be exploded after, if not before, marriage? My disappointment at college had shown me the futility of romantic love. Now I had the opportunity to marry either my dashing attorney or the somewhat prosaic friend that I had known so long. Would marriage with either of them be what it should be? I determined to be in no hurry to make this momentous decision, and meantime to become as well acquainted as possible with both my suitors.

I began now to observe my married friends and to analyze the cause of their happiness or unhappiness. I soon decided that there was just one general rule that seemed to prevail throughout, and this was that an abiding respect and a deep unity of tastes and interests were to be found in every marriage worthy of the name, and that a lack of these underlay not only the unhappy marriage of my father and mother, but also most of such marriages.

How did this conclusion apply to me and my suitors? I was compelled to admit that it put my friend of the dazzling characteristics out of the running, for by no stretch of the imagination could I think that his tastes and interests were at all similar to mine. He had repeatedly expressed his preference for hotel life, and had said that home with all the duties and responsibilities it entailed was something that he did not care about. He had pointed out the freedom and the opportunities for self-culture and social work that hotel life gave to women, and had announced his intention of giving his wife room to develop her individuality.

I had always listened to these opinions with amusement, never taking them too seriously, but when the question of marrying him was to be decided I could no longer dismiss his ideas with a smile. That he would willingly give up this pet idea of his if I made that a condition of our engagement I did not doubt, but would that settle the question? The fundamental principle was there, and no mere yielding of a cherished plan could affect it.

Another thing was to be considered, something which in my girlhood I would never have allowed myself to think about, and that was the question of the children I might have. If I had not seen the necessity of putting aside for my own sake all petty considerations and all fleeting ambitions, the duty laid upon me of securing the best possible heritage for those whose lives I would be responsible for would surely have compelled me to do so. When this test was applied to the more magnetic of my two lovers I knew at once that he fell before it, while I was compelled to admit that every test applied to my other lover only served to accentuate his real worth.

During the months when I hesitated and vacillated that steadfast friend who was to become the world and all to me remained stanch and true, even though I often appeared indifferent to him. He brought me the very book I wished to read, discussed with me the play in which I was most interested, escorted me to the lecture or recital I desired to attend, and did it all without putting me under a feeling of obligation.

One bleak November afternoon he stopped in on his way home from his office, saying that he was quite unable to resist the thought of our cozy library with its cheerful open fire. My mother soon left us there together, and then for the first time in months he broached the subject of his love. I was not a little surprised to feel myself trembling with emotion at this juncture. Suddenly I realized that this congenial man with the quiet self-control, the unquestioned character and habits, was indeed the right man, even though he were lacking in those superficial attractions that had so long possessed my imagination.

And then another phase of the question was suddenly presented to my mind, and I who had so carefully weighed the respective merits of my suitors found myself doubting my own fitness for wifehood, and heard a new and utterly unknown self falteringly express these doubts to my lover. That he did not share in my misgivings was but another evidence of his unwavering loyalty and proved the turning point in my life. I no longer doubted nor hesitated; but, realizing that I had much to learn, I set about preparing myself for the responsibilities I was to assume, responsibilities that have been glorified for me because they have been shared by the right man.

Molly Porter

(Margaret Dean Stevens)

This is Bess Streeter Aldrich's response to a *Harper's Weekly* request for articles about the people in readers' hometowns. The narrator of this story, which appeared in December 1914 under her pen name, is probably the most folksy, or chatty, of any Aldrich created, paralleled only by the male narrator in "The Lions in the Way" (1917).

The character of Molly Porter would appear in a secondary role in "Welcome Home, Hal" (*Ladies Home Journal,* September 1934), and in *The Rim of the Prairie* (New York: D. Appleton & Company, 1925).

When I saw the question in *Harper's Weekly* about the folks in our town I thought right away about Molly Porter. It's always that way in our town,—the first person you think of is Molly Porter. Our town has seven hundred and eighty nine folks, including babies and Tom Davis who's foolish, but if you took a popular vote Molly Porter would get it all right, I guess.

She's Fred Porter's wife and she's thirty seven years old. She's just *awful* fat. Her face is honestly as big as a *punkin's* and freckled *to beat.*

She always looks nice and neat as wax when she's at home doing her work, but when she gets dressed up to go to church she looks just *comical.*

Fred Porter is a goodlooking man and has the best general merchandise store in town. Most any girl around here would have jumped at the chance to have him fourteen years ago when he married Molly. But what do you know about this? *Molly was his mother's hired girl.* Fred just looked over the heads of Fernetta Myeres (pretty as a doll) and Angie Beeman (a 160 in her own name) and married Molly. His mother cried and took on something terrible but Dad Porter said he didn't know Fred had so much sense and turned the store over to him.

In the whole town everyone goes to Molly Porter for things. When there's a new baby the doctor looks around as he comes in the door and says "Has Molly got here yet?" When anyone dies Molly stands by until the time to close his eyes and fold his hands.

When that silly little Edie Sheffer got into trouble with Ray Horton she never told her mother but went up to Molly's and told *her*. Molly just reached up and got her blue plaid shawl off the hook behind the kitchen door and went down to Bebe's barn where Ray was hanging around with a lot of fellows and had him walk out toward the cemetery with her. She talked to him right out about *babies* and *being a father* 'till Ray got to wiping his sleeve across his eyes,—and that week he married Edie and Molly got him a job in Fred's store.

Molly can get her washing out by eight o'clock and like as not go over and help Grandma Thompson with her's. She always has the lightest rolls and the fluffiest cake at the church suppers. She can make a suit for the school-house janitor's boy out of an old coat of Fred's. When someone comes to your door and says "Molly wants some clothes for a poor family that's camped out on the edge of town," you just scurry and hand them over without a word. When a mother is sick, Molly takes the children home with her, and takes care of them. She never had any babies of her own but sometimes she is taking care of five at once.

And she says, "*I seen*" and "*I have went.*"

There are only two churches in our town and, *believe me,* there is something doing when the Cambellites and the Methodists get to arguing. It's always Molly that pours oil on the troubled waters. When the school board decided not to give any Thanksgiving vacation, the teachers and children were just *hopping* mad. Molly went over to see Lem Parsons, the president, and got him to change his vote. She's a born diplomat. When the suffragists get to running the government Molly will make a good Ambassador to Russia.

Yes, Molly Porter used to be a hired girl and she says "*I have saw*" but she will do just *anything* for *anybody.*

The Old Crowd

(Margaret Dean Stevens)

The idea of a class reunion twenty or twenty-five years after college graduation is one to which, with variations, Aldrich often returned. "The Old Crowd," published in *Ladies World* (June 1915), was the first of these stories, followed by "The Rosemary of Remembrance" (1917), "Mother's Excitement over Father's Old Sweetheart" (1919), and "Fagots for the Fire" (*Today's Housewife*, 1924).

The western sun, shining through the dense leaves of the old oaks, cast little farewell glints of color that danced and quivered over the green velvet slope of the campus. It was as though, feeling the delicious excitement of the day, he was loath to leave.

Excitement, however, was scarcely to be expected from one who had looked upon the same picture for fifty-eight successive years; the geraniums lifting scarlet faces in their prim conventional beds, the ivy clinging loyally to old buildings, the chattering sparrows on moss-covered cannon, the winding walks, leaf-shadowed and cool, where strolled young men and maidens, with a mingling of parents and "old grads."

True, the appearance of the gay-voiced throng changed from year to year. There had been Junes of hoop-skirts when maidens moved slowly and primly; Junes when gowns trailed gracefully in soft-clinging folds; Junes when ruffles fluttered everywhere; Junes of pure white and Junes of as variegated colors as so many sweet peas and hollyhocks.

But to the sun, so many miles away, the change counted for naught, and with his kindly eye he saw only, year after year, the same sweet maidens with their dream-filled eyes and the same hopeful virile young men—Eternal Youth forever loitering under the old oaks.

As the last flickering rays withdrew, five women who had been seated on a grassy knoll near the new Science Building, arose to their feet with varying degrees of agility, for one is not apt to be especially brisk on her twenty-fifth Commencement anniversary.

"Oh, girls, *were* we as dainty and sweet and pretty as the girls we've seen today?" the Minister's Wife asked earnestly. She was a faded little woman with a face of haunting wistfulness.

"Speak for yourself, Sadie, but I know *one* that wasn't," and the Farmer's Wife laughed good-naturedly with a characteristic little crinkling of the eyelids. She was fat and she was dressed more for comfort than style, but her gray hair curled about a placid, motherly face, and one had only to look into her eyes to feel the charm of a peaceful life.

On the chapel steps a little knot of girls were singing in high girlish voices:

"Say, sisters, say,

When we are far away—"

"Why, Polly"—the Governor's Wife turned to her—"it's the same old song you wrote!"

"Yes," she said, and there was a happy moisture behind her glasses. "How it all comes back! I sat on the top step of the stairs over the old hall and wrote the words while the girls were practicing. Eunice kept sticking her head up over the banisters to ask me if I had another verse ready. Why, it seems like yesterday, and yet over there my daughter is singing that same song."

The five were unconsciously humming the air now.

"Do you know," the Millionaire's Wife broke in suddenly, "once at the opera, in Paris, when Sembrich was singing the 'Casta Diva,' some freak of memory put our old song into my mind and I saw as plainly as though it were on the stage before me, the long rows of girls in their old-fashioned mackintoshes crouching along in the rain under the Delta's windows."

The Farmer's Wife reached over and pressed the other's slender jeweled hand with her own rough one.

"I know, dear," she said; "I've had the old times come back the same way. Only," she added, "I've usually been in the hen-house or cutting up pumpkins on the back porch."

The others laughed and began slowly moving across the campus toward the Teacher's suite of rooms, for it was time to dress for the evening concert.

They were an odd little group. The Millionaire's Wife, regal and stately in her Paquin gown, had drawn the arm of the Minister's Wife through her own and was calling her Sadie. The latter looked more faded than ever in contrast to her well-groomed companion, but she carried herself with a certain little queenly air that all the made-over garments of all the years had not been able to destroy.

The Farmer's Wife, puffing and perspiring, but beaming her happiness at being with the old crowd again, was an anomaly in dress. She wore a gray silk of excellent material and a hat with a really beautiful plume, but she carried an out-of-date sunshade and her shoes were a sight. She was even then laughingly explaining to the Governor's Wife and the Teacher how comfortable her shoes were, and how she had managed to sneak them into her trunk when her daughters were not looking.

The Governor's Wife was a plump, near-sighted woman with something almost child-like in the open candor of her face and a certain shyness in her manner.

The Teacher looked ten years younger than the Governor's Wife and might almost have passed for a daughter of the Farmer's Wife. More than any of the others had she retained her girlish looks. She was a blond of the type that seems to stay the same age for a decade. As a member of her Alma Mater's faculty, she was as great a chaperon favorite with this year's class as she had been for the class of eighteen Junes before. It was she who had been the instigator of the reunion. It had been her untiring efforts and emphatic insistence upon the old "Mystic Seven" meeting again, that had brought them all together.

The Army Officer's Widow was not present, for she was with her married daughter in the Philippines. The Doctor's Wife was not present, for she was dead.

"It looks like rain," the hostess announced a few moments later.

"Say, girls"—the Governor's Wife looked up from the shoe she was buttoning—"wouldn't it be nice if we could just stay here and visit instead of going to the concert?"

"Well, let's," the Minister's Wife said, with more enthusiasm than good English, as she paused with a hairpin in her hand.

"Count my vote in favor of that, too," chimed in the Millionaire's Wife.

"Oh, thank goodness!" said the Farmer's Wife. "I won't have to squeeze into that gray silk again, or put on my new shoes."

She sighed so contentedly as she folded her kimono about her and dropped into a chair, that the others all laughed.

"Oh, Polly," someone said, "you haven't changed a bit. You're heavier, of course, but you never did care for clothes, did you?"

"Heavier?" she answered. "Say, do you know what's the matter with us and with this reunion? We're not acting like *ourselves*. I'm Mrs. Perry, an old married woman, to you, instead of Polly Woodberry, and you seem to me like four strange ladies, who used to know some friends of mine and can still recall anecdotes about them. Now let's *be* the old Mystic Seven, instead of talking about them. 'Heavier?' Humph, Ruth Wayman, twenty-five years ago you would have said, 'Polly, where in the world did you get such gobs and oodles of fat?'"

They all laughed again. It was just what they needed to clear the atmosphere. It was true—there had been an unexplainable restraint all the afternoon.

"Down with your hair!" she continued gayly. "Who will follow Daniel Boone?" There was a merry chatter as, girl fashion, they pulled down and braided their hair. With the braids hanging down their backs, even though some proved to be graying and scanty, there came a feeling of the returning intimacy of their girlhood.

"Down on the floor by the fireplace," the Farmer's Wife went on dramatically, and added, "all except me. I'll sit in this low chair, for if I got down there, you'd have to hire a derrick to get me up."

"No-sir-ee-bob"—the Teacher forgot her eighteen years of teaching proper forms of English. "Down you come, too, old girl, with your gobs and oodles of fat."

The four seized her and pulled her down beside them, compromising only by allowing her a half-dozen sofa pillows.

"Do you remember the house-party," the Governor's Wife was saying— "the time we stayed up all night and talked of our futures?"

"And Sadie went out about four A.M. to weed the radish bed to keep awake?"

"And the time Will came to call on Mame and we tied the picture of her home beau on a string and lowered it through the stove-pipe hole into Will's lap?"

"And the night Eunice pretended to have the nightmare and walk in her sleep?"

They were all talking at once, familiarly, intimately. It was as though the years had been turned back. Forgotten were the grown sons and daughters; forgotten the work, the wealth, the poverty, the joys, the sorrows of a quarter century. They were the old crowd living in the old times. The rain was on the roof.

As the evening wore on, the talk turned into more serious channels. Someone spoke of the crosses they must all have borne.

"Nell"—the Millionaire's Wife turned to the Teacher— "tell us why you didn't. You could have, I know."

The teacher smiled at the other's enigmatical way of asking, but knew what she meant.

"This afternoon I wouldn't have told you," she answered frankly. "I haven't confided much in people since the old days, but to-night you have me hypnotized into thinking it just as easy as ever to talk to you girls." She paused. "Yes, I've had my cross. There was a man and I cared; I think he cared, too, but something happened—no matter what, now. Anyway, I couldn't seem to care for anyone after that. Only"—she flushed girlishly— "he has asked me this spring to marry him. I haven't answered him yet, but— I think not. It seems too late now." She sat for some time looking into the fire, the Millionaire's Wife patting her hand sympathetically.

"My cross is so *silly*," the Governor's Wife said with an embarrassed little laugh. "It's just too foolish for words, but it's there inside of me and I can't help it, so I might as well tell you. Part of it is that Will is so *good-looking*." She brought it out forcibly, as though she defied them to think it was not worth worrying about.

"You see, it's like this: I didn't think anything about it when we first married. I never was good-looking, but I had youth and a fresh complexion and good eyes, anyway. But when the boys came, I kept getting more shape-less, and gray hairs and wrinkles came, and then I had to wear spectacles. I tried to wear nose-glasses, but they simply wouldn't stay on my turned-up nose." And she deprecatingly touched the guilty member. "Will was always handsome, and now at fifty he's just splendid. And look at me! I'm just 'Mother' to Will and three great, big, strapping boys, all fine-looking, like their father. You don't know what I suffer," she went on defiantly, "when I have to stand in the receiving-line and meet strangers. I feel so dowdy and homely and backward, and when Will says, 'Let me introduce you to my wife,' it seems to me that they are saying to themselves, '*Your wife!*' And when we're at any social function or in any town where Will is speaking, it just seems to me that people are saying, 'How fine-looking the Governor is, but his wife—have you seen her? Isn't she just the *limit*?'" She was half laughing, but there was an earnest little note in her voice.

"Why, Mame!" the Minister's Wife said reproachfully. " 'Pretty is as pretty does,' and no doubt you look better to Will than anyone else in the world."

"That's just it," she said quickly. "Will seems to think I'm all right and goes on dragging me out with him every place. I tried to tell him once, and he said, 'Why, Mother, did you want some new clothes? You go and get what you want, and don't think of the expense this time at all.' Men don't understand. It isn't *clothes*—it's the way you carry them."

She went on stubbornly: "I want to be Will's wife, but I don't want to be the Governor's wife. I wasn't cut out for it. I was happier in the old home, where we used to live, in Masonville. The executive house is too big and the servants worry me, and the ladies who call seem so formal. I want to go back to Masonville and tie a towel around my big head and clean house and serve at the Ladies' Aid suppers and run in and see Grandma Thompson every day! It won't be long until this term is over, and"—she bent forward mysteriously and whispered—"I'm just *praying* that Will will be defeated!"

They couldn't help laughing—she seemed so tragic in the recital of her little trials—more earnest because it was the first time she had spoken of that which had been in her heart so long.

"Seeing this is a genuine testimony meeting," the Minister's Wife laughed, "I must feel it to be my duty to be one of the first to speak." Her laugh changed suddenly to a sigh. "Isn't it queer," she asked, "how we are turned around in life? How I would love the going about and meeting cultured people and attending club meetings! Instead, I have been tucked away in the funniest little towns for twenty-three years. I get so *sick* of them sometimes, I could fly! You girls can't know what this trip has meant to me. I've looked forward to it for a year, scarcely daring to plan about it for fear something might happen at the last moment. And now I suppose that I'll look back upon it for all the years to come. Oh, don't understand that I've been the discontented whining kind," and she laughed brightly with a bird-like toss of her head. "I've thought too much of Dick for that. It's only that there has always been something in me that has craved travel and books and music and the flesh-pots of Egypt, that all the Conferences and Ministerial Associations haven't entirely taken out of me.

"Dick always thinks that the Lord sends him to each charge—but I don't know; sometimes I think the bishops and elders have a whole lot more to do with it than the Lord.

"You girls with your homes, you don't know what it means to move and move. Why, I'd give anything for a two-roomed house that was *mine!* I've packed and packed our Lares and Penates until I know just how to fit them together like a puzzle. I know the red sofa pillow is always around my cut-glass vase, and the silver baking-dish, that my Sunday-school class gave me, is wrapped in towels inside the bread-pan." She was laughing, but the tears were very near the surface.

"We buried one baby in Waycross and one in Huntsville," she went on, after a minute, "and the other three children are getting through school on almost nothing, but we would send them if we had to go hungry. Think of my telling you all this, when I believe I was the proudest spirited of us all. Why, girls, I couldn't even have afforded to come on this trip, but Polly sent me the money, bless her heart! How we quarreled over it in our letters, but when she threatened to get on the train and come after me, I gave in."

The Farmer's Wife began talking, to cover the embarrassment of the moment.

"Well, girls, since you've been talking, I've been trying to think what my greatest cross has been and for the life of me I can't decide whether it's my getting as big as a hippopotamus, or raising turkeys, or Ed's old Aunt Phoebe. The turkeys—how I despise the creatures!—haven't even hen-sense, and that's the last word in stupidity. Aunt Phoebe has lived with us for fourteen years and I've had to bear her just like Christian bore his burden, and, honestly, sometimes she has sagged most terribly. Poor old soul! She has nowhere else to go and not for worlds would I have her know what a trial she is.

"Seriously, I can't say very much about crosses. But I've had hardships. When we went to Kansas, you know we took up raw land and, girls, for ten or a dozen years it was just nothing but windstorms and new babies and grasshoppers and whooping cough and crops drying up and measles and seventeen-year locusts and pink-eye. Seems like we'd no sooner be out of one thing than into another, but when things went wrong, we'd always try to see the funny side if there was one. Of course you just *can't* see a wildly humorous situation in the facts that the hogs have died with the cholera, and one of the boys has fallen off a shed and broken his arm, and a sand-storm has blown up right after you have cleaned house. Ed would always say: 'Cheer up, Polly! The worst is yet to come.'

"Why, one summer, pie-plant and tomatoes were the only things we had in the garden. Sakes alive! We had tomato sauce and tomato preserves and tomato pie, and you wouldn't know there were so many things you could concoct out of tomatoes. I think that was the summer I began to get fat," she said laughingly. "But we stuck," she continued, "and bought land of those who left, until now—well, the children are all getting good educations, and we have six hundred and forty acres and a nice big house and an auto and a piano and a cream separator and a phonograph and a kodak and a chafing-dish and a potato-bug catcher and a patent egg-beater—" and the sentence trailed into laughter to join the others.

It was sometime before the Millionaire's Wife spoke, and, when she did, it was with a seriousness that everyone felt.

"I don't know just what to call my cross," she began, "but I've missed something, somewhere. I'm not contented. There doesn't seem to be any real motive for doing anything. I've had too much of some things—and not enough of others," she added vaguely, almost bitterly. "You girls have all shouldered responsibilities and hard work and assumed obligations cheerfully. And I haven't. I'm the only failure in the crowd; and I don't know what the trouble has been."

She turned suddenly to the others with an impatient little gesture—there was a touch of self scorn in her voice.

"Yes, I do, too," she said passionately. "I'm only pretending to you that I don't know. I've even pretended to myself that it wasn't my fault. It was. I know what my cross is and the most awful thing about it is that I made it myself. You have had yours thrust upon you, but I tell you I built mine with my own hands. I brand myself a shirk before you all. I have *shirked mother-hood.*" She brought out the words almost fiercely.

"I was born to be a mother," she went on. "I could have mothered a whole brood. But the life we have led, there seemed to be no—oh, why make excuses! They are so futile and not really true. If there had been children, perhaps George—" It was all she said. They recalled afterward that it was the only mention she made of her husband during the reunion.

"I've tried the last year or two, since I realized, to make up for it," she said more calmly. "I've given to hospitals and been on all sorts of charitable boards. But it isn't enough. It is no great sacrifice. It will never right the wrong. What will I say when God asks me where are my children? I think I will begin to tell Him of the money I've given to children's homes and He will say: 'But where are your own?'" She shivered slightly, and held her hands toward the embers of the dying fire.

There was a solemn, almost dramatic silence. The Minister's Wife leaned against the Governor's Wife. "After all, it doesn't make a bit of difference *where* one lives," she murmured.

The Farmer's Wife was wiping her glasses. Putting them on, she reached up to a stand for her hand-bag.

"It's past midnight," she said, drawing something from the bag. "But before we go to bed, I have a letter to read to you and I'm afraid it will be hard to do it." She paused. "Eunice wrote it to us nearly two years ago. I was to read it at the reunion the last thing before we parted."

They all started a little, yet it seemed a fitting close to the evening—this voice from the dead. There was a little stir among the women. The Teacher drew back into the shadows.

The Farmer's Wife began: " 'Dear Girls,' " and stopped to clear her throat. " 'To think of you having a reunion without me. How I would love to be there! If people can come back—but they just *can't*, and so there is no use in speaking of it. And the worst of it is, I can't even think of you that night, can I? You'll think of me, won't you? That helps some. Of course there is just a possibility that I will be there and Polly won't have to read this, but it doesn't look that way now.

" 'There is so much that I would like to say to you all. At first I was rebellious. It seemed that it just couldn't be. It wasn't just nor right. But I've fought that all down, and only one thing bitter remains: Doctor and the girls. What will they do? If there were only relatives that in a measure could take my place, but there is no one. I have thought and thought until it has become a perfect obsession with me. Three little girls—think of it! Fifteen and thirteen and nine.

" 'At first I couldn't bear to think of Doctor marrying again—no good wife can be real unselfish in her thoughts of that. But lately, it doesn't seem to matter. Nothing matters but a good mother for three little motherless girls.

" 'Write to them, girls, all of you, won't you? Tell them to be good girls, to do the right thing. Ask them to write their little troubles to you. There is no truer, nobler set of friends anywhere than the old "Mystic Seven."

" 'You remember the old song? I'm thinking of it now:
"Say, sister, say,
When I am far away—"

" 'Only it has a deeper meaning now.

" 'Good-bye,

Eunice.' "

They were all frankly sobbing—all but the Teacher.

She sat quietly in the shadow. When she leaned forward into the light, there was a sweet, warm look in her eyes.

"Girls, I have something to tell you," she said simply. "I have changed my mind. I am going to marry the Doctor."

Grandpa Statler

(Margaret Dean Stevens)

In this sketch published in *Harper's Weekly* (26 June 1915) Aldrich writes of her grandfather, Zimri Streeter, for the first time. He becomes, for her, the archetypal older pioneer hero—massive and gnarled, wise and witty, and devoted to land and country. He would reappear in *The Rim of the Prairie* (New York: D. Appleton & Company, 1925), *Song of Years* (New York: D. Appleton-Century, 1939), "The Soldier Vote in '64," *Scholastic* (November 1944), and "I Remember," *Journey into Christmas* (New York: Appleton-Century-Crofts, 1949).

I wish you could have known Grandpa Statler. A tall gaunt man he was—as big and massive as the native timber in whose clearing stood his weather beaten house. And he was the wittiest man I ever knew.

The Hon. Ezekial Statler I ought to call him for he was the first representative to the state legislature from Nemaha County—but the whole country side and half the young raw state knew him as Grandpa Statler.

To fully appreciate Grandpa's wit one must also have known Grandma Statler. She was the background against which his droll sayings stood forth. They were like a vaudeville team—with no disrespect to the dear old dead. Grandma—fretful, energetic, humorless, intolerant of wasting time in fun making. Grandpa—easy-going, droll, lounging in his chair by the fire, picking up every little saying of his partner's to bandy it about with a sly wit. There was never any loud laughing on his part, just a twinkle in his sharp blue eyes appreciative of his listening audience and a noiseless chuckle that apparently undulated over his huge body from head to foot. And while we youngsters would be convulsed with laughter at his wit, Grandma would be hustling, bustling, darting in and out, scolding at Grandpa, finding fault with him, with the chore boy, with the handleless well-sweep, the weather, the broken fences.

Perhaps Grandpa's wit would seem tame now. Primitive it may have been like the new country. But like the home-made inventions of those days, it was original. And clean. Crude, perhaps, but clean as the ozone of the forest.

One story that was told of him in the early legislature was that some young lawyer with grandiose eloquence attempted to kill a bill Grandpa was trying to get through. His oratory soared and swelled, and with a last impressive effort he quoted from his Cicero:

"*Hic, hic, sunt senatu—*" etc.

Grandpa, gaunt and shaggy in his Sunday home-spun, gained the floor and began:

"We have listened to the gentleman from Otoe with sadness and wondered how sich a brilliant young man could fly so fur from the mark, but now we know what's the matter of him. Down Nemaha way 'hic hic' means jist one thing—" He got no further—the House was roaring and Grandpa's bill went through.

A cancer developed on his hand and he had it amputated. Later he won a wager when he bet with a stranger that no matter how severe the winter, he hadn't worn a pair of mittens for four years. As the disease crept upward, his arm was amputated. When it broke out on his forehead he said to me:

"Chunk," (his nickname for me. I was as thin as a rail). "Chunk, will you sit by me when they take this off?"—tapping his head.

There came a day when he made no effort to get out to the chair by the fire. Grandma, not to lose the lessening light, sat by the window darning stockings.

"Chunk," he said, nodding his shaggy gray head out toward her, "we never could get her to see much fun in life, could we?" Almost the old chuckle undulated over his huge frame, shrunken under the patchwork quilt.

A little later: "Chunk, how do ye reckon it'll be? Psalms and harps and Sunday clothes and prayer meetings? *No—no fun?*"

And lower, with his fading eyes on the little bent industrious figure: "It'll be mighty lonesome—settin round—waitin—for her." They were the last words spoken by the wittiest man I ever knew.

The Heart o' the Giver

(Margaret Dean Stevens)

Events from Aldrich's childhood surface in this story, published in the December 1915 issue of *Modern Priscilla*. One of these events seems almost a photographic recollection of herself as a child taking noon dinner to her father at the Cedar Falls flour mill. He would brush flour off the bench so that she could sit and eat beside him without getting her skirts covered with flour. In this story, the father brushes away wood shavings and sawdust for his daughter, who as an adult recalls a photograph of herself barefoot at the age she was taking her father his lunch. Bess Streeter was probably barefoot, too. Aldrich's use of a Scottish maxim, part of which furnishes the title, is reminiscent of her childhood, as well: her mother and grandmother seem to have been fond of quoting these old sayings, and Aldrich often makes her point with them.

Aldrich's mother's name was Mary, and she may have been called Molly. Here Mary Freemore's husband addresses her as "Molly," and this is one of several stories using "Molly," a name that also appears in the 1914 "Molly Porter" and in all of the "Mother (Molly) Mason" stories (*The American Magazine,* 1918, 1919, 1920). These narratives depict women whom obviously Aldrich enjoyed for their work habits and sense of humor—again, like her own mother.

Along with the Christmas theme, which often recurred in her works, Aldrich returns to a concern that appears in her first major story in 1911, "The Little House Next Door." The notion that wealth unravels the bonds of happiness that hold a couple together when they are young and poor appears later in "The Woman Nell Cutter Was Afraid Of" (*The American Magazine*, 1922).

$\mathbf{M}$rs. John Stanley Freemore, in her modish suit and furs of silver fox, seemed an incongruous object walking along the New England country road. It was almost as though one of Reynolds' languid ladies had been cut out and pasted in the foreground of a Corot. Not that Mrs. Freemore looked languid, however. Her vigorous step and erect shoulders gave mute evidence that the many years of her social life had held time for a certain amount of physical training.

The fact was, Mrs. John Stanley Freemore was running away and she felt as elated over her little escapade as a mischievous child.

"Of course, I shall phone back as soon as I get there," she was thinking. "They will send a limousine for me and I can get back in time to dress for the dinner. What a tame ending," she added, rather drily. It was so seldom of late years that life had anything that was not executed precisely in accordance with prearranged plans.

So the walk along the country road over which the soft, new snow was lying, took on something of the air of an adventure. True, this seemed no adventurous highway to the laughing crowd of young skaters who passed her, nor to the stolid mail carrier driving by, but they, of course, were not running away from a Christmas dinner at the new country house of the Parker-Moore's. Not that it was Christmas day, but when one knows the people who composed Mrs. John Stanley Freemore's exclusive circle, one finds that they seem to possess the power of changing almost anything, even to the moving of Christmas day to the twenty-fourth.

It was rather clever of Mrs. Moore to bring them down to The Willows, Mary Freemore was thinking as she breathed in the fresh crisp air. Not a soul had given a real country Christmas party for years. From which statement you will deduct how limited the circle must have been.

"A country Christmas, a country Christmas," she repeated rhythmically to herself as she swung vigorously along the track made by some venturesome spirit who had been trying his sleigh on the new fallen snow. A country Christmas! How she used to love them! After all, Mrs. Moore's select affair, in spite of its rustic setting, was no real country party. To merely send in advance a coterie of trained servants and bid them to make ready a country party was only an unsuccessful imitation. Now a *real* country party was in a low-ceilinged old farmhouse. The floors were scrubbed to a shining whiteness, there were rag rugs and splint-bottomed chairs. A few ears of corn hung from the beams and the windows were full of geraniums, Martha Washington's, and sweet Lady Jane Gray's. There was a hasty supper for the family, then push the table and chairs against the wall, get the molasses ready for the taffy,—here was old Ezekial Potter now with his fiddle. Then upstairs to dress by the dim light—putting on one's new blue dimity—a whispered voice from the stairway. "Hurry, Mary, don't stop to primp any longer, here's John Freemore." *John Freemore!* Who was no multi-millionaire at all but a struggling young lumber clerk.

And with the agility with which the mind works, hers had leaped the quarter century and was telling her that to-day John was coming home from some business trip out to Chicago, or had he said Indianapolis? She had left a note for him telling him of the Moore's house-party, including an invitation for him to come down. Of course, he wouldn't come, but it had been the courteous thing to ask him. She prided herself not a little on that, always doing the courteous thing by him. No, their trouble had held no disgusting intrigue, nor had it been one of those affairs that are dragged out into the open where all who run may read. Ah! well! It was his own fault—their drifting apart. For a long time she had tried to keep up the pretense that a little flame of love still flickered. But why use so much of one's energy to fan that which gave out so feeble a warmth? So she had turned away and let it die to ashes. For years now they had been as hopelessly asunder as though there were no potency in the sacred phrase, "Whom God hath joined."

And what in her life had taken the place of that which was dead? She turned almost involuntarily and looked back at the fading gables of The Willows far across the snow-clad fields. As she stood for a moment looking at what seemed to be the symbol of her social achievements, there came to her one of those moments of weariness when the very soul seems to droop. Turning again, she resumed her journey, but less energetically, as though admitting to herself for the first time the need of peace in a heart that was growing old and cold and discontented.

For a moment she stopped in front of a farmhouse to watch two little girls who were making "butterflies" in the snow. They lay down on their backs and spread out their arms to form the wings.

"*I* used to do that," she thought rather wistfully. When she went on, it was to recall the Christmas she had spent with Aunt Lucretia, who was not a real aunt but her mother's old school chum.

She hadn't seen Aunt Lucretia for—oh, she was ashamed to count the years. But she had never forgotten her nor her many kindnesses. She and John had even stored their household goods there when they moved. Well, she had repaid it many times. Never a Christmas but she had sent some gift. One year it had been a thimble set with Olivine from Florence. Once there was a little Swiss clock from Lucerne. Only a few days ago she had chosen an amethyst brooch in an odd silver filigree. She hoped they had expressed it right away. As for not coming to see her before, the time had gone so quickly, she had been so busy, there had been so many trips—Oh, why make excuses! They were so futile and not really true.

When she had heard how very close was The Willows to Rock Bend, in that hour of the afternoon when everyone had been pursuing his own pleasure with the freedom that made Mrs. Moore a popular hostess, she had started across the country to call on Aunt Lucretia.

That she would be welcomed she was sure for had she not recently received a note, delicately smelling of lavender, and giving her a quaint little assurance that if ever the mood seized her in which she would again like to visit the old house in the New Hampshire hills, Aunt Lucretia Rayburn would gladly welcome her and as best she could try to take the place of home folks.

How sweet to be welcomed by "Home Folks." Not for years had she heard the homely old words used.

Unconsciously she quickened her footsteps and even as she did so, in the early descending dusk, saw the lights flash in the windows of a sturdy old Colonial house on the edge of the village.

Sweet indeed was her welcome. Physically tired she was from the walk of greater length than had been her custom. But as she rested in the chintz-covered chair there seemed to be a fatigue upon her greater than from her recent excursion. It was as though she had played harder than she knew, and like a tired child, had come home at nightfall to a mother's comforting lap.

"And you will stay all night with us, dear girl?" Aunt Lucretia's peaceful voice was saying. May Freemore looked through the little panes of the window across the fields where the snow was falling leisurely as though there were no need to hurry when the whole winter was before it.

Behind that long indistinct row of trees on the banks of Crystal Lake stood The Willows in which they were even now beginning to dress for dinner. The company would be unusually brilliant for a house-party, the table would be beautiful in its Christmas roses and shaded candles, the service would be perfect. Mrs. Moore's new chef—Pierre, had she called him?—would be in his happiest mood.

A past-mistress in the art of inventing delicate regrets, there would be no difficulty in giving some reason for not returning, if, indeed, she chose to remain. But did she really wish to?

Gadski was to sing,—or was it tonight that the choir boys were coming down from St. Andrew's to sing their Christmas carols? It had been rumored that Santa Claus, laden with gifts, was to alight on the lawn in a biplane.

What was stealing over her senses like incense from a long discarded shrine? The homely old-fashioned smell of doughnuts and cinnamon cake. Her mother had let her twist the doughnuts and drop them into the sizzling grease. And what was that other odor? *Catnip!* She had forgotten there *was* such an herb. Mother used to steep it for the children when they had colds. She steeped in a kettle with a piece of the rim broken out. It was shaped like a bird,—that broken place.

She turned suddenly to the little Dresden-china lady by the fireplace.

"If you will keep me, I will stay," she said with a rare smile that gave her rather sad face its haunting sweetness.

The winter evening had brought with it an ink-like darkness, but so cheerful was the flickering log and the light from the fat, old lamps, that the shadows crept into the corners of the room where they lay waiting until the flames should grow feeble and die.

Lucretia Rayburn sat by the table sewing, her soft blue-veined hands putting the last delicate stitches into an apron for Katie, her housekeeper's little girl.

The scarred-face old Seth Thomas clock was ticking off the moments that Mary Freemore had been up in her room looking over the contents of the box that had been accidentally left behind when their household goods were stored. Aunt Lucretia had written about it but Mary Freemore must have forgotten all about it, for it had been up in the north closet for—was it over twenty years? Dear, dear, how time does fly! There was probably nothing of any value in it anyway.

The door opened and Mary Freemore, her hands filled with an odd assortment, came into the room.

"Aunt Lucretia," she said slowly with an embarrassment oddly foreign to her manner. "I have opened that box and looked the things all over. I am glad you kept it for me. I had forgotten all about it. There were—keepsakes in it." She paused. In a moment she began speaking almost as though to herself. "We used to have such good times. Such a plain old house as we lived in and such simple little pleasure, and yet—how happy we were!"

Lucretia Rayburn gave her a quick bird-like glance.

"Do you remember father's saw-mill?" she continued reminiscently. "I used to take his dinner to him. Here is an old tintype of me as I looked then. I went barefooted and wore my hair in two braids. I used to go down past the place where the wild blackberries grew. Father would brush the clean shavings and sawdust off a bench and we would spread out the dinner. There would be baked potatoes, and bread and butter, and slices of ham, and the berries I had picked. I have never tasted anything so good since." Lucretia Rayburn smiled at the thought of the dinners that Mary Freemore had attended.

"And at Christmas time what fun we had! I remember one time when it snowed so hard that father and mother couldn't get to town, so all we had was what they could make at home. I think we never had such a good time. Father made me a little cupboard with doors that opened and shut and two cunning little drawers. Mother made me a doll quilt, some aprons and two doll hats. One of the hats was blue trimmed with chicken feathers and the other was red with a bunch of dried 'liveforevers' for trimming. Here is the quilt, the doll quilt that my mother pieced thirty-five years ago." She smoothed the little blocks of faded red and white.

"Then she baked each of us our favorite dish," she went on more brightly, "and put it on a chair by our stocking. She made me my favorite caraway cakes and a plate of doughnuts for Nellie. There was a platter of ginger cookies for Bob, and for father an immense custard baked in a milk-pan." And she laughed her charming silvery laugh. Sobering suddenly, "Ah, me, Aunt Lucretia," she said, "what wouldn't I give to be a little girl and get a wooden cupboard and some caraway cakes!"

She sat thinking for a few moments and then resumed: "And when I was first married the Christmas times were just as happy. I remember one better than any of the others. It was the Christmas before the baby came." She paused, shaken from saying that which had been so deeply locked in her heart. "On the Christmas I was speaking of," she went on bravely, "we had such a good time—John and I. We hung up our stockings in the little white cottage. I gave John some handkerchiefs and a copy of Robert Elsmere, and two shirts that I made myself. Such a time as I had with the buttonholes." She smiled at the recollection. "He gave me these things. I found them in the box tonight." She touched tenderly a pair of worn gray slippers, a faded piece of music and a picture in a tarnished silver frame.

"Then—" she glanced almost shyly at the older woman and spoke softly, "the baby was coming, you know. John said it would be a *boy* and I said it would be a *girl*. So, just for fun,"—she paused—"I bought this dolly for her." She unrolled from a silk scarf an old-fashioned doll with a little scarlet painted mouth and neatly waving china hair. It wore a dress that had been in style a quarter of a century before. She held it in the hollow of her arm as one would a baby,—as she would have held her own baby had it lived.

"And John,—" she smiled, looking suddenly girlish, "John bought a toy for *him*. His present was a funny little wooden donkey. It was absurdly painted blue and every time a slight motion jarred it, it began wagging its head. I never knew what became of that, either. I guess we lost it when we moved. You don't think—" she looked at the old lady almost pleadingly, "you don't think it was foolish—our getting the toys like that, do you?"

"No," said Lucretia Rayburn, the pink in her cheeks deepening. "I don't. I think it was just sweet."

Mary Freemore stroked the glossy back waves of the doll's hair.

"Ah, me! How very different now." She spoke again as though to herself. "It used to be so much fun to keep the secret of what we were getting for each other—John and I. We would keep the little things hidden, and then on Christmas eve do them up in all sorts of odd-shaped bundles. Why, I remember once when he gave me a thimble and it was in a hat box." She smiled at the thought. "But now," she spoke bitterly, "oh, I still get a gift. This year it was a tiara. I've even seen it for I was called to Tiffany's to decide about a setting. Aunt Lucretia," she broke off passionately, "it is a tragedy to know what you are going to get." She stopped suddenly as though ashamed of her display of feeling. "I am going to tell you something," she went on more calmly, "I never told a soul before. I was happier with these little things," she touched the picture and the faded music, "than with all—." She left the sentence unfinished, throwing out her hands in a little expressive gesture.

Lucretia Rayburn took a few stitches in the white apron as she said in her mild old voice: "My old grandfather used to say in his quaint Scotch speech, " 'It's na the gift ava that counts. It's the heart o' the giver.' "

"Yes," said Mary Freemore tremulously. "He was right."

The sound of sleighbells came closer and stopped at the gate.

"It's Martha and little Katie coming from the Christmas tree," the little, old lady said, smiling happily as those natures do to whom another's pleasure means something.

Mary Freeman hastily gathered up the collection of trinkets and took them to her room. Descending, she found Katie with wind-blown hair and hard, red cheeks hanging her stocking by the fireplace.

"Did you have a good time, Katie," she asked graciously.

"Oh, yes, ma'am," the answer came shyly, "there was speaking and singing and—oh, the tree! It glistened and shone like fairyland." The eyes of the child had brought home the reflected sparkle of the shimmering twigs. After a whispered consultation with her mother, she came closer to Mary Freemore.

"You will hang up your stocking, too, won't you?" she ventured timidly.

The woman smiled. "Why, yes, I might," she said. "It has been years and year since I hung up my stocking, but I believe I will tonight."

"You'd better," Katie was dancing about, "for I know something—" and clasped a fat hand over her too talkative lips.

A little later Mary Freemore was going to her room perplexed with the thought that she had nothing with her to put in Katie's stocking.

"How provoking," she said to herself. "If I had known there was a child here—" and in her mind she ran over any possible gift. In her fur hat was a dull scarab she had picked up in Assonau on a Nile trip and there was her wrist watch,—both as unsuitable as they were valuable.

"Of course I can send her a gift, but I want something tonight in her stocking."

She opened the door of her room and on the walnut bureau the china doll sat smiling.

"No, no." she said aloud in answer to the thought. "I will buy her a beautiful doll, but now that I have found it, I couldn't give her my own baby's."

Pausing on the threshold of the room, she gazed, fascinated, at the doll in its old-fashioned pink tarlatan dress, a whimsical feeling possessing her that her baby was near and was watching.

"How long has it been since I have given anyone a gift that was a sacrifice on my part?" she thought.

To her sensitive imagination it almost seemed that the doll was holding out plump little china arms.

"Perhaps it is the secret of the Christmas spirit—to part with that which one holds dearest."

With almost a sob Mary Freemore was across the room. Gathering the doll in her arms, she felt her way down the dark stairway and placed it by Katie's stocking.

O n Christmas night one light shone in the Freemore's town house. It was in John Freemore's den on the third floor. Making no noise as she walked down the hall with its soft rugs, Mary Freemore came quietly to the door which was slightly open. She paused, partly to make sure that John was alone and partly from agitation over what hung on the balance of the moment.

John was alone, for he sat in front of the fire stretched out in a great leather chair, his eyes shaded from the light of the flames. Christmas night, and alone in the barn of a house they chose to call home! A great pity for him took possession of her and her hand trembled as she pushed the door farther open.

And then all other feelings were overcome by one of amazement. On the other side of the fireplace, resting on a table, stood a little Christmas tree. That it had been hastily arranged, she was sure, for it was crudely tied with ropes and braced by heavy books. A few candles sputtered and burned low in their sockets as though loath to relinquish the joy of their burning. A handful of carnations was stuck through the branches and vied in coloring with the flame of the candles. A little white angel tilted and swung somewhat shakily from the top branch. Peanut shells littered the Kermanshaw rug and there were traces of popcorn on the Russian leather of the huge davenport. Several chairs were overturned and a brocaded portière had been thrown over them to make a tent.

"John," the voice of the woman broke into the reverie of the man in the chair.

He sprang up in confusion.

"Molly!" He was plainly surprised and even embarrassed.

"I thought you were up in the country." He began picking up the chairs and speaking quickly in marked contrast to his usual deliberate speech. "It was a little Christmas treat for one of the stablemen's boys. His mother died last year. I went out there and found the father hadn't done anything for the boy. Seems like every little fellow at Christmas time—. The kid seemed pleased."

He was clumsily folding the brocaded portière.

"I got a few things together. His father sawed off the limb. I found a few things around the house,—some fruit and candy, and a little wooden donkey I've been keeping since—since—Oh, Molly, a do you remember the Christmas I bought that little donkey?"

With a cry the woman was by him, her arms stealing up to his neck. He drew her to him and for the first time in oh, many, many years—whispered "Little Mother."

It was far into the night that they talked by the fireside; talked of the long journey they had come, of the lost path, and whether there were any crossroads back to it.

"There is no way back for just one, but when two people are looking for it," the woman said hopefully, "they can find it."

He stroked her hand tenderly, this man of few words. "We will hunt for it then"—he said, softly—"together."

Up in the country hills the pale Christmas stars danced and twinkled with happiness as they looked into the old plain bedroom, where a little girl with wind-blown curls and hard, red cheeks lay dreaming of the day that was gone. Clasped in her arms was an old-fashioned doll with scarlet-painted lips and neatly waving china hair.

Through a loft window on one of the finest stables in the city, the rays of the Christmas moon fell like a benediction over a motherless boy who sighed contentedly in his sleep. Standing on the bedpost in the full light of the silver rays, a little donkey, absurdly painted blue, nodded and wagged his wooden head.

Mother o' Earth

(Margaret Dean Stevens)

Published in *Delineator* of July 1916, "Mother o' Earth"
has ties with several Aldrich stories that offer glimpses of
the household helper named Tillie, who later appeared
much more fully characterized in the "Mother Mason"
series (*The American Magazine*, 1918, 1919, 1920).

An activity that Aldrich must have known well and en-
joyed is described early in "Mother o' Earth" when Marcia
Compton slides down an old, round-topped haystack.
The joy and excitement of this descent reappeared in *The
Rim of the Prairie* (New York: D. Appleton & Company,
1925).

The Rim of the Prairie and "Mother o' Earth" share
another favorite theme of Aldrich's: young women who
believe they are smart to marry for money rather than
for love. "The Little House Next Door" (1911), "Through
the Hawthorn Hedge" (1919), "The Present Generation"
(*American Magazine*, May 1922), and "The Victory of
Connie Lee" (*American Magazine*, October 1923) all deal
with the temptation of marriage as a means to wealth.

If the most noted surgeon in the city says that one is to
go to the country for the Summer to rest and rusticate—one goes. Particularly is this so if the famous surgeon's dictum is seconded by the very
wealthy uncle with whom one lives and whom it is exceedingly wise policy to
obey.

That this should be necessary, that one should have "nerves" at twenty-
three, is a matter for astonishment and regret. But even "twenty-three," if she

has autoed and dined and danced a little too strenuously, must pay the price when Life, the stern keeper of the toll, steps forth and demands his fee.

Which bit of philosophy brings us to the top of a very huge haystack where Marcia Compton in an old-rose dress settled herself and peered down the perilous slope. That she was torn between her desire to try the long descent and a cautious fear of the consequences showed itself in the hesitancy with which she took the plunge. Apparently her love of excitement won over any wariness in her character, for she finally threw out both arms, stiffened herself, and moved downward.

Now, according to laws immutable, the tendency of all falling bodies is to accelerate in speed. That Nature is no respecter of persons, soon became apparent to the girl, after she had landed in a perfect whirlwind of swirling dust, old-rose ruffles and chaff, the man who had just rounded the stack heard her let forth a feminine squeal as she sank down on some of the débris that had accompanied her.

"Well," he said dryly, "did you intend going on through to China?"

"I *did* plan to," she looked up at him mischievously; "but I got a stopover." In that momentary upward glance Marcia's brain tabulated a series of quick impressions which began with overalls, went on to blue shirt, strong hands, broad shoulders, square jaw, big mouth, good teeth, and stopped at his eyes—"blue-gray," she thought afterward, "and they would bore a hole through manganese steel."

"Didn't you know that you might have given your ankles an ugly twist?" he asked.

"I might have—but I *didn't*, you see." Which remark epitomized her attitude toward life.

"Little city girls," he added impressively, "have no business to take risky plunges like that."

"It wasn't a business matter, really," she said airily, "and perhaps I'm not a city girl."

"Oh, yes, you are."

"How do you know?"

"Country girls do not wear high-heeled pinkish slippers with white buckles when they climb haystacks."

"Oh, I don't know! There are the mail-order catalogs."

"I'll prove it another way."

"Do it."

"Answer three simple questions that every country girl knows before she starts school. First, what is that growing on the other side of the fence?"

She hesitated a moment—then tossed her head.

"Pooh! That's easy."

"Well—what?"

"Oats."

"Good! It happens to be wheat. Second, when do we plant Winter wheat?"

She looked about helplessly. "*Winter* wheat?" she asked peevishly. "Why—in the *Winter.*"

The man controlled his features perfectly, save that his eyes twinkled.

"Third—what is a silo?"

She was reckless now. "It's—a vegetable," she said bravely. "But I've never eaten it—have you?"

He threw back his head and laughed—a prolonged, virile laugh. "You little numskull!"

Now, there are many ways of saying the same thing, and this epithet, which might have seemed unusual, to say the least, was given in such a tone of voice that plainly said, "but, anyway, you're charming,"—that she could hardly take exception to it. But it is policy to take a conversation at its face value, so "I must be going in," she said coldly. "Dinner will be served."

"You had better hurry," he smiled down at her. "The silos might be overdone."

Chin in air, she marched on. At the corner of the house, under pretext of catching her skirt on a rosebush, she half turned and shot a glance backward from under dark eyelashes. He was watching her, standing tall, straight, immobile, like a soldier at attention.

"Grandma Cox," she said, affecting indifference as she went into the house, "who is the man that comes on this place sometimes—some one besides your hired man?"

"Who do you mean, honey? Now, you must mean Alec. Oh, my stars, honey, Alec Brown! He lives on the next farm over the hill."

"Is he—has he a family?"

"He lives with his father and mother. He's thirty-five or thereabouts. He ain't never married," she added dryly.

"What kind of a man is he?" asked the girl, in a tone of voice that assumed unconcern as to the answer.

"God never made a better," Grandma said shortly.

"Well, he's made oodles of politer ones," Marcia retorted.

Nor was she ready to retract her statement the next evening. As she sat with Grandma and her daughter-in-law, Mrs. Cox, on the porch, the low picket gate was opened by a tall man in immaculate white flannels. In the time that it took for him to stride up the grassy path, Marcia had decided that he carried himself well, and that, in spite of his recent rudeness, there was an element of excitement in his advent. Formal introductions followed, and of course he had to smile down at her and say, "How is the sliding on Mont Blanc to-day?"

"I didn't try it," she dimpled back, contrary to her determination to hold herself aloof. "The altitude is too enervating."

They all sat for some time, discussing topics of local interest. Grandma herself was strangely silent. Usually so voluble, she seemed to put all her energy into rocking. When she rose to go in, Mrs. Cox spoke of setting her bread, and excused herself, too.

"Now," said the irrepressible Alec Brown, as though he had waited for this moment, "I am going to give you your first lesson in intensive farming."

"Oh, you *are?*"

"You will kindly proceed," he said, totally ignoring the tone of her voice, "to walk down to that field with me and look at the grain.

"This," he continued, a few minutes later, reaching through the fence and pulling a bunch of grain, "is wheat, w-h-e-a-t, wheat. If thousands and thousands of us farmers in the mid and northwestern States didn't raise this, where would you, my lady of Urbs, get your bread and rolls and buns and shredded biscuits?"

"I don't care much for them, anyway."

He turned and looked at her. "What do you like?"

"Oh, salads—smarty ones best of all, and sweet things—chocolates and ices."

"Just as I would have thought. Now, while you are here, you ought to be a sensible girl and eat good, wholesome things!"

She pounded her fists together. "I hate being advised to be sensible, and I'm not an invalid."

He surveyed her critically. "No, you scarcely look it. But what's this Mrs. Cox says about your being here for your health?"

"Oh, it's so silly! I was just a little tired, and in an auto accident—scarcely scratched, but I was ordered here to rest—as if I hadn't rested enough the very first day!"

"Now, we will go down to the silo," he said, and turning her around, he conducted her unceremoniously through the barnyard to the huge cylindrical-shaped tank.

"This is a silo. Now, what is it?" he asked pleasantly, placing his hand upon it. A little furtive smile lurked in the corners of his handsome mouth.

"A silo," she found herself repeating, much to her vexation.

"Correct. It does not grow in gardens. They seldom cook it. They almost never eat it. It is built for holding ensilage. What is ensilage? You do not know, do you?" he forestalled her answer. "All right. The subject for to-morrow evening's lesson will be ensilage."

To-morrow evening? Well, the nerve!

They strolled back to the porch, where they sat talking for some time, the girl a mixture of resentment and interest. He was certainly not her idea of a farmer. He quoted Ibsen, said he enjoyed the "Trovatore" music better than "Aïda," and showed out a dozen characteristics that were contrary to what she would have expected. All this of course was because he had been a college man.

But why, oh, why, would a college man shut himself up on a farm?

"You're no farmer," she said to him suddenly, the next evening.

He smiled in his quick, boyish way. " 'Apparel doth oft proclaim the man,' " he quoted.

"But you've two kinds of apparel," she retorted. "You're somebody in disguise."

"Hist!" he said, "I'm the Kaiser," and he held two upstanding fox-tail grasses jauntily to his upper-lip. "But, why?" he asked, suddenly serious, his keen eyes upon her. "Why not a farmer?"

She was immediately confused. "You're not what I—you're not my idea of one."

"No," he said a little scornfully, "you belong to that class of the big S who thinks a farmer a brainless nonentity. You move in your little two-by-four soft-cushioned orbit, and what can you know of us and our lives? What, in fact, do you know of the really exquisite things of life—the cycle of the seasons, the lives of the wood-folk, the lure of the streams? Is there any pleasure in your artificial, theater-going, dance life, that can compare with these?"

"You're unjust to us," she said, aroused. "Almost all of the young people in our set go to the country for the Summer."

"And how?" There was contempt in his voice. "By sending a retinue of servants on ahead to get the dance-floors and the bridge-tables ready."

"*No,* sir!" She was thoroughly angry now. "We do what all healthy young people would do—auto and golf and boat."

"Do you get up to see a June sunrise?" he asked gently, in contrast to his recent scorn. "Do you listen for the call of the bob-whites in the wheat? Have you found the oriole's nest? Watched the glint of a flicker's wing? Glimpsed a scarlet tanager in the green pines? Discovered the pools where the catfish lie? Sighted a yellow perch against gray stones? Learned how the white birch sheds its bark, how the maple drops its leaves? Reveled in the lazy shimmer of the silver cottonwoods? Have you heard the beech-trees sing in Summer? Do you know the heartache of the mourning dove, the plaint of the whippoorwill? Do you know the habits of the chipmunk? Have you studied the blending of the colors on the butterfly's wing? Learned how the great horned owl courts its mate? Have you gathered the little wind-flowers and the wild oxlips?"

"Do you do all these things?" the girl asked, her eyes moon-filled and luminous.

"I used to—when I had time," he answered rather wistfully.

Impulsively the girl leaned toward him with a charming little gesture of abandon.

"Let's take time," she said.

The warm Summer days went by on green-and-gold wings. Each one saw Alec Brown at work with his men, directing the care of the stock, the plowing of the corn, the cutting of the alfalfa. Each evening saw him, scrupulously cleansed from his wrestle with the soil, immaculately clothed, coming down the path from the hill beyond the stile.

From long, dreamy days of ease, Marcia slowly emerged into busy, housewifely ways. So gradual was this transition that she could not have told when the change took place. She had known how hard Alec was working, had seen the accomplishing of so many tasks by Mrs. Cox, Grandma and Tillie, the little maid, that she had found herself to be the only drone in the community. From a few little self-imposed duties, she had come to find pleasure in the completion of some larger ones.

"I *churned!*" she called out to Alec one evening, as he came up the path. So delighted was she with her piece of news that she ran to meet him like a happy child. It was her greatest charm, he thought—her spontaneity—her odd little impulsive way.

It had led her into raptures over a bed of lilies in a shady cove, the first sprays of goldenrod by the roadside, the sunsets they had watched together, the baby rabbits they had found. The girl seemed to expand under the white magic of the lore of stream and wood, like a little plant home again to its native soil.

There had been a few days of pouring rain when the farm work was stopped, and Alec in raincoat and cap had come down the path, bringing with him the fresh breath of woodland and meadow. They had built a tiny fire in the grate, "to take away the dampness," Marcia had said, but she knew it was really because she wanted to see Alec stretched out in a big chair in front of a fire. He had brought some old worn volumes of Emerson, Keats and Tennyson, and while Marcia in a low rocking-chair busied herself with her embroidery, he had read snatches from them, commenting upon them occasionally in a slow, hesitating way as though for the first time he were speaking to another human being his thoughts of them.

And there had been one unforgetable afternoon of gray mist when Alec had come for her with an invitation from his mother. They had taken a roundabout path through the woods and arrived at the old gabled house, wet and laughing like two runaway children after a lark. The father and mother had greeted Marcia as only two old people who have dispensed hospitality for years, could do. There had been a cheerful supper and a cozy, intimate evening in which Marcia had sung a few simple, old-time songs at Alec's request. When it came time to leave, the mother in her sweet, unaffected way had given Marcia a motherly kiss. Her "Come again, dear; we all like to have you," affected the girl unaccountably. That had been the first time she had found it hard to raise her eyes to Alec's.

It was late in September when the letter arrived from her aunt, bidding her return. There had been a few nights of light frost, a day or two of flurrying leaves, just enough hint of the coming Autumn to remind Marcia that the curtain would soon ring down on this strange Summer of hers.

Then September laughed at the fancy and called back the sunniest of her days and the balmiest of her evenings.

To Marcia, the letter came like a note written in a foreign language, so far away had grown to seem the interests which until recently had been hers. It contained countless plans for the Fall and Winter, in which parties, gowns, Palm Beach and Jerry Adams were all mentioned numerous times.

Marcia sat on the front steps by a riotous growth of asters, survivors of the chill nights. "Jerry Adams," she said aloud contemptuously, "with his everlasting, 'Oh, I say, now, Marcia.' " And, ápropos of nothing, she sat for a long time, chin in hand, looking out across the close-cropped meadow, somberly green in the September twilight.

So it was a pensive Marcia that slowly mounted the narrow stairs. For a few moments she stood, hand on the door-knob, looking in at the homely comfort of the old-fashioned room that had been hers for the Summer. It was the first time a room had meant anything to her. Rooms become dear only when they take upon themselves some of the best that is in us. And it was here that all that was best in Marcia Compton had been nourished.

To dress for the last evening she took from its wrappings a gown of lace and silver—a silky, cobwebby thing.

"How silly and out of place!" she said to the girl in the glass, as she bound her dark hair with silver and platinum bands. The girl in the mirror was evidently of the same opinion, for she suddenly stared back and retorted, "Just like *you*, Marcia Compton—silly and out of place!"

So unlike the Marcia who had worn simple pinks and whites all Summer, did she look when she came down-stairs, that Alec, who had never been given to saying complimentary things, was startled into something of appreciation.

"Whew!" he said. "Where's your pumpkin? Do you vanish at twelve?"

"Oh—this?" with a little careless motion to her dress. "This is to celebrate. It's a joyous occasion. I've a piece of good news to tell you." They were walking down the familiar path to the stile. "But you must wait until we get to the hill," she laughed.

At the stile she ran lightly up the steps where she poised at the top like a silver-and-white butterfly.

"Ladies and gentle*men*," she said, "this is to announce the departure of the lovely Miss Compton to her urban habitat. His Royal Sawbones—peace to his ashes—tells her uncle that she ought to be sane and sound by this time. If she's not, she's rustic enough, anyway."

Alec caught her hand as she came down the steps.

"When?"

"To-morrow."

"Then this is the end of the Summer—the end of the perfect day?"

"Yes," she said soberly, a little breathlessly; and for no reason at all, she turned and went back a step, where she seated herself. "You've made my enforced stay here pleasant for me," she went on hurriedly. "I want to thank you. I want to say—something else, too. It's been more than just pleasant. It's changed my view-point. You've taught me things. I don't mean just about blue jays and trees. It's hard to explain. You may not understand—but the whole Summer has broadened me—my opinion of people. I—see things—differently.

He had walked to the side of the steps where she was sitting. It brought his big square shoulders only a little above hers. She glanced up at him—a silent figure he stood, one foot on the lower step.

"Shall I say it now, Marcia?" he asked quietly.

Hand at her throat, she gave him one brave, fleeting glance, and then turned away.

"Yes—say—it."

"I love you, dear."

"And—I—"

"Go on, dear."

"Love—you."

But when he would have taken her, she stopped him with a little cry: "No, no—wait! I must tell you first. I have a confession—you will despise it in me. You hate pretense so. I'm so ashamed to tell you."

The blood seemed to drop away from the man's heart.

"What is it?" he asked, his voice strained.

With lowered eyes she said, "Oh, Alec, *I was born and brought up on a farm.*" He would have laughed from sheer relief at her words, had she not brought out the little disclosure so tragically.

"I've pretended so," she went on in a little tense voice. "I lived on a farm until I was fifteen. I used to know all those things I let you and Mrs. Cox teach me. I'm *so* sorry I've deceived you. I have raised chickens—and churned—and not know a silo? Why, Alec, my playhouse was right *under the nose of a silo.*"

"What was your object in keeping it, Marcia?" he asked.

"Oh, don't you *see?* I was ashamed of it. I never wanted any one to know it."

Then she told him of her childhood days on a poor, sandy farm, of her longing for the outside world, her parents' death, the coming of her uncle's wife to choose one of the children, the years spent at finishing-schools to "make a lady" of her.

"I've been such a *snob!*" she said with downcast eyes. "And worse—I've been wicked. Aunt Julia didn't want me to write to my brother and sisters.

And oh, Alec—*I promised!* It was knowing you, that made me know how wicked I had been.

"My conscience had sometimes hurt me—but not so very much, either," she added truthfully, "for I was always having so much to do, and so many places to go. But this Summer—I've thought so much of my little sister. She was nine when I came away with Aunt Julia, and she's seventeen now—and just think how she may be *needing* me!"

He took her little, cold, clenched fists in his big, firm hands. "See here, dear. All this that you have told me seems very tragic and very wicked to you. But my heart goes out to my little fifteen-year-old, orphaned Marcia. Later we can find these sisters and brother and make amends to them in some way. Just now, the big thing is that you care for me. Tell me this, dear—you would come here to live?"

"Yes," she said simply, "I would, now. I fought it for a long time. I thought you—were caring. And then I found I—was caring, too. But—I wasn't going to let myself—"

"Marry a country jake?"

"You're not jakey," she said, "you're perfectly splendid."

"It's my turn to talk now," he said. "I'll have to begin away back with a farm boy who went away from home to take up a profession. He worked so hard that as the years went by he found himself quite the top of that profession. Always he was planning to go back some Summer. Well, he went. The Summer was perfect. For there was the girl, you know—his dream-girl. He found that he loved her from the bottoms of her foolish little patent leathers to the two-inch scar up under her hair."

"The *scar?*" She raised big astonished eyes to his. "Why, no one knows of the scar—but the nurses—and—and—"

"And the surgeon who sewed it." He was smiling quizzically, tenderly, at her.

"Dr. Brown?" she said—a world of wonder in her voice. "You—not you—you're not Dr. Blaine Brown?"

"Dr. Blaine *Alexander* Brown," he corrected, enjoying her incredulity.

"And—you—sent me here?" she asked.

"That was my prescription," he laughed.

"But you said you—fought me?"

"Yes, I had seen you a few times. For some reason or other your face haunted me. I tried to throw off the attraction it had for me, but just the same you tagged me around unmercifully. You see I was as loath to let myself care for a society girl as you were to like a farmer. When you were brought to the hospital I didn't see you until you were anesthetized. And when you lay on the table, you weren't a 'case' to me—you were—just you. I wanted more than anything in the world to know you. I gave your uncle Mrs. Cox's address. Then I thought of the Summer I had wished for so often—and I told the staff I would be gone for the rest of the Summer. So, just like the old wolf in 'Red Riding Hood,' I ran around through the woods and got to the grandmother's house first. And when Red Riding Hood arrived on the scene, the wolf looked very innocent in his farmer togs with a ten-days' tan on his hospital features."

The girl looked up. "What big sharp teeth you have, grandmother!"

"The better to eat you, my dear," said the wolf, as he gathered the girl close.

The Cat Is on the Mat

(Margaret Dean Stevens)

Delineator published "The Cat Is on the Mat" in October 1916. The story's theme recurs in "Marcia Loses Her Job" in *Mother Mason* (New York: D. Appleton & Company, 1924). Episodes from this story also appear in "Marcia Mason's Lucky Star" (*American Magazine,* March 1920) and "Proving Marcia Born Lucky" in *Mother Mason.*

To sit quietly, all alone, in a launch securely anchored to shore, is surely no sin. Especially guileless would such a proceeding seem to be if the occupant chanced to be a charming girl—a girl as dainty and trim as the little launch in which she sat, which was very dainty and trim indeed.

But, if the launch chanced not to be the girl's—nor a relative's, nor a friend's—in short, if said charming girl had come tiptoeing into the launch not knowing whose it was—ay, there's the rub!

That she was enjoying this cool usurpation of another's property seemed apparent, for she sat gazing out over the water as contentedly as though she had just bought and paid for the gay little boat. She had on an old-rose gown of the daintiest, most melting shade in the whole category of colors—the shade her cheeks would be if she blushed. But she had no thought of blushing, this bold little pirate on another's ship. Instead, she threw back her hat of old-rose tulle, as though to make herself more comfortable.

The old-rose hat formed a big circle behind her fluffy dark hair that curled and fluttered with the brisk little lake breeze—a circle that looked like a rosy halo behind a roguish Madonna's head, thought the man who came down the sandy slope of the little cove.

The girl's face showed surprise and chagrin in exactly equal amounts. At the same time her cheeks flew little old-rose flags, which, in Youth's signal-code, is a variable sign, meaning almost anything.

For a few moments they looked at each other without a word, the man standing straight and tall, smiling down at the strange girl in his boat. Her eyes dropped before the steady gaze of his keen blue ones, which, somehow, seemed more disconcerting because of the clear, thick eyeglasses which he wore.

"I feel," she said in a moment, "just as though I had been in the jam jar."

"Shall I slap your hands?" he asked pleasantly. She put them hastily behind her.

"Oh, please, kind sir, I'll never do it again!" she said, smiling adorably. "I had been walking and wanted to sit down—and you shouldn't have left such a dear little boat right under my nose to tempt me."

"That *was* thoughtless of me. I should have taken it under my arm over to town. I apologize."

"You see, I had an enormously important question to decide," she explained, "and when I sat down here, I said I would not leave until I had come to a decision. Give me just one minute"—she looked up at him demurely—"so I'll not break my promise to myself." She looked over the man's head, evidently thinking of her decision, while he continued untying his boat.

"Take your time," he said. "You should never decide anything too hastily." As he spoke, the wavering little noise of the engine developed into a steady "put-put-put" and they were moving out into the lake.

"Oh," said the girl, genuinely embarrassed, "I was going to get out! I—"

"In order to keep your promise to yourself, you will have to stay in for a little while, until I take this package and the mail up to camp."

The girl sank back on the cushions reluctantly, distressed. "I *could* jump overboard," she suggested.

"I wouldn't," he said placidly. "I'd have to fish you out, and you'd just spoil all that—pink stuff."

Although she had settled herself among the cushions again, she was visibly annoyed. There had been nothing wrong in their informal, joking conversation at the cove, but to make away with her in this high-handed fashion was carrying things too far; she would show him that to her it was not the huge, mirth-provoking joke he evidently thought it to be.

"Peach of a day," the man remarked, and she turned toward him with a just-came-back-to-earth expression.

"Beg pardon?" she said coldly.

"Lovely day," he said, with a boyish grin. So those were to be her tactics, were they? Miss Prim from Conventionville! So be it! He would pay no more attention to her. He lapsed into a long silence, devoting himself assiduously to his engine.

Now, as in her own small circle the girl was a much-liked young person and not at all used to dividing attention with a little black engine that said nothing but "sput-sput-sput," she grew somewhat piqued at the prolonged taciturnity of the good-looking young man who was making away with her.

"It's a fine little launch," she said, rather inanely.

The man looked up, intending to say, "What, are you still here?" but seeing the merry expression in her dark eyes, he became friendly again.

"You'd enjoy it mightily if you'd forget the conventions and let yourself."

"I will," she said quickly. "I walked into the trap myself. I ought not to make such a fuss over my punishment, had I?"

" 'Punishment'?"

"Well, reprimand, then," she conceded, dimpling.

"About that question you had to decide?" he said in a moment. "What sort of a chap is he?"

" 'Chap'? You're uncanny! How did you know it was about a man?"

"It always is, isn't it?"

"No, it isn't," she said warmly. "I've had lots of things to decide that had nothing to do with a man."

"You?"

"Of course! One was whether I should let myself be dependent upon rich relatives, or work."

"The decision is obvious."

"What was it?" she asked.

"Rich uncle—society girl."

"What makes you think so?"

"Oh, the general—well, the pink stuff."

"You *are* densely masculine!" She laughed a gay little rippling laugh. "I'd have you know I *labor* for my bread and butter. This is my hard-earned vacation. As for the pink stuff, a real sure-enough society girl could tell you in a minute it was home-made."

By the time they had reached camp, they had discussed and settled a dozen questions. When the launch came to a purring stop at a landing, the man stood up, carefully carrying a package which he covered from the rays of the afternoon sun.

"Smuggled diamonds?" she asked.

"Weenies," he answered, and they laughed for the sheer joy of the laughing.

As he sat down, he snapped open his watch in the quick, alert way she had noticed about him. "It's only four o'clock," he said. "I've discovered a place a mile farther up where the wild phlox grows unbelievably thick. I'd like very much to show it to you. I'll deliver you safely back at the spot from which I kidnapped you, in time for dinner." He looked over at her and smiled in his frank, open way. "Up or down?"

The girl made a fluttery little motion with her hands. "Up," she said.

"Thank you. Now, before we start, I will tell you who I am, my residence, occupation, political party—"

"Oh, don't!" the girl broke in impulsively. "It would spoil all this! The minute I know who you are, I'll find out that my roommate's uncle is your chum's brother-in-law, and there'll be no more adventure."

The man threw back his head and let forth a hearty, virile laugh.

"How far do you live from here?" she went on.

"Several hundred miles to the east."

"And I several hundred to the west. You'll never see me again, will you?"

"No," he said, so decidedly that she added hastily:

"Of course not. It will be just one mysterious page out of each of our life books. It will end when the sun goes down. I have a plan. I'd like—oh, *how* I'd like to ask some one's advice about that problem! All the people I could discuss it with are so—so prejudiced. If I don't know who you are nor where you're from—I could ask you about it—you'd be a totally disinterested person and maybe what you'd say would help me. And what if you had something I could help *you* about!"

"As a matter of fact," he said, smiling at her impulsiveness, "I came out here to decide a problem."

"Is she very nice and sweet?"

"Oh, very." And they laughed again, because it was Summer-time and Youth-time.

When they had gathered armfuls of the wild phlox and seated themselves where it billowed away on every side, the girl said: "Now, let's take up our problems. You're a disembodied spirit, I'm a wood sprite. When the sun goes down you dissolve in the western sky; I disappear under a clump of early goldenrod."

"I appreciate your offer, Wood Sprite, but my problem is merely a business one—just a decision to make between two positions offered me. I'll just have to thrash it out myself in the next day or two. Now, let's hear yours'. It's much more interesting, I anticipate."

"Well, Mr. Disembodied Spirit, could you stretch your imagination to think of a man wanting very much to marry me?"

"I'll try." Again he smiled down into her merry dark eyes.

"Because if you could, then I can tell you about it. I'm twenty-three. I ought to know what love is when I see it—but I'm not sure I do. I'll tell you this very frankly—and it seems so good and honest to say it out loud to some one—I'd *love* a home. I'm crazy about waffle-irons and percolators, and I'd rather make white ruffled dining-room curtains than *eat!* I don't like my work any more. I don't like to go outdoors when it rains or snows. I'd much rather stay in my own house and bake cunning little raisin cakes and polish the silver."

There was a great deal more that she told this disembodied spirit. She was very truthful about it—she made it very clear to him that she was not at all sure whether she was loving the man or the thought of the house that she would keep.

"It seems all mixed up," she finished candidly. "Maybe I don't care at all and just imagine I do—and maybe I really care and don't know it. There ought to be some sort of acid-test that one could apply."

"There are tests," the man said thoughtfully. "I suppose the thought of poverty is one of them."

"Oh, dear!" she said, "he isn't a bit poor."

"It isn't love," he said gravely, "at least, not the type that knows no questioning." Suddenly he faced her. "I *was* thinking of something besides a business problem out here. No girl has ever appealed to me as much as the ideal I placed for her. At thirty-five I have about come to the conclusion that the type of love I have dreamed of is going to pass me by. It is just recently— this Summer—that I have been thinking of putting aside that dream—and asking a girl I have known a long time—I am rather fond of her—"

All the way down the lake the easy banter of the earlier afternoon seemed not to return. The man was very quiet, busied with his own thoughts. The girl was pensive, thinking, now that the glamour of the adventure was nearly over, how unwise she had been.

When they stepped out of the launch the man said, "You promised the page would end when the sun went down. Let's walk up there for the last paragraph."

They went up the sandy slope to a grassy knoll where a silver birch stood sentinel.

"It's been a very interesting page," he said.

The sun sank lower; there was only a piece of it left. Impulsively the girl slipped her hand into the man's. His own closed over it.

"Good-by, Disembodied Spirit," she said. "Just think, I don't even know your real name!"

"I know yours," he said, still holding the friendly little hand. "You're Babbie. I shall always think of you as Babbie. I met you as the Little Minister did, in Caddam Wood."

"I'll not see you again," she said hurriedly; "this is the last line." The sun disappeared. "Turn the page," she said gaily.

"All right," he said, "but there are other pages. I'm going to see you again. I want to see you to-morrow. After all, I'll have to know your name—I can't just ask for Babbie. And where are you staying?"

"If I'm Babbie, I may live up in a tree," she said merrily. Then she shook her head. "No, this is my page of adventure. To-morrow's page will be prosaic again. . . . I'll pin a note on this birch and tell you my name."

At two o'clock the next afternoon the man unpinned a note from the friendly birch. It read:

> You will always remain Mr. Disembodied Spirit to me, for I found a telegram awaiting me and I am leaving at noon. After all, we had to write 'finis' at the end of the page of adventure.
>
> Barbara Kendall.
>
> P.S. You had better marry her if she's *very* nice.

A month later Barbara Kendall in a smart gray suit and gray toque with two audaciously scarlet wings on it, alighted from the 2:15 train at Watertown, Iowa, and giving her check to the baggageman, hurried to the street-car that would take her to the high-school building. She managed to breeze into town at the eleventh hour and to slip gaily into the assembly-room as a little electric-bell sounded. She had only time to wave her hand across the room to a score of her co-workers, among them Inez Walker, her roommate, and to give Miss Hippman, her principal, an impetuous hug.

"Hippy, I'm gladder'n anything to see you! Sit in front of me and let some of your intellectual rays shine on me, and the new 'Supe' will think I am a handy volume of the encyclopedia."

As the electric-bell ceased jangling, the new superintendent opened the door of his office suite and came briskly onto the platform. He was very tall. He had keen blue eyes, the more disconcerting for a pair of thick eyeglasses which he wore.

Ninety-two pairs of eyes were upon him, ninety-two faces were turned expectantly toward him. The ninety-third pair of eyes dropped, startled; the ninety-third face flushed as brilliant as the scarlet wings above it, and then went pale.

The next minute he was speaking: "We want the keynote of the year's work to be cooperation." But other things were whirligigging themselves in Barbara Kendall's brain—a ridiculous jumble of phrases: "Cooperation among pupils, parents, teachers and superintendent." "Sput-sput-sput."—"Developing the child's initiative."—"A place where the wild phlox grows unbelievably thick."—"The old order of blindly following the teacher has passed away."—"I don't like my work any more, I want a home." And on and on and on, through a nightmare a half-hour long.

It was only at the close of the meeting when announcements were made that Barbara roused herself. "There are three late changes," his familiar-strange voice was saying: "Miss Short, of the third grade, Lowell, is transferred to the fifth grade, Whittier; Miss Miner, of seventh grade, Holmes, is transferred to seventh at Lowell; Miss Kendall, of first grade, Longfellow, is transferred to first grade at Lafayette."

All other things were suddenly forgotten in the fact that she was to go to Lafayette, to leave Hippy. Why, she couldn't teach without Hippy's guiding hand!

"Oh, Hippy!" she moaned, "why has he done that?"

"I don't know, dear. They love you so down there. What shall we do without you?" Go up and talk to him. Perhaps he can arrange it some other way."

The dark eyes snapped. "Not in four hundred years!"

"Then I'll go." And Miss Hippman shouldered her portly self through the maze of chattering teachers.

Barbara looked wildly about for a chance to escape without passing that tall figure ensconced by the door. The doors in the rear of the room were locked, "contrary to fire orders," she thought hotly. Well, she might as well walk up and face the music now. It was impossible to keep out of his way for any length of time.

"He will probably say 'I met Miss Kendall in the Summer,' and some of the girls will hear, so I'll have to make some explanation," she thought, when she was within a few feet of him, but she advanced resolutely.

Miss Andrews, the Latin teacher, stopped her. When she went on toward him, he was holding out his hand as he had held it out ninety-two times before.

"*This* is Miss Kendall," said dear old Hippy, in her kind, cordial, frank way.

Barbara raised dark eyes that were meant to be indifferently cordial, but which only succeeded in being carefully miserable. There was an awful moment—it seemed a quarter of an hour long!

"Miss Kendall?" he repeated interestedly. "Then you are one of those transferred, are you not?"

"I believe so," she said stiffly—and it was over!

She got to her boarding-house as quickly as she could. After endless greetings from Mrs. Hoover she went to her room and threw herself in a little crumpled heap on the familiar bed.

"How *could* he?" she moaned. "How *could* he act that way after that afternoon? Oh, it's horrible that I'm here! If I could only get a job a thousand miles away! But positions don't hang on bushes in September. He had not *wanted* to remember that page in the book, he took this way to show me it was distasteful to him!"

Suddenly she thought of something—it brought her bolt upright, clutching the spread. Of course—the girl—the girl who was very nice and sweet. He was engaged to her now. But, even so, why couldn't he have referred to that day like a human being? She wouldn't have mooned around and talked to him about it; just a casual reference to it, and they could have dropped it. She knew her place.

The door opened below and she heard Inez's gay voice. She was busily unpacking when Inez blew in.

"Oh, Barbe, you dear thing! If you knew how perfectly Astorbiltish you look in that swell suit! Isn't he the grand man? I'm simply 'over came.' Did you ever see a grander profile and what do you know about his not being married?"

Barbara slammed a dresser-drawer. "Inez, I might as well tell you on the start—I hate him!"

"Oh, Barbe, just because he transferred you? But that's nothing against him. What are you to him? Just a cog in the machinery. Now, *me*—I'd do anything he asked. If he smiled at me in that wonderful way and said: 'Miss Walker, I'd rather you would be janitor of Whittier,' I'd say: 'I'd love it! I'd rather sweep than teach, any day!'"

And so on through dinner-time it went—the praises of the new "Supe."

"He has splendid executive ability," said Miss Hippman.

"*Absolutely* the most heavenly smile and *also* a *magnificent* jaw," said Inez.

"Slush and *also* piffle!" said Barbara.

Miss Hippman's interview with the head of the schools had availed naught; Miss Kendall was to be transferred, he had told her principal, with his "heavenly smile." So the next morning saw a very sulky Barbara trudging with her books and pictures over to Lafayette. She had said good-by to Hippy, whose tears had run down her plump cheeks, and she was met at the Lafayette by Miss Neiderhauser with the grim statement—"I hope you understand that I require my teachers to keep their plan books strictly up to date."—There are principals and principals!

In the hall she met the new superintendent. She tossed him an airy little nod, to which he responded pleasantly, "Getting settled, Miss Kendall?"

"Yes, thank you," said Barbara. (A mean-faced little imp, hovering unseen in the atmosphere, leaned low. "But there are other pages—this doesn't end it," he whispered, and howled in a fit of fiendish laughter.)

So the moving finger, having writ the seasons of the year, moved on. Barbara nursed her children through Columbus spells, Thanksgiving and Christmas fevers and a siege of Eskimo life. She brought them safely out of valentineitis into a convalescent period of robin red-breasts and bursting lilac buds. She worked conscientiously, and her relations with the superintendent were very businesslike, very courteous, and very cool.

"I wish I could get a position next year in Honduras or Hongkong," said Barbara one evening to the other four.

"You'll have to decide to-morrow whether you'll stay or not," said Rose Raymond. "The cat was on the mat to-day with the paper for next year's signatures."

It is well to insert here, for the uninitiated, that in all well-managed schools there is some statement by which it becomes known to the teachers that the superintendent is in the building. The teacher who first sees him passes the information on to the others. So, if you are a superintendent and chance to meet a small boy tiptoeing about from room to room, carrying a scrap of paper on which is scrawled "Scotland's burning," the chances are that there is no conflagration whatever, but that the expression has reference to your being in the building. The particular sentence by which the Watertown, Iowa, teachers knew that the superintendent had hung his hat in the principal's office, was the time-honored and concise statement: "The cat is on the mat."

So, when Rose Raymond said the cat was on the mat to-day with the paper for next year's signatures, Barbara knew that the time had come to pass in her resignation.

"All right, let the cat come," she said tartly to the others, "I'm ready for him and when I tell him I'm not signing, I'll proceed to relieve my mind of a few other things, too."

"Still peeved over your transfer, Barby?" asked Inez gaily. "Now, *me—I'd* wash the Whittier windows for Mr. John Marshfield if he asked me to."

"Oh, *you*," said Barbara acridly, "*you'd* eat oats out of his hand!"

Spring arrived, bag and baggage, the next day. She opened the school-room windows and blew warm breaths of mellow earth and buds into the rooms. Barbara had worn an immaculate white suit in honor of the arrival—it turned in at the throat, showing the lovely contour of her face. And by way of completing a very satisfactory picture she had stuck a bunch of lilacs in her belt.

The Kindergartners had just started home, when one little girl returned to knock on Barbara's door and say "Mith Thmith thent me back to thay the cat ith on the mat." She shrilled it out just as Mr. John Marshfield came briskly up to the door.

"What's this?" he asked blithely.

"Oh, nothing—they have found Mamie Jones's kitty," Barbara fibbed, and she had the grace to blush.

"I'll be back a little later, Miss Kendall," he said in his businesslike way, as he started up-stairs.

Barbara's pupils had gone when he returned. She seemed not to hear him until he came quite close.

"Well, Miss Kendall"—he was tapping the paper for signatures against his hand—"are you signing with us?"

Barbara filled in a green leaf carefully. "No," she said, "I'm not."

"Is it—it's not on account of that chap, is it?"

"Just what do you mean, Mr. Marshfield?"

"You know what I mean."

"I'm afraid not."

He tried new tactics. "Why are you resigning?"

She looked up at him for a fleeting, miserable glance. "If you *must* know," she said, half angry, half frightened, "it's because—the year hasn't been pleasant. You've not—you've picked on me," she finished in a little tragic voice, for the tears were very near the surface.

"Picked on you? I? *Picked* on you?" He repeated the childish phrase in astonishment.

"Yes," she said. "I have been sorry enough for that day without any added punishment. But it seems that you found it necessary to transfer me and to haunt this building to criticize me and to require me to hand in lesson-plans to you when no one else did and—" Her voice trailed off.

"So I've haunted this building, have I? I've criticized you, have I? I've asked you an unnecessary number of times for plans, have I?"

"What *is* this?" she asked with the first trace of her old mischievousness. "That psychology exam you were going to give us?"

"No," he said hotly, "it isn't. But I'll make it clear to you what it is. Good heavens! I've haunted this building because you were in it. I transferred you so I could see you everyday. Every morning this year at eight-fifteen I've locked my office door and tiptoed to the window like a High School boy and watched you go by. I've been crazy,—stark crazy about you! I've asked you to hand in lesson-plans just to see your handwriting. I've been loony enough to think you might write something in them or on the margin about last Summer! I've walked past your boarding-house—" He gave a dry laugh.

"Last Summer when I had read your note, I chased around to the cottages until I found some one that knew you. When she told me you taught at Watertown, Iowa, I couldn't get away fast enough to telegraph the school board my acceptance. Of course, my first impulse was to write you, but the thought of the surprise that my presence here would give you seemed too good to forfeit. When that meeting was over I was as excited and happy as a kid. Then—you came up like a small iceberg, and not only wouldn't mention that day in the Summer, but made it so very apparent that I was not to mention it either, and—all year—" He walked over to the window and back. "I suppose there's only one thing it means. You're not going to marry that chap, are you?"

"No," she said very low. She was filling in another leaf.

"Babbie," he said, "didn't that day, that wonderful, unforgetable day, mean *anything* to you?"

"Did it?" she asked. "Well, at least enough, so that when *you* didn't mention it, made it so very apparent that *I* was not to, and acted like a—a cold-storage plant—I was—quite wretched."

"You care?" he challenged her.

"I—don't think so."

"You're afraid to say so! Why? You do care. You care as much as I do."

"Well," she said, "of course, if it's—cooperation—you want—"

He drew her to him for three wild, sweet seconds.

"Oh, goodness!" she whispered, pulling herself away, "I forgot—Herbie Folsom—watering the plants."

In truth, Herbie was at that moment standing quite near, a look of curiosity on his large fat face, the watering-pot full to overflowing, spilling a steady stream down his trousers' leg.

"Herbie, you go out in the yard and water something," said Herbie's superintendent. When they were alone, he took her hands again. "You dear little—"

The door opened, and the janitor deposited a pail, two brooms and a mop.

"Jim," said his superior officer, "I'll be busy in here for a half-hour or so. Suppose you do all the other rooms first."

"Yes, sir." Jim withdrew.

"You sweet—"

The door was opened again, and Herbie, having hastily dashed a gallon of water against the nearest tree-trunk, was back, ready for more excitement.

"Herbie," said the head of the school system, "you take that watering-pot and *go home.* Water your yard until bedtime if you want to, but *don't come back here!* "

I t was nearly time for dinner to be served at Mrs. Hoover's boarding-house.

Inez, lounging in the window-seat, announced: "Here comes Barbara, and—oh, my stars and stripes forever, girls!—*he's* walking up this way with her!"

They were all at the top of the stairs to meet her, crowding about to ask questions.

"Did you sign, Barbe?"

"No."

"Does he know why?"

"Yes."

"What did he say? Does he know what you're going to do next year?"

"Oh, yes, he knows." Barbara bent to tie her shoe, her ears showing pink under the chic black toque.

"What did he walk up this way for?"

"Oh, I don't know. I guess he was trying to find out who started that cat-on-the-mat idea."

"How does he know about that?"

"I told him."

"Barbara!"

"Barbara!" It was Miss Hippman with her most principal-y voice. "Stop making up things and tell us just *what* he said to you."

Barbara faced her tormentors. "Well, the cat is on the mat—go on down and ask him, sillies. He told me to send you all down; he has something to tell you. I think it is something about the position he has advised me to take next year."

The Light o' Day

(Margaret Dean Stevens)

The setting of "The Light o' Day" was typical of times when restaurants were few and unmarried people took their meals in boardinghouses. Aldrich was familiar with this lifestyle, for she and Charles Aldrich met at the Robbins' Nest, a boardinghouse in Marshalltown, Iowa. In Aldrich's 1925 book, *The Rim of the Prairie* (New York: D. Appleton & Company), the dining room of the Bee House is an important feature. As in *Rim*, a teacher is a central character in "The Light o' Day," which appeared in *Woman's Home Companion* of November 1916.

M r. James Mortimer Smith was eating buckwheat cakes. That they were very good cakes it seems certain, for the number that Tillie had brought in to him was appalling.

Nevertheless James Mortimer was grouchy.

He had risen to face a bleak, snowy morning, an uneventful day, a monotonous career, a dull life. And so biased was his mind over the fact that this was a dinky little Western burg, that everybody in it was a rube, that he was the biggest mutt of all for coming out to it, that he had accompanied his dressing with a sarcastic monologue.

By the time he had pounded back his thick, dark hair with a stiff brush, he was saying to his surly, good-looking self in the glass, "I've got the quarry-slave-scourged-to-his-dungeon act down for sure, I have. Just nine days in this town and crying for home and mother. Why, in the dev—" He glanced hastily at a picture on the dresser. "Beg your pardon! I was about to remark, 'Why, in the development of my career was I hornswoggled into coming out here into the "wild and woolly"?' "

The "wild and woolly" was a thriving little city of about thirty thousand peaceable and more or less cultivated Iowa people, but of course there *are* individuals who still have primitive ideas of the Middle West.

By the time he had put on his dark serge coat he was muttering, "Rankin said I'd have a little of everything to do in the office at first, did he? Well, by George, he was right! I've done a little of everything—I've oiled the adding machine and I've taken a mouse out of the trap." And by the time he had clapped on his hat and had started toward the boardinghouse he was saying, "Well, come on, Jimmie, don't loiter. 'What if thou withdraw from the living, and no friend take note of thy departure?'"

At the boarding house the familiar subdued chatter greeted him, intermingled with the odor of Mrs. Watts's good coffee. Yes, she did serve good feeds, he had to admit. But better a spoonful of tea in Pittsburgh than a quart of coffee in Wallace, Iowa.

He had jerked out his chair, unmindful of the languishing look that Tillie bestowed upon him, or of the rapidity with which she rushed her idol's order through. All of which brings us by a circuitous route back to the griddle cakes.

While he was consuming those unnumbered morsels, his mind kept up a running fire of criticism concerning everything in sight but the cakes. It was principally turned toward Major Shorts, at the end of the table: "You're sure an entertaining old duck, Major. Now, that Civil War of yours that you conducted, just how did you happen to decide it in favor of the North?"

Then it percolated through his brain that there were many more plates laid than usual and that there was conversation in the air relative to the fact that the teachers were back after the holidays.

So that was it, was it? There were to be pedagogues all about him. Now, that was nice, wasn't it? A bunch of school-ma'ams, and he, James Mortimer Smith, in their midst. Mrs. Watts couldn't even give him a place out at the other table where the doctors and dentists and a decent lawyer chap were, but had to wedge him in between this old dry-goods stiff, and a medieval history. There was even a new place constructed right across from him. No doubt another of the tribe would sit there and emit wise sayings.

They had arrived in large shoals by this time—about a dozen of them. As James Mortimer Smith finished his coffee, he had come to a definite conclusion:

"Well, by George, this is a hennery for fair! I'll listen to all these talking report cards until the end of my week, and when that is up, then you bet I'll—"

The door opened and *she* came in.

"Stay some more weeks," he finished.

She hung up her coat and came toward his table pausing a moment to speak to someone. ("Come on! Oh, please, come on!") Then straight toward him she floated and took the seat opposite. He didn't know whether he put his napkin in his pocket or threw it under the table. As a matter of fact, he laid it very neatly beside his plate, which all goes to prove that habit is stronger than emotion.

Mrs. Watts introduced them, and although he fully expected to hear her say "Miss Venus," she did nothing of the kind. She said in her matter-of-fact way, "Mr. Smith—Miss Abbott."

Dragging his reluctant self away from the table, he got his coat and hat and stepped out on the windswept porch. Gee, it was a great morning! Just bracing enough to be right. Neat little town, this, too—and not so slow. Those fellows out at the other table, now,—hadn't they said something about a skating party?

Miss Abbott! And what was her first name? It ought to fit her, that was sure. He couldn't imagine Henrietta, or Evelyn, or Eleanor—he detested Eleanor. How gold-brown her hair was and how woodsy she had looked! Not *back-woodsy*, understand, that suit had cut to it,—but like a wood sprite or a water nymph or someone you had dreamed about but had never seen.

Noontime and luncheon took on the nature of an adventure. When Mrs. Watts volunteered the information that Miss Abbott was going to take her luncheons in the Lowell District, where she taught, his depression was akin to some of his long-ago childish disappointments.

So she was really a teacher! Well, what did you know about that?

Dinner time was only about six weeks distant. When it finally arrived and James Mortimer was in his place, his heart, which he had always assured himself was under very good control, fairly turned over every time the door opened. When the dessert was being served, a Miss Black, whose manner was stiffer than starch, ventured the remark that Eleanor had been invited to dinner by one of her patrons. So her name was Eleanor! Stunning name, that, when you stopped to think about it. Just suited her—euphonious and sort of laughing-like.

The next morning she had been there and gone when he arrived. What luck! You could bet *that* wouldn't happen again. Then there was that Sahara Desert of a luncheon to be lived through.

Six o'clock and dinner! And she was in her place in a pippin of a pale blue dress. Her eyes were gray-blue like cornflowers—and her hair! If he could only touch one of those riotous fluffy strands! Yet, if he had his choice between that and taking her perky little chin with its V-shaped crevice in the cup of his hand, he believed he'd vote for the chin.

All of this wild day-dreaming in the back of his mind persisted in accompanying the general conversation, of which there was a great deal, for everyone seemed in a peculiarly jovial mood. J. M. S., himself, never at a loss for something to say, and in a drink-to-me-only-with-thine-eyes mood, was doing his share. So that when Doctor Merner called from the other table:

"Anybody in there want to try skating to-night?" "Do *you?*" said Jim Smith, unabashed, across to that cleft in her chin. It must have wanted to, for it dimpled in a little and seemed to help her adorable mouth to say, "Yes."

Then everyone became very jolly and informal—just like a big family planning an outing. They went off down the street to the foot of Iowa Avenue, where a series of boathouses, standing shiveringly in the frozen river, gave a partial protection from the cold while skates were buckled on. As Jim took Eleanor Abbott's hands in his own big ones and glided out over the smooth glare, he thought of the grouch which he had acquired the day before as a thing belonging to another decade.

"Do you know," he said, bending down to look at her, "just yesterday I despised this town, kicked myself for coming, and had a genuine grouch on?"

"I had the same experience," she said honestly. "I did *so* hate to come back. We'd had such a pleasant vacation at my cousin's; and Holton's Primer, and the life of the Eskimo, and Johnny Pringle's sniffing seemed so sort of monotonous."

"Where is your home?" he asked.

"I have none," she said; "I'm a nomad, a Wandering Jew, a man without a country. I spend my holidays at my cousin's. My spring vacations I usually spend here." [Oh, joy!] "And in summers I teach as much as I can in teachers' institutes."

"You?" he said incredulously, looking down at her little self.

"Why not?" she demanded. "I've been teaching three years and a half, ever since I graduated from Teachers' College. Now tell me something about *you*. Three things about you I know, though."

"Which three?"

"Well, first, I know that you are the new man with the Rankin Company; second, I know you are from Pittsburgh; third, I know you have a picture of a lovely girl in a gray silver frame on your dresser."

He stubbed his skate awkwardly on a piece of weed growing out of the ice. "The dickens you do!"

"Yes," she went on imperturbably. "She has big brown eyes. She is looking over her shoulder. She has on a white lace dress and is holding a bunch of roses in her arms."

"You are uncanny. Do you happen by any chance to operate a clairvoyant's studio when you are not teaching Johnny Pringle?"

"Oh, no," she laughed. "It's very simple. Mrs. Morford, your landlady, tells Tillie, and Tillie never lets any piece of gossip about any of us get away."

"Now, . . . about that picture," he began rather lamely, and they both laughed.

"Don't bother. I know just how it is," she said serenely. "Of course you don't care the snap of your finger about her. You just want me to understand that you've known her all your life and happened to have such a good picture of her that you put it in a frame. I have one on my dressing table, too. I talk to it sometimes."

"Just one question," he asked. "Is he a school professor?"

She made a little grimace. "Oh, no," she said frankly, "not at all." And they laughed again for the sheer joy of the laughing.

The moon was up, now, flooding the crystal ribbon and making long slim shadows that danced grotesquely ahead of them like two pale spirits out for a lark.

"Beats dancing?" he questioned.

"Doesn't it?"

"I haven't skated since—let's see—my last skate was from Rotterdam to The Hague, that's fifteen miles."

"Oh!" she said. "You've been abroad?"

"Studied and hiked around a little." Then, in explanation, "The money petered out. Now I'm in the Rankin Company with my eyes and ears open. Did you ever oil an adding machine?" he asked suddenly, and, when she looked up in surprise, "or take a mouse out of a trap?"

They went up the silvery stream to the two-mile bend. At the end of the first mile they had been acquainted a year. At the end of the second, five years. When they stopped to rest at the Log Cabin on the return trip they had clipped off fifteen years; and when he unbuckled her skates at the boathouse they had known each other centuries before in some old Druid wood.

When James Mortimer Smith went up the stairs at the Morfords', he was singing "I Love a Lassie" under his breath. As he swung open his door he ventured, a little louder, "She's as sweet as the heather, the bonny, bonny,—" and snapped on the lights. The song ended abruptly. From a gray silver frame a girl in a white lace gown was looking reproachfully at him over an armful of roses.

Eleanor Abbott did not turn on the lights. She stood braiding her gold-brown hair in the silver moonshine that swept across her room.

For a few moments she stood in front of her mirror peering into its moonlighted depths. Suddenly, like a naughty child, she reached out her finger and cautiously pushed a photograph backward until it fell with a thump behind her dressing table. Whereupon she ran to her bed and, jumping in, buried her face in a pillow.

Winter turned to spring with a smell of loam, a bursting of buds and a mating of birds. The allurement of it all was in the air. Even as the robins twittered their love-songs in the old oak in front of the squatty brick boarding house, so the contagion spread until there was a veritable epidemic. Even Tillie and the milkman stood out by the back gate so often, digging their heels into the ground, that the sod looked as if a gopher had been at work.

By the time the children were putting great masses of lilacs and apple blossoms on their teachers' desks, Eleanor Abbott had handed her resignation to the board. There was no formal announcement of her engagement to Jim Smith, only as the blossoms told it and the birds sang it.

Spring turned to summer with a blaze of color running riotous over the boarding-house porch. But the teachers were not there; they had scattered like so many leaves.

Long after the climbing roses had withered, the vines looking in at the old-fashioned dining-room windows one Saturday evening saw Eleanor Abbott again in her accustomed place. From a summer at the cousin's spent in preparation for her coming marriage, she had come to Wallace for a day or two in response to a letter from Jim urging her to look over a house with him.

He had not told her where the house was,—would not, in fact, when she interrogated him at intervals,—put her off with, "Maybe you won't like it."

So, after they had left the boarding house, every corner they turned was a matter for delicious anticipation to Eleanor. When he suddenly took her arm and marched her, square-corner fashion, between low hedges and up a long cement walk, "Oh, Jim," she said, clapping her hands like a little girl, "how *dear!*" And again, "Oh, Jim, I used to go by here the year I taught at the Whittier. It was being built then. I loved it every time I passed it. And *we* can have it?"

"Yes, it's for you to say," he said quietly, as though his answer held a hidden meaning. "We're to let Jamison know by to-morrow night."

The house was nothing unusual, a story and a half, bungalow style. It has its duplicate in almost every city of the Union, with only the loving touches of the people who call it home to differentiate it from the others. Up the steps they passed and to the wide porch. Jim inserted the key, was turning it, as Eleanor touched his arm. "Oh, wait, Jim!" she said breathlessly. "Wait just a minute. It's such a—such a big thing in my life—I want to take it slowly."

"Take your time." He stopped to examine a porch pillar minutely. "Left their hooks for the hammock," he said in a matter-of-fact tone, to hide his own emotion.

"I guess it's because I've not had a real home for so many years," she said apologetically as she crossed the threshold. They entered a reception-hall, bare of furnishings, but, even so, it seemed to hold out warm, welcoming hands.

He took her little chin in the cup of his hand and bent to it. "Evening," he whispered as he kissed her, "and I've just come home. Great, isn't it?" She clung to him a moment with another breathless "Oh, Jim!" and then turned to the survey of the room.

"Oh, how *pretty* it will be," she said happily: "a soft green and gray rug, green and russet pillows on the built-in seat, and—oh, Jim, *could* we have a clock on the stairway?"

"Sure thing, and Longfellow's poem tacked on the front," he laughed.

They turned to the left, where pillars separated the hall from the living-room.

"A *fireplace!*" the girl exclaimed. "And built-in bookcases on either side! Oh, it will be so *dear* in here—warm, soft tans and browns in wall paper and rug, creamy curtains, and old-rose pillows on the davenport, our books in the low cases, and hyacinths in a silver dish on the library table. Jim,"—she turned toward him—"honestly, I don't know whether I'm loving you or the house."

"Well, love away," he laughed, "so long as I go with it."

To the dining-room was but a few steps. The slanting rays of the sun were flickering unsteadily over the floor.

"Blue," she announced decisively, "Delft and cornflower blue, and brass candlesticks on the buffet. My mother's dishes that she left me have delicate little sprays of cornflowers on them, and the curtains shall have borders to match. And, Jim, *shall* we have a round or a square table?"

"Well, Mis-s-Sabbott," he said, in imitation of Tillie, "the point is—could you get a square meal on a round table?"

Pushing open the swing-door, the kitchen seemed fairly to shout at them, "Now, what do you think of *me?*" It was small, but as snowy-white and charming as enamel, aluminum, and glass could make it.

"Do you know," she said suddenly, when she had finished inspecting the last convenience, "do you know, even if we could afford it, I would no more think of having a maid to take care of this dear little house than I'd fly!"

"Wouldn't you, Eleanor?" he spoke soberly.

"Well, I guess *not,*" she responded, with a charming little toss of her head.

Passing out through a short entry, they came again to the little reception-hall.

"Now, up-stairs," the man said.

There were three bedrooms and the bath. At the door of one room, Eleanor said, "Gray, gray and poppies. I have all the old-fashioned things that were my mother's. I'll put a soft gray finish on the old furniture and cover the chairs with cretonne splashed with poppies. And the best part of all, the expense will be so small."

He smiled at her: "You're a great financier, Eleanor."

"I've had to be," she answered simply.

At the door of another room she paused, thinking hard. At last she announced: "Mother's best old walnut set, left just as it is. It can't be improved. We'll have a big braided rug, and the wall paper shall be yellow with a little pin-stripe. I have some pictures in old walnut frames, oval you know, and a queer old hassock. I'll make snowy-white ruffled curtains. It will be peaceful and restful. Your mother will enjoy it when she comes to see us. Is she old-fashioned, Jim?"

He glanced out of the window across the chimney tops of the neighboring houses. "No," he said in a moment, "not very."

The third chamber was over the living-room and was identical in size. From its windows one looked down upon the green lawn and into the branches of a silver maple. She paused and looked out thoughtfully.

Tenderly he put his arms about her. His very tenderness brought her tears. "I want my mother," she sobbed brokenly. He smoothed back her hair as gently as a woman, until she looked up, smiling through her wet lashes.

"Now, come," he said, drawing her to the little alcove in the hallway. "I want to talk to you." There was a built-in seat under the double windows, and upon this he drew her down beside him.

"Eleanor," he spoke abruptly, "you've heard of Henry F. Close?"

"Henry F. Close?" she repeated. "Why, of course. Everyone has." It was a name that carried almost the significance that the Rockefeller and Carnegie names carry. "But, why," she spoke, perplexed, "why do you speak of him?"

"Because," he said simply, "he is my stepfather."

"Stepfather?" she repeated questioningly, almost as though failing to comprehend the word.

"Yes, my mother's husband, you know." He spoke as one would to a child.

"But, Jim,"—she was apparently still failing to understand—"you've told me your mother was a widow."

"No, dear," he said patiently, "I never said that. I told you my father died when I was twelve. It's true I purposely withheld it from you that my mother was married again. At first it was purely for business reasons that I told no one. My stepfather is backing the Rankin Company, and neither he nor the company wanted it known. Only Rankin himself knows it. The name Smith, you know, happening to be honestly mine, was something of a mask in itself." He smiled at her, then sobered suddenly.

"You must know first," he began, "that, rich as my stepfather is, it has never meant anything to me as far as the future was concerned. He made that plain to my mother when he married her. I have made my home with them whenever I wanted to; and a mighty slim excuse of a home it is, too," he added bitterly. "There was more *home* to the seven-roomed house we had when I was a kid and my father was a country lawyer than there is in the whole combination of the four estates Henry Close keeps up. Well, what I want to tell you is the proposition of a wedding gift he has made to us." He cleared his throat, almost in embarrassment, now that the clear gray-blue eyes of the girl were upon him. "When I went back East he called me into his library and said in his short, snappy way: 'Jim, I'll make you a wedding present that's worth while, if you want it. You can take it or let it alone. I'll give you as long as you live the use of so many shares in the Blank Consolidation Company. You can't sell it—the income is yours. If you take it, you've got to get out of the business. With that much money you wouldn't be worth anything to us.' He's blunt, you know. 'They say you're making good out there. There might be the managership someday if you stick. If you take the business, you don't get the money. If you take the money, you don't need the business.' That's all, Eleanor, except to tell you what the income from that stock would be." He wrote something on the back of an envelope and handed it to her.

"Oh!" she said, astounded, as though the amount were beyond her comprehension.

"It's a big decision," he went on. "I've given it a great deal of thought. I've been greatly disturbed by it." The very formality of his speech, usually so careless in its construction, showed the stress of his emotion. "All the way back on the train I pictured to myself the delight of telling you—the things I could do for you. I'd give you a lovely house. I'd take you abroad. I thought of you in beautiful gowns. I went back to work. I got intensely interested in some plans in the office. I've been working on them evenings. I've had my salary raised twice." He got up abruptly and stood above her. His voice rose passionately. "Well—I've found myself. I've located my manhood. *I don't want his money!*" He was pacing restlessly back and forth now. "What would I be doing for you?" he asked her gruffly. "Nothing—not a thing! The old man is long-headed. *He* knows. We'd be living on charity. We'd be idlers, social apes, parasites. Well," he said more gently, as though somewhat ashamed of his recent passion, "it's a big decision, and we must weigh it well." He stopped and looked down at the girl, but she kept her eyes lowered so that he could not read them.

"I'm sorry, dear," his voice broke to its tenderest quality; "you were so happy and untroubled this evening. You don't need to decide right now. Think it over to-night and to-morrow, so that we can tell Jamison about the house." He smiled down at her bent head. "It's for you to say. Paris gowns and Palm Beach," he said whimsically, "or my manhood and this," he made a gesture which took in the modest little house.

"Do you know," he said gently, when she did not speak, "a little verse I read long ago and had not thought of for years has been running through my mind:

'Give me your hand, your hand to hold,
    Here where the life ways part;
Shall we fare this way to the light o' day,
    Or that to the night, sweetheart?'

But the question is," he added very low, as though speaking to himself, "*which* way?"

W hile he was speaking the girl had been watching an old man down in the alley hitching a bob-tailed horse to an ancient surrey. As he tied his horse and put on his coat with the slow movements of age, she unfastened the screen and leaned out. "Oh, Mr. Jamison!" she called. The old man looked up to nod and smile at her. "We've decided about the house," she called down to him, "and we'll just keep the key."

Turning to the man who stood close behind her she laughed up at him adorably. And when he took her—"You foolish boy, to have let it worry you," she said tenderly. "As if I didn't know which is the way to the light o' day!"

Concerning the Best Man

(Margaret Dean Stevens)

"Concerning the Best Man" is the only story Aldrich wrote in letter form. She sold this story in 1915 to *Modern Priscilla*, whose editors seem to have held stories for about two years before publishing them. In April 1917 an unsigned editorial in the magazine discusses whether or not this journal, devoted to needlecrafts, should have any fiction. It acknowledges that in a recent survey most readers responded they would like to retain the one or two fiction pieces usually included; however, neither that issue nor following issues contained either short stories or serials as they had previously, nor did Aldrich sell any more pieces to this magazine. The April 1917 *Modern Priscilla* was devoted to weddings and would have been a logical place for "Concerning the Best Man" to have been published.

Aldrich said that she sold every story she wrote; this one was sold but not published. The copy that appears here was taken from a revised manuscript and is probably the one from which Mrs. Aldrich's final copy for *Modern Priscilla* was prepared. Across the top she has written "Modern Priscilla."

Dear Ruth:

They didn't receive my letter and there is no one to meet me. I have telephoned to the house, and Pauline's father is coming right down with the car. He says the whole crowd is out to a dinner given for the bridal party. They thought I was coming on the late train.

Will write you each day as I promised.

Hastily,
Betty.

Sat. A.M.

My Dear Ruth:

I think I am coming home, that is I would if I had any excuse under the sun. And I may yet. Anyway I wish I hadn't come.

It was positively rude of Pauline not to tell me who the doctor's best man was to be, when I was to be her maid. Even if she didn't know that I ever knew him she ought to have mentioned his name.

This is the way it happened. The dinner crowd came home before the dance. The girls all came upstairs to see me and help me dress. I was glad the blue gown "set" me so well, as old mammy used to say.

Of all the chattering and laughing, you can imagine! The dance was to be informal, you know, just given by Jack Bradley, Dick Worthing and some of those men. Jack Bradley has just come back from "across the pond" where he has been nosing around in musty out-of-the-way places; and young Dick Worthing, an army surgeon you remember, is here on a furlough from Manilla.

There were to be no cars, for it was such a heavenly night, the whole crowd was going to walk over. The men were waiting below and all the girls had gone down but two or three of us. As we turned on the stair landing, my heart stood still a minute, and my first thought was to run right back up the big stairway and *never* come down. Then I threw up my head (you know my great grandmother shot an Indian in pioneer days. P.S. I hope you see the connection.) and I remember as I went on, I kept saying to myself, "I will not let it make any difference. I will *not*." For across the crowd by the reception hall door there loomed the one man in the whole world that I didn't want to see then—or ever.

Pauline introduced a lot of people to me and then the first thing I knew was presenting the doctor's best man, Mr. Carhart, and he was saying he was glad to know me, and then in Pauline's sweetest voice she said, "And Mr. Carhart is to walk over to the dance with you, Betty," and added thoughtfully, "I'm sure he will take good care of you."

That horrid man said he was quite sure he would, and I plainly saw a twinkle (the old twinkle) in his eyes.

We walked along in the most awful silence for a way, and then he said, "Really, I couldn't help it you know, Betty."

"Miss Holbrook," I just snapped out.

"Miss Holbrook," he repeated quite humble.

"I should like to ask you one question, Mr. Carhart," and I know that my tone of voice must have awed him, "Did you or did you not know that I was to be here?" You must remember that I am a judge's daughter.

"I did, Miss Holbrook," the prisoner at the bar answered.

"Then why did you come?" I demanded.

"I came because Jim Abbott is the best friend I have in the world and because he wanted me, Betty." I let it pass that time. "And besides I wanted to," he added, which I thought entirely uncalled for.

"You might have told them we used to be. . . ."

"What?" he said, almost stopping.

"Acquaintances," I finished hotly.

"Oh," he said, "Acquaintances," and neither of us spoke again.

Afterawhile I took a tiny little peep up at him, and he was looking straight ahead, and his jaw looked just like iron.

Just then the crowd came up, and we all went in together.

As we were starting to dance, I said quickly so no one would hear, "So long as no one in the party knows about that year that we. . . ."

"Were acquaintances," he put in.

I nodded, "I should prefer now to continue. . . ."

"I think I have my cue perfectly," he said, and the orchestra began.

After the first dance, which we got through somehow, Pauline and the doctor came up, and Pauline said, "You two people dance together just beautifully." And the doctor said, "Yes, we were both noticing it."

I saw that wretched twinkle again, and the owner of it said, "Perhaps Miss Holbrook and I have danced together in some other world."

How I wanted to answer with something cutting, but with the others there, all I said was "Then you remember much better than I, Mr. Carhart."

After that he went away and did not come back until his last dance. He quite devoted himself to Madge Turner. *I* think she's rather forward, but no doubt that's the style he likes.

It was so late after the dance that we all went back to our rooms soon.

I haven't seen him this morning. Someone said he and Dick Worthing, Jack Bradley, and Pauline's brother John had gone to play tennis.

I've been with Pauline opening some of her gifts. They are just beautiful.

It's luncheon time. The tennis players will not be here.

I shall stay through the houseparty and wedding, Ruth, but to some people I shall be exceedingly cold.

Betty.

Sun. A.M.

Dear Ruth,

I just came in from a drive with Jack Bradley. He drove tandem, and we went out the loveliest shady country road. Quite a way out we met Bob Carhart riding one of the Van Sant horses. Jack pulled up to talk, and I was quite pleasant, I thought, but Bob, I mean Mr. Carhart, acted in a hurry to go. Speaking in plain English, he acted positively surly.

Last night Dick Worthing gave a dinner for twelve of us. Dick took in Pauline, the doctor took me, and Bob had Madge Turner up at the other end of the table.

During the course of the dinner, the question was brought up concerning the attitude of the modern girl in times of physical danger. Jack Bradley said he never saw a girl that didn't either scream or do something foolish when danger was near.

John Van Sant said so, too. Dick Worthing had seen a native girl on the island killed in some terrible accident, and although conscious, she had not uttered a sound. Jack Bradley said he had been speaking of American girls. Someone asked Bob Carhart his opinion. Everybody leaned forward to listen, just as though what he was going to say would be important. People have fallen into the habit of paying attention to what he says since he made his big speeches against that corporation. I, myself, would not humor him in that way.

He picked up a glass and absently looked into it.

"Several years ago," he said, "I was spending the winter in Florida in a little out of the way town on the coast." I kept my eyes on Pauline's pearly brooch, just to have something by which to steady myself, for I grew afraid of what he was going to say.

"I sailed across the inlet one day, anchored, and started on foot across the peninsula, to the ocean."

Pauline's brooch moved out of my perspective as she turned to fix a little green candle shade, but I stared stonily at the place where the pearls had been.

"As I plunged into the jungle, I saw a young girl." Jack Bradley gasped and clutched his heart, but no one paid any attention to him. "She wore a riding habit. Her horse had thrown her in such a manner that her foot and ankle had been caught cruelly between two palmetto logs. She had been lying there for some time, and added to the pain of her fractured ankle, was the horror of spending the night in that wild jungle. My point is merely that in the face of these dangers, she neither screamed nor acted foolish as Jack says."

The conversation changed immediately, but I was nervous all through the rest of the courses. Why did he have to drag that in before them all? Of course no one knew, but some men would have respected a girl's feelings.

> Goodbye for today,
> Betty.

Mon. A.M.

Dear Ruth:

We had a nice quiet Sunday night, that is if you call about a dozen or more people laughing and talking on the veranda, quiet.

The long French windows were raised, and the big grand piano moved over by them. Madge Turner played, a little too brilliantly I thought for the occasion, for it was all so beautiful and still out there. The moon shone down through the big oaks on the lawn and cut the veranda into patches of light and shadow. The night was so still that we could hear the river noises. And the chimes on the old Catholic Cathedral were playing.

I sat on the steps with Marion Huntley. Some one came and stood in the shadow of the pillar not far off. I don't know who it was, for I wouldn't look.

John Van Sant brought out his violin and played the Intermezzo from Cavalleria Rusticana. No matter how badly it's played that always makes me want to cry, the part about "Mother hear us while our tears are falling," and John plays well.

Madge played again and then they insisted that I should sing. I didn't want to, for I didn't feel like it at all, but like Yellow Dog Dingo in Kipling, "I had to." And then in a wild moment I sat down and began to sing Asthore. Of all carelessness! Think, after all that happened down there at the beach, choosing deliberately to sing:

> "The waves still are singing to the shore
> As they sang in the happy days of yore."

The crowd was very nice about the song and wanted something more, but I got away as soon as I could.

Concerning the Best Man

We are to have rehearsal for the ceremony this P.M. It's to be a home wedding, you know.

I wish every day you could have come, but am well aware of the fact that young Phillip, Junior, is taking his share of your time.

Will try to tell you all I can about everything.

With much love,
Betty.

Tues. A.M.

My Dear Ruth:

Rehearsals went off finely. The line of march is to be through the library and two parlors. We had lots of fun the first time we rehearsed. The men didn't get to their places by the big east windows as soon as the maids did, and so ran all the way through the reception hall. Once Jack Bradley, who was taking Pauline's father's place for the rehearsal, came in tangoing with the bride.

Last night was the tally-ho party. We had just a lovely time. Maybe I enjoyed myself so much because I sat up front behind the bugler and the best man was away somewhere in the back.

When the party came home, we had cakes and ices on the veranda, and everybody sang and we all felt jolly. I was feeling a little more kindly toward Bob Carhart, just beginning to think he might not have been so much to blame for being here, when I passed him on the stair landing, and he was whistling Asthore in a very cheerful manner. *Now* he need never expect me to act even friendly.

With love,
Betty.

Tues. P.M.

Dear Ruth:

I was going to write a few lines before dinner and finish in the morning. I just have to write for I'm so furious. The most wretched thing happened this P.M. You know uncle has a sister-in-law, a little old lady, who lives over in Hillsburgh, and he wanted me to go over and see her while I was here.

This P.M. I took the trolley to go over and had gone a block or two when Bob Carhart got on. He came over and sat down by me, and, of course, I was obliged to talk to him. We discussed improvements in electric cars.

The courthouse is still in the old town of Hillsburgh, and Bob was going over to get the doctor's license. When the old conductor came to collect fares, he grinned and said, "You're the fourth couple I've taken over today." That was embarrassing enough, but to have had Dick Worthing get on just in time to hear him, was unbearable.

I shall be glad when the wedding is over, and it will be necessary no longer to put up with such indignities.

Wed. A.M.

We went up the river in John Van Sant's launch last night, and took supper. There was a slight chill in the air, so the men built a big campfire, and after supper we all sat around it.

Dick Worthing told some of his army experiences, all full of wild animals and mausers and natives and dynamite. The moon was under a cloud and the big shadows came out of the woods and up the river bank and pressed up close to the fire as though they were cold. We could hear the water lapping against the launch, and away over somewhere an owl mourned and mourned.

And this was Pauline's last evening as Pauline Van Sant. I watched her as the fire played over her face, and she looked so serene and happy. I wondered how she could. If I were in her place I know I would have been nervous and serious and afraid to go on. Uncle told me once I was an extremist and that I must try to get over being so uncertain in my moods. And even old Mammy used to say "Law, chile, you'se like a teeter boa'd, you'se away up or away down." But maybe if my mother had lived, had always been with me, like Pauline's, like all the girls', things wouldn't be so tangled and hard to understand.

The one little tiny place that Bob Carhart still has in my . . . consideration, is because, he too, lost his parents long ago, and with all his money, and has had no home. I looked across the fire at him, and he was watching the doctor with such a queer look on his face, neither the iron jaw nor the twinkle, that something somewhere in me said, "Betty Holbrook, you can at least be pleasant and kind." And I knew I was going to be.

Well, the moon came out, and it was so beautiful that we came down very slowly in the launch. Everyone seemed loathe to let the evening go. It was as though we were leaving behind us with the big shadows something that was dear. Jack Bradley helped me into my white sweater, and I sat with him by the wheel where the spray tossed over me.

That night I was nearly asleep when Pauline came in, and we lay and talked a long time.

She told me a great deal about the doctor, how kind he had been to her, and when she had begun to care: but here was one thing she couldn't begin to tell me and that was how *much* she cared. That must be very beautiful.

Then she told me there was just one thing to mar her happiness, that another man cared for her too, but she was sure he would some day find someone who would make him very happy.

She spoke of Bob once and how much the doctor thought of him.

"Betty," she said, "You haven't any home except with your uncle. I wish you could marry a man like Bob Carhart, but he told Dr. a long time ago that there was only once he had cared for anyone and that was for that little girl in Florida he told us about that night."

I didn't answer Pauline, and she spoke to me again and thought I was asleep, for I lay quite still. When I was sure she slept, I crept over to the window and looked up at the stars a long time as though Mother might be nearer then.

   Betty.

Thurs. A.M.

My Dear Ruth:

Oh, so beautiful as it was, the wedding. Last night was the most perfect night of my life.

We were so busy all day with the decorations. We hung the parlors and library in ferns and banked the mantels with roses. The breakfast room we hung in white. That was where the bridal party was to be served. The big front stairway was massed with ferns and bridal wreath.

There were caterers' wagons and express wagons, and messenger boys coming and going all day, while the phone rang constantly.

Finally the last rose nodded in its place and the house grew quiet, for everyone had gone to rest. Jack Bradley broke the stillness once by going down the hall past the doctor's door singing "Just before the Battle," and, of course, everyone laughed. Then all was still for a long time. Marion Huntley and I dressed slowly and sat down in the big window seat.

Finally a door slammed somewhere, and at the same time a cab crunched on the gravel driveway. More wheels followed, and there was laughing and talking down stairs. In the back hall, the half-frightened, half-laughing maids were straightening their ropes of ferns and carnations. The old rector came out of Pauline's room and I caught a flutter of a white veil. The old gentleman stopped to speak to the maids, some of whom he had christened.

From down below came the first strains of the harp and violins playing the Lohengrin. The talking below stopped. John Van Sant spoke to the maids, and they started down through the long rooms to the canopy of roses in the big east windows. Then I followed, and back of me came Pauline and her father. Pauline, all sweet and beautiful in her shimmering white veil, her eyes shining straight into the doctor's. Then I saw something I shall never forget, a man standing in the doorway, a man whose face had gone ashy white as he looked at the bride. It was Jack Bradley.

The voice of the old rector rose trembling and solemn, "Dearly beloved." The harpist barely touched the notes of an old love song. Then the doctor was saying, "I, James, take thee, Pauline." I closed my eyes at "Until death us do part." At "Thereto I plight thee my troth," I looked up at and quickly away from the eyes of the best man.

It was soon all over, the ceremony, the congratulations and the supper. We were helping Pauline into her going away gown, and Madge was locking a suitcase. Then we left Pauline with her mother and went down to the guests.

The doctor and Bob came down with the grips, and then Pauline came to the landing with her bridal bouquet. All the maids held up their hands, and that bouquet fell into mine, though Pauline may have aimed it. Then everyone very foolishly congratulated me on being the next bride.

This is the part I want to tell you the best of all and I can't, for I don't know myself, just how it happened. As bridesmaid, I had to get into the car with the doctor and Pauline and the best man. When we went to the station, the crowd all went into the train. It was in there that I discovered I had that enormous bouquet in my hands, but no one seemed to notice it.

Bob and I were the last of the party to get off, and when we got outside, after some last words of goodbye, the other cars were leaving. We two stood alone a few minutes and waited until the train started, Pauline and the doctor in the vestibule waving their hands. I don't know why it was. It may have been that the nervous strain of the week had been so great, it may have been that it just dawned over me that I was losing Pauline forever, Pauline, who had been like my sister. And then again it *may* have been Providence instead of Pauline, but as the train moved, I just stood there and cried all to myself.

A few minutes before, Bob Carhart would have been the last man in the world I would have wanted to see me doing such a babyish thing, but as I stood there looking up the track with the tears rolling down my face, I wasn't one bit sorry. It's awful to admit it, but I was glad he was there with me.

He hadn't seen me at first, I mean what a foolish thing I was doing, for he too was looking after the departing train. When he looked down he said two things and one was teasing, and one was stern: "Why, little girl, what's the matter?" and "Betty, Come here." And I went. And then that absurd shower bouquet must have been in the way for Bob said "Give this thing to me."

"It's unlucky to touch it," I sobbed.

"I'll take the risk," he laughed.

And there in the shadow of the old station, on a track covered with tar and cinders, with a box car on one side and a truck load of cabbage on the other, the miserable misunderstanding of the years gone by, was righted.

Then something funny happened. The train which I thought gone, had merely been on a side track and now came back on the main line straight past us. The doctor and Pauline were still in the vestibule and waving their hands at us, for I saw them myself through my tears, [from the] lapel of the best man's dress suit.

"Bob," I said, "why do you suppose the doctor and Pauline didn't look surprised when they saw us, for they didn't know we met before?"

"Don't scold," he said. "I told them."

"And Pauline knew about us when she got me down here?" I demanded.

The best man nodded, with the old twinkle in his eyes.

And the bridesmaid didn't even care.

Your very happy,

Betty.

The Rosemary of Remembrance

(Margaret Dean Stevens)

"The Rosemary of Remembrance" is one of several Aldrich stories dealing with a class reunion twenty years or so after college graduation. It was published in November 1917 by *Black Cat Magazine*.

Robert Dudley, broker, clean-cut, good-looking and forty, sat at his Circassian walnut desk in the best office suite in the new Metropolitan Building in the biggest city on the western coast.

He was looking over his personal afternoon mail, which had come later than usual, and frowning a little at the delay, for he had been ready to leave the office. As he cut open and read the last letter, the frown on his face relaxed its hold, lessened and disappeared. The letter was headed "Central University. Mathematics Department, Thomas J. McCullough, Professor." It said:

"Dear Old Bob:

Are you aware (of course you're not) that this is the year the old crowd promised to meet again at Commencement? As Flo and I are the only ones that married in our own crowd and also the only ones to live at the old stand, the reunion is to be at our home.

It's Flo's idea that just the crowd itself is to be present, so we are writing all the others to kindly leave superfluous husbands, wives and babies at home. Naturally, we are putting it more delicately than that, but as you have none of the above, I didn't mince matters.

Of course, you should have married long ago, you old sardine, but we'll forgive you. Come along, don't fail, under any consideration, to be with us June first,

For the sake of auld lang syne.

Tom McCullough."

There was no semblance of a frown now. Instead, a smile that suddenly broke out of its hiding place gave Bob Dudley's face a singularly boyish look.

There was another sheet of paper that had come out of the envelope,—a carbon copy. It was signed "Flo McCullough," and said:

"Dear Folks:

Tom is writing the letters to you about our reunion. I am adding a note to each. Forgive the carbon copy idea, but I'm the busiest woman in the U. S. A., and I wanted to tell you all the same thing anyway, excepting Bob and Nell.

You know Bob has never married! Nell has never married! Nuff said! Whatever happened, I don't know,—guess no one does,—but let's do our best to get them to fix it up at the reunion. Don't let them suspect, but leave them alone a good deal, etc.,—and if it accomplishes its mission, this reunion will be the best ever. All come."

The smile, which had spread, was the forerunner of a chuckle, then a burst that shook Bob Dudley in one of those 110-volt laughs which come occasionally from a quiet, unemotional man.

That Flo McCullough, in her great hurry, had enclosed one of the carbon copies in his own letter, seemed the season's best joke. He sat back in his big swivel chair and let his mind "turn the leaves of fancy" as it recalled to him the members of the old crowd. His mental vision brought them all before him one by one,—only half consciously did he reserve Nell Russell for the last. He found himself recalling her in various settings,—coming across the windswept, leafy campus, in a scarlet cape and tam cap,—breezing in to dinner at the old Gibson boarding house, late, out of breath, good-natured and sunny. He had cared,—Lord, yes, he had cared. That misunderstanding,—how trivial and foolish it had been—something to do with a red-haired fellow in the old Philomathian Literary Society.

Into his reminiscent dreams came the office boy. "Mr. Dudley, Mrs. Dudley said to tell you that her and the little boys was waitin' for you."

Ay,—there's the joke! Flo McCullough had evidently never heard that Bob Dudley had been married three years and was the proud father of as obstreperous a pair of twins as ever poked pencils and button hooks down the registers.

Robert Dudley stuck the letter in his pocket, locked his desk and took the elevator down. A big car waited his coming. In the tonneau sat a sweet-faced, daintily gowned lady, who clutched two little duplicates to keep them from throwing themselves out bodily at their daddy.

"Hello, there, Goose Grease and Lightning," he greeted them, and to his wife, "Could you stand a good joke?"

"I might risk it," she admitted.

But it was not until they were on the porch of the big brick and stucco house that he produced the letter. He handed her Tom McCullough's with no comment. She read it through until she came to the statement that Bob had no wife nor children. "Well,—I must say—I like *that!*" she announced.

And then—yes, it does seem incredible,—he handed her the carbon copy. At the same time he shook again with his 110-laugh. When she had read it through, because she was merry-hearted and liked a good story, she laughed too; but it wasn't 110, more like 40.

"Now," he said decisively, "I'm *going* and I intend to be just what they expect me to be,—a single man."

When she gasped at the audacity of it, he went into the details of his plans. He was going to turn the tables on the old crowd and pose as unmarried until the last evening, when he would tell them the joke. If she thought the journey and the plan unwise she gave no utterance to it, merely pulled the handiest twin to her and hid her face in his fat, warm neck.

So, it came about, that on the morning of June first, Bob Dudley, very well groomed and prosperous looking, with something that resembled laughter in his eyes, sat in the smoker of an east bound train as it pulled out of Omaha. An hour out, at a little country station, a fat, shabby man with an old-fashioned telescope valise climbed onto the train.

"Fat Matt, as I live," said Bob Dudley to the huge fellow who came lumbering down the aisle. They wrung each other's hands long and vigorously.

Matt Jones in the old days had been proportioned between fat and bones as the ratio of four to one. Now it was sixteen to one in favor of the fat. He edited a country newspaper and still paid rent, but was the most contented man in the county.

When they had visited for awhile, Bob suggested their going back through the coaches. There was a possibility that they might run across someone else. Through two coaches they passed, recognized by no one nor seeing anyone they knew. In the third, half-way down, sat a lady, chin in hand, looking intently out of the window. She wore a smart tailored suit and from her small hat rose a pair of jaunty wings. Something in the tilt of her head and the gold-brown of her hair caught the attention of the two men.

"Matt," Bob half turned to him, "who's that girl?"

"Nell Russell," he whispered back and got so red in the face that Bob would have laughed aloud if his own heart had not been pounding strangely.

"How do you do, Nell?" He spoke in as matter-of-fact a tone as though he had been seeing her all these years.

She glanced up, a faint pink travelling over her face, but kept her poise perfectly as she put out her hand. Seats were quickly arranged so that they might all talk together. It was noticeable that most of Nell Russell's remarks were addressed to Fat Matt and it was toward him that she usually looked.

They lunched together in the diner and when the girl inadvertently said, "Bob, here's your favorite cantaloupe," she looked genuinely distressed at the slip.

It was late afternoon when the train pulled into Watertown. The station was a mass of moving students, class colors, arriving parents and old grads.

"Brings it all back, doesn't it, Nell?" Bob asked as he took her grips.

Flo and Tom were watching for them—Flo, plump and matronly, Tom as tall and cadaverous looking as though he ate his mathematics.

"How am I ever going to get you all into my car?" he asked as he led the way to where a little car of very modest price and very immodest notoriety waited. "If any of you crack a joke about it, I'll tip you all out when I turn the corner at Dry Run."

"It's an elegant little car, Tom," said Bob, at which they all laughed immoderately.

Matt and Tom sat in the front seat where Matt oozed over the sides. The others filled the back seat.

"Anybody else here?" they asked.

"Everybody that can come," Flo informed them. "There are nine of us now. Molly Fletcher is here and Jim Caldwell and Ethel Dotson and Jen Grier."

The little car bounced merrily over familiar roads lined with unfamiliar residences, past new dormitories and boarding houses, and slackened in front of the campus that smiled gently at them like a kind old mother whose sweet face welcomed them home.

There were artistic new entrances to the driveways, a half dozen new buildings, and a strange campanile pointed its finger obelisk-like to the blue sky; but the older buildings, the trees, the paths under them, the very grass, seemed waiting to bestow upon the wanderers the rosemary of remembrance.

Bob Dudley involuntarily looked across Flo to Nell Russell. She turned big blue eyes to him that were moist with memory. "Oh," she breathed, "it's rather like a grave yard, after all, where our youth lies dead." Of which statement Flo made a mental note to tell Tom the minute she had him alone.

They stopped in front of a low, roomy bungalow whose long porch held two hammocks and numberless rockers. Three people were sitting there, but all rose and came down the steps. Little Jen Grier came first, tinier than ever, with the same quick-motioned ways that had won for her the name of Jenny Wren. She had been saucy, too, like her namesake, quick-witted and sharp-tongued, and in the joking way with which Fate handles us, she had married a minister.

Ethel Dotson, heavy and slow-moving, came forward a little shyly. She was the wife of the governor of a southern state, but in her heart she despised the life and the executive mansion and longed to be back in her own home.

Jim Caldwell had broadened, too, from the slim college boy to a plump, well-fed dentist. As Bob Dudley shook Jim Caldwell's hand he said, "Good Heavings! Is *everybody* fat?"

"All except me," said a voice above them; and Molly Fletcher stood in the doorway, literally filling it from side to side. She was a sight, but her good-natured face beamed happiness behind her big spectacles. The years of hard work on a Kansas farm had left her with the philosophy that "Although for a dozen years it was just nothing but windstorms and new babies and grasshoppers and whooping-cough and crops drying up and measles and seventeen-year locusts and pink-eye, it was all for our good, I guess."

The hour that followed was not an unqualified success. After the travellers had dressed and returned to the porch, things seemed to lag. The reunion seemed not to have lived quite up to its expectations. The old crowd was nothing but a group of nearly-to-middle-age people who politely and with forced jocularity recalled anecdotes of some especially jolly young folks they had once known. After all, you can't entice Youth from her hiding place when your mind is on a growing boy's examinations or an unfinished job of printing or the setting hens that were to come off to-day.

At ten minutes of six Flo announced that they had better start as they were to go several blocks to their dinner. It was an odd looking little procession that they made. Flo led the way with plump, dapper Jim Caldwell and quiet, tranquil Ethel Dotson. Fat Matt and little Jen Grier were behind them, looking like De Wolf Hopper and his tiniest ballet dancer. Tom McCullough, gaunt, and as long as a geometrical equation, was painfully trying to suit his step to huge Molly Fletcher's waddling gait.

Bob Dudley and Nell Russell, slightly conscious that the others had purposely left them behind, were bringing up in the rear. Although their conversation consisted largely in generalizations on the improved condition of College Hill, although he was apparently saying, "They have converted

Prexie's old house into an isolation hospital," and she was answering, "What a good idea,"—what mentally passed between them was, "Do you remember that seat under the oak, Nell?" and, "Oh, *do* I, Bob?"

As the little procession followed Flo's lead, crossing one corner of the campus to a row of old houses that stood modestly facing a short side street, it gradually percolated through someone's head that she was taking them to Gibson's. Immediately they were all exclaiming the same thing: "Surely, Ma Gibson doesn't keep boarders yet!"

"Goodness sakes, no!" Flo informed them. "She is over eighty and lives out in the country with her son. A young couple lives here. They use the old dining room for a laundry, but when I told them about the reunion and how we'd like to eat here for old times' sake they took out the tubs and boiler and we fitted it up as nearly like it used to be as we could."

They turned into the familiar old basement dining room.

"Same old ivy. Same old screen door. Same old bumble-bee hanging around," Jim Caldwell said as he went in.

The kitchen door swung open and Flo's biggest surprise stood before them. Lizzie! Tall, angular Lizzie,—her pale hair drawn as tightly back and pinned with as countless a number of wire hairpins, her apron as big and stiffly starched, her eyes shining as kindly over huge cheek bones, as ever. They were all shaking hands with her and listening to her explanation: "Yes, I been married fourteen year come Christmas—livin' up to Hanley—'j'ever see such foolishness—me leavin' my old man and chickens to come down and cook for you—but Mis' McCullough she would have it—"

Youth, who had eluded them up to this moment, seemed to slip in shyly from the kitchen with Lizzie. For the first time they began to feel young. In hilarity that was no longer forced they sat down in their own old places. Only for a moment were they sobered by the thought of the two who were absent. Lou Reeves was not there, for she was teaching in the Philippines. Bert Morrison was not there, for he was dead.

As the meal progressed, all restraint vanished. Gone were the years and the newly formed ties,—forgotten were the hardships and joys, the hours of failure and the hours of triumph. They were the old crowd. The band was playing La Paloma on the campus. Lizzie was in the kitchen. Youth was in their midst.

And Youth abided. So much in the spirit of the occasion were they that by unanimous vote they decided to cut the class play and continue their old time visit on the McCullough's ample porch.

The laughter that rang out from that porch was so infectious that more than one passing student grinned in sympathy. Long-neglected episodes were brought to light,—the evening was replete with "Do you remember?"

"Remember, Tom, in Latin class, reading *'Hic, hic, sunt senatu,'* and Bob whispering, 'Sit down, old man, you're drunk?' "

"Remember your note, Matt, that you pinned on the laundry you sent to the washerwoman:

> *'If all the shirts I've sent to thee*
> *Should be delivered home to me,—*
> *Ah, well! The dresser would not hold*
> *So many shirts as there would be*
> *If all my shirts came home to me'?"*

"That reminds me of Molly's touching ode to our china-painting teacher when that craze first struck:

> *'The hours I've spent with thee, dear heart,*
> *Are as a string of daubs to me,*
> *I count them over, every one apart,*
> *My Crockery,—my Crockery.'* "

Far into the evening they sat in reminiscent mood. No one enjoyed it more keenly than Nell Russell. Temperamental, emotional, she seemed to throw her whole soul into living over her youth. Gay and sparkling, she was vaguely conscious that Bob Dudley's eyes were upon her with something of the same expression in them that had been there for her in the old days.

So apparent was this to the others, also, that no one was surprised when the two lingered after the crowd had dispersed. Romance-loving Flo, in her own room, whispered rapturously to her practical husband, "It's working, Tom,—oh, *joy!*"

That "it" was "working" became more evident as snatches of low-toned conversation from the porch were wafted to her.

"I *did* care—with every fibre of feeling—" came from Bob, and Nell's softer tones, "But how was *I* to know?" And a little later:

"Good-night, Bob."

"Good-night, dear."

"Tom," Flo whispered, *"he kissed her!"*

"Hear it?" he growled, sleepily.

"No,—but I *felt* it," she retorted.

When Bob Dudley went to the room which he was to share with Jim Caldwell in the house next door, he realized that Nell Russell seemed as much a part of his life as she had been in the days long gone by. *Had she really ever been out of it?* At any rate, the college setting, the old crowd, the moonlight night, all had woven a magic spell, the charm of which he was enjoying more than his fancy had dreamed.

"Jim, a fellow can make an awful ass of himself," he said enigmatically to his yawning bedfellow.

As the second day wore on with its alumni reunion, parade, ball game and picnic supper on the river bluff, Bob Dudley found himself dreading more and more to break the news of his marriage to the crowd. The joke that had appeared so hilariously funny in California, now seemed harder to carry through than he had anticipated. Instinctively he knew that, for the rest of his stay, his status would be lowered in the eyes of the people whose faith he wished to keep.

And Nell?

He chose the evening of that second day to enlighten them.

With apparently an unintentional slip of the tongue, he said, "Just before I left home I was arguing that same thing with my wife—"

It was like a hand grenade in their midst.

"Your *what?*" "What's that?" "What are you saying?" came the shrapnel return.

Everyone looked involuntarily at Nell Russell and as quickly looked away. She had glanced up at Bob, startled,—then a flush, painful in its intensity, slipped over her face as she dropped her eyes away from them all.

Bob Dudley explained with more elaborate finish than quite necessary, how it had seemed a joke when reading Tom's letter to let them think him still single,—that he had been married three years before in California,—he hoped they would all visit him sometime—

But no joke ever lay in such a flat, punctured condition as that one. Disappointment showed plainly in more than one face, but above all, sympathy,—sympathy for poor, proud Nell who wanted none.

"The whole thing's spoiled," wailed Flo McCullough to her liege lord. "And that poor Nell—she has cared for him *so*—how *could* he—"

"Well, cheer up,—it's love's labour lost," advised Tom, who was secretly as disappointed as she.

Another day of Commencement activities came, in which everyone in the crowd took a feverish interest as though to keep from thinking of the romance that was no longer romantic. And when in the evening Bob and Nell deliberately broke away for a long stroll out toward the country, something akin to disgust swept through the mind of the most loyal friend.

There was a noticeable frigidity in the air when the two came back to the porch, although Molly Fletcher, with characteristic good spirits was as talkative as ever.

Nell looked very sweet and thoughtful as she sat down in the shadow of the vines. Bob perched on the rail near by. Suddenly, with an impulsive movement, he reached down and took her hand. Everyone felt uncomfortable and embarrassed. Fat Matt wheezed to Tom McCullough, "The mutts!"

"People," said Bob Dudley, and his voice had a queer foreign note in it, "I have something to say—and I want to say it to all of you here first. It's going to be hard—you're going to censure me—I take all the blame—you are in no way to think hard of Nell." He raised his head suddenly with almost an arrogant gesture. "Sometimes," he went on in a moment, "a man makes a mistake and the only thing for him to do is to acknowledge that mistake and—rectify it if he can."

Everyone was staring at him as though hypnotized, all but Nell. She had her head in the hand that Bob was not holding. "Long ago—I made a mistake—" His voice was tense. "Nell and I were engaged—I—something came up—an unbelievably small thing it seems now in the light of the years that are ours. Three years ago I married—" He began picking nervously at the Crimson Ramblers. "When Tom's letter came and I realized that none of you had heard of my marriage, the temptation came to me to keep up the pretense for awhile—to see Nell as I used to—here—at the old school—with all of you. I let my wife read Tom's letter—she even knows what I planned to do." He paused. Everyone felt the import of the moment. All eyes were fixed upon him. There was no sound but Fat Matt's asthmatic breathing.

"Well,—" he went on, "I found Nell unchanged—and caring for me—just as I know I have cared for her all these years. Nothing else matters now." He suddenly stood up, big and dark against the rose vines. "Again I beg of you not to be harsh in your judgement when I tell you that Nell and I are leaving in the morning and we go—together."

It was like the third big act in a drama. They sat there stunned,—these kind, simple, common folk, to whom sex problems and the divorce court had come no closer than newspaper reading. The tragedy of it, the overwhelming bigness of the step Bob and Nell were taking, left them in a half-anaesthetized condition.

Just as little Jen Grier, who had been working her hands together, was moistening her dry lips to speak, Bob turned to Nell and touched his hand gently to her bowed head.

"Don't you think we had better go in the morning, mamma?"

"Yes, I think so, father," came in muffled tones.

"Mamma! Father! What do you mean?" They were shrill, nerve-tense questions, like the staccato bark of dogs.

"I mean," Bob said deliberately, "that just because you didn't know that Nell and I were married three years ago is no reason—"

They were no longer a *stunned* audience. They were a *stung* audience,—and between the two lies many a ripe egg and tomato can. None of these commodities being commonly kept on a university professor's front porch, the audience substituted numerous hammock and porch pillows and a choice collection of epithets.

"You see," Bob Dudley was defending Mrs. Dudley with one arm, "first I got Tom's letter; then Nell's, addressed to Miss Nell Russell, at Seattle where she last taught, was forwarded to her. Then we knew for sure that none of you had heard we were married. Speaks well for our correspondence, doesn't it? And when Flo generously put one of her carbon copies in my letter so that we knew you were all expecting a regular Mary Pickford reel from us,—we decided to put on a good performance so not to disappoint you. I had hard work persuading Nell to leave the twins—"

"Twins?" It was Fat Matt, the machinery of whose mind had suddenly begun to work. "You mean you two folks are married and own a pair of twins? Well, you old *double-barrelled* mutts!"

The Patient House

Aldrich sold this story to *The Designer* in June of 1917
when she was still using her Margaret Dean Stevens pseu-
donym; however, by the time it was published in April
1918, she had decided to publish under her real name.

Aldrich believed that evoking the senses was important
in writing, which is the reason she often used scent in
both her short stories and her books. Here, as in "Their
House of Dreams" (1918), she surrounds the setting for a
home with the fragrance of an apple orchard in bloom.

Dr. Charles Westlake, bag in hand, walked down the
aisle of the only passenger coach on the afternoon local. Thinking over the
peculiarities of the case he had just attended, he came almost to her seat
before he saw her. That she had seen him, however, was evident, for she was
holding out a prettily gloved hand and smiling at him with all her old
friendliness. He took them both—the hand in his own big one and the smile
to his heart. That the former had not been his own to keep forever was now
his life's tragedy—a shadow that dogged his waking hours—a wraith that
mocked him in the night-time.

But so ordinary are the things the lips say to keep the heart from speaking, that "How do you do? What brings you here this warm afternoon?" was
his commonplace greeting.

"I'm going up to the little town of Tiller," she responded as she made
room for him beside her.

"Well," he said bravely—one might as well face the grim facts—"well, it is
Mrs. George Merrifield, now, is it?"

She dimpled. "Mrs. George Merrifield sounds awfully married, doesn't it?"

Would he ever be able to forget that little trick of her eyes smiling first before they communicated their mirth to her lips?

"How about you?" she asked in her sympathetic way. "You have been in dreary places in your Red Cross work, haven't you?"

"Yes," he said gravely, "the year was full of heart-breaking experiences." That the greatest was his own personal one, he did not add.

He had been near the French frontier when the letter from his aunt came. It had contained a newspaper picture of the girl he loved. There had burned into his mind the words underneath the likeness: "A Bride of To-day. Mrs. George Merrifield (née Miss Shirley Bennett.)" And "Didn't you use to know this girl?" had appeared in his aunt's hasty scrawl across the corner of the picture.

D̲r̲. Charles Westlake had put away the little slip of paper and gone on with his work, wishing that a stray German bullet would wander his way. But whom the gods wish to punish they sometimes merely let live. And now, only a few days after the arrival home, they had connived to bring about this meeting just by way of further torture. No doubt they were howling with glee at the pain this little experience would cause him.

"By the way, Shirley," he was saying, so easily did the old familiar name come to him, "you know you have several hours to wait in my home town. Your train leaves at 10:05. I can't think of you in that stuffy hotel. You must come home with me. You will be much more comfortable."

"You are as thoughtful as ever," she said looking gratefully up at him. "But you said your aunt was not at home."

"That isn't to make a bit of difference. Anna, who has kept house for us for years, seems almost like another aunt to me. She will have my dinner ready and it will be better than the one at the hotel anyway."

So a half-hour later the two were in the cool, screened porch eating the most palatable of meals, which old Anna had prepared for the doctor.

It even turned out to be a gay little affair. The plum-trees, heavy with blossoms, tapped gaily on the screen, sending showers of petals over the stone flagging. And not even the shadowy presence of George Merrifield could keep the fragrance of the May evening and the cozy intimacy of the little tea-table from combining to weave a magical spell. From speaking of the friends which they held in common in the city, the conversation gradually became more reminiscent, which is equivalent to saying more dangerous.

"Do you remember the evening we drove to Bellwood?" the girl asked once.

"Do I remember my name?" He smiled grimly. "What a night! Just about the kind this promises to be. Shirley,—what do you say? Will you drive again to-night or—won't your conscience let you?"

The eyes flashed their laugh to her lips.

"Conscience," she asked mockingly, "tell me—would you hurt?" She paused as though listening and shook her head solemnly. "It doesn't say a word. It either wouldn't hurt, or it's too horror-stricken to answer. The only way I can find out what it means is to try it."

He chose to drive the horse, for the days that had been his and Shirley's were before his automobile days.

Past the outskirts of the overgrown town to the highway, they went. Several times they stopped so that the girl might gather armfuls of wild crab-apple blossoms. She was like a child brimming over with happiness. It was easy to imagine that things were as they had been, that nothing seemed incongruous, nothing except the narrow gold circle on Shirley's left hand.

"One doesn't half enjoy the little things along the roadside in a car," she said as the horse ambled along between colonies of little green shoots.

"Doesn't Mr. Merrifield ever drive a horse?" he asked rather stiffly.

"Oh, no," she laughed. "It would be too much trouble. Always a car and a chauffeur to do the work."

When they were approaching the limits of the town on their return trip, she noticed a house in an orchard.

"Whose pretty little home?" she exclaimed enthusiastically. It was one of her most charming traits, that genuine interest in everything about her.

He turned and looked at her a moment. Never had she appeared sweeter to him. Never had his grief seemed more poignant.

"I'm going to stop here a few moments," he said suddenly. "I want you to see that house." She looked up at him, startled at the foreign note in his voice, then with no comment, she got out and went with him.

Up through an apple orchard, billowy in its pink and white waves, they passed to the house on the summit of the knoll. It was a queer little rambling cottage that the trees held lovingly in their midst.

"Why, no one lives here," she said surprised. "How *can* the owner stay away in apple-blossom time?"

"No," the man said, "no one has ever lived here. Before it was finished the man who built it—died." He smiled grimly at his words.

With apparent ease he unfastened the door and they stepped in. To the girl's surprise the house was partly furnished. Simple craftsman furniture stood in place, a huge library table, bookcases, and chairs in the living-room—a tasteful buffet in the dining-room with its rows of gaunt windows.

"And the man *died?*" she asked in awe.

"Well," he said with a little gesture of abandon, "part of him lived, but most of him died!"

"Was it—" she looked up mischievously, "because of 'a rag and a bone and a hank of hair'?"

He shook his head. "I can't allow you to malign her."

"Do you know," she said suddenly, a little timidly, "it's the kind of home I always wanted."

"Don't say things just to be polite, Shirley," he said acridly.

"I'm *not*," she spoke gently. "When I was a little girl I dreamed of a house in an apple orchard. I wanted windows just everywhere—so the blossoms would feel friendly. I wanted a bed of larkspur in the back yard and sweet peas up and down the path. I wanted a little chintz curtain across a corner cupboard in the kitchen and a fat little clock on the shelf. I wanted to keep the pans all nice and shiny. I wanted a cozy little house," she said very low "just—like this."

"You dreamed that," he said, sarcasm creeping in, "and then chose the Merrifield mansion that could put this in its pocket!"

"The Merrifield house is very grand," she said turning to look out of one of the small-paned windows. "There are elegant Bokhara and Kermanshah rugs, and Corots and Reynoldses on the walls, and ivories in cabinets and the most beautiful damasks I have ever seen. The butler is as stiff as Rameses the Second. Sometimes," she looked up audaciously, "sometimes, I feel like throwing a salad fork at him." His face relaxed from its strained look. Yes, he believed her. It was not like the Shirley he had known to succumb easily to the solemnity of the Merrifield traditions.

"Well," she said with a little catch in her voice, as they stepped out on the broad porch again, "it's a very, very dear little house. Why don't *you* buy it? All you would need would be some rugs and dishes and curtains and a bride."

"It's hard work to choose all four, you know," he said smiling at her matronly little way of trying to advise him, just as she used to do.

They stood for a few moments on the steps looking down into the deepening dusk of the trees. The moon came slowly sailing into sight. The gods were calling out all their reserves, it seemed—the May night, the blossoms the fragrance—and now they had sent the moon to aid at the inquisition.

"Sit down a few moments," he spoke almost harshly. And when they were seated, "I'm going to tell you all about it," he said, abruptly. "It can't harm you. If you were unhappy, I'd be more than a cad to talk this way. But I can see you are blissfully happy. This *is* my house." The girl made a little gesture with her hands.

"When I was in college," he went on, "I used to think, like every healthy young fellow, of the girl I was to marry. I used to plan and dream about her—how she would look, what she would say. Then—I did a foolish thing—a thing an alienist might commit me to an asylum for doing. I built a house for her. My uncle was a carpenter and I had worked with him in vacations from the time I was a little kid. I thought I would build a little house that would be all ready for her when I should meet her. I was as sure I would meet her as—religion itself." He was speaking gently. The girl sat very passive with her hands clasped in her lap.

"I have always loved this hill," he went on quietly. "When I was a boy I used to fly my kites here or lie in the grass and watch the clouds."

He paused and when the girl did not answer, he spoke again. "I decided to practice here in my home town. I had a very little capital that my parents left me. So I bought this land—and I started my house. The furniture I made myself. Then—I met the girl. She was just home from a year abroad. She was everything I had dreamed—and more. I was so simple in my love for her, that for a time I didn't realize that I needed ever so much more than love and a little house to offer her. When I realized it—knew that love didn't count for much until the time when I could give her all the things that other men had to offer her—I came up here and told *that* to the old orchard, too."

For the first time the girl spoke. With a visible effort it came. "Why didn't you tell it to the girl, instead?"

"Because," he answered gently, "I was so sure that she knew we were meant for each other, that I let our friendship remain—just friendship—until I could give her those things. I know perfectly well that I made ghastly blunders all along. I thought she cared, I thought she knew, and when I went away, I couldn't blame her, of course—but she didn't wait—" his voice broke for a moment. "Well," he said whimsically, "the little house was a simple greenhorn, country-joke sort of house like the fellow who built it. It didn't know any better. It—just waited."

The girl's eyes were full of tears. She started to speak, but her lips trembled and she gave it up.

"Well," the man said, rising quickly like a soldier called to duty, "it will soon be train time."

Together they walked down through the fragrant orchard. As the man untied the hitching-strap, the girl lingered by the gate looking back at the little house standing lonely on the top of the hill.

"Nice little house," she said.

At the house again, the doctor found a call awaiting him. "I'm so sorry. I'll have to go, Shirley." He was getting his bags. "It isn't quite time for your train. But my call is for four miles in the country, so I'll have to take you to the station right away."

The girl looked about helplessly as though trying to think of the answer to something that was puzzling her.

"I'd rather wait here," she said impulsively. "I'm not a bit afraid to go down alone. I want to write a letter. Couldn't I stay and write after you've gone?"

"Why, of course," he said, "if you'd rather. I'll stop and get one of the little Thompson boys to walk down with you. Well, good-by—little girl." He took both of her hands for a moment. "Forget what I told you. You're so sympathetic, I suppose you'll pity me. Don't do it. I'll work so hard I won't have time to think. I'll sell the little house. It ought not to be deprived of its life-mission, to make somebody happy, ought it? And I hope that you'll always be as happy as you are now."

He was gone, the rear light of his roadster twinkling palely in the moonlight. "As happy as I am now," she repeated, her hand at her throat.

It was nearly daylight when the doctor drove into the garage. The birds were stirring, getting ready to greet the dawn. All the way home he had thought of the girl. It was going to be harder than before, now that she had been here and he had seen her in the setting of the apple orchard. Tired from his night's work, he walked wearily into the old-fashioned living-room and snapped on the lights. His desk was open, and in the precise way he had of keeping his things in order, he walked over to close it. A note addressed to him in the girl's hand lay before him. The fingers that were steady with the surgeon's knife trembled as he tore open the envelope.

"My Dear Charles:

"I have had something on my mind all evening. I wanted to tell you about it—I *ought* to have told you—I tried to on the steps of the little house,—but—it wouldn't come. I can write it, though. Here it is: I don't care one single bit for George Merrifield—at least I don't love him. George Merrifield doesn't care one single bit for me,—at least he doesn't love me. Now, that I've told you that much, I want to talk it over with you. I will come back from Tiller to-morrow evening. If I could see you between trains again, just a few minutes' talk with you might help me.

"Shirley."

His mind, already tired from the night's vigil, worked laboriously over all the scenes of the previous evening. How characteristic of Shirley to cover this sickening thing with her gay little mood! Painstakingly he went over and over her little note with its hidden meaning. Puritanically, he shrank from what it might mean. To his credit, his thoughts came back after every toilsome journey to the decision that he must in some way help her to see that there had been no mistake where she believed one existed.

The day, with its round of professional visits, drew to a close. No call, however, would keep him from meeting Shirley's train. She needed him in this hour of her heart's travail as much as the young wife had needed him the night before.

It was a quieter, more constrained Shirley that he handed into his car. Quite naturally, she seemed to avoid meeting his eyes. Instinctively, he turned toward the apple orchard and stopped the car by the little gate. Without a word he helped her out, and led the way up through the pink and white clouds from which lazy little showers of summer snowflakes floated.

At the steps of the little house he said gravely, "Now, tell me about it."

"Do you know—I can't," she said. "When I was away from you—it seemed easy—but now that I'm here again—I'm afraid."

"If you'd think of me as a physician," he suggested, "and remember just that I am going to help, somehow—"

"Well, Doctor," she said at length, "I felt it coming on some time ago, but it didn't become acute until—" she turned her head away, "until the night I was bridesmaid at my cousin's wedding."

When she paused he spoke questioningly as though to help her.

"Yes. When she married George Merrifield, you know."

With a little exasperated movement, she threw out her hands. "Goodness gracious! Did you honestly think I could marry that *old stiff?*"

"Shirley, what are you talking about?"

"Oh, nothing," she said in a little frightened voice, now that the moment had come, "that is—nothing but that I'm not married. I never was, and I guess I never will be—."

"But—why—how—you said you were."

"Oh, no, I didn't say so," she shook her head smiling.

"You said so—of course, I know I'm a regular Mrs. Sapphira for letting you think so—but yesterday I met her in the city—your aunt I mean, not Sapphira—and she told me about sending that picture—."

"You silly," she burst forth, "if you'd written me one little tiny line about it, I could have told you the society editor got the two photographs interchanged. It was corrected with apologies in the next issue—."

When he only continued to look at her with half-dazed comprehension, she said, "I know it wasn't dignified—nor correct—nor lady-like to come up here to see you, but I'd been visiting my cousin—."

He came out of his anesthetized condition.

When he had gathered her close and kissed wonderingly her lips and eyes, she said quietly, "I know one thing. If I had that dear little house like yours, *I* wouldn't be so stingy with it."

The Box behind the Door

This is the first story Aldrich sold using her full name, Bess Streeter Aldrich. When she sent this story to the editors of *McCall's* she told them that she had written for several years under the name of Margaret Dean Stevens but that she now wanted to begin using her rightful name. An editor responded that she should contact magazines holding any of her manuscripts and request that they change to her new name before they published her work.

"The Box behind the Door" appeared in May 1918 and is an early version of many of the ideas in *The Rim of the Prairie* (New York: D. Appleton & Company, 1925).

Alan Gray Seymore unrolled a bright-colored Navajo and placed it on the floor of the one-roomed cabin. The rug was his own— the cabin his for as much of the summer as he should choose to remain; that period of occupancy depending on the length of time it might take him to write his text-book on psychology.

The cabin had been something of a find. All year at Western University he had hoped for just such a secluded place where he might work undisturbed by the strident voices of summer-school students. He had found it beckoning to him from a grassy knoll in a wandering, gipsy-like apple orchard.

With incredulous wonderment, the old couple who lived down in the clearing had rented it to him and directed him "down the road a bit to Marthy Flagg's" for his meals.

He had brought his belongings out from town that afternoon and was making short work of settling. The Navajo disposed of, he placed his books and papers on the cheap pine table, arranged his typewriter in the best light, and took his clothes out of their case. Deciding to improvise a closet, he swung the door back. A little trunk stood there, a home-made, rude affair covered with an untanned calfskin. The initials "J. C." were worked out on the top with brass-headed tacks.

He tried the lid—he had a right to know with what sort of objects he was living—and it flew open with amazing readiness. He almost laughed aloud at the contents. There were a doll and doll clothes, books of various kinds, paper ladies, a game or two—all the little treasures that might belong to a small girl.

He reached down and brought up a volume. It was *Little Prudy's Captain Horace*. On the fly-leaf, in heavy, pressed-in letters, was written "Jean Craddock—aged eight." Craddock was the name of the old couple. Their little girl, then. Dead, perhaps, or, if living, middle-aged. No doubt a grandmother now—these country girls married young. He wondered vaguely why they didn't have the chest with its keepsakes down at the house.

The text-book progressed with amazing rapidity in the days that followed. In the setting of the old apple orchard whose solitude was broken only by the happy calls of birds or the sharp gossip of insect folk, the book almost wrote itself from the data that Alan had collected.

As he worked busily in the midst of his scattered papers he stopped occasionally from sheer arm weariness rather than brain-fag. At these times, he found himself whimsically talking to the ancient little chest—for, gradually the faint aroma of mint and sassafras and dead violets that came from the depths of the box wrought a magic spell that, with its sorcery, brought to life an enchanting little girl who had owned the paper ladies and the old-fashioned doll with its painted cheeks and neatly waving china hair.

On the fourth day, as he went carefully through the books, he came to the diaries. With no more compunction than he would have shown at reading the life of some bygone character, he set about perusing the memoranda. They were charming:

> "Some of the apple blossoms came out this morning, and I ran out to the orchard and looked up to the sky and said, 'Please, God, don't make anything in heaven smell sweeter'n apple blossoms, because we couldn't stand it.'
>
> "I said something cross to-day and I feel sore and sick and mean. I have thought this to myself, that mean words are bad fairies that go out to hurt other people and then they come back and hurt you worse."

So little Jean Craddock, too, in the long-ago, had found her boomerang.

"I love the yellow dandelions in the grass and the white daisies and the lavender crocuses. They are for everybody—but the sweet, sweet violets are mine. The angels made them just for me and hid them in the hollow by the creek."

When she was twelve, with true feminine instinct, the mind of Jean Craddock had dwelt upon worldly things.

"When I grow up, I am going to have a hat that is lacy and white like the inside of silky milkweed pods. I am going to have other beautiful things, but best of all, I am going to have a dress of pink silk as pale as the first little anemones, and with it I am going to wear a string of pearls."

The winter she was fifteen, she wrote of love.

"Love comes to a person in waves. Sometimes you don't think about it—you just think about school and having fun and things to eat and skating on the creek— and then, all of a sudden, you think of love."

Alan Seymore looked off through the old gnarled apple trees. Yes, that was the way. You just think about your book and your lectures and the canoe you are having made—and then, all of a sudden, you think of love, how if you ever did meet the girl that was like your dream-girl—

In the summer, Jean Craddock's dreams took on more definite form. "I can see him when I sit under the apple trees," she had written, "at least most of him. I can see his shoulders and the square kind of chin he has and the way his head looks in the back—but, try as hard as I can, I never can see right in his face. But, anyway, I know this: When I see him I shall know him."

"Dear little Jean Craddock,—aged fifteen," said Alan, "I hope with all my heart that you knew him when you saw him."

He turned the page. "I am sixteen to-day. They have told me. It is in five more days—" Then followed a blurred place where something had been painstakingly erased. It ended simply—broken-heartedly, it seemed—"Good-by, little Jean Craddock, dear little Jean Craddock—I love you—good-by."

He was so startled that he read it all over. What was it? What happened to her? Did she die? Did they marry her to some one against her will? For Heaven's sake, what became of her? He turned the pages, but their blankness laughed up at him and mocked him.

At the end of the second week, the tragic ending (if tragic it were) had grown less significant in Alan's mind—and Jean Craddock was once more a charming little personality to whom he read the rapidly increasing pages of his text-book.

The afternoon was dark, with big, puffy black clouds that rose in the west and glowered down on the straggling old orchard. Alan threw down his manuscript and stretched himself lazily.

"Well, little Jean Craddock," he said aloud, "thus endeth the eighth chapter." Big drops began spattering here and there, like birdshot. So he got up and closed the cabin door, then walked across to the window, where he stood looking out at the swaying trees. Suddenly, he heard some one singing in the rain:

" 'Skies are only bright and fair in your eyes of blue.

Song is only sweet, my dear, when I sing of you!' "

The voice came nearer and rose in a crescendo of sweetness:

" 'Spring hath many a rose to wear'—" The singing stopped; the owner of the voice was unmistakably kicking at the door of the cabin. As the door began to yield, she took up her song where she had dropped it:

"Kissed of sun and dew; they are only sweet, my dear!"—Wide-eyed, she stopped.

" 'When they bloom for you,' " finished Alan Seymore—which was rather nimble for a professor of psychology.

She looked distractingly pretty in the doorway. She was wearing a simple white dress under her raincoat, which, disdainful of the weather, was flying wide open. Bare-headed, with drops glistening on the gold-brown of her hair, she seemed to have floated out of the clouds that brought the shower. There was a faint odor of violets—

"I beg your pardon," she said, distressed. She might have added "The nerve of you!" for her eyes looked it.

It was Alan Seymore's turn to feel uncomfortable. In answer to the questioning expression of her face, he defended himself with, "I have rented this place of Mr. Craddock."

"Grappy rented my playhouse?" she flashed out angrily. "Why, of course." She smiled so that he felt an intense relief. "He didn't know that I was coming. It has been seven years since I was here. I am Jean Craddock," she added.

"I am Alan Seymore," he volunteered, "and, if I intrude, please tell me. I could make other plans."

"Oh, no indeed." She was friendly again. "For the moment, I had forgotten that I was too old to play here. But—I left some things—" She turned to look about inquiringly.

"I must confess," he said, bending over the box, "I raised the lid. You know I thought there might be dead men's bones in there."

She gave a merry little rippling laugh, and then sobered suddenly. "Do you know—you were right. The girl in there is dead."

"You mean Jean Craddock, aged eight? You see, I lifted out a book to see whose property it was."

"I mean Jean Craddock, aged sixteen. I have come to see if I can bring her back to life or whether she is quite dead."

It was a most unusual experience. Yesterday, the diaries in the trunk; to-day, the girl kneeling there by it—as though the genii had tapped on the chest and there had arisen the girl of long ago.

As the shower ceased to drop its shrapnel on the cabin roof, the girl jumped up. "She's alive," she asserted joyously. "Alive—and she can stay a week."

Alan watched her go down through the orchard toward the old house in the clearing—the sun shining through the rain-spangled branches on the gold-brown of her hair. "Jean Craddock," he said softly, "not dead nor over forty—but alive and—twenty-three."

That was Tuesday. On Wednesday he awoke with a vague, delightful feeling. All day his mind reverted to the new thing in his life. In the evening he walked briskly around by the house in the clearing. She was crossing the barnyard. When she saw him, she waved her basket gaily and called, "I'm hunting for eggs. Do you like to?"

"It's my favorite pastime," said the grouchiest member of Western faculty.

On Thursday, they went berrying. On Friday, they took Alan's runabout and drove to the big woods for pine cones and spruce bark. On Saturday, they got out the old water-soaked punt and went fishing—all of which had nothing in particular to do with the writing of psychology texts.

Sunday evening they drove aimlessly, contentedly, over the long, brown highways. When he was helping her out of the car—it happened. It was only for a moment that he caught her to him and kissed her with, "I love you, little Jean Craddock"—only for a moment that she clung to him. Then she said, "Oh, no, no," and sped through the yard that led to the old house.

On Monday morning when Alan opened the cabin door, he picked up her note. It said, "I am leaving this morning, instead of to-night as I had planned. Please believe that it is better so."

As he stood, stupid and uncomprehending, the morning train whistled in. It woke him to action. Speeding down to the village station in the run-about, he saw the train pulling out. He felt he wanted to be dragged along with it. But she would not—she would not go out of his life like this.

When Alan returned to the house in the clearing, he found the old people in the garden together. When he asked where Jean had gone, he was bewildered to meet with an instant rebuff.

"That I will not tell ye," the old man gruffed out.

"But—I love her," explained Alan, as though it settled the matter.

The old man took his pipe from his mouth. "Love!" he said—"Huh!" and replaced his pipe.

Alan turned to the grandmother, who had been crying. She looked timidly at her husband and said, "I canna tell ye."

When school opened in September, the professor of psychology, apparently unchanged, took his place at Western. Over and over the details of that week in the summer went through his mind. Through it all, his faith never wavered. The memory of her charm, her childlike purity, her loveliness, permitted no thought but that she was all she had seemed.

In November, he went back to the farmhouse. After an unsuccessful interview with the old man, Alan tramped up through fallen leaves to the cabin. As he came back in the deepening dusk, the grandmother stepped out from the shadow of a tree.

"Pa's out milkin'," she said breathlessly. "Here it is."

The slip of paper contained an address in an eastern city.

With fine disregard for work, Alan told his President he had been called east.

He determined to call on Fritz Emerson of his old college class. At a more suitable hour, after lunch, he would find Jean.

He easily found the great brokerage suite, and his welcome was greater than he had imagined. Little Fritz wrung his hand and pounded him on the back.

"Married, Alan?" he asked.

"Not guilty. How about you, Fritzie?"

"Not yet—but soon," and launched into a panegyric on the qualities of one Miss Marjorie Wilmarth, in the midst of which he became suddenly imbued with the noble desire to have Alan meet Miss Wilmarth and the girls that composed her set. That afternoon, there was to be a tea-drinking stunt of some sort at Marjorie's home—wouldn't he come?

Alan felt compelled to accede to the plan. Through the unfamiliar avenues they rode, stopping in front of one of the castle-like structures that lined the drive. Dreading the ordeal, Alan entered the house in tow of the little man, who bounced along like a rubber ball.

Soft lights, sweet music, delicate colors, made up the combination of sensations that assailed him.

A few feet away stood a laughing, animated group of young people. In their midst, in pink "as pale as the first little anemones," stood Jean Craddock.

As though hypnotically compelled, she turned and met Alan's eyes. Dazed, uncomprehending, her own clung to his. The color slipped from her face, but she kept her perfect poise.

Fritz gaily piloted Alan toward the group. "Marjorie, I want Mr. Seymore to know you. Alan, Miss Wilmarth—my fiancée."

Jean Craddock extended her hand.

"Old college classmate, you know, people. Knows more than all the rest of us in this bunch put together. Can't give us but a few minutes—looking up an old girl of his this afternoon. Lucky girl, I say—" and on and on in his little, piping voice.

Alan stood straight, immobile. Would the confounded lunk-head never stop?

It seemed hours before they found a corner to themselves in the gallery. Marjorie Wilmarth raised miserable eyes to Alan.

"That girl—was it—"

"Yes—you."

"How did you find me?" He explained in the briefest way. Tears sprang to her eyes. "Granny did that for me?" She was unconscious of the slip. "Oh, I've so much to tell you—so many things to explain—if we only had more time—they may come in here any minute—" Her sentences were tripping over each other.

With folded arms, the man stood looking down at her.

"I'll tell you all about me, now," she went on. "I'll begin back when I was a little girl—no—before I was born. Grappy Craddock and Grandfather Wilmarth were great friends as boys. Later Grappy had one daughter and Grandfather Wilmarth three sons. One of the sons went out to Grappy's to spend the summer vacation. He was twenty. She—my mother—she was only seventeen, you know—Grappy made him marry her. After the marriage, the son, my father, started back east and was killed in a wreck. When I was born, my mother died. I lived with Grappy until I was sixteen. Then the Wilmarths suddenly decided they wanted me, but Grappy didn't want to give me up. They left it finally to my own decision. Of course, I wasn't long in deciding. It seemed like the enchanted garden to me. My mother's death, the Wilmarths' immense wealth, Grappy's poverty, my decision to leave him—those things all made Grappy bitter. He won't mention the Wilmarth name, nor allow Granny to either. He has always called me Jean Craddock just as my mother was called. When they told me on my sixteenth birthday, I was wild to come—but just at the last minute I was sorry for the little Jean Craddock I was leaving behind. I had to change my name—everything changed—my ideas—my ideals—life itself. The Wilmarths made me promise not to go back—but last summer I went. They thought I was with Alene Palmer at her home. I wanted to see Grappy and Granny. I wanted to see if there was any of the old Jean left. I—" She suddenly covered her face with her hands. "I'm sorry—I went."

His lips were pressed, as if waiting to get himself well in hand.

"Why?" he asked in a moment.

She turned her face away. "You know."

When he spoke again it was to ask very low: "Don't you care for Fritz?"

"He is good to me," she evaded, with pitiful eyes. "And he represents all the things I have grown used to having. I was engaged to him before—last summer. I wasn't—in love with him—but—it seemed all right."

"Doesn't it seem all right, now?"

"Oh, now," she admitted, simply.

"Would you be happy with me?" he asked suddenly.

When she remained silent, he said, "It seems preposterous—to compare all this that you have with what I could give you—the four things I could share with you."

"What four things?"

"My salary—it's twenty-four hundred dollars a year—and a seven-roomed bungalow—and a dinky runabout of last year's model—and—and love."

"And—love." She repeated it after him, very low. In a moment, she said in a little tense voice: "Last summer when I left Granny's I thought I put everything out of my mind—the apple orchard—you. But I learned something—there are bridges that won't burn."

Neither spoke for a moment, after her confession. Suddenly, she looked up at him. "I want to be fair to you. I want to be fair to Fritz. But most of all, I think I want to be fair to Marjorie Wilmarth and Jean Craddock. I can't go on like this—" For the first time she smiled with a touch of her old mischievousness. "Marjorie Wilmarth likes the flesh-pots of Egypt—Jean Craddock believed in good things and simple things—"

"And love."

"Yes," she said bravely, "she did." In a moment, she asked, "Could you come out to Granny's again in May?"

"Yes."

"I'm going to give them equal chances—those two girls. I'm going to give them until May to know which may survive. I'll come to Granny's some time in the first week of May—and, whichever way it is, I will tell you." They went to join the crowd.

May came, slowly—shyly. For two evenings after the westbound train passed through, Alan sat on the seat formed by the roots of the apple trees, with his eyes glued on the house in the clearing.

On the third, "Pleasant evening, Mr. Seymore," she said suddenly at his back, and laughed like a child at his surprise.

"Well," he questioned, his hands clenched at the import of the moment, "which are you?"

"I'm just a girl," she said humbly, "who has come many hundred miles to ask a very wise man four questions."

"What are they?"

"The first one is—what will twenty-four hundred dollars a year buy?"

"Twenty-four hundred dollars a year will buy for a family nourishing food, sufficient clothing, a few friendly books and a bit of good music."

"And what will a seven-roomed bungalow hold?"

"It will hold two people who love each other, and leave room for a little boy, some time, who will pull his daddy's papers off the desk and throw his mother's thread down the registers."

She leaned her cheek suddenly against the shaggy gray bark of the tree. In a moment, she went on: "And where can one go in a dinky runabout of last year's model?"

"One can go out in the peace of the good green country—out where the wild roses tangle on the hillside and where the sumac burns scarlet in the timber."

"And what—is love?"

"It is dreams come true," he said gently.

"Well," she said, with a queer little laugh, "you certainly have the most uncanny way of bringing Jean Craddock back to life—and if you really think you want me, I'm afraid you'll have to take me pretty soon, for when I told them, they made such a fuss—I didn't bring anything but a comb and two handkerchiefs and a toothbrush—"

He held her close without a word.

A discriminating co-ed ran up the stairs of the dormitory and burst into the room from which came an odor of fudge.

"The biggest piece of news since the flood."

"Well," said her pessimistic room-mate coolly, "ready—aim—fire."

"I told you I suspected it—you said 'piffle,' remember—and now it's come. Seymore's married!"

"No!"

"Honest as Mary Pickford's curls. They were on the car. Introduced Prof. Gates to her—'Professor Gates, I want you to meet my wife'—just like that. He looked perfectly grand—and she's a beauty."

The pessimistic room-mate sank limply to the floor where she gave a very poor imitation of a dying fish.

Miss Livingston's Nephew

The nephew in this story is an attorney. Aldrich's husband was both attorney and banker, which is undoubtedly why bankers and lawyers are among her most warmly drawn characters. The young woman who meets Miss Livingston's nephew holds the same position—assistant supervisor of the Primary Department at a teaching college—that Aldrich held before her marriage.

A ploy Aldrich enjoyed working with was mistaken identities. She uses it here and in "The Cat Is on the Mat" (1916), "The Patient House" (1916), and "Marcia Mason's Lucky Star" (*The American Magazine*, March 1920). "Miss Livingston's Nephew" was published by *The Designer* in May 1918.

The antique street-car stopped like a patient old horse at the edge of the campus. Seventeen people swung themselves down. Apparently they all knew where they were going; in reality, the seventeenth did not, for he had never visited this particular college before. But, as his ten commandments were "Look out for number one," and his catechism "The Lord helps him who helps himself," he swung along as breezily independent as the blithest freshman, which was very breezy indeed.

Up the curving walk he went, between the crescent-shaped beds of gladioli, and briskly up the steps of the massive stone building that stood first in the quadrangle.

Down the long hall he strode until he came to the last of the classroom doors. It was slightly ajar. For a moment he paused. Had he known what was happening to him just then, the *sang-froid* of this well-poised young man would have been somewhat shaken. Old Mother Fate, seeing him pause, held his hand tightly on the doorknob until he began pushing it. He swung the door back. Rows of young girls, shoals of them, note-books in hand, sat around the walls. A group of children in the center of the room watched a small boy who was declaring "It was large. It was hard. A piece of it fell on my tail."

The eyes of the children and the eyes of the acres of girls turned from this thrilling declaration. Mr. Miles Livingston, hat in hand, apparently filled the doorway.

There was a solemn pause. Old Mother Fate beckoned with her bony forefinger to a girl who immediately rose and came toward Mr. Miles Livingston. Whereupon old Mother Fate gave a toothless grin and muttered, as she ambled away, "There! *That* job's done!"

The girl was in blue with a big white collar of sheer stuff that turned away from the firm little chin and the rose-pink of her face. Her brown hair was drawn smoothly back, but little curls jumped out and nodded from all sorts of hiding-places, in the coil, around her forehead, behind one ear. With big cornflower-blue eyes she looked questioningly at the intruder.

"*I will run and tell Henny-Penny,*" said the youthful gossiper in the center of the room.

"I beg pardon," said Mr. Miles Livingston, and although he closed the muffler, his voice boomed to the four corners of the room. "This is evidently not the president's office?"

"It is *not*," said the girl, the rose-pink deepening.

The girl stepped out and closed the door. "The executive building," she said, and her voice was like a thrush's that had decided to talk instead of sing, "is over—that way. It is connected with this building by a concrete bridge."

She began a series of intricate directions, and although the consensus of opinion among members of the State Bar Association was that Mr. Miles Livingston was far from dull, he seemed to have suddenly acquired an impenetrable density. Altogether, he appeared so far from comprehending where to find his destination that, in sheer desperation, the girl said, "I'll walk over that way with you"—which goes to prove that stupidity has its own place in the scheme of things.

"It's an odd arrangement, this bridge," he mentioned sociably.

"The students call it the Bridge of Sighs," she remarked coolly.

He ventured a sidelong glance. Her profile was exquisite—a profile led by a resolute little chin that seemed in absolute command of any frivolousness as to dimples or wistfulness as to eyes. At the end of a corridor she said concisely, "That is the president's office."

"I see it—and I thank you very much. I hope leaving your lesson like this has not inconvenienced you nor queered you in any way with your teacher."

"My teacher!" The cornflower eyes darkened. "I," she said, and the perky little chin went into the air at least an inch, "am the Assistant Supervisor of the Primary Department of the Training-School of Midwest Teachers' College."

"A thousand apologies," he smiled down at her. "And once—in London—" he murmured as though speaking to himself, "I met the tutor of foreign languages to his Royal Highness the Prince of Wales."

That, of course, was unpardonable. With a curt little inclination of the head, she turned and crossed the Bridge of Sighs.

At the door of her classroom she paused long enough to let the color in her cheeks slip away before she stepped in.

"*They all ran into Foxy-Loxy's den and they never came out,*" finished the orator.

A number of surreptitious smiles greeted her. It irritated her. She would show those sixty-seven girls what authority was hers.

"The lesson is closed," she said abruptly. "You will please hand in on Monday morning a well-written paper on Dramatization as a Means to the Interpretation of Reading."

The smiles ceased, and because her own student days were not far in the past, Nadine Taylor knew that she had nipped in the bud many a boat-ride and tennis game.

In her own office, with its plaster cast of "The Laughing Child" and its low-hung copy of "The Song of The Lark," she set herself to the prosaic task of looking over a portion of the lesson plans.

There was a vigorous knock, not at all like the timid approach of one of the sixty-seven. When she had opened the door, he said, "It *was* rude, and I came back to apologize, but you know it was such a great big title for such a—little kid." And because he had not improved matters in the least, they both laughed.

When he had given her the small engraved card which read "Miles Livingston, Attorney-at-Law, Des Moines," and explained that he had stopped at Mount Logan to see a relative, she looked up cordially.

"Oh, you are Miss Livingston's nephew. I have heard her speak of you. I'm so sorry, Miss Livingston has gone to Wymore College to give her monthly lecture on the classics." Surely it was forgivable to stand and talk with any relative of the sensible, gray-haired Miss Livingston, loved and honored by faculty and students alike.

He gravely looked his disappointment. "And I don't know a soul here," he said regretfully. "What would you advise me to do until my train leaves at ten-thirty-five?"

"The Y. M. C. A. meets at six-thirty," she suggested politely.

"Yes. And then I could go to the library after that and read Plutarch's 'Lives' and Fox's 'Book of Martyrs,' couldn't I?" He was looking over the girl's head to the motor-powered lawn-mower clipping its way across the green sloping campus.

"Let's do it," he said suddenly, dropping his dark eyes to the girl's cornflower-blue ones.

"Do what?" she asked, startled.

"Go somewhere to dinner. There must be some sort of eating-place around here."

"Really, I'm not just accustomed—" she began stiffly.

"Of course not," he assured her. "Let me put it to you this way: Suppose my aunt were here. I would take her out to dinner as a matter of course. Before committing that nephewly act, I would have had her call on you with me that I might apologize for my seeming rudeness, and we would have asked you to complete our little party. Now, with only the aunt eliminated—?" He paused hopefully. Miles Livingston had not studied persuasive argument for naught.

The girl looked thoughtfully at the plaster cast of "The Laughing Child." Wouldn't Miss Livingston appreciate this courtesy? So, "It is hypothetical in the extreme, but for Miss Livingston's sake, I'll go," said the jury. And the plaster cast grinned like a little maniac.

I t was a gay little dinner-party they had at Wild Rose Inn, chaperoned by the shadowy presence of the sensible, gray-haired teacher of English literature. When it was over and he had taken her back to the home of Professor and Mrs. Evans, where she roomed, they sat on the moon-swept porch in the merriest of conversations.

"Good-by, little Miss Supervisor of the Pleasant-Hours Department of The-Best-Time-I've-Had-For-Ages," he said, as she stood above him on the step. "I'm going to drop in again. I'd like to surprise my aunt."

On Saturday morning the mild little adventure, viewed without moonlight and other distracting accessories, seemed unwise in the extreme. As penance she spent most of the glorious day in her office, devoting herself assiduously to October outlines on "Columbus," "The Squirrel," and other adventurous gentlemen.

In the days that followed, she acquired palpitation of the conscience every time she met the large and placid Miss Livingston. Of course, when he came again, he would tell his aunt. One thing was certain, though, when he came again, she would be pleasant, but cool—very cool.

Four red-and-yellow-leafy weeks had gone by and the shadows from the old oaks were growing long and wavering on the afternoon of the third Friday in October. Nadine Taylor, in an immaculate white suit with a saucy black velvet tie, had just dismissed an embryonic teacher whose tender heart, at a slight criticism, had set her tear-ducts to working.

"Stony-hearted one," said a voice that sounded hauntingly familiar, "what have you been doing to the lachrymose maiden who just passed me?"

"Oh!" she said, genuinely distressed. "Didn't I tell you? I thought I *did*—your aunt goes the third Friday of every month."

"The third Friday of every month," he repeated, astonished. "I'll always remember that. My mistake is very humiliating. Where shall we go?" he added.

The extreme frigidity which was to develop on Nadine's part in case Mr. Livingston came again, resolved itself quite suddenly into the philosophy that one might as well be hung for a sheep as a lamb. So they went up the river to Linger Longer Inn, making the trip in the gay little launch that was coining money in the golden Indian-summer days. They came home laden with yellow maple boughs, shimmering silvery birches and the scarlet flame of the sumac. To the merry-eyed girl who looked at him over that riotous mass, he said "Good-by, little Miss Supervisor of the Wood-Sprite Department of the Elves-That-Haunt-The-Hills. I'll remember surely, now, the third Friday in *every* month."

November seemed to the residents of Mount Logan one long, sunless, rainy, disconsolate decade.

With characteristic exuberance of spirits, that in truth drooped a little under the continued weeping of the elements, Nadine enthused her department with "Pit-a-pat. See the Lovely Raindrops," and other songs and games.

The third Friday was more disagreeable than the preceding days, the clouds discharging liquid exasperatingly all day long. Nadine, in her tightly buttoned raincoat, trudged steadily along under the dripping elms toward her room. She stepped aside to let a hurrying pedestrian go by, but the hurrying pedestrian's big hand closed over her umbrella handle.

"My aunt—" he began lamely.

"Your aunt," she said tartly, "is going to take steps to bring you before the feeble-minded commission, for you certainly know that she has resigned and gone to Wymore as head of the English Department."

"Even if I did know, you needn't be so spoffish," he argued. "I've a case up at Greenwood, and I'll have to stop here between trains every few weeks. So what are you going to do about *that?*"

The months marched by with steady rhythm.

The assistant supervisor of all this activity was very busy. And very happy.

It was May now and "the little leaves were dancing in the silver of the sun." Nadine closed her desk and tore "Thursday, May eleventh," from the calendar, the pink deepening in her cheeks, for the "Friday, May twelfth," that stared redly at her, was to bring Miles Livingston again. December had brought him, and January and February, to say nothing of March and April, "as regularly as the Woman's Foreign Missionary Society," he had said.

She put on her hat with its blue cornflowers like her eyes, and started home. Seeing the athletic director looming on the horizon, she turned hastily and took a roundabout way through the campus, for she wanted to be alone with the little flock of memories that the months had left.

There was one memory that persisted in being noticed. They had been alone in the Evans living-room while a March blizzard rapped spitefully on the windows. Standing in front of the fireplace, Miles Livingston had said, "Little Miss Supervisor, wouldn't you like a pretty bungalow like this of your own?"

She had bent down to the fire to hide the vision in her eyes and answered gaily, "Yes, I would, and when I get to be head supervisor I'm going to have one—a dear little house with built-in bookcases and beamed ceilings and window-boxes." "I do so want to work up to that position," she had said. "Every day I think of Whittier's lines:

" 'Let my mortal dream come true,
With the work I fain would do;
Clothe with life the weak intent,
Let me be the thing I meant.' "

He had been very grave as he said quietly: "The thing you meant to be and the thing God meant you to be are not the same, little Nadine Taylor."

It set her pulses to pounding now as she thought of it. And to-morrow he was coming. His letter, written in a piratical hand, had been characteristic:

"In the merry month of May, Mount Logan, like that country despised of my high-school days, must be divided into three parts: those who eat decorously at tables in their own homes, after the manner of civilized tribes; those who eat at the various inns which do haunt the banks of the river, and those who eat out of market-baskets. Can't we take our supper in one—a big basket with flappy tops?"

It had closed with "I've something to tell you, so be prepared, little Miss Mother-Confessor."

She went up the Evanses' steps, humming the children's apple-blossom song, and opened the door. A letter lay on the hall table. It was from Wymore, from Miss Livingston. Strange, too, for they had not known each other intimately, never corresponded.

There were some preliminaries, and then: "I wonder if you will do me a favor? You seem just the one to ask. My nephew's fiancée from Greenwood is spending the day with me. She is going to be in Mount Logan Friday evening until the southbound Iowa Central leaves. She will arrive on the five-forty-five on her way to Des Moines to surprise my nephew. I'd like to have you meet her if not inconvenient, otherwise the wait would be tedious. Her name is Laura Lalan. She is a dear little thing. We are all so glad. My nephew has been something of a gay Lothario. He will settle down now, of course."

The words danced diabolically before her. There was a pounding in her throat and she couldn't seem to concentrate her thoughts. From the chaotic jumble of her mind, naked, leering truths picked themselves out. He was engaged to a girl in Greenwood. His case hadn't pertained to law. It was the variety of "case" that Noah Webster fails to mention. And she trusted Noah Webster—and Miles Livingston. It was clear, hideously, sickeningly clear. He had come each time to have a place to wait, pleasanter, no doubt, than sitting in the station. He was going to tell her about it. He had said so in his letter.

The hall clock struck. Mechanically she went up-stairs to the blue-and-white room. There were roses there that he had sent—sent to pay her for the time she had spent to entertain him between trains. A sudden fury seized her—a sense of the loss of her self-respect. The thoughts she had harbored! She put her hands to her hot cheeks. Thank goodness, he'd never know! She had let herself adore the way he laughed, the way he bit his lip when he was thinking, the way—oh, he was so thoroughly *likable*. So this was what Tennyson meant when he wrote "A sorrow's crown of sorrow is remembering happier days." She dropped down by the side of the bed, a forlorn, crumpled heap. A verse she had read and liked merely for its rhythm came to her. Now it was a prayer. "O God," she said, "wilt Thou blot out before mine eye the little path that he came by!"

Suddenly she sat up. Like a flash it had come. Where had her wits been? They were coming on the *same day*, tomorrow—he at four-twenty, she at five-forty-five. So Miss Laura Lalan was going to surprise her fiancé, was she? Well, it would be a surprise, all right. They'd make a cozy little family party of it. She laughed hysterically. She wouldn't tell him who was coming; just send him to the train to meet her friend's friend. It wouldn't be kind. But all's fair in love and war, and this was war. When he found out who it was, perhaps he wouldn't bring her out at all, just telephone some silly excuse for not coming back. Oh, well, so much the better!

All day Friday she went about her work with the letter in her waist— miserable little Cleopatra concealing the asp. She stayed at her desk until there was no one in the building but the janitors. When Miles Livingston, big and clean-cut, stood in her office doorway, she wanted to put her head on his blue serge coat and cry. But the letter hissed—no, crackled—and she told him what he was to do.

He was disgruntled and he told her so. But she only said in a businesslike way, "You'll know her. She is to wear a dark blue suit and a hat with a red silk scarf on it. She's light and fluffy."

"What's her name?"

"My friend didn't mention it." One might as well complete the list of vices.

"Very well, little Miss Kaiser Wilhelm, I'll get your feathery friend with the red sofa-cover on her head, but you let me do the speaking to Mrs. Hanson about that picnic supper. You're pale. By George, you've no business working as late as this."

"You'd better hurry. It's five-twenty now," she said crisply.

In her room she dressed in light blue linen. When she heard the train whistle, she decided she looked ghastly, hastily tore off the blue and got into a soft rose-colored dress.

At the sound of voices below, she breathed a little prayer for composure, and started down. Even so walked Marie Antoinette out onto the balcony at Versailles. Half-way down she stopped.

Unceremoniously, Miles Livingston was coming through the vestibule to the foot of the stairs.

"Didn't she come?"

"Yes. She's on the porch with your athletic director. I've asked him to go—had Mrs. Hanson put up supper for four. Come on down. I want to tell you something before we go out there." He was very sober.

She took a step down. "Oh, don't," she said in a queer little voice. "Never mind. I know all about it. I've deceived you. I thought—I—was hurt—because you didn't—tell me. It made me want to punish you. I'm sorry."

"I should have told you long ago. I've just let things drift along. You won't let it make any difference between us, will you?" It is a very old question. No doubt Napoleon put it to Josephine. Probably Jacob asked it of Rachel when he took Leah to wife. They made no answers—only smiled, woman-wise—Rachel and Josephine and Nadine Taylor.

When Miles Livingston saw the pathetic little smile that was meant to be friendly and cheerful, he burst out with, "I'm all kinds of a cad. It's a beastly shame to have allowed you to hear it from some one else. Who told you?"

"Your aunt. She wrote me yesterday. She said Miss Lalan was a dear girl. I *am* a little disappointed that—you didn't think enough of our friendship to tell me—but it's all right—and I congrat-u-late—"

"Nadine, would you mind telling me just what you are talking about?"

"Why—Miss Laura Lalan—your aunt said—she *is* your fiancée, isn't she?"

"The dickens she is! Listen, dear."

"Sh-h."

"I won't. I've 'sh-h'd' long enough." He reached up and pulled the little old-rose girl down to the bottom step, her hands held fast in his. "Good Heavens, child! I never saw this Miss Lola-Lulu from Honolulu before. I have no wild desire to see her again. I never saw Miss Livingston. Begging her pardon, I never heard of her until you mentioned her. She isn't my aunt. I told you I had a confession to make. If you'll recall the exact words of our first conversation, at no time did I say she was my aunt. *I* said 'I stopped to see a relative.' I did—George Marshall, a young freshman—and I found he had gone home. *You* said, 'Oh, you're Miss Livingston's nephew,' and became cordial immediately. Now, answer me, would you have gone to dinner with me that first night if I had told you she wasn't my aunt?"

She shook her head.

"You see, I had to. It was the only way. I knew you were the girl for me that first afternoon."

The girl-for-him gasped.

"And then I kept putting off telling you after Miss Livingston resigned. I wanted you to know me well enough to trust me without any recommendations from relatives. I can tell you, though, that my family lives in Pittsburgh and is distressingly decent."

He took the girl very gently in his arms. "I love you, dear. You do trust me now, don't you. And—love me—just a little, sweetheart?"

"Well," she said in a little, shaky voice, "I'm not sure—maybe I do—anyway, this is the first time in twenty-four hours I haven't wanted to scratch that Miss Laura Lalan's eyes out."

He drew her close and kissed her, when she suddenly pulled away from him in confusion.

The athletic director was standing in the vestibule—his golf cap held decorously in front of his eyes.

"Toot-toot! Honk-honk!" he said. "Sorry to break in on this Sothern and Marlowe balcony scene, but there's a freckle-faced kid been out on the porch for half an hour hanging onto a big market-basket that looks good to Miss Lalan and me."

Their House of Dreams

This is one of Aldrich's longest short stories, described by *The People's Home Journal* as a novelette. The original idea for this story, published in July 1918, probably came from the 1912 sinking of the *Titanic* or the 1915 sinking of the *Lusitania*. Such events were the kinds of "germs," as Aldrich called them, from which she took ideas to create stories.

Chapter I.

With a solid silver spoon, Noel Hilliard was eating grapefruit from a Haviland plate, exactly placed on a cluny-edged damask breakfast cloth. Not everyone who eats grapefruit from thin china is as wholesome looking, as near to being handsome as Noel Hilliard, just twenty-six. When all the world is young, when that world is enriched with such accessories as solid silver and damask, one is likely to be having a very, very good time. This young man was having it.

Life to Noel was bounded on the north by a gun and a fishing-rod, on the east by a launch and a canoe, on the south by a golf bag and a tennis racket, and on the west by a saddle-horse and a long, low, gray car. And if a Peggy sat in the low-backed car, it was not on a truss of hay—and be assured it was not always the same Peggy. Blue, brown, gray-eyed Peggies—it did not matter much to Noel so long as the eyes laughed and flashed merry glints.

Decent, clean-cut, big-hearted he was, but no weather-vane on a red barn veered more to the wind than he to the breeze of his attractions.

All of which has nothing to do with the sudden sharp ringing of a bell upstairs in Noel's own room. With a boyish grin he dropped his napkin, overturned his chair, and sprang through a side door down the veranda steps.

"By George!" he laughed. "Caught the little beggar! Who'd have thought he'd have the nerve to prowl around in broad daylight!"

The continued sound of the bell grew fainter as he ran through the vine-covered pergola and over the sweet-smelling, close-cropped grass. An impenetrable hedge formed the back boundary line of the grounds. Whoever had been thieving around the place must have been coming in over the low gateway between the high hedges. With characteristic interest in the undertaking, Noel had perfected a trap that posed innocently as a part of the gate. The crowning touch of this masterpiece was the hidden wire that would ring a bell in his own room. To be sure, he was not in his own room very much of the time, but the fates had been kind in permitting him to hear the present commotion.

He passed the garage. "One of those kids that live across the links, I'll bet—the little rascal!"

He passed the greenhouse—rounded the corner of the stable—and stopped astounded.

A girl crouched low on top of the gate. Soft tendrils of hair blew about her face. Brown eyes, that were meant to smile, looked frightened. A tremulous mouth above a boyish chin was attempting to hold itself steady. Her arms were full of goldenrod; a book or two lay on the grass.

Noel folded his arms and stood looking across at her. Their eyes were on a level. For a moment neither spoke.

"Well," he said dryly. "*You're* caught."

"So—I s-see."

She attempted to raise herself but only succeeded in spilling a box of watercolors—little round paints that rolled irritatingly in every direction. Distressed, she began an explanation:

"I was gathering goldenrod—I'm one of the new teachers in the Lafayette School—we have to be in the building at eight-thirty. When I found it was near that time I was desperate, and attempted to take a short cut through your grounds. "Oh," she burst out, "if you just *knew* Miss Neiderhauser you'd understand! When you're late she looks at you with her gray-green eyes—and you shrink—and shrivel—"

"Miss Neiderhauser! Good heavens! Twenty years ago she looked at me with those gray-green eyes! It dwarfed my nature. I never got over it. I'll have you there in two minutes"—he was unfastening the clasp set so cunningly in the gate. She was obliged to put her hand on his shoulder to steady herself.

She seemed sweet and dainty and woodsy. There was a faint odor of violets. It made him clumsy.

"Now then," he helped her down; "you pick up the pieces of the wreck and I'll get my car around." He was hurrying toward the garage and running out the low, gray car that began to purr with a proper sense of its importance.

She looked at her wrist-watch. "Eight-twenty! Do you *think* you can make it?"

"If we don't we'll take a straight shoot over Pine Bluff into the ravine. Think how remorseful she'll be when they find us!"

Not until they had gone the length of the driveway and turned into the street did Noel take time to explain the reason for the trap. "And it works, doesn't it? You'll write me a testimonial, won't you, when I get it patented?" He was looking down at her. Suddenly he threw back his head and let forth a howl. "Think of the paper this evening: 'Prominent Teacher Caught in Trap. Rescued by Gallant Hero. Saved from Execution at Hands of Principal.'"

"You *wouldn't tell!*" she was genuinely fearful for a moment until she saw the sparkle in his eyes. Relieved, she laughed—a gay little rippling laugh. "Your headlines are fakes. I'm not prominent, for I've been here only five weeks. And *you're* not gallant or you wouldn't have stood there with your arms folded and looked me over."

"Were you frightened?"

"Terribly."

He stole a sidelong glance at her. Profile, led by a determined little chin—exquisite. Hair, dark brown and fluffy. Coloring—brilliant and natural.

"We're about to casually approach the ogress," he announced as they turned into Capitol Avenue. "Think how embarrassing that we don't know each other's names! I'll begin: Noel Goodwin Hilliard. Noel for grandfather; Goodwin for mother; Hilliard for father. Next!"

She laughed. "Leah Lindsey, from Center Junction, Center County."

"Hurrah for Center Junction! Here we are. Hist, there *she* is! Run, Miss Leah Lindsey!"

She gave him a hurried, warm, "Thank you very much," and went briskly up the long walk. A book lay on the seat of the car. He picked it up and started to get out, thought better of it, and placed the volume under the cushion. Shooing several dozen small boys off the running-board, he started home.

Leah Lindsey! Euphonious, certainly. Sounded like she looked; sort of rippling and sweet and laughinglike. Awfully young for a teacher.

"Cute little thing," he decided. And who was a better judge than Noel Goodwin Hilliard?

At home again, he finished his breakfast, related the episode to his interested semi-invalid mother, and began his usual active, if useless, day. This included exercising his riding horse, playing a round of golf with Bob Summers, doing some errands for Emily Vance and Jean Robertson, his married half-sisters, helping to install a new billiard table, and conscientiously sitting for a whole hour in a big Circassian walnut chair in the office of the Hilliard Lumber and Coal Company. That those two very useful commodities would have moved in and out of their respective sheds and bins whether or not he honored the office with his presence, is neither here nor there. When John Hilliard died he left the business running "on high," and, no thanks to his charming son, gears had not been shifted. The property was held in trust, not to be divided among the children until after Mrs. Hilliard's death, a satisfactory enough arrangement to Noel, whose income amply covered such necessities of life as gasoline and theater tickets.

In the evening, after this strenuous day, Noel kept a concert date with Miss Katherine Knox, whom two kind and affectionate families, including Miss Knox herself, had decided he was to marry. That there was no formal engagement yet, was excused on both sides by the statement that the young folks wanted to be free to have a good time for awhile, which was a polite way of saying that Noel wasn't ready. However, in his careless, amiable way, Noel intended to marry Kathie.

The next evening found young Mr. Hilliard in the long gray car at the front of the old Burton home where, by some occult means known only to himself, he had discovered that Miss Lindsey had a room. There were several girls on the front porch, among them The One, who looked very charming in pink; out of the corner of his trained eye he could see that. He stopped just a moment to fuss with a perfectly reliable speedometer in order to give her a chance to leave the bunch and start down toward the car. But as she seemed to have no notion of doing it, he bounced out with sudden decision, took the book which was to be the password, and swung boldly up to the porch.

"I beg pardon—I have the honor," he said formally, "of returning a work of science and art that has been lost to the world for many years. It is known as 'Holton's Primer.'"

"Oh, that must be mine!" Miss Lindsay said briskly, reaching for the book. "I lost it near the schoolhouse. Thank you very much."

Not on your life, young lady! He had not chased around a mile or more inquiring where she lived to be backed off the stage like this. So he looked straight into the brown eyes and said, "Yes, it's yours, Miss Lindsey, and I have come to take you riding again."

She flushed, of course, and laughed at her own defeat, introduced him to "the girls" and explained that Mr. Hilliard had taken pity on her and kept her from being late the morning before. As for a ride, she thanked him, but she was going to a lecture with the girls. Oh, no, she didn't want to cut it. Why—yes—perhaps she might ride some other time.

"Some other time," as translated to suit Noel Hilliard, meant the next evening. Even then she succeeded, somehow, in taking along one of the girls, a vociferous young person who was greatly impressed with the car and wanted coquettishly to know what this was for and why you turned that.

When the girls got out he detained Miss Lindsey long enough to ask her to ride again the next evening alone. No, she couldn't. She was going to help Mrs. Burton with a dress. No, nor the next. Well, she had some work to do. Now, Leah Lindsey could not know, of course, that Noel Hilliard as a little boy was one of those children who, saying at eight o'clock in the morning, "My rocking-horse needs a new tail," is found also at five o'clock in the afternoon insisting doggedly, "My rocking-horse *does* need a new tail." With the same persistency he now insisted upon wanting to know just when she *would* go? It seemed that Miss Lindsey could not be persuaded to accept for any school night—but next Saturday afternoon if it was convenient—and a nice day—she might ride out into the country far enough to get some wild flowers for school.

Chapter II.

On Saturday afternoon at two minutes of two, Noel rounded the curve in front of the Burton boarding-house. Miss Lindsey, in a brown corduroy suit and small rough hat over her fluffy hair, came down the steps. She did not know—and it is just as well—that the sight set Noel's heart to pumping more vigorously than Miss Katherine Knox's presence had ever done. He was startled, himself, at the activity of that hitherto remarkably placid organ.

"Whither away, Miss Lindsey-Woolsey?" he greeted her cheerfully to cover an unusual embarrassment.

He turned the nose of the gray car toward the Big Woods, a haunt beloved of his boyhood days. The afternoon was glorious. Blue of the sky, bronze of the oaks, gold of the maples, silver of the shimmering cottonwoods, scarlet of the sumac. The girl was radiant, as much a part of the autumn day as the gentians. In her nut brown suit she looked like a wood sprite.

"You belong outdoors," Noel said as she came toward him. "You seem part of the country."

"Thanks." Her eyes flashed merry glints above the gorgeous mass of sumac. "Honesty is always the best policy. I know I'm countrified."

When the girl had appeased her insatiable longing for the growing things of the woodland, she said rather wistfully, "Well, when you come to the 'end of the perfect day,' you usually turn around and go home again."

For answer Noel walked to the car and brought out an unquestionably high-priced lunch basket.

"Please don't scold. You wouldn't have the heart to protest if I told you there was fried chicken, would you?"

It made a more intimate affair of the trip, naturally, as Noel had divined. But when, nearing home again, he sought to make another engagement with her, she put him off. No, she wasn't at all peeved about the lunch, she just didn't know when she'd be at liberty again; no, her time all belonged to the school board.

"Great guns! Fine chance you have of making me swallow that! I know what's the matter. You're engaged."

"No, I'm not," she said quietly; "but you are."

"I am *not*," he answered crossly. "Somebody has been handing you a neat little fairy tale." But even as he spoke, visions of his mother and Emily and Jean and their husbands and children and various Knoxes who all harbored the idea, rose before him.

When they had gone a little way in rather strained silence the girl said simply, "I'm really very grateful to you for wanting to be kind to me. This trip has been lovely. I hope I am making it clear to you how perfect the day has been. But I don't want you to ask me any more—or come for me." She looked up at him with grave, sweet eyes. It percolated through Noel Hilliard's head that she *meant* it. For a young man who was rapturously welcomed by all the girls he knew and by seven-tenths of the mothers, the conviction came as a shock.

"Why not? Can't you give me your reasons?"

"I'd rather leave it just as it is—your taking my word for it that it's best."

"Impossible! Why can't I come?"

"If you insist, I'll tell you, but I warn you that I'll hurt your feelings." That chin—he rather liked the way it was holding itself.

He guided the car toward a row of scrub oak farther on at the side of the road.

"If my feelings are going to be hurt I don't want to be driving." He looked toward her expectantly. "Ready—aim—fire!"

"Well," she was embarrassed but undismayed—"you and I live in altogether different worlds."

"Piffle!" he interrupted her; but she went steadily on:

"My entire salary is about what you spend on shows, candy and flowers. I have to work. My grandparents—they are getting old. I am helping them and the time isn't far distant when I must take the entire responsibility. Not that I fear it—you mustn't think that." She was flushed and very much in earnest. Noel thought that he had never seen her look so beautiful. "So, I must *live* for my work. I have only a small amount of time out of school, and I want that to be spent advantageously in study, in service for someone, or in friendships that may mean something to me. You"—she paused and lifted dark, serious eyes to him—"you can bring me nothing. You have no occupation—no work of any kind. Your life is entirely without an objective. You are not exactly—lazy. You are too active for that. But your activity is all along selfish lines. If that same energy were directed in the right channels you might bring something worthwhile to a friendship. If I were to see you often it would mean nothing to me but play—pleasant, perhaps, but productive of nothing. That's the reason," she finished simply.

"Then I take it that if I carried a tin dinner-pail and had callouses on my hands I could qualify as a friend of yours?"

"If you choose to put it that way."

He looked at her quietly for a moment so that she flushed and her eyes fell before his clear gray ones. "Noel," he said presently, "you and I will take this bold woman home and then we will sit down and think it over."

In the days that followed, what the girl had said bothered him to such an extent that, to regain his poise, he was frequently obliged to seek the company of Miss Knox, who had no foolish scruples about young men who would neither toil nor spin.

The more he thought about it, the more it rankled. There was one thing certain—no little snip of a school teacher could tell *him* where to get off. *He simply would not see her again.* The decision lost some of its point when it occurred to him that this was just what she herself had dictated. She had the most beautiful eyes! There was a little V-shaped cleft in her chin—

It was a square purple box that held the huge bunch of violets. "These didn't cost a cent," he wrote. "Picked them myself in our greenhouse, with my own busy hands. Calloused all over 'em. Mother is going to ask you to dinner for Friday night. Please don't take your spite out on mother, for she's nice. I leave my world about six o'clock and arrive in your world a few minutes later to get you. Respectfully yours, No (el) Good (win) Hilliard."

He felt sure that she would accept under such circumstances. He had told her of his mother's delicate health and the invitation from mother later would undoubtedly bring her. It was very true that Mrs. Hilliard wanted her to come, for she wanted anything that Noel wanted.

"Shall we go around and climb over the back gate?" he asked her on Friday night. He was in the gayest of moods; the girl had accepted and there was an element of personal success in having won his point. That was all a josh about not wanting to see him. He knew girls.

If he felt a distinct pride in the beautiful rooms—the sweeping stairway, the wide fireplace, the Oriental rugs and tapestry hangings—it was a natural one. Miss Lindsey, fitted into the picture as completely as if a part of it. In a soft old-rose silk, simply made, her dark hair framing her piquant face, she was charming.

Mrs. Hilliard welcomed the guest and apparently aroused her interest and sympathy by her weakness. But after the pleasant evening, when Noel took Leah Lindsey home, he made the fatal mistake of inferring that her statement about not seeing him had been revoked.

"Now you are taking advantage of your very sweet mother's hospitality," she said at the porch. "Conditions haven't changed in the least. I'm just as busy—busier in fact. And you're"—she paused.

"Just as lazy—lazier in fact," he finished with sarcastic emphasis.

"How well you put it!" she scoffed.

For a week he stayed away from her, but confessed rather sheepishly to the chap in his mirror that the punishment was all his own. It was just his luck, of course, to be away when she made her call on his mother.

Then, to the pleasure and surprise of a rheumatic old gentleman who lived across the street from the Lafayette School, young Mr. Hilliard dropped in to see him late one afternoon—the pleasure over the visitor's sympathetic call being tempered somewhat by the young man's incoherent farewells and hasty exit.

"You are the original little traction engine for work, Leah Lindsey," he said as he caught up with her after his solicitous call on the old gentleman.

"Work never hurt anyone," she remarked crisply.

"Meaning me, of course, stony-hearted one. I'm thinking of going to work. The janitorship of the Lafayette School appeals to me."

"You?" she retorted. "You couldn't hold down Jim Mullen's job two days."

Chapter III.

In the gray November weeks that followed, Noel found his interest in Leah Lindsey never flagging. She was sweet and sincere and frank—oh, yes, she was frank all right. He fought for every engagement he had with her. She was always busy, always visiting patrons, always preparing some special work; never ready to "fritter her time away," as she told him. When on rare occasions he succeeded in getting her out in the car or on a long hike, she captivated him with her charm and childlike pleasure in everything.

As the winter came on he grew restless and moody. In January he went to the hunting lodge for a week's shoot and stayed two days. The last of January, he took his gentle, delicate mother to Bermuda. He wrote Katherine Knox a dozen hastily scratched letters and Leah Lindsey one; but he was three days composing it.

When he brought his mother home, the sight of Katherine Knox, elegantly gowned, in her electric car, elicited a friendly "Hello, Kathie." The sight of Leah Lindsey coming down the Lafayette walk in her crisp, rose-colored linen, a splotch of white chalk by the cleft in her chin, brought a suffocating pounding in his throat. It was disconcerting, to say the least; so disturbing, in fact, that, to the surprise of the Hilliard Company managers, Noel volunteered to go west on a mission connected with the business.

A laboriously written, ink-spotted letter from Emily's oldest boy, beginning: "Deer Unkle Noel, Skool is leting out 2 weeks suner on Acount a scarlt Fever Gee Ime glad," had the effect of causing his "Deer Unkle" to nearly break his neck making train connections to get home—actions that were, to say the least, slightly inconsistent for a young man who had run away.

He arrived on Friday, to be hilariously greeted with the news that he was just in time for the dinner and theater party Katherine was giving that night for her friend from the East.

When he went to the dinner and received the crowd's enthusiastic welcome, he wondered vaguely what proportion of the great satisfaction he felt in life came from the pleasure in being with the dinner guests and how much came from the promise he had succeeded in getting from Leah Lindsey that she would go for a trip into the country the following afternoon. She had protested that she had to pack—and finish some work—and go down to see Jimmie Nelson's mother—and the train left at eight-something—and—

"See here, Leah Lindsey," he had said, "I chased home fourteen hundred miles to see you before you left, and I don't intend to be balked. I'll come for you at three o'clock."

With this anticipated trip in his mind and the comradely feeling toward his old crowd, he was enjoying himself immensely with the gay little theater party that filled two boxes. Glancing over the audience he saw the high-school science teacher, a decent, good-looking chap, coming down the aisle with a dark-haired girl in a rose-colored gown.

Bob Summers leaned jauntily over to Noel. "What's the matter with you, Pete? You look as if you'd like to kill somebody."

"Men school teachers," Noel returned irritably, "are a crime! The government ought to abolish them."

Saturday afternoon! A May Saturday afternoon!

Blue of the sky, green of the new wheat, yellow of the flowering currants, pink of the apple buds, white of the cherry blossoms!

"Where are we going?" Leah asked.

"Where would you like to go?" He would have started to the moon if she had wished.

"Well," she said with a gay little laugh:

> I like a road that leads away to prospects white and fair;
> A road that is an ordered road, like a nun's evening
>   prayer;
> But best of all I like a road that leads to God knows
>   where.

He was mightily pleased; but that was not unusual. She had a way of pleasing him. For answer he turned the car to the west, where they drove for a long time down "an ordered road" as straight as the king's highway; then to the north on one less noisy, more sheltered, and again to the west down a little loitering grass-grown road.

"Here it is!" she exclaimed happily:

You come upon it suddenly, you cannot seek it out;
But when you see it, gone at once is every lurking doubt.

Up and up the car climbed over the grassy road, not as on a steep hill, but a steady slope so gradual that only when Noel stopped the car did she realize that they were on the top of such an elevation. In three directions they could look over the fertile country with its prosperous farm homes. Acres of plowed land and acres of green wheat divided the land into checkerboard squares. Far to the north the silver thread of a river shone through willows. The spires of three country churches pointed upward, remindingly, to the heavenly blue of the sky. To the east, only a smoky haze told tales of the city. On the south side of the road a sloping apple orchard, like a great pink-and-white nosegay, filled the girl with ecstasy.

"Oh!" Leah Lindsey stood up in the car. "Did you ever see such a beauty place?"

"Can you *see* anything up there?" he asked. "Anything that isn't there?"

"Of course! A house—a little low house! How absurd a tall one would be. It's shingled—and stained—the sides are apple-blossom white and the roof is green, as if all the leaves from the apple trees had tumbled on it. There are windows everywhere for the blossoms to look in. Inside the house there are gay chintz curtains and books and a corner cupboard and shiny pans and clean milkcrocks! And down the back path are hollyhocks and blue cornflowers!"

"Tattling," Noel said in a moment, "isn't my particular vice; but I'm going to tell you this: I brought—another girl—out here once and asked her the same questions. And she said it looked lonesome and horrid, and she couldn't see anything but rotten apples and mosquitoes."

"I pronounce judgment upon that girl," Leah said solemnly, raising her hand. "I condemn and sentence her to wear expensive gowns and jewels and ride in a closed car on hot city pavements forever and ever."

With plenty of merriment and chatter they ate their luncheon under the apple trees which showered their petals down on the snowy cloth. They gathered armsful of white blossoms and tightly closed baby buds of pink.

With the setting of the sun, the warm May evening took on a slight chill. At the car again, Noel helped the girl into her scarlet sweater. Her gaiety seemed to have dimmed with the dropping of the sun.

"Tired?" he asked her.

"A little," she admitted.

As they were ready to leave, she turned to the orchard. "Well, good-by, you Most-Beautiful-Place-in-the-World. Do not forget me. When I get to be supervisor, I'll come back and buy you and build my little house. What's that about 'the bird to its nest and the heart to its home?' " She stood looking at the long green slope where the gray shadows were falling now. "How perfectly sinful for those people not to have a house there! I wonder who owns it?"

"I do," Noel said quietly.

All the way home the spontaneous merriment and gay banter of the afternoon did not return. The girl made a few desultory attempts at conversation, then ceased her effort. Noel drove steadily, grimly, silently. There was nothing to say but one thing, and that he could not, in honor, say.

At home again, after taking Leah to her train, his mother called to him: "Noel! Katherine and her friend and Bob were here. They were looking everywhere for you. Katherine wanted you to 'phone as soon as you got back."

Chapter IV.

Life at best is not simple. The observation is trite enough, to be sure—as trite as Adam. But true—as true as Eve.

Here was Noel Hilliard, healthy, clever enough, rich—no one to insist that he do thus and so—a few months ago lazily contented with the thought that some time in the future when he got ready to marry, the girl would be Katherine Knox. From the time they had been in high school, the subtle atmosphere of a future betrothal had enveloped them. He had gone with a dozen other girls in the meantime, Katherine looking on in her half-amused, wholly tolerant way; but always she had been "his girl." And now, quite suddenly, his heart, his mind, his very being had all turned traitor; turned their back deliberately, as it were, on the girl he had known for years, and wanted no one but Leah Lindsey.

After Leah had gone, Noel made an honest effort to assume the same attitude toward life that he had held before he knew her. But life grinned impishly at him. He tried stopping at the Knox home frequently. Aristocratic Mrs. Knox treated him like a son. Capable, jolly Mr. Knox joked with him as he had always done. Katherine was full of her usual chatter of social events past and those to come—a trait that seemed more in evidence than he had ever known it to be. Leah, now—! No, by George! At least he wouldn't be cad enough to continually compare them. With every call he realized how out of the question it was for him to hurt Katherine, to disappoint her parents. By a hundred tiny strands as minute as spider threads, he knew he was securely bound.

On a warm June day, Noel took his mother, Emily, Katherine, and Mrs. Knox in the Vance's big car to attend a wedding at Miles City. It was a seventeen-mile drive, so for the mother's sake they remained all night. Starting home in the early afternoon Emily said, "Aren't we close to the town where that nice Miss Lindsey lives? Let's go around and see her."

Now, Noel knew to the fraction of a mile how close they were to the town where that nice Miss Lindsey lived; but it was the last place on earth he wanted to take the family and neighbors. To protest would only be to arouse suspicion, so, when the others seconded it with no comments, he turned the car.

A small boy on a street corner of the straggling town motioned them toward a fine old home at the edge of the town. As they went up the driveway, Leah Lindsey, in a pink gingham dress and white collar, stepped out on the porch. She was plainly surprised, but kept her poise perfectly and became cordial at once, bringing out chairs and making Mrs. Hilliard comfortable with cushions and a fan.

"What a beautiful old place!" "Yes, isn't it!" Emily and Mrs. Knox were impressed with the old-fashioned home and grounds.

"I've always loved it," Leah said, flushing at the lavish praise.

The women conversed for a while, Noel watching the girl, so unconsciously lovely, and thinking how appropriate a setting in which to find her.

Suddenly, with an impulsive little gesture of her hands, she said, "Oh, people—I'm deceiving you! I'm so *ashamed* of myself! You will all despise me for it. I'm so sorry. This isn't my home! It's Judge Hayes's. Grandmother and I take care of the house when he is away. We—my grandparents and I— live over there, just beyond the hedge. My grandfather is Judge Hayes's gardener." She paused and looked from one to the other. "When you drove in, I was coming out to lock the house. You all have such beautiful homes something"—she put her hand to her throat—"*something* in me was base enough to let you go on thinking—what you did."

She was looking at them with wide, distressed eyes. Noel felt a sudden hot mist in his own. He wanted to take her in his arms—there, before them all.

"When I was a little girl," she went on, "I used to come here with grandfather and sit on the terrace steps and pretend it was my home. My pretending," she gave a little deprecatory smile, "my foolish make-believe has all come back on me to-day. Now, if you can forgive me, I want you to walk over to our house and meet my grandparents and have some tea."

Noel swept his glance over the other women. He felt angry for having brought them to witness this wonderful girl's humiliation. He was furious at Emily for her stiff, "Oh, I see!"—furious at Katherine for her cold stare, at Mrs. Knox for walking away. But mother—mothers always did right—toward her he felt a sudden rush of tenderness when she said, "Why, my dear, of course we'll forgive you. You were very brave to correct the impression. You mustn't bother about the tea; but we'll enjoy meeting your grandparents."

N oel helped his mother across the cool grass, sweet from its recent mowing. The others walked ahead, Emily and Katherine and Mrs. Knox in their expensive motor things—Leah Lindsey in the fresh pink gingham with its immaculate collar and cuffs turned back from the firm roundness of her throat and elbows.

"Ah, me!" the mother said. "The lies we live and have not the courage to acknowledge!"

"She is absolutely incapable of wrongdoing, mother!" And mothers are wise.

It was a little old-fashioned house, an upright and an ell, set in the midst of roses and honeysuckles, hollyhocks and dahlias. At a pansy bed, Mrs. Hilliard stopped. "Pansies for thoughts!" she said, "thoughts of my girlhood long ago."

Leah stooped and picked a purple velvety one, fastening it in the lace at the older woman's throat. "They are very sweet thoughts, I am sure."

Into the house with its shabby furnishings she took them. They almost filled the little front room. The grandmother came in from the backyard where she had been taking some baby chickens off the nest. She was wrinkled and stooped, her hands were rough and worn. Shy she was and ill at ease, but Leah took her sunbonnet and made her sit down. When the granddaughter said, "Granny, I want these friends to have some of your good sugar-cookies with their tea," the old woman became herself. That meant something to do for some one.

The half hour that they spent there was not an unqualified success. Emily and Mrs. Knox assumed cool patronizing airs; Katherine a gushing one. In spite of her naturally sweet manner, Leah was plainly nervous. Noel was too hot with anger to rally his usual fund of humor that might have bridged the chasm. When they were leaving, he said his farewells last; and because he was afraid he might say too much he said too little.

Over and over on the drive home he kept remembering his disgustingly formal "Good-by, Miss Leah Lindsey. We've enjoyed this very much." By his unusual silence the others would probably construe all sorts of things. Well, let them—hanged if he cared!

In the evening he broke an engagement with Bob Summers and settled down in a hammock on the side porch. Hands under his head he lay and watched the June moon swing into view. Was there no honorable way out? Wasn't the honorable way, after all, the truthful way? Leah's face in its different moods came between him and the moonlight— saucy and piquant, eager and interested, tender and distressed. How brave she was about working and helping the old folks! She wouldn't have to teach long—some decent chap would marry her, of course—maybe that science teacher. Not by a long shot, he wouldn't! Perspiration came out on his forehead. He sat up, his head in his hands. "Gosh!" he groaned sincerely, if inelegantly, "who'd ever have thought this would happen to *me?*"

"In trouble, dear?" his mother spoke from the doorway.

"No—nothing," he threw himself back in the hammock.

Chapter V.

In a moment she came down and seated herself near him in a porch chair. "Noel," she said quietly, "you know—Miss Lindsey—she didn't realize that she was helping me—to get courage—to tell you something." She stopped as if to gather strength. "Listen, Noel. No matter what I am going to tell you— no matter how much I may hurt you—remember this—mother loves you— has always loved you—and—oh, God!—I hope I am doing right. I've lived a lie, Noel, so long that it has sapped my strength, eaten at my very soul! And now—to-night—I am going to tell you. Dear, you are not really my own boy."

"What, mother?" his mind had heard only words.

"You are not my own boy. Oh, Noel—to live a lie! I wish I hadn't."

He had not moved. His hands were still behind his head. He was gazing at her, fascinated. Thoughts of insanity came to him.

"Are you—ill—mother?"

"No, dear—not ill, only truthful for the first time. Don't you remember, Noel, how I always talked to you about the wrong of untruthfulness more than anything? Think of it—I—who lived a lie with every breath; but it was because I knew—I *knew.*"

Frozen though he seemed, it was characteristic of him to want to get at the heart of it.

"What—do you—mean?"

"I'll tell you, dear; but, oh! be patient with mother. Remember I have suffered a thousand punishments of my own. I was a second wife, you know. Father's first wife had been beautiful and she had had Emily and Jean. I was not beautiful and I had no baby. Then, after several years, I had a baby boy— not—not you. I was in poor health, and when the baby was two months old father, the baby and I, with my nurse went abroad. I didn't want to, but father thought it would help me. He always had his way, you know. We no more than got there and were settled at Lucerne when he had to come back. There was a cablegram—something about business. We stayed for four months and started home on the *Shamrock*. You've been told about it's going down and how ill I was so long after. I've never talked about it. They thought it was on account of the memory of the shock. But it was not that. It was because my lie began then. My little baby was drowned—the nurse had him in her arms—I was trying to get to her to take him myself. A wave swept them off. Oh, Noel, my little baby—I can see him yet." It had been twenty-six years and she was still grieving.

"I was thrown into the sea, but got on to a plank somehow. A woman— your own mother, I suppose, Noel—was trying to get on, too. She was holding you—a little baby—and I reached to help her. I got hold of you by your little dress—but she—slipped off. They took us off together—you and me. I was suffering from shock and remember nothing until I regained consciousness in a hospital. I kept calling for my baby and they brought you to me. I told them you were not my child—that my baby had been drowned— but they only humored me in it; thought my mind was wandering. Strangely enough you had on a little bib with 'B. M. H.' embroidered on it. 'Mrs. Hilliard and infant' had been on the passenger list, and here they were. Well—lying there in bed—so ill—I just accepted what they said. I kept you. I would never have another baby—father would not know—a few months make a vast change in a tiny child. So I brought you home—and kept my lie to myself. I honestly think I was hardly responsible for my decision at first; but after a while the enormity of the thing came over me. Somewhere other relatives were mourning for *you!* But I was afraid then to tell—afraid of father's grief and anger. My decision must stand—and, besides, I had grown to love you. So, always, I've carried this in my life. It was what kept me ill— the consciousness of the lie. You'll wonder why I told you at all after all these years. I hardly know myself. I may be doing you an unnecessary wrong; but, someway, I don't feel so. For myself—I am glad—it seems good—as if to-morrow I would be well."

She came to him and with a tender little word of endearment, stooped and kissed him, leaving him with, "Whatever you do, Noel, don't live a lie."

For a long time he did not move. The library clock struck midnight—and one—and two. Still he lay, his hands clasped behind his head. Clouds dropped over the moon. It grew chilly. Some time between two and three there were lights and footsteps, people talking. They were calling him. He got up stiffly asking, "What is it?" Upstairs the housekeeper was telephoning; a maid farther down the hall stood whimpering. The nurse met him at the head of the stairs. The woman who was not his mother was dead.

In the days immediately following, Noel Hilliard walked as one asleep, or, rather, as one who stands aside and watches himself. There were flowers and tearful people and the hushed silence of the big rooms. Katherine brought roses. Leah Lindsey sent a little box of pansies.

There were no relieving tears for Noel—Only a tense grief that was half remorse. If he had only known! If he had only said something to her that night—told her she had done right to tell him—made her understand that he felt no bitterness toward her—only love! Every one thought the motor trip must have overtaxed her strength. Perhaps it had; but only Noel knew the prophetic words, "For myself—I am glad—it seems good—as if to-morrow I should be well."

The Saturday after it was all over, he got out the car and turned toward the farm—the eighty acres that had belonged to mother and which she had given him on his twenty-first birthday. He had taken his boyish sorrows there and, to-day, he would thrash out the problem that was tormenting him. In a measure the keen edge of the shock that he was not a Hilliard had worn off, but there was another phase of it with which to reckon.

Over the road that he had taken Leah! It seemed years instead of a short three weeks. When he turned down the little grassy road the verse she had quoted came to him clearly:

You come upon it suddenly, you cannot seek it out;
But when you see it, gone at once is every lingering doubt.

Mechanically, at the top of the long hill, he got out of the car and went through the orchard to the green sloping knoll.

For hours he lay on the grass, his auto cap over his eyes. Over and over in an unending chain of argument went his thoughts. He was not a Hilliard; therefore, not one cent of the property was his. If he kept the information to himself no one would be the wiser. "Whatever you do, Noel, don't live a lie!" What had she in mind: the thought of his telling that he was not a Hilliard? Or, had she guessed his love for Leah Lindsey? How foolish, how utterly foolish, to let one-third of the Hilliard fortune go. It was splitting hairs. He had been raised a Hilliard; to everyone he *was* a Hilliard. And yet, the will had read: "to go to my children, to be divided equally."

Well, *he* was not one of the children. The memory of John Hilliard rose before him—the man who was not his father. Strangely enough, there was an element of relief in that thought. It helped account for many things: the antagonistic views they so often held; the lack of sympathy between them. John Hilliard had abhorred a lie; but was not a lie sometimes justifiable? Or was it enough that a family had taken a little waif from the sea—a baby that otherwise would have drowned—and given him everything that he could wish for twenty-six years? So back he came in an unending circle to the fact that he was not a Hilliard and the property did not rightfully belong to him. He stood up.

"All right," he said. "I'm game."

There were numerous bewildering things to encounter in the next few days. There were two tearful, incredulous sisters to face, a firm of astounded attorneys who talked of "proof" and "technicalities."

"No, her mind was not wandering," Noel repeated wearily. "She was clear and definite in all her detailed statements. She left me as if happy and relieved to get it off her mind. There is no law under which a man is required to accept property that he doesn't want, is there?" No, there was none, but papers waiving all future claims must be signed.

"All right; get them ready."

"Great heavens, girls, turn off the weeps!" he said later to Jean and Emily. "You act as if I were a starving newsboy. Haven't I got a cracking good eighty? I feel very different about keeping that. Knowing all the circumstances, mother gave me that. And at the rate hogs and corn are selling, I'll come to town some day in my nice green lumber wagon and buy you all out."

"Noel, you're not going to *live* out there, are you?"

"I are."

"But Katherine? Oh, Noel, it would kill her!" It was Emily.

"No—Katherine wouldn't *stand* for it." It was Jean.

"Katherine won't need to," he said quietly. "I talked with her last night—

and—she wouldn't marry a farmer anyway. So, drop it, please, and don't spill any tears over me."

And a little later, "Noel, you'll take part of these rugs and things, won't you?"

"You bet," he answered blithely. "I need 'em in my business. And one thing more I'd like to borrow."

"Yes—what is it?" they asked eagerly.

"The name, 'Hilliard,' although," he grinned cheerfully, "I suppose 'A rose by any other name would smell as sweet!' No, I can't pick out the things just now. I'm going up the road a ways. Yes, I'll be back to-morrow and you can help me pack the things. I'm going to work this week. Got to get my alfalfa cut."

It was seventy-six miles to Center Junction. The gray car behaved beautifully. When it slipped noiselessly up the gravel driveway it was just four o'clock. There was no one in sight. Noel walked over to the cottage. Leah was up at the big house working. Judge Hayes was away, the grandmother told him.

He threw his motor coat and cap into the car as he went by. Up the steps, and his fine courage was oozing. Who was he—a man with a borrowed name—to hope—Across the porch—there might be some one else! Unceremoniously, he pushed the screen door open and stepped quietly into the hall. She was not in the first room. At the door of the second room he stopped. If Leah Lindsey was working, it was not noticeable. In a house cap and big apron that buttoned up behind like a little girl's, she sat in a forlorn heap by the window, her head in her arm on the low window ledge. An idle broom stood guard over an equally idle dustcloth. And because his heart was in his throat, Noel said flippantly, "Hello, central."

Frightened, she looked quickly around, the color slipping from her face.

"You?" she said in a queer little voice.

"Listen, Leah Lindsey!" The color had suddenly swept from his own face. He did not stir from the doorway. "What would you say if I told you not a cent of the Hilliard property came to me—that I had nothing but that eighty acres and had to—work?"

"I'd say," she said simply, "it was the best thing in the world that could happen to you."

He was across the room, gathering her up in his arms. "I love you, Leah Lindsey! I've loved you ever since the morning I caught you in my trap." He was too much in earnest to smile at the recollection. "The money won't make any difference to you, will it? I'll work so hard for you—and be so good to you. We'll build that house—that little dream house—by the apple orchard. You can love me, can't you—if you try—"

"What about—*her*?" she stopped him.

"Katherine? I'd forgotten you are entitled to an explanation on that score. Well, don't worry. Kathy doesn't want to marry a farmer any more than her mother wants her to—nor any more than the farmer wants her to. Now, let's forget Katherine Knox and talk about Leah Lindsey." He had his hand under her chin. "You do care, don't you?"

"I wonder," she said slowly, "if I dare tell you the exact truth?"

"You couldn't tell a fib to save yourself."

"Oh, couldn't I? All right, Mr. Noel Hilliard. I think, then, you had better know that last fall when I told you I didn't want to have anything to do with you—those reasons I gave you were not the real ones at all. It was because—from that first morning—I was afraid I might care and I wouldn't play with fire."

"Why, Leah Lindsey, you little liar!" He drew her close and kissed her.

"Do you realize, woman," he said to the top of her fluffy head, "that you are promising to marry a—a workingman?"

"I'll risk it," she said, snuggling closer.

There were countless things to discuss. Sitting on the old-fashioned sofa they made their plans.

Leah was going back to school and wait. Yes, she was *not*. That little house would be built and finished by October—shiny pans, milk crocks and everything. "Quarrel number one," Noel teased her, "and I win."

"You must come over and see granny and grandpa before you go. When do you have to start back?"

"I'll spend the evening with you and go early in the morning. Is there a hotel here?"

"Yes, but not very good. You can stay here at Judge Hayes's. He will be home on the evening train and he will want you to. I want you to like him, Noel. He has done so much for me—sent me away to school and been just like a father to me. He's had a very lonely life, too. He lost his wife and baby boy at sea years ago. Maybe you've heard of the *Shamrock* disaster? It was before I was born; but I've heard lots about it, of course, for the whole community was sorrow-stricken with Judge Hayes. That is his wife's picture up there."

Dazed, Noel rose and walked across the room to stand, fascinated, gazing at the picture. A young woman, no older than Leah, looked down at him with tender eyes over the top of a fat little baby's fuzzy head. The girl joined him.

"What was the baby's name, Leah?"

"Why—I don't—yes, I do, Bruce. Bruce Maynard Hayes for Mr. Hayes. Just think, Noel, to lose his young wife and baby! And never to marry! I've always tried to be so kind to him; but I never in the world can repay him for all he's done for me."

Awed, solemn, almost uncomprehending, the man slipped his arm about the girl. "I think, sweetheart—together—we can."

Then he told her.

Mother's Dash for Liberty

Bess Streeter Aldrich felt that "Mother's Dash for Liberty" was one of her most important sales, for she had been trying to place stories with the highly regarded *American Magazine* for five years before they accepted this one, for December 1918. She originally named this mother's adventure "Freedom from Her Mountain Height," but changed the title before she sent it to *The American*. This is the first of the series of stories published in *The American* which would later become Aldrich's first book, *Mother Mason* (New York: D. Appleton & Company, 1924).

Mother sat in front of her Circassian walnut dressing table, her f—, no, *plump* form enveloped in a lavender and green, chrysanthemum-covered, stork-bordered kimono, and surveyed herself in the glass.

Mother was Mrs. Henry Y. Mason, and in Springtown, Iowa, when one says "Henry Y." it conveys, proportionately, the same significance that it carries when the rest of the world says "John D."

It was eleven o'clock at night, which is late for Springtown. Mother had set her bread before climbing, rather pantingly, the wide mahogany stairs. There is something symbolical in that statement, illustrative of Mother's life. She had been promoted to a mahogany stairway, but she had clung to her own bread-making.

Three diamond rings just removed from Mother's plump hand lay on the Cluny-edged cover of the dressing table. These represented epochs in the family life. The modest little diamond stood for the day that Henry left bookkeeping behind and became assistant cashier. The middle-sized diamond belonged to his cashier days. The big, bold diamond was Henry Y. as president of the First National Bank of Springtown.

Mother was tired and nervous to-night. She felt irritable, old, and grieved—all of which was utterly foreign to her usual sunny disposition.

She took off the glasses that covered her blue eyes. It was just her luck, she thought crossly, that she couldn't even wear eyeglasses. They simply would not stay on her nose. Deprecatingly she wrinkled that fat, broad member. Then she removed and laid on the table a thick, grayish braid of silky hair that had formed her very good-looking coiffure, and let down a limited, not to say scant, amount of locks that were fastened on as Nature—then evidently in parsimonious mood—had intended.

With apparent disgust she leaned forward under the lights that glowed rosily from their Dresden holders and scanned the features which looked back at her from the clear, oh, *very* clear beveled glass. She might have seen that her skin was as fair and soft and pink as a girl's, that her mouth and eyes showed deep-seated humor, that her face radiated character. But in her unusual mood of introspection she could find nothing but flaws. The eyes looked weak and near-sighted without their glasses. The chin—like a two-part story, that chin gave every evidence of stopping, and then to one's surprise went merrily on. She leaned closer to the glass. Two sprightly, little hairs reared themselves from her chin's cushionlike surface.

"Well," Mother said dryly, reaching for manicure scissors, "that is *the limit!*" Living with a houseful of young people as she did, Mother's English had in no way been neglected.

Then, as though to let Fate do its worst, and looking cautiously around— for she was very sensitive about it—Mother took from her mouth a lower plate of artificial teeth. Immediately, out of obedience to nature's law that there shall be no vacuum, Mother's soft lower lip rushed in to fill the void.

"Pretty creature, am I not?" she grumbled.

J ust at this point, we opine, everyone who reads this little harmless tale will say, "Ah! No doubt the president of the First National Bank is showing symptoms of being attracted elsewhere!" Not so. Mother had only to turn her plump self around to see the long figure of that highly efficient financier stretched out in its black-and-white checked tennis-flannel nightgown, sleeping the sleep of the model citizen and father.

No, Mother had only reached one of those occasional signboards in life that say "Fagged! Relax! Let up! Nothing doing!" She was suffering from a slight attack of mental and spiritual *ennui*, which is a polite way of saying that her digestion was getting sluggish. She was fifty-two, not exactly senile, but certainly not as gay as, say, *twenty*-two.

Just then the connoisseur of mortgages rolled over heavily like a sleepy porpoise and muttered something that sounded like "Ain oo cum bed?"

Fifty-two! she went on thinking, and she had never had a day to herself to do just as she liked. From that day, twenty-five years ago, when the nurse had laid the red and colicky Bob in her arms, her time belonged to others. In memory she could see Henry's white, drawn face as he knelt by her bed and said:

"Molly, you'll never, *never* have to go through this again."

But she had! Oh land, yes! Bob was twenty-five, Katherine was twenty-one, Marcia eighteen, Eleanor sixteen, and Junior twelve—all healthy, good-looking, fun-loving and thoughtless. She had been a slave to them, of course. She ought to know it by this time, everyone had told her so.

But it wasn't just the family. There was the church—and the club—and the Library Board. Oh, she was hemmed in on all sides! Always, everyone thought, Mrs. Mason would do this and that and the other thing. Why did people think she could attend to so many duties? She was just an *easy mark!* This week, for instance: this was Monday night; to-morrow afternoon she was to lead the missionary meeting; to-morrow night the Marstons were coming to play Somerset. They came every Tuesday night. She and John Marston would bid wildly against Sarah Marston's and Henry's slower playing, and Henry and Sarah would probably win. Henry's bidding was like his banking—calm, studied, conservative. Then she would serve sandwiches and fruit salad and coffee. Why did she rack her brain to think of dainty new things to feed them every Tuesday night, just to hear them say, "Lordy, Molly, your things melt in the mouth!"

Wednesday, the Woman's Club was to meet with her, and besides entertaining she had to get her paper into better shape to read. It had been Mrs. Hayes's date, but she couldn't have them—or didn't want them—and of course they had asked to come to Mrs. Mason's. Well, being an easy mark, *she* could put all the chairs away afterward and pick up the ballots strewn around.

Wednesday night was the church supper. Why had *she* baked the beans and made the coffee for *years?* Thursday afternoon the Library Board must meet, and Thursday night Junior's Sunday-school class was to have a party in the basement of the church. She must go whether she felt like it or not, and help with the refreshments and play "Going to Jerusalem" until she was all out of breath and—oh, *why* did she have to keep on doing so many things for others? It was as though she had no personality. Never a day to herself to do just as she liked!

Tired and cross, she brushed her hair spitefully. Then her eyes fell upon a motto-calendar, silver-framed, on the dresser. In gay red letters it flaunted itself:

> . . . Know ye not
> Who would be free themselves must strike the blow?
> Byron: *Childe Harold.*

Could message be more personal? Underneath the calendar the detested lower plate of teeth reposed in a little Japanese dish which was their nightly bed. She picked them up and held them distastefully in her hand, so uncannily human, so blatantly artificial. And suddenly, born of rebellious mood and childish desire, was brought forth a plan.

She rose from her chair and undressed. Then she knelt by the side of the bed and said her prayer, a little rambling, vague complaint: "Oh, Lord; I'm so tired of the same things—and everybody expects so much of me—and there are so many things to do—and it won't be just a lie—if You know all about it—and why I did it— Amen."

And maybe, to the Good One who heard her, she seemed only a very fat little girl with a thin little pigtail hanging down her back.

Mother rose stiffly from her knees, snapped out the lights, and lay down beside the president of the First National Bank, who mumbled drowsily, "Hut time ist?"

At the breakfast table, Mother casually announced, as though she were accustomed to these gay little jaunts, that she was taking the nine-twenty train for Capitol City. It was like a hand grenade in their midst.

"*You*, Mother?" . . . "Why?" . . . "What for?" . . . "You can't! It's Missionary Day!" came the shrapnel return.

"She's going to see Doctor Reeve about her plate." Father had been previously informed, it seemed.

"Her plate?" . . . "What plate?" . . . "Card plate?" . . . "Haviland plate?" . . . "Home plate?" Everyone giggled. The Great American Family thoroughly appreciates its own wit.

"Sh!" Marcia tapped her own pretty mouth.

> "The hours I've spent with Doctor Reeve
> Are but a china set to me—
> I count them over, every one apart,
> My Crockery! My Crockery!"

They all laughed hilariously, all but Mother. They were not cruel, not even impertinent. But they were intensely fun-loving, a trait inherited from Mother herself. Strangely enough, Humor, Mother's faithful partner for fifty-two years, had suddenly turned tail and fled, leaving only a lifeless mask which she surveyed in tragic dignity. Very well, let them make fun of her if they so wished.

There was some discussion as to which one should take Mother to the train. She settled it herself; there was a reason why she chose to walk. On analysis, she would have discovered that this reason was not to interrupt the new sensation of feeling sorry for herself.

She would have liked to make the trip to the station in mournful solitude, but Henry must have been watching for her, for he grabbed his hat and came running down the bank steps as she passed.

"Have you got plenty of blank checks?" he wanted to know.

All the way down Main Street Henry chatted sociably. When the train whistled in he said, "Well, Mother, we'll meet you to-night on the five-fifty"—and kissed her. In ordinary times a tender kiss from any member of her family had the effect of melting Mother into a substance resembling putty; but to-day she had no more feeling for her tribe than the cement platform on which she stood.

As she settled herself in the car, Henry came to the window and said something. There was a storm sash and she couldn't hear. So he shouted it: "You sure you got plenty of blank checks?"

"Yes, yes!"

She nodded irritably as though he had said something insulting.

At Capitol City Mother went immediately to the Delevan—rather timidly, to be sure, for Father had always been with her when they registered.

"Single rooms, two, three and four dollars," said the jaunty clerk.

"Four dollars," said Mother boldly, as befitted the wife of Henry Y. Mason.

There was a little time to shop before lunch, so she walked over to Sterling's and bought one nightgown, one kimono, and one pair of soft slippers. After lunch she sent a telegram to Henry:

Find lots to be done. Home Friday night.

Well, she had cut loose, burned her bridges! For three days she would escape that long list of energy-killing things. She would think of no one but herself, do nothing but what she wished to do.

In the afternoon she sauntered past the movie theaters, reading the bill-boards. To the hurrying passerby she was only a heavily-built, motherly-looking person in a Hudson seal coat and small gray velvet hat. In reality she was Freedom-from-Her-Mountain-Height.

In the theatre, as she took nibbles from a box of candy and listened to the orchestra, if any thought of the missionary meeting with its lesson on "Our Work Among the Burmese Women" came to her, it was in pity for the femi-nine population of Burma who knew not the rapture of complete liberty.

She laughed delightedly and wept frankly over the joys and sorrows of the popular star, who whisked energetically through seven reels.

Out of the theatre again, she loitered by the plate glass windows of the big stores, went in and out as fancy dictated, and bought a few things—always for herself.

When she returned to the Delevan there was a long-distance call for her. It was Henry: "This you, Mother? Say, I could just as well come down on the night train and stay with you until you're all through your work."

"Oh, no, no," she assured him. "I'm perfectly all right. I'm *fine*. I wouldn't *think* of it."

"You got plenty of blank checks?"

"Yes, *yes!*" Mother was smiling into the transmitter. Her grouch was as much a thing of the past as the Battle of Gettysburg.

At dinner she ordered food for the first time in her life without running her finger up and down the price column. After resting a while in complete comfort, she sallied forth again. A famous tenor was singing at the Audito-rium. His "Mother Machree" gave her a momentary twinge of conscience-itis, but she quickly recovered. Even Mother Machree may have had one wild fling in her life.

There were two more whole days of complete emancipation. Club after-noon, when she should have read her paper on "Pottery—Ancient and Modern," she was attending "The Vampire." She had always wondered just what that particular blood-sucking animal was like, and she was finding out.

When she left the theatre it was snowing, and by dinner time there was a good imitation of a blizzard. But after dining she struggled through the wind and snow to a theatre where a merry troupe demonstrated how one may effectively kick and sing at the same time. *Now,* Mother thought, as she watched the twinkling heels, the women were clearing up that awful mess of church-supper dishes and wondering how it happened that they had fallen short of chicken and had three times as many noodles as they needed. Thank her stars, *she* had escaped it!

On Thursday she took a long street-car ride, read comfortably in her room, went to two movies and attended an art exhibit. The Library Board was meeting at home, of course, and listening half the afternoon to the Rev. Mr. Patterson tell how he started a library at Beaver Junction forty years ago. Then Junior's class was cavorting through those never-ending games of "Tin-Tin-Come-In" and "Beast-Bird-Fish-or-Fowl." Well, thank fortune, some other mother was getting a dose of assisting Miss Jenkins with her irrepressibles.

Friday morning Mother went up to Doctor Reeve's office. Friday afternoon she went home. On the train she reviewed her pleasurable three days. She had solved the problem. Life need never again become too strenuous. How simple it all was. The foolish part was that she had never thought of the plan before. She had only to slip away in peace and solitude when a week piled up with duties as the past one had. Good sense told her that she would not do it often, but it would always lie there before her—the way of beatific escape.

The train was rumbling through the cut in the Bluffs now, where lay the ghosts of many dead picnics, rounding the curve toward the water tank, slowing at the familiar station. There they were, Henry and Marcia and Eleanor—assembled as if they were about to greet the President of the United States. Junior, hanging by one arm and leg from a telephone pole, was waving his cap like a friendly orang-outang.

They kissed her rapturously—the girls and Junior. Henry's kiss, while resembling less a combustion, was frankly tender.

"Your dental work hurt you, Mother?"

"Oh, not a great deal." She was cheerfully brave.

They hung about her, all talking at once as they moved in a tight little bunch toward the car.

"Kathie's got two girls home from the University for over Sunday," they were telling her. "We had Tillie bake a cake and make mayonnaise and dress chickens for dinner to-night, but Papa wouldn't let her fry 'em—wants you to do it. And, Mama, you've got to lead Missionary Meeting next Tuesday, Mrs. Fat Perkins said to tell you. They didn't have it last Tuesday."

"And to-night's paper said in the club notes that Mrs. Mason would read her paper on dishes, or kettles, or something like that next Wednesday."

"Oh, Muz!" It was Junior jumping backward in front of them and shouting. "We didn't have our party—Miss Jenkins said you'd be back to help next Thursday. Ain't that dandy?"

"They put off the library meeting till you got home, too."

"Did they?" A tidal wave of chuckles were forming somewhere in Mother's stout interior. "Did they by any possible chance have the church supper?"

"No, they never," they were all answering. "It was so blizzardy and they phoned around, and they said anyway you weren't here to do the beans and coffee. It's next Wednesday."

"Oh, I guess you didn't miss much, Molly." Henry gave her substantial arm a friendly squeeze and beamed down at her. The Marstons are coming tonight."

The tidal wave rolled in—or up. Mother was laughing hysterically. Humor, her faithful partner of fifty-two years, had returned from his mysterious vacation, and with the rest of the family had met Mother at the station.

Mother sat in front of her Circassian walnut dressing table. It was eleven o'clock. She had just come up-stairs after setting the bread. She removed the heavy gray braid, laid it on the dresser and let down her scant hair. Then she took from her mouth the detested thing—so luridly red, so ghastly white—and surveyed it critically to see whether there remained a visible trace of the minute defect that Doctor Reeve's assistant in four minutes had ground down in his laboratory.

As she laid the plate in its Japanese dish, her eyes fell upon the silver-framed calendar. The old date was now ancient history. Mother removed the card and slipped the new page into place. In black and gilt it grinned impishly up at her:

Freedom is only in the Land of Dreams.

Schiller.

Mother got into her nightgown and knelt by the bed to say her prayer. It was neither vague and wandering, nor was it a complaint. It was a concise little expression of gratitude, direct and sincere: "Dear Lord: I always felt that You must have a humorous side and now I am sure of it. The joke's on me. And, Lord, I'll be good and never be cross again about doing all the little everyday things for the folks about me. Amen."

Then she rose, snapped off the lights, and lay down beside the president of the First National Bank, who mumbled sleepily, "Hut time ist?"

The Lions in the Way

"The Lions in the Way" is the only story Aldrich wrote from a male first-person point of view. This tale of a dentist was originally titled "Lower Left Bicuspid," but the editor of *People's Home Journal* changed it. The editor subtitled it, "A little comedy staged in a dentist's chair." It was published in February 1919.

Did anybody ever read anything written by a dentist? I never did, barring, of course, professional themes and pamphlets. Physicians break into print every little while, but for modesty the shrinking violet isn't in it with us Knights of the Chair of Torture. And I don't believe that it's because our lives are so humdrum that we never see anything worth writing about. We're far from being a glum set, even if we *are* accused of looking down in the mouth so much—that joke was invented when little Cain cut his first tooth!

We're a typical little mid-western town. You know the kind: the three-doctor, two-dentist variety where everybody knows how much Mrs. Groceryman Smith paid for her new carpet, and how many cigars Doc Merrill smokes in a day.

The Williscroft girls were the town belles and, believe me, they were A-No. 1 girls. Margaret was the older by a year or so—sweet as a peach and soft-spoken in a gentle, ladylike way. She had light brown hair and deep blue eyes and a fluttery way with her hands that you always noticed.

Barbara was more spirited. She had dark brown hair and eyes to match, and she wasn't so gentle in her talk—not that she talked loud and boisterously; but with more ginger and snap. Where Margaret seemed like a picture and droopy, Barbara was chic and breezy.

168

The Williscroft family lived on the last street in town, named "Elm Boulevard" by Mrs. Sarah Williscroft when Dad Williscroft held a seat in the town council. There was one half-grown elm to about seventeen butternut trees, but Elm Boulevard looked better on the stationery. Personally, I think "Butternut Boulevard" would have been more catchy.

The house was big and fine, one of those roomy, porchy houses with a wide hall through the center. There were two cupolas and a porte cochere, which certainly made Glenville look metropolitan. Three big lions had to be passed before one entered the house—two stone ones at the front steps and Mrs. Sarah Williscroft.

She sure did hold the steering wheel of that household. Dad W. furnished the gasoline and kept up all repairs, but Mrs. Sarah laid out all routes. A big, gray-haired, high-and-mighty woman she was, and hard as enamel.

Mr. Willis Williscroft had risen through nails and stoves and waffle-irons to the presidency of the First National Bank. He was his own boss there, at any rate, and no Wall Street millionaire had anything in the way of a shell-like reserve over our First National president. When he got shut up in his little iron cage, he looked for all the world like an old crow hopping about with his claws full of mortgages and other dainty tidbits.

The rivalry between the two banks would make a good story in itself. It took on moral, religious, and civic features, and even extended to the maids in the kitchens and the men in the yards. When the Williscrofts built the new house and furnished it newly on both upper and lower jaws, President Mason of the State Bank bought an auto. It would make you laugh to see it now: chain driven, two lungs, with engine chugging like a cornsheller, but we thought it a wonder then. As soon as Dad Williscroft had recovered from ulceration of the root—root of all evil, you know—over his new house, Mrs. Sarah bundled herself and the girls off to the Bermudas, which was quite some jaunt for a Glenville inhabitant.

The only persons seemingly not affected by this rivalry were Margaret and Barbe. It was as though, sensiblelike, they remembered that their polish was, after all, just stove polish.

Of course, with all this in-growing aristocracy of the elder Williscrofts, it is needless to say that, in their parents' eyes, there was scarcely anyone in Glenville good enough for the girls to associate with. There were few enough girls, goodness knows, who could pass the stone lions unchallenged; and as for the men around town, you could count, perhaps a scant half dozen. Myself—I kept a copy of our family tree in my coat pocket, and, as I went up the steps, I always had my hand on it ready to show Mrs. Sarah if she should ask for it.

And, believe me, there wasn't a fellow but found his nerve shattered after sitting on the edge of a brocaded Louis-something chair all the evening, within earshot of Mrs. Sarah. There was just one young man, in fact, who seemed to pass muster with her, and that was Louie Meacham. This Louie boy could sit on the Louis chairs until the bottoms dropped out and not get the icy conversation from his idol's mother.

It was Margaret that he had his fishy eyes on, and I never saw him look at her that I didn't feel like handing him a swift slap. If there was ever a piece of poor bridgework, he was it. And you couldn't put your forceps on a thing wrong with him: smooth, suave, courteous—most ladylike fellow you ever saw. Didn't drink, didn't smoke, didn't do anything sporty—in Glenville. Best-heeled young chap in town, too. Father had left him the Glenville Emporium and several good town properties, to say nothing of a corking good hundred and sixty acres just out of town. And, you can bet, he'd have several times that amount before he shuffled off. "Good business ability," old Willis Williscroft called it. "Sneaking unscrupulous stinginess and graft," I called it. He'd cheat his grandmother out of her cuspids and smile that chessy-cat smile all the time he was doing it.

And so, while Margaret was away at school, Louie smiled on Mrs. Williscroft and waited. And when she returned, and he asked Mr. and Mrs. Sarah Williscroft for their elder daughter's hand, they were both willing and thanked Providence that such a nice well-to-do young man wanted their girl. Oh, shucks!

This is where John Prescott comes in. I wish I could tell you he was the son of the rival bank president. But I'll go you one better. He was the son of the rival bank president's gardener! Speaking of the ground beneath your feet!

As a little chap, John had helped his father in State Bank Mason's garden, stopping long enough to look at the little Williscroft girls whenever they rode by in their pony cart.

To him, Margaret was always the princess and Barbe her lady-in-waiting. And when John Prescott got through high school and went away to take a civil engineering course, he had sixteen dollars and forty cents and a picture of Margaret, snapped under a tree at a Sunday-school picnic. Their mother had allowed the girls to mingle with the ragtag and bobtail, and John and

Margaret had taken a long walk together. My! Margaret must have looked sweet, with her light brown curls and her deep blue eyes, looking up at John as he took her picture with the camera he had borrowed for that very purpose.

It was the one thing she kept from her mother, John's writing to her all the time she was away at school. But, sometimes, the one thing is—the one thing.

They say the day she told her mother, in her sweet, gentle way, that John Prescott was the only man in the world for her, and that she couldn't, oh! she really *couldn't* think of marrying Louie Meacham, her mother became right then and there all the avenging angels combined to sit in judgment on that poor little sinner.

"But, Mother—" she managed to say during the tirade.

"But Mother—" echoed Barbe.

But—Mrs. Sarah just froze into a composite of every iceberg in the Arctic Ocean, and looked defiantly through her lorgnette. Margaret took her punishment of words as she had taken her spankings—quietly and sobbingly—and wrote John that her mother was getting old and couldn't bear to see her go away from Glenville, that she guessed it had all been an idle dream. She wouldn't have made him a very good wife, anyway—she wouldn't really—only please not to forget her and please to keep that little picture and this new one she was sending, no matter how many wives he might have. And never a word about "the scum of the earth," and "an ignorant old gardener," or a "washerwoman mother." I'll bet sixteen ounces of gold-plate that Mrs. S. W.'s conscience hurt her good and plenty after that tirade, for down in her heart she knew as well as the rest of us that old man Prescott was a good, honest man, well-educated too, for his limited advantages, and that Mrs. Prescott's washing was a sacrifice laid on the altar of her son's education.

It didn't take John Prescott, in Candle, Alaska, U.S.A., very long to read between the lines of that little stilted letter, and when he opened the picture and saw the dark blue eyes looking up at him again and the curls tumbling out in spite of the young lady's coiffure, he took the next boat up the Kewalik, which was only a small matter of three weeks later, and in a short time blew into Glenville with all the breeziness of the wind that comes over the Kotzebue Sound.

Didn't look like he'd been out of civilization, either. Was about half a year ahead of us Glenville fellows in his smart serge suit and ahead-of-date hat. I had never seen him, you know, until he came into the office to have some work done, but I'd heard a great deal about him from Barbe, and I took a shine to him the minute he swung open the door.

He was a tall, broad-shouldered chap, clean-cut and vigorous looking. The more I talked with him the better I liked him. He made Louie Meacham seem like a nickel's worth of scrap fillings. And I despised myself like I despised Louie. We were both in the same boat, insipid, spineless fellows, Louie measuring polka-dot calico and matching shades of pink baby ribbon, and I pulling old Mrs. Abe Miller's last molar. But John Prescott was a man, with a man's work to do, and he wanted to take Margaret with him into all the nooks and corners of the world while he did that work. If it had been Barbe, now, with her quick, energetic ways and her spunk! But Margaret, with her housekeeping tastes, and her fluttery hands! Funny, isn't it?

John had hardly walked up Water Street to the little one-story cottage where he had spent his boyhood, until the news was noised up one street and down another. It traveled by the grocery boy up Elm Boulevard and in through the kitchen window where it found its way out to the east porch and straight to Mrs. Sarah who was making a dinner list of Glenville's elect.

So it happened that when John Prescott went striding up between the stone lions a few hours later, he was met at the door with the information that Margaret had retired with a headache. But, dictator that she was, Mrs. Sarah couldn't keep Barbe out of the way, too, and Barbe did her best to be gracious and pleasant.

"I'm going to see her," John Prescott said to me, "if I have to set the house on fire to get her out."

"And I'll think of some way for him to meet her if I have to commit forgery to do it. If she'd just see him once, it would be all off with her, I know. He's perfectly dandy; I'm ready to run away with him myself. The only thing that prevents me is that *he* doesn't want me," declared Barbe.

Of course, her mother wasn't keeping Margaret in by force, as one would a child; but she had played so on her feelings that Margaret had grown to think it her duty not to see him, and in her own sweet, gentle way Margaret was a little obstinate, too.

I was seeing John Prescott every day, for he had two or three teeth to be looked after.

"I haven't been mixing up with many finger bowls or white spats or dentists," he said in his jovial way. When he wasn't at the office he was with "the folks" at home. Took his mother out riding every day in the most comfortable carriage he could find at Beed's livery barn. Jerked off his nifty blue suit and got into some old overalls and helped his father in the garden.

"Makes me feel like a little kid again," he said to me, "to see Dad trimming the grapevines with the same old clippers and Mother just inside the kitchen frying the potatoes for supper."

"Barbe," I said one day when I met her on Main Street, "without absolutely prevaricating, could you give the impression at home that John Prescott was leaving on the noon train tomorrow?"

"I could," Barbe replied serenely.

"Could you get Margaret to come down to the office in the afternoon after the train had gone?"

"I could not," she said emphatically, "short of dumping her into a wheelbarrow and trundling her down—unless of course there was sufficient reason."

"Hasn't she any dental work to be done?"

"None that I've heard her speak of." It was true. I had examined her teeth and they were as sound as a squirrel's.

"Haven't you any work to be done?" I asked pointedly.

She shook her head. "No, not a bit."

"Open your mouth," I commanded. She looked surprised but obeyed.

"Barbe Williscroft," I exclaimed, "there's an awful cavity in one of your lower left bicuspids. It's a wonder it hasn't given you an awful lot of trouble."

She looked astounded for the fraction of a second, then the brown eyes sparkled. "It has," she said. "It has kept me awake nights. I've concealed it from my family so as not to worry them."

"You ought to have it attended to right away."

"I will," she said. "When?"

"The only open date I have this week is tomorrow afternoon at four o'clock. I expect a patient at two-thirty, but I shall be just about through with him at four."

"But maybe Marg—I mean, maybe I'll have to come alone," she suggested, wrinkling her nose in a funny little way she had.

"Well," I said soberly, "that cavity is so deep that you might have to take an anesthetic before I could work on it, and in such a case someone ought to be with you."

"Perhaps I'd better bring Mamma?" she said dimpling.

"Oh, no," I protested in haste. "It won't be as bad as that—just a whiff, more like a *sister* anesthetic. But you mustn't let her light out and leave you all alone. Tell her not to fall into a panic when you lose consciousness."

I was more worried the next afternoon than I had been the day I almost pulled old Miss Haley's jaw out of joint. Now that I had started the ball rolling I didn't want to make an idiot of myself.

John Prescott came in, more low-spirited than usual.

"Say, Doc," he said, "I've just heard about this Louie Meacham deal."

"Oh, piffle! *That* for Louie Meacham," I said—and several other things which I will not set down at this time.

John and I chatted along with the work a good deal that afternoon, and before I knew it my little brass clock had struck four. I was as nervous as I had been at my first clinic. I heard the outer door open, and stepped out, carefully closing the door between the two waiting rooms.

There they both were, and, say, they looked good to me! Margaret was sweeter than I had ever seen her, all in pale blue like a little droopy butterfly. Barbe looked as trim as you please. She had on a white suit and one of those hats that looks like the suit. It's made out of tatting or gingham or crochet or something like that. I don't know what you call 'em.

" 'Prithee, Rosalind and Celia,' " I said, " 'whither away?' "

" 'Peace, fool, where learned you that?' " retorted Barbe in her quick way.

"There," said Margaret, "that's the first time she has said anything since we started. She has an awful tooth, Doctor. We've all been scolding her for letting it go so long. She held her handkerchief over her mouth all the way. Do you think it has affected her jaw?"

"Affected my mind, more like," growled Barbe. She wouldn't look at me but stood with her back to me gazing out of the window.

"I'll see her in just a moment," I said, "as soon as this patient is out of the chair."

I went back to the operating room. I was as cold as a pineapple ice. I couldn't have filled a nerve channel at the point of a pistol.

"Say," I said to John, and I bet I looked foolish, "There's a ticklish job right here. I might hit a nerve, you know. Better let me give you a whiff for a minute."

"Not for mine," he said. "Had the tendon of Achilles on my left foot nearly severed up on Lost River. George! but that was a hurt, with no one but a lazy native to get me to a road house. No, thanks. Think I can stand it. Mush on."

I had lost, but I would play the rest of my hand anyway. I stepped back of the chair and, quick as a cat, clapped the whiff-net over his face. He was off in a minute.

"Girls," I cried, rushing out excitedly, "I need your help! Margaret, come into the operating room and help me. Barbe, run for Doc Merrill."

Margaret made a swift jump to the inner room and Barbe darted out of the door. I bolted through the laboratory to stop her.

"Hist!" I whistled; "Barbe!" I caught her and pulled her into the laboratory. "It's just a plot, you know."

"Oh," she said. "But you gave me a scare! What am I to do?"

"Stay here with me. He'll come round in a second. I'll look through this keyhole and see—"

"You will not look through any keyhole," she said, and got between me and the door.

"Oh!" she cried. She was wringing her hands; "now you've gone and done it! She'll give in as soon as she talks with him, and go out there to live in Alaska or Australia."

"If she marries Louie Meacham," I said, "she'll live in misery!"

"And I'll lose my Marge," she wailed. "I wish you had never done it."

Now isn't that just like a girl?

"My own Marge," she was moaning, "I just can't lose her! I'll die."

"Let's die together," I said and reached for the bichloride.

"Don't be flippant," she sobbed. That took all the flippancy out of me. To think of Barbe Williscroft sobbing, Barbe, who was always so gay and full of spirit!

"Why, Barbe!" I said. I started to put my arms around her, but first I unpinned that gingham-or-tatting hat and threw it under my worktable. The thing was in the road.

"Why, Barbe," I cried, "you sweet girl, you sweet little girl! I've loved you—and *loved* you ever since I knew you, but never so much as this minute. You've always seemed so gay and happy. You seemed never to need me—or anybody. But to see you crying—you *do* need me, don't you! You will need me after Margaret goes, won't you? You do love me don't you, little-girl-of-my-heart? Tell me."

And then *the* miracle happened. Barbe nodded her head, down on the lapel of my white office coat. I kissed the top of her fluffy head.

Then she raised her head and her nose wrinkled. "How about that lower left bicuspid?" she dimpled.

I took her perky chin in my hand. "Open, please?" I said. "Good piece of work! And now, little-girl-that-pays-her-debts, my fee."

She gave me two. The first was sweet and timid as if it came from the heart of a rose. But the other clung and throbbed as though it came from the heart of a woman who loved.

We all went to Elm Boulevard together and straight up to the lions—stone and otherwise. I let John go first, seeing he was an out-of-town guest, so to speak. Besides, I could talk to Barbe all I pleased, if we brought up the rear of the procession.

I don't know whether Mrs. W. had been at the point of giving in anyway or whether such an avalanche of prospective sons-in-law struck her dumb. It couldn't have been John's casual remarks about the gold mines he was developing. At any rate she accepted us as graciously as though she had all along planned these two identical matches. But when she asked Barbe about her tooth, that saucy miss said: "You know, Mother, a tooth always stops aching as soon as you get inside the dentist's door."

Through the Hawthorn Hedge

The scene of the young woman putting candy on the
porch roof to cool would find its way into Aldrich's novel
Miss Bishop (New York: D. Appleton-Century Company,
1933). Aldrich often wrote about young women, and
occasionally young men, who had been orphaned and
reared by grandparents, as she does in this story, published in *McCall's* of March 1919.

Mrs. Corvin's boarding-house stood dark and silent,
its windows lighted palely by the cold glimmer of the street lamp. Only one
gleam of yellow light, hidden by the black bulk of the house on the corner,
fell upon the snowy roof of the side porch, and in its ray stood a girl.

She was a distractingly pretty girl, in a soft, rose-colored kimono and the
most frivolous of gray suède slippers. A thick braid of fluffy brown hair hung
to her waist, and the band of white flannel around her neck detracted
nothing from the rose-pink of her cheeks or the Irish blue of her wide eyes.

"Mrs. Watson!" she called in a voice that had seen lusty service in basket-
ball. "Mrs. Wa-AT-son!" But no window in the next house gave forth a
glimmer. Everyone had gone to the lecture. An automobile rolled swiftly by
on the paved street at the front, the purring of the engine dying away in the
distance, and silence closed upon her again.

Something clammy lighted on her nose. Horrors! It was beginning to
snow again! "Hoo-hoo-oo!" she called. Her voice came back to her thinly,
echoing from the heedless walls. No answer came from the deserted street.
She was beginning to shiver, and a cough strangled her voice in her throat.

She ran once more to the edge of the roof. She could jump. "Yes, and
break my ankles," she thought, "and faint and be covered with snow when

the girls come home. They'd think I was the wood-pile." She laughed nervously, and shivered again.

So this was the way they all felt, was it?—Babes in the Wood—Princess in the Tower—and she, on the roof of the porch of a boarding-house! Irrepressible laughter bubbled again, tangled with something like a sob. Ages went past, it seemed, while she huddled there.

The sound of steps on the side street at last seemed to stun her, so that she made no sound. A man was passing quickly with long, swift strides. Through the muffling sensation of nightmare she struggled for her voice. "Hoo-oo," she called frantically. "Help me—please—hoo-oo! Help me, won't you?"

The man stopped immediately, turned, and came gingerly through the snowdrifts in the Watsons' back yard. "What is it?" he asked a bit impatiently, stopping under the clothesline and looking up at the girl. "What's wanted?"

The girl leaned down toward him. "I'm so sorry to bother you—but everyone has gone to the lecture—and I feel so silly to tell you—but—I got out on the roof to cool some candy—and it locked—the window, you know—and I've got a sore throat—and I'm so cold—" Her voice trailed off.

The man said something to himself. She caught an astonished exclamation. Then—"Where can I get a ladder?"

"There's one in the barn, I think—but you see—even if I get down—I can't get in—for the night latches are on."

"Couldn't you go into some friend's house until your people come home?"

She waved a despairing hand. "Look at them! Everybody's gone to the lecture. I suppose you were going too?"

"I had intended to," he admitted, "but that's all right. Say, I have it—I'll get you down and take you over to the Auditorium and you can find your parents."

"Goodness gracious!" she laughed hysterically. "I have on a kimono—and my hair is hanging down my back—and I'm a public-school teacher."

He threw back his head and laughed, too. "I beg your pardon. You look like a little girl, up there."

He began trying doors and windows. "I guess you'll have to come up and break my window," she called as he came back from a fruitless trip.

"If we are going to break windows," he suggested, "it might better be downstairs here. You'll want your own room as warm as it can be."

He strode off to the barn, from which he returned with a long ladder balanced across his shoulder. He placed it in a snowdrift by the kitchen wall and held it firmly.

"Come on," he called. "Be careful."

When she was halfway down, one of the inadequate slippers dropped.

"See here," he said, "you can't walk in this wet snow. I'm going to carry you around to that porch."

"You'll be sorry," she warned him. "I smell awful listeriney."

He took her off the ladder and rounded the corner of the house to a small, built-in porch, where he set her on her feet between the refrigerator and a washing-machine. She couldn't see his face. There had only been time for the fleeting impression of his fur-lined coat and his muscular strength—and a certain sense of confidence in his personality. She wondered vaguely if it was true—that a person radiated character like that so one could tell—even a stranger—and in the dark—

"Now then!" he had the big coat off and was putting it around her. "Isn't this a tub? Sit here. Draw that around you. Keep your feet warm. Is there a hatchet here—or an ice-pick?"

"There's a hammer on top of the refrigerator, I think. I'll get it."

"You sit still."

"You're kind of bossy!"

"And it strikes me that you need a little bossing," he retorted.

Crack! Crack! The girl shuddered and put her hands to her ears. Crash!

"Now!" he said decidedly.

The girl stood up. "I've been so much trouble. I'll be good all the rest of my life. I'm so sorry you've missed part of the lecture."

"But you're missing it all."

"Maybe it's just as well," she laughed. "Redfern's a great author, but he's a rank pessimist and a cynic and he might have converted me. Well, I must go in. Three Fiends are haunting me—Tonsillitis, Bronchitis and Pneumonia; and the greatest of these is Pneumonia."

"Promise me you'll take quinine and a hot bath."

"I promise."

Safely inside, the girl touched a nearby switch and flooded the room with light, then turned toward the porch. The effect was of a painting framed by the broken window—one of Reynolds' languid ladies turned mischievous. The gay, chrysanthemum-covered kimono infolded a winsome maiden whose fluffy hair was as wind-blown and tangled as Fanchon the Cricket's. She held out her hand from the picture frame to the man standing in the shadow. He took the little cold hand in his left one.

"I don't know whom to thank." Her eyes questioned him.

"You can thank—John Smith—who was just in town between trains. And it's lucky for you that he was. What's your name, Miss Imprudent?"

"Jane Jones." She made a laughing grimace, so that he knew she was not telling the truth. "Thank you again, Good-by, John Smith."

"Good-by, Jane Jones."

Upstairs again she gave herself a hot bath, took quinine, rubbed her abused throat with evil-smelling drugs—libations on an altar to appease the wrath of the Three Imps—and went to bed. But not to sleep. She loved to entertain the girls with funny anecdotes—and this was rich! How they would laugh! She had her amusing story all ready when they came.

Her roommate opened the door cautiously and tiptoed in. "How's your throat, Honey?"

She sat up, stifling a manufactured yawn. "Fierce. How was John Bruner Redfern?"

"Perfectly grand. He looks just like his pictures. It's mighty queer he's escaped matrimony. His talk was immense! But he was horribly late—we sat and sat—and he had his right hand—his gesturing hand you know—bandaged—and he made no explana—"

But wide-eyed—wild-eyed—the girl in the bed had dropped back on the pillow and pulled the blankets over her head.

The doctor came on Saturday morning. After he had gone, the girl, propped up in bed with two and three-fifths degrees of temperature to her discredit, told the other teachers about her adventure, the names that had been exchanged—everything. They were incredulous. She was fibbing, they told her, but the yawning window, the author's bandaged hand, his late arrival, all attested to the truth of the story.

"Now, isn't that just your luck?" Dora, the roommate, was disgusted. "I could have fallen off the kitchen roof and cracked my head and either the janitor of our school or that foolish Perkins boy would have found me."

All day long the girl lay and paid, in fever, for her escapade. In the late afternoon, after those throbbing, drug-scented hours, a florist's box arrived, directed to Miss Jane Jones, 1424 Sycamore Street.

With that naive interest in each other's affairs which women who are living together display, four excited girls bore the box upstairs to the touching accompaniment of "Here Comes the Bride."

"You silly things!" the girl greeted them, and for the first time resented the old familiarity.

There were roses—a mass of them—Caroline Testout roses, their silvery-rose petals just showing the cherry-red of their hearts. The card bore the magic name, "John Bruner Redfern." Tucked among the flowers was this brief note written in a very piratical hand:

> Which Fiend is it? I earned the right to know. I'm in Mill City over Sunday—at the Hawkeye—and being "kind of bossy" expect an answer to my question.
>
> John B. Redfern.

How should a school-teacher address Genius? Remembering, with mortification, how a school-teacher had addressed Genius, she wrote several ladylike notes—formal, stilted affairs. Suddenly, she tore them all up and wrote hastily:

> It's Tonsilitis. He's horrid. My head feels like a gourd with my neck for the handle. But even that is pleasant in comparison with my chagrin. For me the song should read, "When you come to the end of the *im*perfect day and sit alone with your thoughts." Of course I found out—even last night—who you were. That awful thing I said about you! I'm truly sorry I said it, and more sorry that I can't take it back. And to have made you so late! And your hand was cut! Tonsilitis is light punishment for me. The roses are beautiful. When the Fiend glares, they smile back at him. Thank you for everything.
>
> Margot Jane O'Brien.

On the following Wednesday, Miss O'Brien returned to her boarding-house from a strenuous gathering-up of the loose ends of her school work after two days wasted by that bane of all teachers, a substitute, and found a letter awaiting her. The letter said:

> Margot Jane,
>
> I like your name. (That's *vers libre*.)
>
> The Jane stands for the saucy part of you and the Margot for—some things that are not saucy.

How is the Tonsilitis? Gone. I hope.

Don't worry about the criticism. I have had many, but never one more sincere. I have written about things as I found them and I have not found them rose-colored— Margot Jane.

I wonder if you know a Tom Kennedy in your town? He and I used to play marbles (and hookey) together a hundred years ago. I had been to his house last Friday night when I—passed your kitchen roof. His house seemed to be hermetically sealed, and I did not stop to break a window. If you know anything about him, I'd appreciate hearing.

It was only common courtesy, of course, to answer that "Tom" Kennedy was known as the Honorable T. J. Kennedy and was at present in the state legislature and that the tonsilitis had gone, thank you.

In a week an appreciative answer arrived. Now, Margot Jane O'Brien, Irish as to disposition, eyes, fanciful day-dreams, and the cleft in her chin, was also Scotch, and canny. So she did not answer the letter. The tonsilitis was a thing of the past, the new window-glass was neatly puttied in, and the roses had withered, so to the brief acquaintance she said farewell. But, of course, she could not prevent Mr. John Bruner Redfern's stopping in town again, between trains, to see his friend Kennedy. That he did not see the Hon. T. J. Kennedy was not strange, seeing the august body of lawmakers had not thought of adjourning. That he called on Margot Jane O'Brien instead, was also not strange, for did he know another soul in town?

The months marched by with steady rhythm. In February a primary teacher revels in an orgy of hatchets, valentines and cherry trees, in March literally falls over kites, pussy-willows and seed-boxes, in April supervises the painting of several thousand wild-looking robins whose eyes and beaks and wings mingle sociably.

Consequently, Miss Margot Jane O'Brien, Grade One, was very busy. And very happy. The brief acquaintance had grown into a friendship, fed by letters, warmed, perhaps, by fugitive dreams.

It was May now, and the children were piling creamy-white May blooms and honey-sweet lilacs on Miss O'Brien's desk, and Miss O'Brien knew that the time had come when John Bruner Redfern was to stop once more between trains on his return from the west.

Legislature had adjourned, but it was noticeable that the Sunday the

Through the Hawthorn Hedge

author arrived in town, he very impartially gave the short forenoon to his old playmate and the long afternoon to Margot Jane O'Brien.

The Sunday afternoon was glorious. They walked out to a row of bluffs overlooking the little city, the well-known author and the unknown school-teacher. At the crest of one of the green, rolling hills they sat down on a fallen tree trunk. Below them shimmered the river, worn like a silver sash on the green dress of May.

The afternoon slipped away like the river.

"There are some days so perfect," the girl said in the late afternoon, "that it seems an actual sorrow we can't hold them. Look at it!" She threw out her hands to the panorama. "There's nothing in the world that could improve it to-day. And yet there will come days when the fields will lie brown and parched and days of sodden soil and dripping trees. But the memory of the way it looks to-day will be constant, like our faith that all we hope for will come to us."

The man turned to her. "You have the optimism that has never known rebuffs, the optimism of a child. It's a pleasant life to lead, until you find yourself with a figurative black eye. You called me a cynic once. I'm not. The theory of my life can be summed up in two words: I pay. Things don't come my way tied up in tissue-paper and ribbon, as they do to you. I'm thirty-eight. For the few sincere friends, the small measure of success that is mine, I have sweat blood—and paid."

He paused a moment, then turned to her with his quick, boyish smile. "Live your life of all-things-working-together-for-good if you choose. But for me, I ask of Life mighty few things—and I pay."

While he was speaking, the girl, looking far across the river, had grown a little white around the lips. Now she turned to him Irish-blue eyes that did not see him.

"I pay." She repeated the words half-dreamily, half-scornfully. "Yes—?" It was a slightly questioning, mocking tone. Suddenly she brought her eyes straight to his.

"Listen!" she said in a queer voice. "You'll go to-night on the eastbound nine o'clock. I'll not see you again. I'll hear of you, of course, but you will know nothing more of me. You will only remember that somewhere there is a girl who believed, with you, that 'to pay' was the most honorable thing in the world. . . .

"When I was a tiny girl my father was killed. My mother took me home to her parents. In a few months she died, too. They were humble Scotch people—my grandparents. Grappy was gardener for Judge Maynard, who lived across the alley from us in a house that I thought was a castle. There was a conservatory and two towers and a formal flower-garden and a long, curving driveway. A hawthorn hedge shut out the alley where I lived, and it seemed like a wall around fairyland.

"When Grappy used to go over there to work I'd stand and peek through the hawthorn hedge, and if I saw Mrs. Maynard, in her pretty clothes, drive away, I'd squeeze through the hedge and go over there with Grappy. There was a little summer house there, and the mere sitting in it made me feel beautiful, wealthy and accomplished. I grew to think that everything I wished for in that magic summerhouse would come true. Once I wished for a big doll out there, and the Judge brought me one. That I could take music lessons, and he got me a teacher. That I could go to college, and he made it possible. Almost everything I have had done for me has come from him."

In a moment she went on: "Grappy died first, and last year, Granny. The Judge has been my friend, my guardian, my adviser. Two years ago his wife died—" Involuntarily the girl turned away eyes that had grown dark. "And he wants to marry me—and I—must pay."

She was silent a moment. When she raised her head, a little smile, vague and wistful, was at her lips. "There it is!" She pointed across the river to the edge of the overgrown town. "Do you see it—the big brown house in that clump of oaks? The Judge is out of town. He will be home to-morrow night and I am to tell him then. There is just one evening left to me while I am free. Shall I tell you how I am going to spend it?"

She looked up at him with her whimsical smile.

"I am going to be all Irish to-night. 'There's a wheen things that used to be and now has had their day.' But to-night I am going to bring them all back again. I am going up to the old house where I lived with Granny. Then I'm going to squeeze through the hawthorn hedge into the big garden, and the great-grand-childer of the fairies that danced on the Cushendon downs will help me re-create the atmosphere of my little-girl days. ' 'Twill be sweether than singin' of linnets when May on the meadows is young.' I'm going to the magic summer-house. But I shall never wish there again after to-night, for there is only one thing more I want."

She paused, and the man, his brows drawn, watched her intently. "What—is that?"

"It is all in a little verse I learned years ago. I didn't know the meaning it would some day hold for me:

               'Bid all repining to cease,
                 Speak to my soul in the twilight
                 And grant me my prayer for peace.' "

Neither spoke for a moment. It was the girl again who broke the silence. "Well, Mr. Author," her laugh sounded bright and sincere, "put me in a cyanide bottle, stick a pin through me and place me under a glass case, but when you classify me, please print underneath 'Species—Non-Whiner.' And now we must go, mustn't we?"

All the way home the gay banter of the earlier afternoon did not return. The man, deep in his own thoughts, stalked along silently, grimly. The girl made a few attempts at conversation and then ceased her efforts.

They found the boarding-house deserted, with the calm of a Sunday evening on it. The girl unpinned a note, which dangled from the topmost lilac in a vase on the library table, and read it aloud:

> We've all gone to Summerville. There's cake in one tin
> box in the pantry and buns in another and cold chicken
> and lettuce and salad dressing in the refrigerator.
>
> Ma Corvin.
>
> P. S.—If Mr. Redfern stays to lunch with you, open a jar
> of strawberry jam.

They both laughed. It cleared the atmosphere wonderfully—that jam.

"You'll stay?" the girl asked gaily. "You wouldn't have the heart to keep me from having some jam?"

"An inborn sense of chivalry compels me to accept."

The girl put on an absurd little ruffled apron and gave an ample one of checked gingham to the man.

It turned out to be a merry little affair—that farewell supper. So talkative and vivacious was the girl, that the man entered readily into her mood. When the hands of the homely black clock on the mantel pointed to eight-thirty, the man pushed back his chair. " 'Where duty calls,' you know—'or danger,' " he quoted lightly.

The girl stood up, too, and smiled.

"Well, Margot Jane O'Brien, I've grown rather used to getting your bright letters. You will still write? You won't let—what you told me—make any difference?"

It is a very old question. Napoleon probably put it to Josephine when he divorced her. King Ahasuerus very likely asked it of Vashti when he put her away. But they all smiled—woman-wise—Vashti and Josephine and Margot Jane O'Brien.

"Still write? Oh, no!" she shook her head. "I'm as old-fashioned about those things as—as—a Scotchman."

"Then I'll say good-by and hope with all my heart that your last wish will come true."

"Oh, it will," she returned. "I'm as confident of that as—as an Irishman."

They laughed again. It was going to be a cheerful parting after all. The man stood for a moment looking over the top of her fluffy head, his brows drawn in their characteristic way. "There's one thing I want to tell you. What I said about studying types—I didn't mean—you mustn't think—"

Thirty years before, in a primer class, Johnnie Redfern may have stumbled as incoherently.

"You're trying to tell me," the girl's honest eyes sought and held his—"that your friendliness toward me wasn't as—cold-blooded as that? . . . I'm glad of that. And there's one thing I want to tell you. I don't want you to leave with the impression that I am going to be unhappy. I'm not. I've always been able to make happiness for myself. There will be many compensations. I adore the old house and grounds. And the gardener has a little girl to whom I can be fairy godmother—think of the fun in making her wishes come true! And the Judge has my deepest—respect and—admiration." If her voice faltered for a moment, it was scarcely noticeable, so quickly did she continue: "So you see, everything will be all right, and your theory of honorable payment is—quite right."

She put out her hand. "You must go. I made you late once, but trains won't wait as patiently as audiences."

He took her hand for a moment, straightened himself like a soldier called for duty, said good-by and was gone.

In the twilight, a girl in a white dress, waiting by a hawthorn hedge at the edge of town, suddenly threw back her head to listen. The long wail of the nine o'clock, eastbound train came from across the river. Breathless, she watched it—a tiny toy train against the black background of the bluffs, specks of light shining from each miniature window. As the last little car vanished into the night, she turned, and pushed blindly through the hedge.

Suddenly, the dull ache in her heart became a poignant pain. This was no enchanted garden. The castle was merely a big, dark, lonesome house. The shining knights and ladies were only tall canna and gladioli. The magic lights were but fireflies. Where were her fairies? Years ago they had come at her bidding to assist in making hard things easy. She had not given them a thought since—last winter. She had not needed them. It was true then! They forsake you when you have neglected them.

She passed slowly up the gravel path to the summer house and threw herself down by the rustic seat, a forlorn, crumpled heap. How could she go on? Life was not meant to be like this, with all the glamour, all the enchantment gone! The Judge was so good—so kind. . . . Why, oh why, had she been permitted a glimpse of something infinitely more sweet—and alluring? Just a glimpse—and the door had been shut! Her mind seemed to creep numbly like a broken, wounded thing, from one bitter-sweet memory to another.

Suddenly she sat up. Someone was coming through the iron gateway and crossing the broad, sloping lawn. Frightened, she sprang up and stepped to the doorway. It must be the Judge. He had come home on the nine o'clock train, a day earlier. What could she tell him? What excuse could she give? No whimsical, childish belief in good fairies could aid her in this. She couldn't—

The man seemed taller than the Judge—and broader-shouldered.

"Margot Jane!" he called.

Her hand went to her throat. He had missed his train then.

"I thought you were the Judge." The words sounded strange and far away. "And you were frightened?"

"Terribly." Her voice caught. "I'm sorry you missed your train."

"I didn't miss it. I was there in time. I couldn't go." His arms went around the trembling girl and he drew her gently to him.

"I came back—because I can't let you marry him. It's unthinkable. I know now that, for me, you are Faith and Happiness. I love you, Margot Jane. Could you care for me—if you tried—dear heart?"

Just at first she could not answer. Then, trembling, she whispered—"And I thought—the enchantment—had vanished."

Mother's Excitement over Father's Old Sweetheart

This story, one of four by Aldrich about college reunions, was printed in July 1919 in *The American Magazine.* Having grown up in a college town, Aldrich had attended many graduation activities, which were important civic events that took place over several days each year; she would later recall how exciting these days were. Her "reunion" stories examine the sense of having matured past the "good old days," yet still being able to recapture youth for a few hours.

Aldrich enjoys poking fun at fads of the day and here skewers the Cult of Chaos and Cosmos, as she later would Cosmic Philosophy in "Tillie Cuts Loose," in *The American Magazine* (April 1920).

Mrs Henry Y. Mason's years numbered fifty-two, which means that she stood on that plateau of life where one looks both hopefully forward and longingly back. Life had been very gracious to Mother Mason. It had brought her health, happiness, and Henry; and sometimes in a spasm of loyal devotion, Mother decided that the greatest of these was Henry.

To-night, as she sat knitting by the library table, her heavy figure erect, her plump face, under its graying hair, radiating energy and kindliness, her health was evident.

As for the happiness, the source of a goodly share of it was apparent. Sounds of youthful laughter came with the scent of lilacs through the open windows. They were all out there in the yard: serious-eyed Katherine home from the University for spring vacation, lovely eighteen-year-old Marcia, merry sixteen-year-old Eleanor, and troublesome, lovable twelve-year-old Junior. Even Bob, good, steady Bob, her eldest, was out there, too, just leaving with Mabel, his bride of a year, for the little home two blocks down the street. Yes, Mother had known much happiness.

Which brings us to Henry. That big, calm, conservative president of the Springtown First National Bank was just sitting down on the opposite side of the library table and unfolding the "Evening Journal" when Mother began:

"Henry, you wait a minute. I want to talk to you about something that has been on my mind all day."

Henry looked up politely, but hung on to his paper.

"This morning I was cleaning out the drawers of that old bureau in the attic and I began reading scraps of letters and looking at the pictures of my old college classmates, and I just got hungry to see them all. I kept thinking about my girlhood with those old chums, and I was so homesick to see them I could *taste* it. Why, if I could hear Nettie Fisher laugh and see Julie Todd's shining, happy face!"

She dropped her knitting and turned to her husband.

"Henry, I've a good, big *notion* to plan to go back to Mount Carroll for Commencement."

"Why, sure! Why don't you, Mother?"

Henry prepared to plunge into the paper as though the matter were settled, but it seemed Mother had more to say. For twenty-six years Father had been a patient, silent boulder in the middle of the stream of Mother's chatter.

"You know, Father, Junior would be all right with the girls to look after him. And then there's this: Of course I knew when Bob was married that he'd probably have children—and it's right, too—I wouldn't say this to a soul but you—for I *am* ashamed of it—but ever since the day Mabel told me her secret, and was so happy about it—poor child!—I've just *resented* the thought of being a grandmother. Why, Henry, I don't *feel* like a grand-mother, and I'm not ready to *be* one."

"I don't see any way to stop it, Mother."

Henry stole a surreptitious glance at a tempting editorial.

"Of course not!" Mother was too much in earnest to be frivolous. "But before I'm a grandmother—it'll be in July—I want to go back to Mount Carroll and be a girl again. If I could just get with that old crowd it would bring my youth all back, I know. I'd just live it over. Why, Henry, I'd give the price of the trip to have *five* minutes of real girlish thrill—"

"All right, Mother." Father boldly dismissed the subject. "You just plan to go and get your thrill."

In the busy weeks that followed Mother moved in an exalted state of mind, thinking of nothing but plans to leave the family comfortable and the exquisite pleasure before her. She wrote reams of messages to Julie Todd and Nettie Fisher and Myra Breckenridge and a dozen others. To be sure, they had all possessed other names for a quarter of a century, but Mother deigned to use them only on the outside of the envelopes.

There were clothes to be planned. Mother thought the town dressmaker could make her something suitable, but the girls protested.

"You're not going back there looking *dinky,* Mama, that's sure."

And Henry added his voice, "That's right, Mother; you doll up."

So Marcia and Mother journeyed to Capital City and chose a navy blue tailored suit, and a stunning black and white silk, and a soft gray chiffon gown, "in which she looks *perfectly Astorbiltish," Marcia afterward told the assembled family. These, with hat and gloves and a pair of expensive gray suede shoes that hurt her feet, but made them look like a girl's, came to a ghastly sum in three figures, so that Mother felt almost ill when she wrote on the check, "Henry Y. Mason, per Mrs. H. Y. M."

On the evening before the wonderful journey back to the Land of Youth, Father made his startling announcement. He had been reading quietly in his accustomed place by the library table. Mother, who had been putting pictures of all the family and views of the new house into her grip, came into the library.

"Mother"—Henry put down his magazine—"I've decided to go with you to-morrow and on to Midwestern while you are at Mount Carroll." Father's university was in a state farther east than Mother's Alma Mater. "When you get off at Oxford to change, I'll go right on, and then next Thursday, after Commencement, I'll be on the train coming back, and meet you there."

Mother was delighted, reproaching herself severely, in her tender-hearted way, for not having thought of the same thing. Father had attended to business so strictly all these years that this arrangement had not once occurred to her.

"I've been thinking what you said about seeing your old chums, and, by George! I'd enjoy it, too," Henry went on. "I can't think of anything more pleasurable than meeting Slim Reed and the Benson boys, and old Jim Baker."

So Father got his hat and went back to the bank to attend to some business; for with that nonchalant way a man has of throwing a clean collar into a grip preparatory to a long journey there was nothing for him to do at home.

Kind-hearted Mother's cup of joy was bubbling over. Happy moisture stood in her eyes as she got out Father's things. How well he deserved the trip!

Hurrying back into the library to get a late magazine for him to take along, her eyes fell upon the one he had just been reading. It was the Midwestern University Alumnus. Smiling, Mother picked it up. Under the heading "Class of '89"—that was Father's—there were a couple of commonplace items. Her eyes wandered on. "Class of '90." There was a clever call for a reunion signed by the Class Secretary, Laura Drew Westerman. Mother sat down heavily, and The Thing, after a long hibernating period, awoke and raised its scaly head.

Now, there is in the life of every married woman a faint, far-away, ghostly personage known as The Old Girl. Just how much they had meant to each other, Mother had never known. She did know that every spring and fall for twenty-six years she had cleaned out a box which contained, among other trinkets, an autograph album and a copy of Lucile and a picture of a dark-eyed girl in a ridiculously big-sleeved dress, all marked "To Henry from Laura." Laura Drew was Henry's old girl.

So from this lack of knowledge and the instinct inherited from primal woman had been hatched a little slimy creature, so unworthy of Mother that she had refused to call it by its real name. That had been years ago. With the coming of children and the passing of years, The Thing had shriveled up, both from lack of nourishment and because Mother laughed at it. A Thing like that cannot live in the white light of Humor. But now, quite stunned by the sudden surprise that The Thing was alive, she could only listen passively to what it was saying:

"So! even though he has been kind and loving and good and true to you," It said tragically, for It loves to be tragic, "*across the years she has called to him.*"

On the train the next day, Mother steeled herself to venture, quite casually: "I saw by your Alumnus last night that Laura Drew is to be there."

"Yes, I saw that, too," Father said simply, and the subject was dropped.

On the station platform at Oxford, Mother clung to Father's arm for just a second, he seemed so boyish and enthusiastic. She stood for several minutes by the side of her grips watching the train curve around the bend of the bluff, carrying Father down the road to youth—and Laura Drew.

Then, with characteristic good sense, she determined to put the thought completely out of her mind and devote herself to the resurrection of her own youth. So she walked energetically into the station, spread a paper on the dusty bench, and sat down. Her feet hurt her, but the trim girlish appearance of the gray suede shoes peeping out from under the smart suit was full compensation for all earthly ills.

A little gray-haired, washed-out woman in an out-of-date, limpsy suit was wandering aimlessly around the room. In the course of her ramblings she confronted Mother with a question concerning the train to Mount Carroll. Mother, in turn, interrogated the woman. *It was Julie!* Julie Todd, whose round, happy face Mother had crossed two states to see. Poor Mother!

After the first shock, she drew Julie down beside her on the bench and the two visited until their train came. Julie had no permanent home. Her husband, it seemed, had been unfortunate, first in losing the money his father had left him, and then in having his ability underestimated by a dozen or so employers. He was working just now for a dairyman—it was very hard on him, though—out in all sorts of weather.

There were seven children, unusually smart, too, but their father's bad luck seemed to shadow them. Joe, now, had been in the army, and had left camp for a little while—he had fully intended to go back; but the officers were very disagreeable and unjust about it. And on and on through an endless tale of grievances.

It was late afternoon when the train arrived at Mount Carroll. The station was a mass of moving students, class colors, arriving parents and old grads. Mother's spirits were high.

Em met them and took them to her pretty bungalow on College Hill. Em had never married. She was Miss Emmeline Livingston, head of the English Department, and she talked with the same pure diction to be found in "Boswell's Life of Johnson." Also, she was an ardent follower of a new cult which had for its main idea, as nearly as Mother could ascertain, the conviction that if you lost your money or your appetite or your reputation, you had a perfect right to believe that there had been chaos where there should have been cosmos.

Nettie Fisher and Myra Breckenridge had arrived that morning, and were there to greet Mother and Julie Todd. Nettie Fisher was a widow, beautifully gowned in black. She had enormous wealth; but the broken body of her only boy lay under the poppies in a Flanders' field, and she had come to meet these girlhood friends to try and find surcease for the ache that never stopped.

Myra Breckenridge had no children, dead or living. Her sole claims to distinction seemed to be that she was the champion woman bridge-player of her city, and that her bulldog had taken the blue ribbon for two consecutive years. She wore a slim, flame-colored dress cut on sixteen-year-old lines. Her fight with Time had been persistent, as shown by the array of weapons on her dressing table. But Time was beginning to fight with his back to the wall.

They made an incongruous little group, as far apart now as the stars and the seas; but it had not evidenced itself to Mother, who, with blind loyalty, told herself during dinner that a noticeable stiffness among them would soon wear off.

After dinner, Mother unpacked her grips and hung the pretty gowns in a cedar closet. But the photographs that had been packed with happy anticipation she left in the bag. It would be poor taste to display the views of her cherished sunparlor and fireplace and mahogany stairway to poor Julie, who had no home. It would be cruel to flaunt the photographs of all those lovely daughters and sturdy sons before Nettie, whose only boy had thrown down the flaming torch. So Mother closed the bag and went downstairs to meet the three boys of the old class who had come to call.

One of the boys was a fat judge, with a shining, bald head and a shining, round face behind shining, round tortoise-shell glasses. One was a small, wrinkled, dapper dry-goods merchant. And one was a tall doctor with a Van Dyke beard. This completed the reunion of the Class of '90.

There were numberless seats and chairs on the roomy porch of the bungalow, and it was there that they all sat down. The hour that followed was not an unqualified success. The reunion appeared not to be living up to its expectations. The old crowd was nothing but a group of middle-aged people who were politely discussing orthopedic hospitals and the reconstruction of Rheims. Occasionally, someone referred with forced jocularity to a crowd of jolly young folks they had once known. Ah, well! After all, you can't recapture Youth by trying to throw salt on its tail.

Sensing that things were lagging, Mother proposed that they walk up to the old school, with Em to show them around. They found a dozen unfamiliar buildings, an elaborate new home for the president, and a strange campanile pointing its finger, obelisk-like, to the blue sky. Only the green-sloping campus smiled gently at them like a kind old mother whose sweet face welcomed them home.

O̶n Monday they attended the literary societies' pageant. As the slowly moving lines of brilliantly costumed girls came into view, Mother's heart was throbbing in time to the notes of the bugle. With shining eyes she turned to the little widow.

"Nettie," she said solemnly, "we girls *started* this parade day."

"I know it. We all had big white tissue paper hats with pink roses on them—"

"And we stole the Beta's stuffed monkey so they wouldn't have a mascot—"

"And got up at four o'clock to pick clovers for the chain."

They had made the first chain, and now, gray-haired, they were standing on tiptoe at the edge of the crowd trying to catch a glimpse of the lithe, radiant, marching girls—Eternal Youth forever winding in and out under the shimmering leaves of the old oaks!

It was like that for three days. They seemed always to be on the outskirts of things, looking on. For three days they went everywhere together—class plays, receptions, ball games, musicals—this little lost flock of sheep. For three days Mother exerted herself to the utmost to catch one glimpse of the lost Youth of these men and women. Apparently they saw everything with mature vision, measured everything by the standard of a half-century's experience.

On the evening of the last day Mother gave up. She was through, she thought, as they all sat together on the porch. There was to be a concert by the united musical organizations, and the old crowd was ready to go and sit sedately through the last session. Very well, thought Mother, as she chatted and rocked, she would try no more. They were hopelessly, irrevocably middle-aged. She was convinced at last, disillusioned, she told herself. You can never, never recapture Youth.

Then, quite gradually, so that no one knew just how it began, there came a change. Someone said, "Remember, Myra, the night that red-headed Philomathian came to call on you, and we girls tied a picture of your home beau on a string and let it down through the stove-pipe hole into his lap?"

And someone else said, "Remember, Em, the time you had to read Hamlet's part in 'Shake' class and Professor Browning criticized you so severely, and then said, 'Now you may continue,' and you read in a loud voice, 'Well said, you old mole'?"

And the doctor said, "Remember, Jim, the note you pinned on your laundry to the washlady:

"If all the socks I've sent to thee
Should be delivered home to me,
Ah, well! the bureau would not hold
So many socks as there would be,
If all my socks came home to me"?

And before they were aware, they were going off into gales of laughter.

It came time for the concert, but no one suggested starting. Each succeeding anecdote heightened the merriment so that the undergrads streaming by said patronizingly, "Pipe the old duffers!"

"Remember, boys, the Hallowe'en we girls hid from you, and you had to furnish the supper because you didn't find us by nine o'clock?"

They all began talking at once about it, the men protesting that the girls had come out from the hiding place before nine.

"If you girls hadn't nigged on the time, we'd have found you," the men were arguing. There was a perfect bedlam of voices. Youth, which up to this time had eluded them, had slipped, slyly, unbidden, into their midst. Mother was thrilling to her finger tips.

"It was a night almost as warm as this," the judge said, "and the moon was as gorgeous as it is to-night."

Mother, in the stunning black and white silk, jumped to her feet.

"Let's do it again!" she cried with an impulsive sweep of her hands. "Tonight! It's the nearest to Youth we'll ever come in our whole lives." She turned to the men on the steps. "The rules are the same, boys. Give us fifteen minutes' start, and if you can't find us by nine, we'll come back here and you'll buy the supper. If you find us, we'll buy it. Come on, girls."

As Joan of Arc may have led her armies, so Mother's power over the others seemed to hold. In a wave of excitement, they rose to her bidding. Light of foot, laughing, the five women hurried across one corner of the campus. In the shadow of the oaks Mother stopped them.

"Is the same house still standing?" she asked breathlessly of Em.

"Yes, but others are built up around it now."

"Come on, then!" With unerring feet, down to the same house where they had hidden twenty-nine years before, Mother led them.

"What if someone sees us?" giggled Nettie.

"We should worry!" said the head of the English Department, which was really the most remarkable thing that happened that night.

There it was—a house no longer new—but still standing, and as dark as the others near it. Evidently the occupants had gone to the concert. By the light of the moon they could see its high cellar window, still yawning foolishly open, waiting for them, just as it had waited before.

Against the window they placed a sloping board and climbed slowly up, one by one. Em went first, then Myra, and Nettie, and Julie, and, last, Mother. At least, Mother's intentions were good. The window was about eighteen by twenty; and Mother, quite eighteen by twenty herself, stuck half way in and half way out. Up the street they could hear the old whistle—the boys calling to each other. Laughing hysterically, tugging desperately at her, the other four, after strenuous labor, pulled Mother down into the cellar, where, groping around in the dark, she found the cellar stairs and sat down. They were all shaking with laughter-spasms, that kind of digestion-aiding laughter which comes less often according to the ratio of the number of years you are away from Youth.

For some time, whispering and giggling nervously and saying "Sh!" constantly to each other, they sat in the black cellar.

Suddenly, an electric light snapped on over Mother's head and the door above her opened. "What are you doing in my cellar?" snarled a voice as gruff as the biggest bear's in "Goldilocks."

The giggling died as suddenly as though it had been chloroformed.

Cold as ice, Mother rose and faced the darkness above her. Then she said with all her Woman's Club dignity—which is a special de luxe brand of dignity—"If you will allow us to come up there I think we can make a very satisfactory explanation."

"You can explain to the town marshal," answered the sour voice, and the owner of it slammed the door.

They sat down dismally and waited. They heard the telephone ring and then the wooden shutter of the cellar window was banged down and fastened.

"He needn't have done *that*," Mother said stiffly. It is claimed that housebreakers are often sensitive about their honor.

During the long wait every fiber of Mother's brain concentrated on one word—*disgrace*. If the papers got hold of it! Even if they wrote it up as a joke! Imagine—to be written up as a joke at fifty-two!

There were footsteps overhead, and then the gruff voice, "Come up out of there now!"

Slowly they filed up the narrow dark stairs. Mother went first. As she had led them into this sickening dilemma, so would she be the first to face the music.

"May we have some lights?" she asked frigidly.

"Certainly."

Lights were turned on. Three men stood there: A fat one with tortoise-shell glasses; a little, wrinkled, dapper one, and a tall one with a Van Dyke beard—all fiery red from silent convulsions brought on by ingrowing laughter. As the women filed in, the pent-up laughter rolled forth from the men in shrieks and howls. Then the shouting and the tumult died, for Nettie and Julie were smothering the fat one with someone's sofa pillows, Myra and Em were taking care of the bearded one, and Mother was shaking the little one, while he motioned feebly with his hands that he was ready for peace.

"Kamarad!" gasped the fat judge when he could get his breath. "Anyway, you'll admit we were speaking the truth when we said we could have found you."

"Now, let's dig out," said the doctor, whose respiratory organs were again working, "before the folks that own this house come home from the concert and send us all up."

Breaking out into hilarious laughter at intervals, they walked down to the store at the foot of the hill, and there the girls bought a lunch to make angels weep. It consisted of buns, bananas, wienies, chocolate candy, and dill pickles.

Across pastures, crawling under barbwire fences, went the cavalcade, to build a bonfire down by old Salt Creek. Gone were the years and the family ties. Forgotten were the hours of failure and the hours of triumph. They were the old crowd, singing "Solomon Levi." Youth was in their midst. And the moon, bored to the point of *ennui,* at the countless hordes of students it had seen roasting wienies in that identical spot, brightened at the novel sight of the old duffers taking hold of hands to dance around the huge fire.

As chimes from the campanile striking twelve came faintly through the night, Youth suddenly dropped her festive garments and fled, a Cinderella that could not stay.

The little straggling procession started soberly back across the meadow. Julie's rheumatism was beginning to manifest itself. The head of the English Department was painfully aware that in the place where she had stowed that awful collection of indigestibles there was chaos where there should have been cosmos. Far, far behind the others came the judge and Mother; not from any sentimental memory of their past friendship, but because, being possessors of too, too solid flesh, they were frankly puffed-out.

F̲ather swung off the steps of the train at Oxford and took Mother's bags.

"Well, did you get your thrill, Mother?"

"I most certainly did." Mother was smiling to herself.

They walked down the Pullman to Father's section, which he had chosen with careful regard to Mother's comfort.

"And you—did you have a good time?" Mother questioned when they were seating themselves.

"Fine—just fine!" Father was enthusiasm personified.

A quick little tug at Mother's heart reminded her that The Thing was still alive.

"Were there many of your old classmates back?" she parried, giving herself time to bring out the real question.

"Two, just two." Father was glowing at the happy memory of some unuttered thing. "Just old Jim Baker and I. Jim's kind of down and out—works around the University Cafeteria."

"Was—?" It was coming. Mother braced herself. "Was Laura Drew there?"

"Yes." Father's face shone with the light of unspoken pleasure. "Yes, she was there."

The Thing seemed to bite at Mother's throat and wrap a strangling tail around her heart. With the pleasure with which we turn the knife in our wounds, she asked in a tense little voice:

"Is she—does she seem the same?"

Father drew his rapt gaze from some far-away vision to look at Mother.

"The same?" he repeated, a trifle dazed. Then he said cheerfully, "Why—maybe—I don't know. I didn't see her."

"Didn't *see* her?"

"No. I didn't see much of anybody." Father grew confidential. "The fact is, old Jim Baker and I played checkers 'most all the time for the three days. He got off every morning at eleven and we'd go around to his room. By George! It was nip and tuck for two days. But the last day—*I beat him.*"

"*Checkers!*" Mother breathed but the one word, but the ingredients of which it was composed were incredulity, disgust, merriment, and several dozen others.

Then she laughed, a bubbling, deliciously girlish laugh, and the Thing relaxed its hold on her heart, turned up its toes, and died.

Surreptitiously, Mother reached down and pulled off the expensive suede shoes. "Now," she announced, "there's one grateful bunion in the world."

Then she fixed herself for the long ride to the West. "Henry," she laid a plump hand on Father's arm, "you are *such* a comfort to me. Won't it be nice to get home and settle down to being a grandfather and a grandmother?"

A Long-Distance Call from Jim

The theme of "A Long Distance Call from Jim," which appeared in the August 1919 issue of *The American Magazine,* would be reworked in a later issue of the same magazine (August 1923), in "Meadows Entertains a Celebrity," and in the *Ladies Home Journal* (September 1934) story "Welcome Home, Hal." All three narratives feature characters who admit to a sense of embarrassment about being "small town," followed by recognition of how good such towns really are. Aldrich was a staunch defender of the people who lived in small towns and whose virtues and foibles she knew so well.

To Ella Nora Andrews, calm, unruffled, serenely humming a gay little tune, gathering her school things together—her "Teacher's Manual of Primary Methods," a box of water-colors, and a big bunch of scarlet-flamed sumac—came the sound of the telephone.

Ella Nora, in her crisp blue linen school suit, shifted her working paraphernalia and took down the receiver. Fate is a veritable chameleon for changing shape and color. This morning she had entered the fat, puffy person of asthmatic Mrs. Thomas Tuttle, and was saying:

"That you, Ella? Have you heard the news? Jim Sheldon is coming here the last of the week. He'll be here on Number Eight, Friday afternoon. And get ready now for the climax—he's bringing his bride. Wha' say? Yes, his *wife.* He telephoned Pa from Chicago—imagine anybody telephoning clear from Chicago, Ella! He's waited long enough to get married, I must say. He's thirty-six, if he's a day. I know, because my Eddie's just two months older. Well, we must do something for them, and we'll have to get busy right away. Wha' say? All right; I'll ask Addie Smith and Minnie Adams and Mis' Meeker—she's forever thinking of things to eat—" And on and on went the rasping, wheezing voice of Fate, while, through the window, Ella watched the red and yellow and orange zinnias in the back yard fade and run together into a smudge of prismatic coloring.

Ella hung up the receiver and leaned against the window. There was a pounding in her throat, and she couldn't seem to concentrate her thoughts. The zinnias had brightened somewhat, but were still dancing diabolically with the cosmos behind them. From the chaotic jumble of her mind the naked, leering truth picked itself out: It had happened at last—Jim was married. By which statement one gathers, and rightfully, that Ella had in some indefinable way been prepared for the news she had just heard.

In truth, Ella had been preparing for it for years. She was thirty-one now, and from her twentieth year she had been working consistently on an elaborate defense system that surrounded her heart.

Patiently she had dug the trench of an apparent and complete absorption in her school work. She had piled around it countless sand bags of mere-friendliness toward Jim, put up an intricate entanglement of the barb wire of her sharp wit, and over it all painted the deceiving screen of her evident joy-in-her-freedom. But down under all this complicated protective system was The-Thing-In-Her-Heart, palpitating, vital, strong, held a prisoner for years by the stern edict of her mind, doing penance for having been unwise enough to go wandering out into No Man's Land of Dreams.

Ella waited while the zinnias separated themselves from their background. It had happened. Of course! Hadn't she expected it? Predicted it? James Warren Sheldon, on the staff of an Eastern newspaper, war correspondent, nationally known this past year, was no more a part of land-locked Centerville now than the moon or the North Sea. It had been three years since he had last come breezing into town—tall, lean, brown, virile. Not a day of that short vacation had they missed being together—Ella caught her breath. So this was what Tennyson meant, was it, when he said a sorrow's crown of sorrow as remembering happier days?

The first school-bell rang. When Duty takes Misery by the shoulder and says gruffly, "Oh, cut it! Come on!" so much the better for Misery.

Ella went quickly down the narrow brick walk, leaf strewn now with the red and gold of the Mid-west maple trees, and turned toward the schoolhouse where she had taught for, it seemed to her now, a half-century. Down the street a little girl disentangled her pipe-stem legs from the picket fence and slipped a moist hand into Ella's.

"Miss-sAndrews, where do all the grasshoppers go?"

"I don't know, dear."

Back in the past was Ella's mind, down Childhood Road. She was only eight when Jim Sheldon, a big thirteen-year-old boy, newly orphaned, had come to live across the alley with his aunt and uncle and their little baby, Grace. For years Jim had meant nothing to her but a dreadful scourge, to be borne with as much Christian fortitude as the boils of Job. One of his delicate marks of attention had been a way of dropping unexpectedly out of trees with a weird shriek just at dusk. Ella smiled involuntarily; and the little girl, seeing it, hugged her teacher's hand to her cheek:

"Miss-sAndrews, can you make white cookies out of brown dough?"

"No, dear."

Then there had followed Jim's high-school years, in which he had meant nothing to her, and she had been as unnoticed by Jim as the stilts or velocipede he had discarded. He had gone away to college, and later she to a teachers' training-school, and one unforgettable summer they had accidentally discovered that they held more in common than with anyone else in dull old Centerville. Then Mother died, and from teaching in Capitol City, where she was meeting new people and having new experiences, she had come back home to keep house for Father, and to teach in the same old dingy building where she herself had studied.

"Miss-sAndrews, my birthday's next July, or April—I forget which."

"That's nice, dear."

But Jim, after a few months on the Centerville "Enterprise," had gone out into the world, the journalistic world, and pushed rapidly ahead. Several important commissions had been his. He had written her once from Cuba, and once from Japan. A sudden bitterness seized her, that it could be so—Jim to go where he would and she to stay in stagnant old Centerville.

"Miss-sAndrews, do skunks live in this town?"

"Oh, no, dear!"

This last year the whole country had read Jim's war reports, and at rare intervals she had received a letter from him, interesting and friendly. In the last one he had said he had something to tell her when he got back. Well, *this* was it! And she had wondered—had let herself think that it might mean—A wave of fury, a sense of the loss of her self-respect, swept over her, that she should have allowed her heart to go philandering.

They were at the schoolhouse now. Ella took off her wide blue hat and hung it in the little closet. Then she went over to the corner blackboard and wrote the memory verse for the day:

Goldenrod, what have I learned from you?
To be cheerful and loving, gentle and true.

"Hypocrite!" she said savagely.

The other four women were at Mrs. Tom Tuttle's when Ella arrived. The Tuttle house was very new and displayed a great deal of yellow pine with a varnish smell. Some of the details of the new furnishings, including several lurid fruit pieces in oil, jumped at Ella as she sat down in the shining depths of a golden-oak rocker. Among other bric-a-brac, a painted celluloid collar box of Tom Tuttle's, that had evidently been thought too artistic to be relegated to a mere bedroom, held an advantageous place on the glossy colonade. No better-hearted people than Centerville held were to be found in the whole world admitted Ella to herself as she gazed, fascinated, at the receptacle which had wandered out of Tom Tuttle's boudoir. But *why* did so many of them have such atrocious taste?

There was immediate discussion as to what form of social event Jim's entertainment should take. Mrs. Tom Tuttle wanted an evening party, with all the men, women and children in town.

"I just feel like we couldn't do enough for Jim Sheldon and his bride," she wheezed, her chin trembling and her eyes filling with tears. Emotion of any description—joy, pathos, surprise, sorrow, it made no difference—always set her tear ducts to working.

Mrs. Meeker wanted a real supper with long tables and everybody sitting down at once. To Mrs. Meeker, earth held no sorrow that food could not heal, and life's sweetest moment was the one in which some neighbor said, "I just know this is Mis' Meeker's salad."

"It will be late afternoon when they get here," she argued, "and I'll bet supper would taste mighty good to 'em."

"Supper!" Minnie Adams was witheringly scornful. "Jim Sheldon eats *dinner* at night now."

"Well, I don't care if he does! I can remember the time when he et a good old-fashioned supper. And it's awful silly to call it dinner. 'Breakfast, dinner and supper, created He them.' I believe I could find them very words in the Bible if I set out to hunt."

"What would we serve if we had—an evening meal?" Addie Smith asked hurriedly. Addie was little and pretty and, like many another ultra-pacifist, was mentally a nonentity, the echo of an echo. But she was the doctor's wife and she had more cut glass and china than anyone else in town.

"Potatoes for one thing." Mrs. Meeker was on familiar ground. "I've got a new way; I learned it from Jennie Rhodes when she visited me, and I intended to spring it on the Kensington; but I'm like Mis' Tuttle, nothing's too good for Jim Sheldon and his bride. First, you mash 'em—"

"Jim and his bride?" Ella inquired languidly.

"Oh, you go on, Ella!—and then you put 'em on the plate with an ice-cream mold, and there they stand up just as cute, like little pyramids with a clove at the top."

"A clove! Why, a clove? Why not a clothespin, or a prune? Is there a clove on the top of the pyramids?" Ella's apparently unquenchable spirits were rising.

Minnie Adams insisted on a reception in the town hall. Minnie was very tall and seemed to get thinner toward the top. Even her neck was larger at the base and very long, as though Nature in an absent-minded mood had forgotten what she was doing and gone on making neck.

"But, Minnie," Ella interposed diplomatically, "a reception is so stiff. At least it would be stiff for informal Centerville people to give."

"Oh, I don't think so—and it would show her that we know how to do things right. She's probably a New York girl—or she may be French, for all we know. Good land! I hope not. We'd have to motion out everything we had to say. Anyway, a reception wouldn't be stiff when we got it to going good."

"How do you stop it when you do get it to going?" Mrs. Tuttle wanted to know.

"Maybe it would be like Mrs. Whitman in her new electric car over at Greenwood," Ella suggested. "She couldn't stop it, you know. She went round and round the garage all afternoon calling out to the men every time she went by. And they couldn't make out what she said, and thought she was just showing off."

Everyone laughed. Ella, apparently, was the gayest of all.

"It would be nice to have a picture of Jim up," Addie Smith suggested timidly. As it was Addie's first contribution to the general reserve fund of ideas it should have been met with more respect, but it only called forth from Ella: "Horrors! Addie! You'll be wanting to paste his war articles up on the walls of the hall."

"Speaking of the hall," Mrs. Meeker put in, "I think a lot of Japanese umbrellas and lanterns could be fixed to cover the walls, they're so dingy—"

"And, maybe, we could get Sam Fong to come up and stand under them for atmosphere." It was Ella again, making the others laugh. "Thank goodness, I'll always be like that," she thought to herself, as though she had just made a discovery. "Outside I'll always be gay and silly."

Minnie Adams won. It was to be a reception. Tom Tuttle was to go to the train and get the guests in his car. Minnie had sniffed to herself over this particular detail, Tom's car being of that make which carries a very modest price and a very immodest notoriety. But as Tom had been honored with the telephone message from Jim, there was nothing to do but submit.

If Jim and his wife chose to change their clothes, Tom was to stop with them at his house, and then bring them on over to the hall. There were several hundred other details connected with the soirée, definitely planned, so that the whole thing would move, barrage-like, with the precision of clockwork. For genuine leadership, Marshal Foch had nothing on Mrs. Thomas Tuttle.

Ella found herself swept along on the tidal wave of preparations, hating it, heartsick, loathing the attempt of these kind, simple folk to make of themselves something they were not.

The receiving line was to have been composed of the five who had met at Mrs. Tuttle's, but Ella balked. If this horrible thing had to be, she, at least, didn't purpose to be a member of the shock troops. She compromised by agreeing to take charge of the frappé bowl, far in the rear of the long hall.

On Friday afternoon the old hall over Hodge's Dry Goods Emporium looked, as the "Enterprise" would later describe it, "a bower of loveliness." Under Ella's direction the school children had magnanimously brought in half the maple leaves and at least two-thirds of the blazing sumac in the precinct.

Red-faced, puffy Mrs. Tom Tuttle had on a dark purple silk which gave her the appearance of being about to expire from an apoplectic stroke. Tall, angular Minnie Adams, with an aigrette from her last winter's hat in her hair, had, in defiance of Biblical axiom, by taking thought added a cubit to her stature. Mrs. Meeker's best black silk was slightly awry from much journeying to and fro between the sandwich table and the coffee pot. Addie Smith had on a really beautiful gown purchased at Capitol City.

"If she only doesn't say 'have saw,' " thought Ella.

Ella, herself, was in white—a dainty, sheer dress which she carried with that little indefinable air that no one else in Centerville possessed.

"You look like a bride yourself, Ella." Mrs. Meeker paused in one of her breathless flittings to the kitchen. "I wish to the land it *was* you—you'd 'a' made Jim a real smart wife."

"Ah, madam, I thank you!" Ella bowed in mock solemnity and then laughed gaily, while The-Thing-In-Her-Heart winced and moaned.

The assemblage was noticeably lacking in masculinity. To be sure, a few brave souls were there—Doctor Smith and old Judge Adams and the two ministers and the editor of the "Enterprise." But not for the President of the United States would the majority of the Centerville men have gone through that boiled-shirt ordeal.

It was almost time now. The receiving line nervously eyed the chalk marks which designated the exact spot where, in a few moments, it was to function.

The train whistled in. That was the cue for several dozen different things. Ella's particular response to this signal was to go down two flights of stairs to the cellar under the dry-goods store and bring up part of the cold frappé, which had been packed since noon in an ice-filled tub, as the ice from the old frog pond was too dirty to put into the beverage. She did her assigned task, and then, with taut nerves stood by the rear window of the hall and looked out over the dismal array of boxes and barrels and sheds, waiting—

At a slight commotion on the stairway, she breathed a little prayer for composure and walked over to take her place at the frappé bowl. Even so walked Marie Antoinette out onto the balcony at Versailles.

They were coming in. There was Jim, taller, leaner, browner, his head thrown back with that familiar air, and the boyish smile she knew so well. And—that—*beautiful* girl! She was not over twenty-two or three, lithe, lovely, radiant. She was in gray, a soft, exquisite pearl gray. From the tips of her slender gray-shod feet and the tips of her slender gray-gloved hands to the drooping dove-winged hat, she was perfection.

Jim was shaking hands with Mrs. Tuttle, while his wife stood waiting with a pretty air of shy interest, until, with a protective gesture, he drew her forward.

Ella's feet and hands were cold and her cheeks blazing. She did not know that, in the heightened color of her fair skin, the soft waves of her hair, the cornflower blue of her eyes, and the lovely contour of her face, she was as beautiful as the young girl she envied.

She only knew that everything was going wrong. Mrs. Tuttle, in her atrocious purple dress, had bounced out of the receiving line, thrown her massive arms around the girl and kissed her. Ella shuddered. From experience, she knew what a combustion it had been.

The whole line was breaking up. Everyone was laughing immoderately. She could hear Minnie Adams's high henlike cackle, and Mrs. Meeker's base rumble that always sounded as though she were using a megaphone. And after a few minutes Jim would bring that exquisite creature back here to meet *her* and to drink iceless punch. How characteristic of Centerville was that dirty frog-pond ice! The whole thing was horrible. They were frog-pond ice people, doing things in a frog-pond way. Oh, she was ashamed of Centerville, ashamed of Mrs. Tom Tuttle's effusion, ashamed of her own handmade dress that she had thought so dainty in its white laciness. The girl would laugh at them all. And Jim—because he loved her—Jim would laugh with her. She *could* not endure it!

"Georgiana!" she called to a young girl who had come up the back stairway. "Georgiana Meeker! I'm going to run down and see about the rest of the frappé. Will you come and take charge of the bowl, please?" Some of life's bitterest moments are also its politest.

Ella did not pause until she was in the kind, if cobwebby, seclusion of the cellar. Good sense told her that she would have to go back to face the music eventually, but, for a few moments, away from prying eyes, she would nurse and cuddle the hurt little-girl heart of her. Mechanically, like all faithful souls who work while they grieve, she picked up a chunk of ice to replenish the melting supply in the tub.

Two blue serge legs were coming down the narrow stairway. They seemed to be bringing Jim Sheldon with them. He had to duck his head to get through the doorway. "Where are you, Ella Norer, I adore 'er?"

The little half-dark, wholly dusty cellar seemed electrically charged with the sheer vitality of his presence. He was coming toward her with both hands out. Nervously, Ella dropped the ice. According to laws immutable, the tendency of all falling objects is to descend in a perpendicular line. The frappé was at the lower end of the perpendicular line. Further, in accordance with another of nature's laws that no two objects may occupy the same place at a given time, several quarts of frappé politely slopped out to make way for the ice.

"Oh, Jim!" she said feebly. "I've spoiled the frappé. That was ice from the old frog pond."

He threw back his head and laughed.

"What's a frog or two between friends, Ellanora?" He ran the words of the name together musically, so that they sounded like a caress.

Together they fished out the ice, and after that, with an immaculate handkerchief, he wiped the spots on her dress and dried her hands comfortably.

Then, quite suddenly, a singular thing happened. James Warren Sheldon, somewhat worldly-wise, wholly capable of taking care of himself, plainly embarrassed, dropped Ella's hands. With the way of femininity since the world began, Ella immediately became mistress of the situation.

"It seems nice to see you, Jim. We're all so glad that you took time to come to us. She's a darling—and *so* pretty."

"Isn't she? And she's as sweet as she is pretty." Jim's temporary discomfiture had vanished. "Poor little girl! Her mother died first, and then her daddy was killed in an auto accident the first time I was in France. When I got back, she seemed to cling to me so—"

So that was the way it happened! Wasn't that just like kind-hearted Jim? To Ella there came the fleeting vision of her own independent self. No, assuredly, she had not been of the clinging type.

"Ella, I'm wondering if you'll do something for me. Could you—would it be inconvenient—could I leave her here with you for a few days while I go on a short business trip? She needs mothering so badly; and while you seem a perfect kid to me in most ways, you've always seemed motherly, too. Gee! I remember one time when I busted my head and you spilled liniment and tears all over me." They both laughed, and for a moment Ella gave no thought to the difficult task before her.

Suddenly, Jim caught one of her hands in both of his. "Ella, I didn't seem to realize what you meant to me—until I got out there—in Flanders! Queer, how everything fell away from me out there but the things that count! I always thought a lot of you, but I supposed it was just a good friendship. When it came to me—so clear—its full meaning—I knew if I lived to get back to you I'd tell you what a mistake I had made, and how much I had always cared."

The creeping, crawling horror in Ella's mind twisted around her heart and clutched, biting, at her throat, so that she put her free hand up to it. Not that! Surely not *that*—when it was too late. It wasn't worthy of Jim to talk like this! It was an unbearable thing to see him fall from his pedestal of Right and Honor. Love was big, but Love's ideal was bigger.

She seized the lapels of his coat and spoke swiftly: "Jim, don't say it! As you care for our friendship and the days gone by, never *think* it again—never *think* of thinking it! I did care—and perhaps you did too, and didn't realize it. But that's over. That had to do with your heart; but the thing you've just said now has to do with your *soul!* and—"

"Ella,"—he put his hands over her own that were tugging desperately at his coat, and gave them a little shake—"what are you talking about?"

"Oh, the *immeas*urable wrong of your saying that! After you're married!"

There was a lightning-like change of expression on Jim's face. "Good lord, Ella! I'm not married!" He seemed divided between merriment and the seriousness of the moment. "That's Grace—little Gracie Sheldon, my kid cousin. Do you mean you weren't upstairs when we first came in and straightened matters out? Such a pow-wow!" Jim was laughing boyishly. "It was certainly rich! I thought the dear old souls would eat her up. And you should have seen Grace and Georgiana Meeker fall on each other's necks. It was Tom Tuttle's mistake, and mine too. If I had called her 'Grace' over the 'phone, he'd have known, I suppose, but I said 'Miss Sheldon,' as I naturally call her to other people. And Tom, of course, thought 'Mis' Sheldon' was a newly-acquired bride."

It is a very dizzying process—taking an emotional plunge like that. It left Ella very weak and limp, both physically and mentally.

Jim put his hand under her chin and lifted her scarlet face, but she would not raise her eyes. "No, Ellanora, I'm not married—and you said you cared."

"That was said under—under—a—misconception—of—"

"I'll grant that—but it can never be unsaid." He dropped his voice to its tenderest tone. "Say it again, Ellanora; *without* any misunderstanding."

She lifted the lids from love-brimming eyes: "Oh, Jim! I—I do care."

So it came about that the guest of honor climbed up two flights of stairs a little later, carrying the frappé to his own party. And Ella followed to kiss shyly the familiar-strange little neighbor-girl who had grown into such a charming young lady. Then, with prickly little chills chasing up and down her spine, and her cheeks ablaze, she served to the perspiring multitude a great deal of frappé permanently weakened by several quarts of well-water.

And always, no matter where she was looking, she could see Jim looming up above everyone, shaking hands, laughing; could hear him saying, "Auntie Tuttle, you certainly look good to *me*." And, "Mrs. Meeker, I'll bet forty cents these are your sandwiches. They're worth a trip half around the world."

Oh, the deliciousness of the secret! The surprise of Centerville! Jim had said he would give her just two weeks to get ready, had scouted her notion of finishing the school year, had said she didn't need any new clothes, that they had a *few* dresses left down in New York. Oh, the exquisite joy of knowing she was going with Jim! Everywhere—anywhere! Honolulu, Hongkong, the moon!

With brimming heart Ella looked at the noisy crowd about her. How kind everyone seemed! What a good old place Centerville was! She was recklessly unashamed of a dozen children who had taken possession of a temporarily abandoned sandwich table and were breaking world records in cramming down the spoils; was shamelessly unabashed when old Sandy Wing, over-alled, coal-grimed, wiping his face with a red bandana, came up the back stairway to wring Jim's hand; was audaciously laughter-stricken—with Jim—when Mrs. Meeker hissed across at her, "My good *land* of liberty Ella, there's a lot of little sticks and leaves in the bottom of this frappé bowl!"

The Two Who Were Incompatible

In this story, from *McCall's* (August 1919), Aldrich provides some fun between the Scottish and the Irish, two of her favorite nationalities. She later recasts her Scottish grandmother in *A Lantern in Her Hand* (New York: D. Appleton & Company, 1928) as an Irish woman.

In "The Two Who Were Incompatible," as in "Miss Livingston's Nephew" (1918), the young woman is an assistant supervisor in a primary training school (teachers' college).

An "unco guid mon" of Edinburgh named Douglas Mackenzie once wooed and won Teresa O'Conor amid the whins and silver-hazels of Ballyporeen. Several generations later, the good saints up in high heaven's court gave the couple three chances each to mold the life of a descendant—a baby girl—just born upon the earth.

Douglas Mackenzie first crowned her with hair like the mists around the mountains of Glencoe, when the sun shines through, and immediately Teresa O'Conor gave her eyes the color of the blue-black waters at Kilkee. Then the man, remembering sensibly that the outward appearance is not all, endowed her with a stable, thrifty, Scotch mind, but the woman smiled and slipped an Irish heart into her. For a long time Douglas pondered cannily how he might wisely use his last chance and finally gave her the sturdiest of square Scotch chins, but Teresa laughed and pressed a roguish V-shaped cleft right in the center of it.

Foolishly practical folks there are who will not believe this, but here, on a Sunday afternoon, twenty-six years later, sat Peggy Mackenzie with her misty Glencoe hair and her blue-black Kilkee eyes and her gay granny's dimple in the middle of her "dour grandfaither's" chin. Sure! And what more proof could a body be needin'?

The room where Peggy Mackenzie sat was the rattan-furnished guest-chamber of a shiningly new bungalow, and Peggy was the guest—the very welcome guest—of her old schoolmate, Maxine Haynes, who had been married to Ed Haynes, for one year and three weeks.

Peggy was allowing herself two days of frivolity and then she was going to take the car out to the State College, find a room and boarding place and report for duty as Assistant Supervisor of the primary training school. Sitting in front of the dressing-table and applying a buffer vigorously to her pink nails, she was thinking of the good fortune that had given her a position in the little city where her old chum lived, when Maxine herself came in and dropped down on the rattan-covered cedar chest.

"Peggy," she began, rather breathlessly, "while you're here there is something you must guard against. Please don't interrupt," she begged as Peggy raised wide eyes to hers, "let me explain." And she went on to explain that the something to guard against was one Newton Collins, aged thirty-six, a lawyer, the town's most eligible bachelor—and her husband's best friend. His Sundays were always spent at the Haynes bungalow, and the Haynes' guests of feminine persuasion were always fascinated by him. In fact, two girls had gone away not exactly brokenhearted, but, to say the least, sorry they had come. "And, oh Peggy," Maxine finished, "I was just sick about it—Ed tried to make light of it—but to have a girl visit me and go away *hurt!*"

"Maxie!" Peggy had flown off her chair in a twittering, birdlike way and was across the little room. "Maxie! See here—why are you *warning me?* Don't you know that I'm perfectly immune? I haven't time even to think of a man. I'm wrapped up in my work, completely, irrevocably. Truly, there *is* such a thing as being 'wedded to your art.' No deaconess or missionary ever entered her chosen life-work—or nun her cloister for that matter—with higher ideals than mine. This sounds silly to you I suppose, but think of it, Maxie, seventy-five girls to train this year—in ten years about a thousand. They will go out to influence—we'll say two hundred pupils each. It's like the pebble you know, and the waves—and there's two hundred thousand people I'm to influence."

"My stars! Peggy, you sound like a government bulletin." At which they both laughed and, hearing voices, went out to greet the guest.

Isaac Newton Collins was large and looked lazy, until one discovered that he seldom made unnecessary motions. There could not have been a more complete contrast than the passive-appearing, slow-speaking Collins and the animated Peggy.

That night in the privacy of their white-enameled, delft-blue bedroom, Ed Haynes remarked laconically to his wife: "Newt didn't cotton to her, did he?"

"As much as she did to him," Maxine came to the rescue of her sex. "Did you hear them argue? That's one thing about Peggy. She's no clinging vine. You can trust *her* to hold her own and take care of herself—even with a self-contained, leading lawyer."

"It strikes me she was a little sassy to Newt. He won't stand for that. I lived with him long enough to know that no little snip can tell *him* where to get off." In a moment he added: "Isn't she the young cyclone? Gives me a headache. I never saw anyone bob around and chatter so much."

Unenlightened people there may be who do not know that an assistant supervisor of a primary training-school is a very busy person—except on Sundays. At Maxine's urgent invitation, Peggy came regularly for lunch on that particular day. And, of course, even if you are "wedded to your art," it becomes an unavoidable condition that you must at least hold the usual polite superficial converse with your very best friend's husband's best friend.

It was a queer relationship which existed between Collins and Peggy. Thrown together by a common interest in their two friends, they seemed in some paradoxical way to be genial enemies. Peggy tried conscientiously to treat Collins with the same manner that served her for all masculinity—the new physical director and the janitor and President Welch and the night-watchman. That manner was two-thirds affable, one-third pert, and wholly independent, but with Collins it usually deteriorated into being all pert.

"I'm usually as canny as Scots 'wha hae wi' Wallace bled,' but when I get near you, you rouse all the Irish in me," she told him frankly.

"That's because you are such an inconsistent child," he said coolly.

"I am *not!* *You're* the inconsistent—" Peggy was waxing too hot to finish her sentences. "And you needn't call me a child, either."

"But you're acting like one, you know," he returned placidly, "a hot-headed little girl who has lost her temper." And then they argued about that.

If the weather was such that Collins could be out in his car, he would, as a matter of courtesy, drive around to get her. If he hadn't got the machine out, Peggy would catch the five or six o'clock car downtown, and just about the time Collins was asking, "Where's the cranberry merchant?" or "What's become of Busy-Izzy?" she would breeze gaily in. Five minutes later the two would be disagreeing about the greatest international problem of the day or the most insignificant trifle imaginable.

"Can't you have her come some other night in the week?" Ed wanted to know one evening, after their guests had left. "Newt doesn't like her. They argue and scrap all the time. I've never heard them agree on a single thing."

"Well, I guess not," Maxine was firm. "You try asking *Newt* for another night. Anyway it does him good to have someone around he doesn't like—it's character strengthening. And that's Peggy's one restful day."

"Restful!" Ed was plainly sarcastic. "She's about as restful as a whirling dervish."

With the incompatibility of the two in mind, it was with some misgivings, that the Haynes announced, on a sparkling Sunday, that they must be off immediately after lunch to make Great-Aunt Bell's birthday call. They had forgotten the day entirely until too late for the usual morning visit.

"But you people make yourself 'to hum,'" Ed insisted.

"And be sure to pull the night-latch when you leave," Maxine added.

"Now they can scrap it out," Ed chuckled as they went down the front walk.

The Haynes need not have been unduly concerned. Fifteen minutes after they had gone the two most incompatible people in the world sat in front of the fire-place and the level-headed one had asked the hot-headed one to marry him. To be sure, a hand grenade would have split up the furniture and made unmendable cavities in the hardwood floor and beamed ceiling, but it couldn't have been more of a shock. The proverbial "bolt from the blue" was nothing compared with this.

Peggy raised startled, amazed eyes to Collins and then dropped them immediately, for it is not given to femininity to look unabashed into the muzzle of "The Great Question." She regained her poise almost immediately and said "Oh, no! No, indeed. I couldn't do that. Not at all." Which was, of course, three noes more than she needed to have said.

Collins studied the knuckles of his right hand for a moment and then asked "Why?"

"Well, if you *must* have reasons, in the first place I don't care for you that way and—in the second place I'm completely wrapped up in my work and—"

"And—? Go on."

"I don't like to—but—yes, I will. I want to show my family that there's one member in it that has stability."

"Stability?"

"Yes. It seems dreadful for me to slander them in this way when I love them so. But it's true—I belong to a family of women who have no minds of their own." Her words came with a rush. "They all lack decision and they're a lot of looking-glasses, if you know what I mean. I have three sisters—all married. Take Alice—if Will thinks the Democratic party is going to pieces, you'll hear Alice telling someone in what an awful shape the Democratic party is. Once, in the literary club, when the president asked Marion just *why* she thought Bacon wrote the Shakespeare plays, she said because Roger thought so. I was *so* ashamed." Her cheeks turned pinker with the memory of it. "You see what Mary's-little-lamb-minds they all have. They don't know what strength of mind or firmness of purpose means. They're spineless, jelly-fish women, sweet and lovable and all that, but putty—just putty women." She looked up at him, her eyes snapping—a beautiful, impetuous, little maligner.

"Not one of them," she went on immediately, "ever had strength of mind to carry out what she began. My mother went to college intending to become a teacher. She married father when he was in his junior year—and kept house for him through the rest of his course. Father sent Alice to an art-school and she married Will before she was half through." Contempt hardened Peggy's voice. "Alice's entire conversation begins with these words: 'Will says,' 'Will likes,' 'Will thinks.' Genevieve had a splendid voice. She was going to do wonders with it, and about the time she was on her third scale she married Harold who boarded in the same house. And now all she sings is *Ride a Cock-Horse*. Marion was perfectly crazy to take up nursing. She finished her course, but never took a case—married an interne and does nothing but exchange recipes and quote that grand Roger of hers. So you can see for yourself," she threw out her hands in a little deprecatory gesture, "what they are—putty—just putty."

For a second she paused expecting Collins to interrupt her, then went on sturdily. "Now *I'm* more like father. I have stability and stick-to-itiveness. I have always known, ever since I was a little girl, that I had more strength of mind than the others. I've chosen my work—I love it—and nothing in the world can swerve me from it."

"Is that all?"

"It's enough, isn't it?"

"If you're through, I'd like to go over those points with you," said the attorney in Newton Collins. "You don't care for me because you're wrapped up in your work, and you're wrapped up in your work to show your people that you have stability—in other words, you are showing your Scotch stubbornness. Now, inversely, if you weren't so stubborn, you wouldn't be so wrapped up in your work, and if you weren't so wrapped up in your work you'd care for me."

Peggy gasped. "I never said that."

"I'll grant it, but that is what you mean." And they were off again—arguing about *that*.

Life went on much as before. Peggy made an excuse to stay away one Sunday, admitted to herself it looked cowardly, and went back, choosing to behave as if nothing had happened. Collins occasionally referred to their talk together. There was a Sunday evening in February when the two put lunch on the table before the Haynes' came home. Peggy, in a ridiculously ruffled apron—badge of the Ancient Order of United Housekeepers—remarked blithely: "I despise a big barn of a kitchen but I adore a cute little one like this."

"All right," said Collins amiably, "we'll have a cute little kitchen like this."

"Of course if it amuses you to talk that way, I suppose there's no harm in it."

"It not only amuses me—it fascinates me," he responded cheerfully.

It was about this time that Peggy began talking about the head supervisorship. "I'm going to be head," she would say on every conceivable occasion. "Miss Abercrombie won't stay forever and I'm just living for her place."

They all took it up. Ed would say "When I get to be head supervisor I'm going to buy some steel stock." And Newton Collins would say "I'll have to get some new tires when I get to be head supervisor."

One blowy March Sunday afternoon the Haynes' outer door burst open and a breathless Peggy in squirrel furs stood in the living-room doorway. She waved her muff. "It's come—and *so* much sooner than I could have hoped. Miss Abercrombie's resigned—is leaving at the end of the year. Either Miss Simmons or I will get it—and it won't be Simmons. She's too old, and the girls call her 'Persimmons.' *Personally* I love her, professionally I hate her." She was quite violent in her likes and dislikes—was Peggy Mackenzie.

The first Sunday in April—a day of sunshine and spring with a faint odor of mellow loam and hepaticas in the air—found Peggy at the Haynes' again, but she was pensive and preoccupied. Collins, from the depths of the big leather chair, watched her covertly. No sooner had they left their friends' door than he asked "What is it?"

"What is what?"

"The thing on your mind."

"You're uncanny! There *is* something. I don't think it's really worth bothering about but Mr. Bradley of the State Board sent in his resignation yesterday. They are taking him to a sanitarium tonight. I tried to see him last evening but they wouldn't let him be bothered with business. This may make some difference in my getting it." Long before this, Collins had learned what "it" always meant.

"Oh, dear!" she burst out vehemently, "I want it *so!* Why, if Simmons gets it, she's going to change the whole system."

As they walked across the campus, dainty in its new spring dress, Collins asked, "Will you marry me if you don't get it?"

"Why, of course not."

"But you'll be out of a position and you'll freeze to death and die of hunger!"

"I'll do nothing of the kind, silly. I'll get another position."

On the following Sunday when Collins called with his car, he found Peggy her old gay, independent self. As they took a turn before going to the Haynes', he ventured "Just promise you'll marry me if you don't get it."

She turned mischievous eyes to him. "I might do it to please your childish fancy."

"It pleases me, all right. The case of Collins vs. Mackenzie progresses."

"Very well. I promise."

"You mean it?"

"Yes, I mean it." She was gay with secret laughter. She even gave him a cordial little hand. "And now, Mr. Newton Collins, allow me to break the news to you that yesterday President Welch told me, in the inner sanctum sanctorum of his office that the Governor was going to appoint Mr. Moorehead of Williamsburg and *he's* my father's old partner and would vote for *me* for *Congress.*"

April smiled, and, giving out bold hints that summer was coming, turned to May. On the first day when "all the little leaves were dancing in the silver of the sun," Collins conceived the notion that the four should go picnicking. So, seated on the summit of a bluff, they ate their supper out of a flappy-topped basket, with the silver river below them and the blue sky close and friendly overhead. When they had finished, Maxine, inspired with the idea that they could get fresh eggs at a farmhouse just discernible through the trees, took Ed and the basket and went off.

Collins and Peggy walked down to a clump of wild crab-apple trees to gather blossoms. While they were breaking off huge masses of the lovely flowers, Collins said abruptly: "How about that new member of the Board of Education?"

"It's queer about that," Peggy answered bravely, avoiding his eyes. "It has been several weeks since President Welch told me, but the Governor hasn't yet officially appointed Mr. Moorehead."

"Then you haven't seen tonight's paper."

"No—why?"

"Because," he said casually, "it says the Governor has appointed me!"

"You're teasing me!"

"Oh, am I?" He took a folded paper from his coat pocket and handed it to her.

The color faded from Peggy's face, then returned with interest on the principal. "That," she said disdainfully, "is obtaining something under false pretenses."

"That," he retorted coolly, "is preparing a case with wisdom and fore-sight."

"Did you *ask* him for it?" She was looking steadily at Collins now, with a scornful tilt to her chin.

He grinned boyishly. "The Governor and I have hooked water-melons together."

Incredulously she flared out, "You wouldn't be the means of changing a whole system just to—get me?"

"I'd change the solar system."

She turned abruptly from him to put her head down on the gnarled branch of the crab-apple tree. Her hands were clenched into hard little fists.

"Are you angry?" he asked her back in a moment when the silence was growing strained.

"Yes." Her voice was tense with wrath.

The man stood for a moment looking at her, then he replaced the paper in his blue serge coat and said quietly: "You have no reason to be. The position is yours. I love you—dearly—but of course I wouldn't want you unless you wanted me."

Suddenly a hard fist unclenched and stole out, groping blindly toward him. He had it in his own immediately.

"I'm madder'n a hatter," came a muffled voice, "but it's at—myself. I've known for quite a while I—didn't—want the old position."

Five minutes later when the Lord had recreated the earth, the girl, from the lapel of the man's coat where she had hidden her face in shame at the chaotic condition of her ideals, looked up to say, laughingly, contemptuously: "*I'm* more like father. *I* have stability."

Ed and Maxine, with the basket of eggs, came swinging along the woodsy road. Silhouetted against the fiery arc of the setting sun stood two figures in such close proximity that, while it was only surmise that their two minds held but a single thought, there was direct evidence that their two hearts beat as one. Carefully the Haynes set down the basket of eggs between them, for even in the face of Romance, thirty-six fresh eggs must be treated with extreme politeness. Simultaneously they turned toward each other like Punch and Judy on invisible strings. Then they said in perfect unison, so that it sounded like the last verse of a chorus: "Well *what* do you *know* about *that?* "

And up in high heaven's court—although there are foolishly practical folks who will not believe this—Teresa O'Conor looked roguishly over the tip of her wing at Douglas Mackenzie and said: "Acushla! 'Twill be because of the Kilkee eyes and the dimplin' chin and the Irish heart of her."

The Mason Family Now on Exhibition

One of Aldrich's strengths is her realistic portrayal of senior citizens and how they are sometimes viewed by younger people. In this story, published in *The American Magazine* (November 1919), she creates Grandpa Warner, who would become old Oscar Lutz in *A White Bird Flying* (New York: D. Appleton & Company, 1931). Aldrich has him describe some of her own mother's adventures, which would also appear in *A Lantern in Her Hand* (New York: D. Appleton & Company, 1928). The man on whom Grandpa Warner is at least partially drawn is a Mr. Berger, an early resident of Elmwood, Nebraska.

The Mason household was to entertain company for Sunday dinner. That in itself was nothing unusual, the Sundays in which it occurred probably outnumbering those in which the family ate alone. But on this coming August Sunday, it was the guest-to-be, himself, who was out of the ordinary.

Specifically, he was to be Katherine's company, but the family had been cautioned by Mother that they were by no manner of means to refer to him as Katherine's individual acquisition. Katherine was the eldest Mason daughter, serious-eyed, lithe, lovely—just graduated from the State University.

The coming guest was Keith Baldridge, assistant professor of history in Katherine's Alma Mater. He was thirty-two and unmarried. No, he was not Katherine's fiancé—Katherine's manner dared anyone to suggest it. As a matter of fact, their friendship was at that very delicate stage where the least breath might shrivel the emerging chrysalis, or blow it into a gorgeous-winged creature of Love.

In the meantime, it was going to be an awful strain on the family to have him come. Mother was already feeling the effects of Katherine's attempts to make over the entire family in the four days intervening before his arrival.

"How long's Bald-Head goin' to stay?" Junior wanted to know at the supper table in the middle of the week. Junior was twelve.

"There he goes, Mama," Katherine said plaintively. "Can't you keep him from saying those horrid things?"

"My son," Father addressed him from the head of the table, "have you ever heard of the children in the Bible who were eaten by bears when they said, 'Go up, thou bald head?' " Junior grinned appreciatively, realizing he was not being very violently reproved.

"If you could just know, Mama, how different the Baldridge home is from ours!" Katherine was in the kitchen now, assisting Mother and Tillie. "Our family is so talkative and noisy, and laughs over every little silly thing, and there is so much *confusion*. Why, at their dinners—beside Professor Baldridge there's just his father and an aunt, both *so* aristocratic—at their dinners it's so quiet and the conversation is so *enlightening*—about Rodin, and—and—Wagner—and, oh, maybe Milton's Il Penseroso—you know what I mean—so much more *refined*."

At that word, Mother had an unholy desire to recall to the polished, critical girl before her the days when she used to hang, head downward, from the apple tree, her abbreviated skirts obediently following the direction of her head. But she forbore. Mothers are like that.

"And I wish you could *see* their house. It's not as big as ours, and really no nicer, but, oh! the *atmosphere!* The hangings are gray or mauve or dark purple—and they keep the shades down so much lower than ours—so it's peaceful, you know, like twilight all the time."

"My stars! Ain't that a gloomy way to live, and unhealthy, too, I must say." It was Tillie speaking acridly.

Tillie's status in the Mason family might as well be inserted here. She was an old maid who had gone to country school with Mother when Mother was Molly Warner. Unlike Mother, who had gone to college, Tillie's schooling had ended with the fifth reader. For eighteen years she had been in the household, as much a part of it as Father or the kitchen sink. Homely, ungainly, she worked like a horse for them all, or "slicked up" and went comfortably down-town or to Missionary Meeting with Mother. No, the servant problem had never worried Mother.

So now, with the familiarity which comes from having braided a little girl's hair and officiated at the pulling of her first tooth, Tillie was speaking her mind.

"And pictures!" Katherine went on, ignoring Tillie's disgusted remark. "Why, folks, in one room there's just *one*, a dull, dim, old wood scene, and so *artistic*. You can imagine how Papa's bank calendar in our dining-room just makes me *sick*. And they have a Japanese servant. You never hear him coming, but suddenly he's right there at your elbow, so quiet and—"

"My good land! How spooky!"

"Oh, Tillie, *no!* It's the most exquisite service you ever saw—to have him gliding in and out and anticipating your every wish."

"Well, Kathie, I'll wait table for you, and glad to, but I ain't goin' to do no slippin' around like that heathen, as if I was at a spiritual séance, I can promise you that."

"Thank you, Tillie, and, Tillie, when you pass things to him, please don't say anything to him, he's so used to that unobtrusive kind of being waited on—and he's so quiet and reserved himself."

"Well, if I had a glum man like that, I'd mop the floor with him." Tillie was always going to mop the floor with someone.

At that, Katherine left the kitchen with dignity, which gave Tillie a chance to say, "Ain't she the beatenest! I declare, she riles me so this week!" To which Mother replied, "Don't be too hard on her, Tillie. It's exasperating, I know; but she's nervous. Sakes alive! Don't I remember to this day just how I felt sitting around in a new lavender lawn dress thinking Henry might come. He had a pair of spotted ponies, and went driving furiously past our farm for three different evenings before he had the courage to stop." And Mother laughed at the recollection.

It was a characteristic of Mother's—this being able to project herself into another's personality. In the days that followed she seemed to live a Jekyll-Hyde existence. She was her own exasperated self because of Katherine's constant haranguing about the way things ought to be, and she was Katherine, sensitive, easily affected, standing quiveringly in the wings of the stage at the Great Play—waiting for her cue.

Because of this trait, Mother had known, to her finger tips, the griefs and joys of each member of her family—how Father felt the year bank deposits dropped forty-five per cent, how Junior felt when he made the grammar Nine. Some call it sympathy. Others call it discernment. In reality, it is the concentrated essence of all the mother-wisdom of the ages.

Mother was worried, too. She had never seen Keith Baldridge, and numerous questions of doubt filled her mind. What manner of man was this that lived in a house of perpetual twilight?

The family managed to live through Thursday, Friday and Saturday. The word *Sunday* seemed to have a portentous meaning, as though it were the day set apart for a cyclone, or something was to happen to the sun.

Professor Baldridge was coming in his car sometime in the morning. He had to leave in the afternoon, as he was to go around by Miles City to get his aunt, who was visiting there, and take her home. In truth, that had been his excuse for coming at all.

It came—*Sunday.* To the Mason family it was "The Day." It proved to be a still, hot morning, full of humidity and the buzzing and bumbling of insects.

At the breakfast table Katherine gave the last of her multitudinous directions. "Mama, I wish you'd *muzzle* Junior. Make him promise not to *open* his head."

"My child"—Mother's tone signified that it was making its last patient stand—"Junior shall be the pink of propriety, I assure you; but not for the President of the United States would I frighten one of my children into silence."

Simultaneously, Marcia and Eleanor hooted. "Imagine anybody being able to frighten Junior into silence!" was their combined exclamation.

After breakfast, Katherine, like General Pershing, reviewed her troops, the house and the grounds. From vestibule to back porch, through the big reception hall, library, living-room, sun parlor, everything was immaculate. There was not a flicker of dust in the house. There was not a stick or dead leaf on the lawn.

Marcia, Eleanor, and Junior all trooped off to Sunday-school and Father followed later to church, but Mother and Tillie stood by the guns, preparing ammunition in the form of salad and chicken. Katherine, who by this time was in such a palpitating state of heart that she couldn't assist intelligently at anything, went up-stairs to dress.

When she had finished—she decided on white after having had on a pink and a pale green—she sat down on her cedar chest, with eyes glued on the driveway. For some time she sat there, starting up at the sound of every car. Then she saw someone turning in at the front walk. He was short and slightly stooped. He carried a cane, but seemed to hobble along without using it. He wore store clothes too large for him and a black, wide-brimmed felt hat over his white hair. *It was Grandpa,* Grandpa Warner, who lived with another daughter on his old home farm, and had evidently come to surprise Mother's family.

Katherine started up with a cry. Not that! Oh, not Grandpa *to-day!* It was too cruel! Why, Grandpa monopolized conversation with his reminiscences, and at the table he did unspeakable things with his knife.

The good fairy which is called Memory reminded Katherine of the days when she had slipped her hand into Grandpa's and gone skipping along with him through dewy, honey-sweet clover to drive the cows down to the lower pasture; days when she had snuggled down by him in the old homemade sleigh and been whirled through an elfland of snow-covered trees and ice-locked rivulets; days that seemed then to embody to her all the happiness that time could hold. But she turned coldly away from the wistful fairy, and looked bitterly out upon a day that was unconditionally spoiled.

Carrying herself reluctantly down-stairs, she perfunctorily greeted the old man. Mother, the happy moisture in her eyes, was making a great fuss over him. Temporarily she had forgotten that such a personage as Keith Baldridge existed.

Back in a few moments to her room, Katherine continued her watchful waiting.

A car turned in at the driveway, a long, low, gray car, and Keith Baldridge, in ulster and auto cap, stepped out. At the sight of the figure that was almost never out of her mind, she dropped on her knees by the cedar chest and covered her face with her hands, as though the vision blinded her. And those who think her only ridiculously sentimental do not understand how the heart of a girl goes timidly down the Great White Road to meet its mate.

As for Mother, as Keith Baldridge grasped her hand, her own heart dropped from something like ninety beats to its normal seventy-two. He was big and athletic-looking, and under well-modeled brows shone gray-blue eyes that were unmistakably frank and kind. With that God-given intuition of Mother's, she knew that he was *clean*—clean in mind and soul and body. And quite suddenly she wanted him for her girl, wanted him as ardently and passionately as Katherine herself. Well, she would do everything in her power to make his stay pleasant and to follow out Katherine's desires.

So she hurried to the kitchen to see that everything was just as she knew Katherine wanted it. She saw that the crushed fruit was chilled, that the salad was crisp, that the fried chicken piping hot. The long table looked lovely, she admitted. Just before she called them in, Mother pulled the shades down part way, so that the room seemed "peaceful—you know, like twilight."

They all came trooping in, Father continuing what he had evidently begun on the porch, a cheerful monologue on the income tax law. Bob and Mabel, who had arrived with the new baby in the reed cab that Father Mason had given them, held a prolonged discussion as to where the cab and its wonderful contents could most safely stand during dinner.

With that old-fashioned notion that "men-folks like to talk together," Mother placed Keith Baldridge and Bob and Grandpa up at the end of the table by Father.

As they were being seated, Father said in that sprightly way which always came to him when a royal repast confronted him, "What's the matter with the curtains?" Then, walking over to the windows, with the highly original remark, "Let's have more light on the subject," he snapped the shades up to the limit. The August sun laughed fiendishly at Mother as it flashed across the cut glass and china and the huge low bowl of golden nasturtiums. Mother felt like shaking Father, but of course she couldn't get up and jerk the shades down again, like Xanthippe or Mrs. Caudle.

Tillie, with an exaggerated tiptoeing around the table, began passing the plates as Father served them. Previously, there had been a little tilt between Mother and Katherine over the coffee, the latter wanting it served at the close of the meal, "like real people," but Mother won with, "Father would just ask for it, Kathie, so what's the use?" And now Tillie was saying hospitably, "Will you have coffee, Mr. Bald—Bald—?" At which Junior snorted in his glass of water, and received the look of a lieutenant colonel from Mother.

There was a little interval of silence as the dinner started, then Grandpa looked down the table toward Katherine and said in his old, cracked voice, "Well, Tattern!" It was her childish nickname, put away on the shelf with her dolls and dishes. It sounded particularly silly to-day. "What you goin' to do with yourself now you've graduated?"

"I'm going to teach in the Miles City High School, Grandfather." She had never said Grandfather before; he'd always been "Grandpa" to her, but the exigencies of the occasion seemed to call for the more dignified term.

"What you goin' to teach?"

"History," she said briefly, and flushed to the roots of her hair. Marcia and Eleanor exchanged knowing grins.

"Then git married, I s'pose, and hev no more use fer your history? That makes me think of somethin' that happened back in Illynois. It was a pretty big thing fer anybody from our neck of the woods to go to college, but Abner Hoskins went, and when he was 'most through he got drowned. At the funeral Old Lady Stearns walked round the casket and looked down at the corpse 'n' shook her head 'n' said: 'My! My! What a lot o' good larnin' gone to waste'."

Everyone laughed. Katherine's own contribution to the general fund was of a sickly, artificial variety.

"You came here from Illinois at an early date, I suppose, Mr. Warner?" Keith Baldridge asked.

It was like a match to dynamite—no, like a match to a straw stack, a damp straw stack that would burn all afternoon. Grandpa looked as pleased as a little boy.

"*Yes,* sir— it was 1865. I fought with the old Illynois boys first, 'n' then I loaded up and come, with teams of course. That was a great trip, that was. Yes, *sir!* I mind, fer instance, how we crossed a crick with a steep bank, and the wagon tipped over, 'n' our flour—there was eight sacks—spilled in the water. Well, sir, would you believe them sacks of flour wasn't harmed, we got 'em out so quick? The water 'n' flour made a thin paste on the outside 'n' the rest wasn't hurt. I rec'lect the youngsters runnin' barelegged down the crick after Ma's good goosefeather pillows that was floatin' away."

Two scarlet spots burned on Katherine's cheeks. She raised miserable eyes, that had been fixed steadily upon her plate, to see Keith Baldridge look-ing at Grandpa in amazement. What was he thinking? Comparing Grandpa with his own father, dignified and scholarly?

On and on went Grandpa. "Yes sir—the year I'm tellin' you about now was the year the grasshoppers come, 1874."

Marcia kicked Katherine under the table. "Same old flock has arrived," she whispered.

"They come in the fall, you know, 'n' et the corn, 'n' then the gol-durn things had the gall to stay all winter 'n' hatch in the spring. Why, there wasn't nothin' raised in the gardens that summer but pie plant 'n' tomatoes. You'd be surprised to know how many things to eat you can make outen them two things." There was a great deal more information about the grasshoppers, and then, "Yes sir, me 'n' Ma had the first sod house in Cass County. 'N' poor! Why Job's turkey belonged in Rockefeller's flock by the side o' us. I had one coat, 'n' Ma one dress, fer I don't know how long, 'n' Molly over there"— he pointed with his knife to Mother, who smiled placidly back—"Molly had a little dress made outen flour sacks. The brand of flour had been called 'Hellas,' like some foreign country—Eyetalian or somethin'. Ma got the words all outen the dress but the first four letter of the brand, 'n' there it was right across Molly's back, 'H-E-L-L,' 'n' Mad had to make some kind o' knittin' trimmin' to cover it up."

Everyone laughed hilariously, Mother most of all. Junior shouted as though he were in a grandstand. Katherine gave a very good imitation of a lady laughing while taking a tablespoonful of castor oil.

"Well, Grandpa!" It was Father, when he could speak again. "She's had several dresses of later years that cost like that, but I never saw the word actually printed out on them."

Oh, it was awful! What would he think? He was laughing—but of course he would laugh! He was the personification of courtesy and tact. Talk about Wagner—Il Penseroso—Rodin! To Katherine's sensitive mind there stood behind Keith Baldridge's chair a ghostly, sarcastically-smiling group of college professors, ministers, lawyers, men in purple knickers and white wigs and plumed hats—gentlemen—aristocrats—patricians.

Behind her own chair stood sweaty farmers with scythes, white-floured millers, woodsmen with axes over their shoulders, rough old sea-captains—common folks—*plebeians.*

Her heart was as an icicle within her. All the old longing for Keith Baldridge, all the desire to be near him, died out. With a sickening feeling that she was living in a nightmare, she only wanted the day to be over, so that he would go home, so that she could go to the cool dimness of her own room and be alone.

The dinner was over. Father, with the same nonchalance that he would have displayed had he been dining the Cabinet members, walked coolly into the library, and with the automobile section of the paper over his face prepared to take his Sunday nap.

Katherine, unceremoniously leaving Mr. Baldridge to the rest of the family, slipped out to the kitchen to wipe dishes for Mother and Tillie.

"Why, Kathie, you go right back!" Mother insisted.

"Let me be," she said irritably. "I know what I want to do."

Mother, giving her eldest daughter a swift look, had a savage desire to take her across her knee and spank her, even as in days of yore.

The work done, Katherine walked slowly up the back stairs, bathed and powdered her flushed face, and with a feeling that life held nothing worth while went down to join the family. As she stopped in the vestibule and surveyed the scene it seemed to her that it couldn't have been worse.

The porch seemed as crowded with people as a street fair. Father had finished his nap, and was yawning behind his paper. Eleanor's entire crowd of high-school girls had stopped for her to take the Sunday afternoon walk which took place whether the thermometer stood at zero or 102° in the shade. They were all sitting along on top of the stone railing like a row of magpies.

Bob was wheeling the baby up and down, Mabel watching him, hawk-eyed, as though she suspected him of harboring intentions of tipping the cab over. Mother, red-faced from the dinner work, was calling cheerily to a neighbor woman, "You've lots of grit to get out in this hot sun." Marcia, in the living-room, had just finished "The Mill on the Cliff" record, and was starting "The Sextette from Lucia," the fanfare of the trumpets literally tearing the air.

Grandpa, for Keith Baldridge's benefit, was dilating on the never-ending subject of grasshoppers. As he paused, Tillie, in her best black silk, came around the corner of the porch and sat down near the guest with "Be you any relation to the Baldridges down in East Suffolk, Connecticut?" (Oh, *what* would he think of Tillie, who had waited on him, doing that?) Junior, on the other side of Mr. Baldridge, was making frantic attempts to show him a disgusting eel in an old fish globe that was half full of slimy green water. Even the Maltese cat was croqueting herself in and out through Professor Baldridge's legs. To Katherine's hyper-sensitive state of mind the confusion was as though all Chinatown had broken out.

With a feeling of numb indifference, she stepped out on the porch. Keith Baldridge rose nimbly to his feet. "Now, good people," he said pleasantly, apparently unabashed, "I'm going to take Miss Katherine away for a while in the car. You'll all be here, will you, when I get back?"

Katherine got her auto things and went down the steps with him, no joy in her heart—nothing but a sense of playing her part callously in a scene that would soon end.

It was outrageously hot in the car. "How about going where it's cooler. Is there some woodsy place around here?" he wanted to know.

So Katherine obediently directed him to Springtown's prettiest picnic spot and, almost without conversation, they made a run for its beatific shade. As they walked over to the bank of the river, the man said, "I'm certainly elated over the find I made to-day."

"Find?" Katherine questioned politely.

"Yes—your grandfather. He's a wonderful man. He's promised to come to my home next week and stay several days with me. He's just what I've been looking for, an intelligent man who has lived through the early history of the state and whose memory is so keen that he can recall hundreds of anecdotes. I am working on a history of the state, and my plan is to have it contain stories of vividness and color, little dramatic events which are so often omitted from the state's dull archives. From the moment he began to talk I realized what a gold mine I had struck. I could scarcely refrain from having a pad and pencil in my hand all the time I was listening to him. Why, he's a *great* character—one of the typical pathfinders—sturdy, honorable, and lovable. You must be very proud of him."

"I—am," said Katherine feebly.

"Take, for instance, my chapter on the early political life of the state. Do you know, he told me that one election day, when it came time for the polls to close, every one in the locality had voted but himself. He was miles away, hauling merchandise home from the river. A man got on a horse, rode over into the next county to meet him, then they exchanged places, your grandfather hurrying home on horseback while they held open the polls for him. It so happened that when the votes were counted, there had been a tie, and of course, his vote had decided the issue. Now, isn't that rich?"

Miss Mason acknowledged that it was.

"I'm a little cracked on the subject of these old pioneers," he went on. "To me they were the bravest, the most wonderful people in the world. Look at it!" He threw out his arm to the scene beyond the river. Before them, like a checkerboard, stretched the rolling farmland of the great Mid-West, yellow squares of wheat stubble, brown squares where the fall plowing had been done, dull green squares of corn, vivid green squares where the third crop of alfalfa was growing! Snuggled in the cozy nest of orchards were fine homes and huge barns. The spires of three country churches pointed their guiding fingers to the blue sky.

"Think of it! To have changed an immense area of Indian-inhabited wild land into this! Visualize to yourself, in place of what you see, a far-reaching stretch of prairie land on every side with only the wild grass rippling over it. Now imagine this: You and I are standing here alone in the midst of it, with nothing but a prairie schooner containing a few meager necessities by our side. We're here to stay. From this same prairie we must build our home with our hands, wrest our food, adequately clothe ourselves. It is to be a battle. We must conquer or be conquered. Would you have courage to do it?" He turned to her with his fine, frank smile. And into Katherine Mason's heart came the swift, bitter-sweet knowledge that she could make sod houses and delve in the earth for food and kill wild animals for clothing—with Keith Baldridge.

"And this," he went on again, indicating the landscape, "this is our heritage from the pioneers. From sod houses to such beautiful homes as yours! I can't tell you how much I've enjoyed to be with your family today. It's the typical happy American family. When I think of my own gloomy boyhood, I could fight someone—a lonesome, motherless, little tad studying manners, and 'Thanatopsis' under a tutor. Yours is the kind of home I've always wanted. It's the kind of home I mean to have when I marry—all sunshine— and laughter—and little children—"

He turned to her suddenly and caught her hands. "It was to talk about that more that I brought you out here. With my whole heart—I love you— Katherine."

It was late afternoon when the long gray car turned into the Mason driveway and stopped at the side lawn. In fact it was so much later than Keith Baldridge had planned to leave that he only took time to run up to the porch to say good-by to them all. If he expected the Masons to sit calmly on the porch when he should drive away, he did not yet know the Masons. One and all, excepting Grandpa, who stayed in his rocker, they followed him down the steps, flocking across the green sloping lawn to where his car stood. The cat, seeing the entire family trooping in one direction, came bounding across the yard, tail in air, and rubbed herself coquettishly against the departing guest's trousers. To be sure, she may have been of a curious disposition, that cat; but she was the soul of hospitality.

Tillie came running from the back of the house with a shoebox tied with a string. "It's some chicken sandwiches and cake," she explained. "Come again. I'll fry chicken for you any day."

Keith Baldridge beamed at her, and shook her rough hand vigorously. "I'm mighty glad to hear you say that, for you're going to have a chance to do that very thing next Sunday."

They all shook hands with him a second time. He got into the car and pressed the button that gave life to the monster. The wheels seemed quivering to turn. Just then Grandpa rose from his chair on the porch and excitedly waved his cane. "Say!" he called. He came hobbling over the grass, the late summer sun touching his scraggly gray hair. "Wait a minute, Mr. Baldridge!"

They all turned to watch him apprehensively, he seemed so hurried and anxious. He was close to the family group now. "Say! Mr. Baldridge! I jes' happened to think of somethin' else about them darned grasshoppers!"

They all shouted with laughter—all but Katherine, for she was not there. She had slipped into the front door and up to her room. There she dropped on her knees by the side of her bed and made a little fervent prayer to the God of families. And her prayer was this: That some day—if she lived humbly for the rest of her life—she might be purged from the sin of having been, even in thought, disloyal to Her Own.

Then, hearing the family back on the porch, she rose from her knees and went into the hall. There she leaned over the banisters and called: "Mother! Come up here. I want you."

The Theatrical Sensation of Springtown

One of the names Aldrich uses several times in stories is Eleanor or Ella Nora. The middle name of Aldrich's only daughter is Eleanor, and this seems to be a bit of family fun between them. Norman Rockwell did the paintings for the original *American Magazine* story in December 1919 and catches the two different aspects of this Eleanor's personality, the athletic and the romantic.

In "The Theatrical Sensation" Aldrich weaves into the text the titles of two other of her short stories, the earlier (1917) "Rosemary of Remembrance" and the yet-to-be-written "Great Wide World of Men" (*Women's Home Companion*, May 1950).

No one ever spoke of Eleanor Mason as being pretty. Katherine was of a Madonna-like sweetness and Marcia was undebatably lovely. Eleanor was neither of these; but she was merry-hearted, and a merry heart maketh a cheerful countenance. Instead of being the possessor of large, luminous eyes like the other girls, she had smaller, twinkling ones, like Mother's. Most people laugh first with their mouths, but when anything pleased Eleanor, which was about four hundred times a day, there came a little crinkling at the corner of her lids so that her eyes seemed to laugh before their mirth communicated itself to her generous mouth.

Of the three girls she had always been the most hoydenish. Many an old lady in Springtown could testify to having been nearly frightened out of her wits at the diabolical speed with which Eleanor Mason rode a bicycle. She could hold her own in baseball and she was the star guard of the high-school basket-ball team.

Clothes she considered mere articles of apparel, worn from the necessity of being decently covered. It was sometimes recalled in the family that once, to give Eleanor more pride in her clothes, Mother had sent her to Lizzie Beadle, the town seamstress, with two nice pieces of serge and the instructions to plan both dresses herself. On the way Eleanor had encountered Junior and a crowd of neighborhood boys, who wanted her to pitch for them. She had rushed up to the house of the Beadle lady, thrust the bundle in the door and called out, "Make 'em just alike, Miss Beadle," and taken herself off to the more glowing pleasures of the Mason cow pasture.

Boys she looked upon simply as the male of the species, somewhat to be envied for having been endowed by the gods with stronger right arms and an apparent aptitude for mathematics, denied to Eleanor herself.

To be sure, there was a Land of Romance, but it was peopled with no one she had really ever seen. The Prince and the Sleeping Beauty were there, and Laurie and Amy from the pages of "Little Women," and Babbie and the little minister. If there occasionally walked someone in the shadowy forest that seemed to belong to her, alone, he was too far away and vague to take on any semblance of reality.

Then came Miss Buckwalter, one of the new high-school teachers. Miss Buckwalter's mind contained a great many convolutions that had been made by romantic experiences. Her life, so far, had been divided, like all Gaul, into three parts, which centered respectively about the following characters:

1. The man she had wanted to marry.
2. The man who had wanted to marry her.
3. The man she was going to marry.

Miss Buckwalter taught the English Literature class. And because she was capable of making an extra credit, Eleanor Mason, sixteen and a junior, was scheduled to take English Literature with the seniors. From this class Miss Buckwalter organized the Shakespeare Club, and so cleverly did she manipulate matters that when the members signed the constitution—which document was nearly as long and serious-looking as the Peace Pact—it was discovered there were just fourteen members, evenly divided as to sex.

"That will give them more interest in the club," said Miss Buckwalter. Which deduction showed amazing wisdom.

The Shakespeare Club met every other Friday night in Miss Buckwalter's pretty suite of rooms. And, to make the club more attractive to the young people, she served refreshments. On the way home after the first meeting, tall, lanky Frank Marston said, gosh, he wished she'd speed up a little on the eats, that the part of his wafer that didn't stick in his teeth flew down the front of his coat. But, take it all in all, the club flourished like the cedars of Lebanon.

Thereafter, Eleanor Mason's language was not the language of her forebears. From morning until night she dropped sayings of the Immortal Bard. She answered every innocent question with a flippant Stratford-on-Avon answer. The family accepted it as they had the measles, an epidemic that, heaven willing, would be over some day.

After school hours, immediately following the banging of the front door, they would hear, " 'Oh, Jupiter, how weary are my spirits!' "

To Father's grumbling about Old Man Smith not doing the fall spading to suit him, Eleanor said:

> "Fret till your proud heart break.
> Go, show your slaves how choleric you are,
> And make your bondsmen tremble."

A piece of gossip from Junior brought forth " 'Peace! Fool! Where learned you that?' "

When Tillie came in to say that she believed on her soul when she lifted that wash water she had strained her back, Eleanor told her jauntily that the quality of mercy was not strained, that it droppeth as the gentle dew from heaven upon the earth beneath.

Tillie was disgruntled. "Can't that girl talk sense lately?" she wanted to know.

"Never mind her, Tillie," Father said. "She's only with us in the flesh—her spirit is living with the great international poet who cornered the market."

"Well, couldn't he a-wrote so white folks could understand him?" Tillie retorted acridly. Which, if you stop to think about it, wasn't such a foolish question after all.

Aside from these poetic flights, Eleanor was apparently unchanged. Mother watched her covertly to ascertain whether the boy question had presented itself. But, gay and care free, after every club meeting Eleanor would bring in the half-dozen young people who lived nearest, and together they would eat large quantities of sandwiches in the Mason kitchen. But, "Better a lot of eating in the kitchen than a little sweethearting on the porch," was Mother's motto.

Then came great expectations. The club was to give a play. Miss Buckwalter evolved the idea that it would make a great hit, be good training for the students, and bring in a mint of money for the school library. Thereupon she chose "Romeo and Juliet." And because of Eleanor Mason's keen intelligence, and the fact that her father was president of the school board and would appreciate the honor, Miss Buckwalter selected her for Juliet. She might have spared herself any pains on account of the latter reason, for a duck's back was not more impervious to water than Father to the fact that he had been highly honored.

Mother was disgusted. "I'm provoked through and through," she told Father. For twenty-six years Father had been her exhaust pipe. " 'Romeo and Juliet'! How *perfectly* silly! I talked to Miss Jenkins—she's so sensible—she didn't approve either, said she suggested 'Merchant of Venice,' or 'As You Like It,' as lesser evils; but a road company gave the 'Merchant' here not long ago, and Miss Buckwalter said she couldn't fix a good Forest of Arden when the trees were bare. She claims she will cut the play a great deal—but think of that balcony scene!" Mother threw up her hands despairingly. "Well, I'll not interfere; but you mark my word, Henry, Eleanor will get foolish notions in her head. Why, Father, she's only *sixteen*."

"Well, haven't I heard somewhere that the original Miss Capulet was fourteen?"

Seeing that Mother was too much perturbed to answer him, Father said cheerfully, "Oh, I wouldn't worry, Mother. Eleanor's the most sensible girl we've got, and the teacher will be there with them." Father was one of those old-fashioned souls who think, optimistically, that the teacher, like the king, can do no wrong. But Mother, having taught school herself, knew that teachers were of the earth earthy.

Comes now Andrew Christensen. Andy had arrived with his parents at Ellis Island from a small country noted for dairy products, some fifteen years before. And now, at nineteen, to prove that he was a genuine American, he dressed in the most faddish clothes and specialized in slang. In fact he was so much of a man of the world that, so far as girls were concerned, he seldom deigned to waste his fragrance of the desert air of Springtown, preferring, at ball games, to flaunt various out-of-town girls before his classmates. Mornings before school and on Saturdays he worked in Thompson's combined grocery and meat market. He was big and blond and good-looking. And he was Romeo.

Rehearsals began. To Miss Buckwalter's disappointment, Eleanor Mason was not getting as much out of her part as she had anticipated. Words! Eleanor could reel them all off at the first rehearsal. But when she said,

" 'Wherefore art thou, Romeo? What's Montague? Is it nor hand or foot? What's in a name?' " she might as well, for all the heart she put in it, have said, "Do you like onions? Or prunes? Can you stand the sight of carrots?"

So, with much coaching on Miss Buckwalter's part and much faithful endeavor on Eleanor's, the practice went on. And then—quite suddenly— Eleanor needed no more coaching. They were on the drafty stage of the old opera house, Eleanor standing on a dry-goods box in lieu of a balcony. Andy reached up and took her hand for the first time. A little shiver, as delicious as it was strange, went through her.

" 'Wouldst thou withdraw thy vow?' " said Andy. " 'For what purpose, love?' "

And Eleanor, her honest little heart beating suffocatingly, leaned over the old box and answered softly:

> "My bounty is as boundless as the sea,
> My love as deep; the more I give to thee,
> The more I have, for both are infinite."

And she meant it.

After that rehearsal Mother noted a subtle change in Eleanor. She seemed very subdued. She slipped up to her room a great deal to read. She became fussy about her clothes. She seemed, and Mother knew this to be the most genuine symptom, to have lost her sense of humor.

When Bob dropped in on his way home and wanted to know how Romiet and Julio were coming on, there was no merry crinkle around Eleanor's eyelids, only a very dignified answer from her.

Junior and the crowd of boys with whom she had occasionally been wont to hobnob were as the dust beneath her feet. The Saturday before the play, they came into the house and entreated her long and noisily to come to the pasture and help them make up a nine. But their supplication was met with such withering scorn that when they left Junior stuck his head back in the door to deliver this cutting farewell: "All right for you, Lady Juliet De Snub Nose! You can put this in your pipe and smoke it— this is the last time us boys'll ever ask *you* to do a *darn thing!* "

As for Eleanor, she was living in the rarified atmosphere which the new thing in her life had created. She walked daily in the land of Romance; but where she had hitherto only caught rare glimpses of a faraway shadowy creature, now he had come closer to her through the forest and, behold—it was Andy!

The night of the play, Springtown turned out as small towns always do for home talent and packed the old barnlike opera house to the doors.

The program opened with a piano solo by Marybelle Perkins. Probably Paderewski or Josef Hofmann could have done as well, but the Perkinses wouldn't have admitted it. Then the high-school boys' Glee Club sang "Anchored," and when they ended with "Safe, safe at last, the harbor passed," people were so relieved that the boys were quite reasonably safe at last from their perilous musical journey that they applauded vigorously.

There was a short farce and then—The Play.

There was a great deal of loud and boisterous enmity displayed between the followers and retainers of the respective houses of Capulet and Montague. There was a scene, somewhat hilarious, showing the ball given by Lord Capulet. There was the balcony scene, and the grand finale of the poison and the tombs.

Springtown liked it. True, there were a few discrepancies. One might have been carried back to a long-gone generation on fleeter wings of imagination had he not, through the foliage on the side of the balcony, caught glimpses of "Mr. Tobias S. Thompson, Dealer in Meats and Fancy Groceries." One recognized the portly Mrs. John Marston's old purple velvet coat on her lanky son Frank, and Lord Montague displayed a startling combination of dress-suit coat and sixteenth-century legs. The tomb where lay the bones of the dead Capulets looked like a cross between an automobile hood and a dog kennel. But, taken as a whole, it was a very creditable performance.

Father and Mother Mason sat in the center aisle, sixth row. Across from them sat Mr. and Mrs. Andrew Christensen, Sr., with so many little Christensens that it had taken nearly a day's wages to get tickets and reserved seats. Mr. Christensen was not yet far enough removed from kings and things but that he glowed with pride because Andy was playing opposite the banker's girl.

People whispered to each other that they never knew Eleanor Mason was so pretty. Lithe and lovely in her white costume, Juliet leaned over the balcony. In after years she was never to smell the pungent odor of rose geranium without seeing Andy's face, pale, a little tremulous, turned up to her.

Liquid-like, dulcet-toned, dripped Juliet's:

> "Good-night, good-night. Parting is such sweet sorrow,
> That I could say good-night until the morrow."

The audience clapped and clapped. Miss Buckwalter, in the wings, was elated. "Eleanor never did so well," she said to Miss Jenkins. Only Mother, sixth row, center, moaned over and over in her heart, "Oh, *what* have they done to my little girl?"

The play was over. The audience breathed a long sigh, rose, began laughing and talking. Mother felt a fierce intuitive resentment against Andy. She did not want him to go home alone with her girl. So she used the only weapon of defense she knew, a sandwich. With a hasty mental calculation as to how many buns there would be left for the next day after dividing four dozen into fourteen boys and girls, she invited them all up to the house.

It was an incongruous sight—Romeo and Tybalt and the old nurse and Friar Lawrence, *en costume,* perched on the kitchen sink and table and cabinet, devouring sandwiches. As they were leaving the kitchen, Mother made a casual survey of the trays, and discovered that the answer to her problem in mathematics was "Not any."

The Capulets and the Montagues all flocked out into the big hall. Andy hung back a moment to speak to Eleanor.

"Say, kid, I wanta see you in the morning when I bring the meat. I wanta ask you something when the mob ain't around."

There was only one thing it could mean, Eleanor told herself when she was alone in her room. It was a date for Sunday. She had never had a real "date," the boys just happened in at times. In an ecstasy of emotion she went to bed. For a long time she lay imagining what she would say to the girls when they came for her to go walking Sunday afternoon. She would answer carelessly, "I can't, girls. I'm sorry. Andy's coming."

When she woke with a start the sun was shining in her windows. All about her were evidences of the Great Event—her costume, a crumpled program, her roses in a jar in the hall. She dressed carefully in a softly frilled blue dress and sat down by the window to wait. She didn't want any breakfast. Eating? How commonplace!

There was a sound of the rattly cart that Andy drove. She wished Andy had a nicer job; he was intending to be a traveling man. She heard him go around the house and then, whistling cheerfully, coming back. She went to the window and raised it.

" 'But soft! What light through yonder window breaks?' " he called. " 'It is the east and Juliet is the sun!' "

They both laughed. How easy it was to laugh with Andy.

"Come on down!" he called. "I want to ask you that."

On winged feet of hope, she sped down the front stairs. Andy perched on the stone railing of the big porch, his cap on the back of his blond, curly head.

"Well, Juliet, we're some little actors—what?"

At Eleanor's answering smile, he said: "Say, kiddo, I wanta ask you to help me think of something for my girl's birthday. It's to-morrow and I'm going to see her. She lives over at Greenwood, and she's some swell dame, believe me. There's nobody in this town that's got a look-in with her. I thought maybe you could think of some nifty stunt."

Eleanor bent to her slipper for a moment, so that when she lifted her head it was quite natural that she looked flushed. Her heart was pounding terribly. She felt sick, but she forced a little crooked smile. There was sturdy pioneer blood in Eleanor, the strain that meets crises clear-eyed and bravely. So she said sturdily, "Why, Andy, flowers or books are nice,"

"Nix on the flowers. You won't see little Andy loping up with a bunch of posies. And books—she likes sweller things than reading."

"You wouldn't want to get anything as expensive as a kodak, would you?"

"Sure thing, just the dope. You're some kid. I thought you'd know something right-o. Much obliged. Well, so long, kiddo. See you at the algebra funeral Monday morning."

The little wings of hope were bruised and bleeding when she dragged them back up the stairs. She closed her door and threw herself down on the floor by the window, a little crumpled heap. So this was the end! Andy hadn't meant any of those things he had said. He had sounded so honest and truthful. The beautiful new thing in her life was gone. The hot gushing tears of youth came. Sobs shook her.

Ah, well! At sixteen a broken dream is as cruel as a broken reality, for there is no one to tell you which is reality and which is dream.

As she sat battling with emotions that would not be laid low, she turned in desperation to the long shelf of books near by. Mechanically she reached for a fat little volume and turned the leaves. Here was one called "The Saddest Hour." With a vague hope that the eminently appropriate title would put her own painful thoughts into words, she began:

> The saddest hour of anguish and of loss
>
> Is not that moment of supreme despair
>
> When we can find no least light anywhere—

Surely it couldn't be that life held sadder moments than this. She read hurriedly, avidly. What, then, was the saddest hour? It seemed it was not when we sup on salt of tears, nor even when we drink the gall of memories of days that have passed. Here it was:

But when with eyes that are no longer wet
We look out on the great wide world of men,
  And, smiling, lean toward a bright to-morrow—
To find that we are learning to forget—
  Ah! *then* we face the saddest hour of sorrow.

Then the saddest hour of all would never come to her, for of course she would never, never forget. For a long time she sat by the window looking mournfully out on the bleak landscape. There was some solace in the thought of dying and being buried in her Juliet costume, with a sprig of rose geranium in her hand. Andy would come and when he saw her, dead, in her little white Juliet dress, he'd think how rosemary was for remembrance. . . .

Junior and Runt Perkins and several of the boys of that crowd were coming up the back walk. They came close and stopped under the clothesline. There were eight of them. They were motioning to her. What did they want? She put up her window.

"Oh, *El*-ner, come on down and make up the nine. Shorty Marston had to go to Miles City with his mother. Come on, please. *Please* do, El-ner." Different voices were taking up the refrain.

Eleanor leaned out. The air was mild and damp as though somewhere there had been a gentle rain. There was a faint smell of mellow loam everywhere. Down behind the garage the hens were cackling noisily. The trunks of the maple trees were moist with sap. There was a faint tinge of green on the hill beyond the pasture.

"You can pitch, El-ner, er bat," Runt Perkins called enticingly, "er any old thing."

"Well," she said suddenly, "wait till I change my dress and get a bite to eat."

At noon Father came up the walk proudly carrying the new broom that Mother had told him to get two weeks before. At the back porch he stopped and looked across the alley to the half block of pasture land where in summer he kept his cow. For a few moments he stood watching, then a grin came slowly over his face and he turned and went into the house.

"Mother," he said, "for once in your life you were good and mistaken about one of your offspring."

"Who's that?" Mother withdrew her rumpled head from a coat closet.

"Eleanor. All that Juliet stuff never fazed her. I told you she was the most sensible kid we had. She's out there in the pasture with Junior's bunch, and she's just made a home run. She took it like a sand-hill crane, her hair flying out behind her, and the boys cheering her like little Comanches."

"Well, thank the Lord," said Mother devoutly.

Out in the old pasture lot, the Jilted One was looking out on the great wide world of men, and smiling, and leaning toward a bright to-morrow.

Acknowledgments

"The Box behind the Door," *McCall's* (May 1918): 16.

"The Cat Is on the Mat," *Delineator* 39 (Oct. 1916): 18ff.

"Concerning the Best Man," *Modern Priscilla,* accepted for publication April 1917.

"Grandpa Statler," *Harper's Weekly* 60 (26 June 1915): 606ff.

"The Heart o' the Giver," *Modern Priscilla* (Dec. 1915): 9ff.

"How I Knew When the Right Man Came Along," *Ladies Home Journal* 30, no. 12 (Dec. 1913): 24ff.

"The Light o' Day," *Woman's Home Companion* 43 (Nov. 1916): 21ff.

"The Lions in the Way," *People's Home Journal* (Feb. 1919): 7ff.

"The Little House Next Door," *Ladies Home Journal* 29, no. 4 (28 July 1911): 14ff.

"A Long-Distance Call from Jim," *The American Magazine* 88 (Aug. 1919): 48ff.

"The Madonna of the Purple Dots," *National Home Journal of St. Louis,* accepted for publication 1907.

"The Mason Family Now on Exhibition," *The American Magazine* 88 (Nov. 1919): 45ff.

"Miss Livingston's Nephew," *The Designer* (May 1918): 10ff.

"Molly Porter," *Harper's Weekly* 59, no. 600 (19 Dec. 1914): n.p.

"Mother o' Earth," *Delineator* 39 (July 1916): 11ff.

"Mother's Dash for Liberty," *The American Magazine* (Dec. 1918): 11ff.

"Mother's Excitement over Father's Old Sweetheart," *The American Magazine* 88 (July 1919): 46ff.

"My Life Test," *Ladies Home Journal* 30, no. 2 (Feb. 1913): 17ff.

"The Old Crowd," *Ladies World* 36, no. 6 (June 1915): 5ff.

"The Patient House," *The Designer* (April 1918): 9ff.

"The Rosemary of Remembrance," *Black Cat Magazine* (Nov. 1917): 3ff.

"The Theatrical Sensation of Springtown," *The American Magazine* 88 (Dec. 1919): 50ff.

"Their House of Dreams," *The People's Home Journal* (July 1918): 12ff.

"Through the Hawthorn Hedge," *McCall's* (March 1919): n.p.

"The Two Who Were Incompatible," *McCall's* (Aug. 1919): 5ff.

"What We Think of the Man Who Is Ashamed of His Wife: Is *My* Husband Ashamed of Me?" *Ladies World* (Feb. 1913): 6ff.